SOMETHING
Wicked

CAROL OATES

OMNIFIC PUBLISHING
LOS ANGELES

Omnific Publishing
1901 Avenue of the Stars, 2nd floor
Los Angeles, CA 90067
www.omnificpublishing.com

First Omnific eBook edition, January 2015
First Omnific trade paperback edition, January 2015

The characters and events in this book are fictitious.
Any similarity to real persons, living or dead,
is coincidental and not intended by the author.

Library of Congress Cataloguing-in-Publication Data

Oates, Carol.
  Something Wicked / Carol Oates – 1st ed.
  ISBN: 978-1-623421-62-5
  1. Paranormal — Romance. 2. Vampires — Fiction.
  3. Jack the Ripper — Fiction. 4. United Kingdom — Romance. I. Title

10 9 8 7 6 5 4 3 2 1

Cover Design by Micha Stone and Amy Brokaw
Interior Book Design by Coreen Montagna

Printed in the United States of America

For Eric

Chapter 1

1869

I decided to walk after partaking in an evening at the theater. The air held an unseasonable briskness, and recent rain further exacerbated the treacherous state of the public streets in Dublin, turning dirt to a layer of sludge. After dismissing my carriage, I headed on foot in the direction of the Carlisle Bridge, which would take me to my home on the north side of the city.

It had been a rousing performance of *Hamlet*, and I had dawdled in conversation with other patrons. When I emerged from the theater, the unlit narrow streets were quiet and illuminated only by the moon throwing a ghostly silver light on the area. It leeched all color, leaving shadows of black and gray.

The hypnotic sound of horse hooves clicking on cobbles in the distance echoed through the darkness. It lulled my mind to the point of distraction, and so I was surprised when a pair of hands wrenched me into an alley.

The astounding strength of my assailant caught me unaware. At a virile twenty, I thought myself fit to best any man in a fight. My heart pounded brutally against my ribcage, and my lungs burned. I fought for every breath against the fingers wrapped around my throat.

I fumbled for my pocket watch. Dublin had gained a reputation for violent robberies and the vast gulf that had developed between rich and poor. The rich wallowed in luxury while the poor—those who hadn't already died or emigrated during The Great Hunger—starved. My family did their best to shelter me from such things, but my education in this city had been in more than academia. And I read the *Evening Post*. I thought myself a man of the world.

"I don't want your watch," she snarled up to my face.

A woman.

I hadn't noticed her feminine clothing or shape. She smelled of ripe fruit and flowers. Her breath was so sweet, it bordered on rancid, and something else I couldn't place, almost as if she had been consuming dirt and sugar. Sugar was reserved for the rich.

My leather gloves slipped over silken fabric as I attempted to find purchase. I pushed against her, convinced a woman, especially a lady of means, could not hold me there against my will.

As if to demonstrate her strength once more, she slammed my body against the damp stonework, winding me. The edge of my vision began to darken. The fabric of my shirt collar pulled and ripped with a furious force. The wet grainy flesh of her tongue swirled in a circle on my neck above her fingers, and my own pulse beat heavily against it.

The work of a devil!

I reached into my pocket and touched the gold sovereigns and banknotes there with the intention of offering them in exchange for my life. It grew progressively harder to keep my eyes open or remain standing under my own strength.

My family—my mother, my father, and my young sister came to mind. They would be horrified at the discovery of my lifeless body, if it were discovered at all. Perhaps the *Post* would report the story of a missing student, disappeared into the cold waters of the River Liffey after one too many liquid indulgences. At the memorial, mourners would weep over my absent body, never truly knowing what became of me.

Something pointed scratched against my neck and then roughly and painfully pierced my skin. A dark guttural noise, more like that of a wild animal than a man, escaped my lips. Against every natural reaction in my body, I fought to stay quiet, biting so hard on the inside of my cheek that I tasted blood. In a flash of revelation, I knew blood was the scent I hadn't been able to place. The woman smelled of blood…blood and sweetness, and death.

With my last remaining strength, I pulled my hand from my pocket and pressed it to her neck to push her away. She screamed and flung herself backward, smashing into the opposite wall in a cloud of powdered mortar, howling in agony and grasping at her neck. My legs buckled, and I slid awkwardly to the ground, panting and lacking the will or strength to remain standing. I frantically tried to decipher what I saw before me. The woman had to be an agent of Satan, a demon we had read about in church.

Now that I was free of her chokehold, my vision began to clear. Smoke and blood poured from between her fingers, down her slender, pale wrist, soaking into the lace cuff of her dress. More blood covered her jaw, dripping down her neck. I gagged on the cloying smell of charred flesh. I wanted to run, and yet my legs refused to cooperate. Wetness poured from the wound in my neck, and I knew at least some of the blood that covered her was mine.

No one was coming to rescue me. Any person of sound mind would run in the opposite direction of the hissing, snarling creature before me.

A lady, obviously of wealth and standing, drenched in blood and baying for more—how could such a thing exist? My stomach curled into a tight ball ready to evacuate everything I had consumed recently, and I tasted the burning acid on the back of my tongue. I swallowed down the nausea, refusing to emasculate myself further. If I was to die, I would do it as a man and not a sniveling, sickly wretch.

A fleck of light caught my eye, and I glanced to my right. The bloodied silver money clip lay discarded on the ground beside me, still smoldering. It must have been in my hand when I pushed her away. I'd cut her.

"I'm sorry; I can't help myself." She wept pitifully, with a slight hint of an accent I didn't recognize.

I looked across the small space, stunned to see the creature curled against the wall and weeping into her hands.

"I have tried to resist," she sobbed, "but I'm so thirsty." Her raven hair had been recently attended to; not a strand was out of place from the elaborate twist atop her head.

My heart squeezed out an extra beat, and my breath caught in my throat. *Do demons feel remorse?* Surely not. Her quiet cries seemed to echo off the stone walls. Something deep within me warned not to approach; the sweet angel before me was a lie, and the monster of moments ago was the truth.

I didn't heed it.

Her white gown was suitable for evening wear, and she wore it without a cloak or gloves. She may have come from the same performance I had. Perhaps she had followed me. Mud from the ground and scarlet blood stained the fabric. It brought my attention back to my neck, and I lifted my hand to assess the damage, fighting the rising panic.

A frozen chill slithered down my spine, and my body trembled. Blood seeped from small punctures in my throat. I hadn't imagined it. She had drunk my blood.

"What manner of creature are you?" I demanded.

"Please, don't hurt me," she pleaded, her face still in her hands.

Sanity sank in, and I had an overwhelming desire to leave before the monster made itself known again. Her slim shoulders rattled, at first I thought from her tears, until the quiet musical sound of her laughter grew in volume. I scrambled to my feet with some effort and used the wall behind me for support, intent on running.

In a flash, she was on me again, and this time my back was flat to the damp, freezing ground. The creature straddled my hips and trapped my wrists by my head. For the first time in my life, I wished I believed in heaven, as surely as I would find myself there soon. I panted heavily, every breath forcing out a stream of fog from my lips, and wrestled against her to free myself. Her physical strength proved infinitely greater. She smiled down on me with black eyes threaded with red behind an angelically beautiful face. Yes, angelic. All these years I had been wrong to doubt my faith, for how could I doubt with the Angel of Death before me?

"No pleading?" she asked softly, tilting her head to the left.

I ceased my futile fighting and concentrated on calming the painfully hard beating of my heart. Terror burned through my entire body, but I refused to show her. Instinctively, I seemed to know this was a game to her. She wanted my fear as much as my blood. She might extract one by force, but I would never allow her the other.

"Do with me what you will, demon. I will not succumb to you."

She laughed again, throwing back her head. The sound was mesmerizing and seeped into a deep part of me like fine tendrils strangling my desire to resist her.

The skin of her slim throat had healed to a red scorch. When she looked back to me, her smile had transformed, turned predatory. My stomach twisted violently when she leaned forward, pressing her torso against mine. Her breath tickled over my jaw. I swallowed thickly as she hummed against the skin below my ear.

"You are strong, and you are brave. You show no fear." Smooth, cool lips brushed my ear, followed by moist flesh.

"Kill me if you will, beast, but know this," I warned her blackly. "I will find you again. I will find a way back to this life, and I will destroy you."

She pulled back again to look at me, her face mere inches from mine. I stared into dead eyes, irises tinged with red, the color more intense at the outer edge. Her lips pulled back, and I gasped at the sight of her glistening white teeth. Elongated, pointed canines pressed against plump, ruby flesh. The veins under her skin darkened and thickened.

"Is that a threat?" She watched curiously. Her hips slid over mine, bunching her skirts up between us. Her long fingers readjusted at my wrist, loosening for the briefest moment, before tightening almost unbearably.

I struggled to hold back the scream inching upward from my lungs. "That is an oath I swear to this night." My voice sounded dark, foreign even to me. There was no question in my mind that I believed my words.

"Well then—" she sighed "—we shall have to see to it that you will never leave this life."

Chapter 2

2010

Music floated through the warm, late evening air in Temple Bar as the bustling Dublin city center area transitioned from evening to night.

I dropped a few coins into the empty guitar case of one of the buskers I passed. He had the disheveled clothing and greasy hair of a person who hadn't had a bath in a while. The young man competed enthusiastically for the attention of tourists and locals that populated the bars, restaurants, and bijou shops off the square. He didn't acknowledge the muffled clacking of metal on felt, not that I expected him to. I knew the peace that came with disappearing into a stream of musical notes until nothing else existed.

The square overflowed with humans enjoying the nightlife and the final days of pleasant weather before autumn set in. Some were passing through the cobbled streets and narrow alleys, some sitting on the low steps of the concrete raised area, simply catching up with friends. All were looking for the same thing I wanted, to be part of life. A life I had been disconnected from for one hundred and forty years.

Still, I came here day after day. *Patience isn't a virtue for my kind; it's a curse.* I waited.

The vampire who had turned me had led me back here before she vanished, back to the city of my birth and damnation. Constance — she was always one step ahead of me, and it had been months since I'd picked up her trail. I lingered in the hope she might return one day soon, although I doubted she would.

Beneath my calm exterior, the ever-present desire for blood clawed at my insides, angry talons constantly tormenting me. I stamped it down and took a seat at one of the chrome tables outside a small café I frequented, pulling my rolled up newspaper from my pocket.

Another tourist killing. There were other vampires in the city, demons who stalked the streets with little regard for exposing themselves or the rest of us. Their disregard had progressed to blatant sloppiness. Maybe they were young and unaware of the possible consequences, or maybe they were so old they didn't care anymore. Any other part of the world, and I wouldn't care either. I kept to myself. I stayed away from them for the most part, and they stayed away from me. This recent spate of killings grated on my nerves. Dublin would always be my home, my territory.

"Hi."

"Hello," I said, looking up to the young woman who worked here.

She smiled graciously, flicking the ponytail of her long, dark brown hair over her shoulder. She clicked a pen several times in the brief moment I took to look her over. A nervous habit, I guessed.

"I'll have—"

"Let me guess." She raised an eyebrow. "You'll have a hot black coffee that you won't drink, and a cinnamon pastry that you won't eat."

I wasn't aware she took notice, since I generally took the pastry and passed it on to one of the many needy on my way home. However, her challenging blue eyes and observation told me she did.

"You know, there is a minimum order, but I think we can make an exception since you are a regular," she offered, leaning closer, perhaps so the people at the next table couldn't hear. I caught the scent of cocoa and ground coffee.

"Thank you," I responded, making great effort not to shift away too obviously. "I'll have a black coffee and a cinnamon pastry, please." I shuffled my paper and returned to it, essentially cutting off the conversation, or so I thought.

Her pen clicked again, and I heard a short sigh before she dropped into the seat opposite me. I looked up, shocked. Over the three months I'd been coming to this café, we had barely exchanged more than a please and thank you. I preferred it that way. I wasn't good at small talk with humans.

"I don't mean to pry…" She pressed the fingers of one hand against her temple as though stemming a headache.

"Then please don't."

She huffed at my remark, apparently unmindful of her intrusion, or of breaking the invisible line between customer and acquaintance. Keeping my head tilted to the broadsheet in my hands, I looked up from under my eyelashes to see her scrutinizing me with narrowed eyes. Not something I was used to. Humans didn't like to look too closely, and this human had never given me cause to believe she was any different.

Her eyes remained fixed on me as she placed the notepad on the table between us and laid the pen across the center, clearly with no intention of leaving. She leaned forward as if preparing to speak in confidence again, then hesitated and grimaced, pressing her lips together tightly and sitting back once more.

"Can I help you with something?" I asked.

"Yes." She smiled, and I couldn't put my finger on why it made me uncomfortable. The girl was beautiful in a non-obvious way, and American, given her accent. The light from the café interior and the square reflected off her shiny hair, and her eyes gleamed with health. I guessed her age at around twenty, and judging by the toned upper arms and shoulders revealed by her tank top, she kept herself in shape.

Despite her calm outward appearance, her heartbeat picked up pace and the color rose in her cheeks, indicating a rise in body temperature. Her pupils dilated infinitesimally when her gaze flickered to my mouth and back to my eyes, fixing me with look I recognized as hunger. A human male wouldn't consciously pick up on such markers, but then, I wasn't a human male.

She was physically attracted to me, but her determined focus indicated it was more than carnal desire. She wanted something else from *me*. Something she appeared to believe only I could give her. Every cell in my body reacted to that need, shattering the monotony of my nightly routine.

Contrary to my usual disposition, I wanted to hear what she had to say. I closed my newspaper, flattening and folding it three times and then placing it on the table beside her notepad. The table became neutral territory between us.

"You are always impeccably dressed. The whole shabby jeans casual look you have going on here is clearly intentional." She waved her hand up and down my body, and I wasn't entirely sure if she was trying to be insulting or complementary. "I've never see you anything but clean shaven, and you have a manicure." She inclined her body again placing her forearms on the table and interlacing her fingers.

Her eyes stayed defiantly on mine as if she was silently challenging me to look away first.

"Every day you come here, and you always leave a big tip. That, and your clothes, tell me money isn't an issue for you."

I had no idea where she was going with this, but I was intrigued to find out, so I moved closer to the table, mirroring her. I was over six feet tall, so my arms were longer than hers, and when I interlaced my fingers, it brought our knuckles only inches apart. A challenge of my own, but she didn't pull away. In fact, she inched closer, and I could almost feel the heat from her skin. The hairs along my arms prickled, and I drew back.

The girl was observant and not altogether wrong. Money wasn't a consideration for me. She was right about that, and my appearance too. I preferred to dress casually, but it didn't mean I couldn't appreciate quality. She was mistaken about my nails. It's wasn't a manicure; my smooth rounded nails were a side effect of my affliction.

"I wondered if you are ill, because you're always so pale." She paused. I imagined she was waiting for confirmation, which I didn't give.

Yes, I was sick, but not in the sense she meant. When I didn't respond, her tongue peeked out and swept across her top lip quickly, followed by a brief pout. The corner of my mouth twitched. I couldn't help being amused by this girl, even though I shouldn't encourage her.

"Your eyes are very distinctive."

I instinctively averted my gaze, although my eyes were their usual dark brown, an uninteresting shade of mud.

There was one night some weeks ago when a fight broke out in the square while I was paying this waitress for my coffee. Some young men were scrapping over nothing after having too much to drink. Blood was spilled, and my true vampire nature emerged for the briefest instant. My eyes turned black tinged with red. It'd been too long since I'd fed. I reeled myself in and left. At the time, I'd had no idea she noticed my physical reaction. I was unprepared, then and now.

I had to force myself to remain when every compulsion told me to take her away from here and deal with her. There was a reason vampires didn't expose ourselves to humanity. The hunter would become the hunted, and we would be forced to defend ourselves. Humans outnumbered vampires because humans were food and only an imbecile would obliterate their own food supply by killing or turning them in any great numbers. Suspicions of our existence were one thing, but knowledge, anything that couldn't be written off as fantasy or delusion, was usually a death sentence.

"It's a rare genetic abnormality," I explained quickly and coolly.

"Ari!" another young woman—blond and far too thin—called from the door of the café, catching my companion's attention.

I'd never taken note of her name before.

Ari's head whipped around to the other woman, exposing a long, slender neck the color of pale golden caramel. I swallowed thickly when my eyes were drawn to the pulsing below the smooth skin. I felt the sting of my teeth biting into the flesh at the back of my lips. My control was instantaneous. Although I knew this young human alone couldn't be a threat to me, my body automatically reacted otherwise.

"I'll be there in a second," Ari answered. The café was busy as always, and yet she appeared in no hurry to attend to other customers. "So, where were we?" she started brightly, as if we were old friends, when she turned her attention back to me. "Oh yeah, you were saying you have a rare genetic abnormality?"

I nodded once swiftly, recognizing that the most prudent course for her sake would be to leave immediately and never return. Something about the girl I had never noted before held me there. The way she looked at me as if she were staring right through all my pretenses was both riveting and very dangerous.

She sighed again, this time accompanied by a confused expression that caused her brow to crinkle and then smooth. For some reason I was sure it was bogus.

"How rare exactly?" She pursed her lips. I recognized a test when I saw it.

She knew I was lying. A tingle raced up my spine, and the hairs on the back of my neck stood, because she'd been watching closer than I'd given her credit for. Perhaps she wanted me to deny what she'd already guessed—that I was something other than human. Why confront me now? What had prompted this bold step? *How rare exactly?* I was all too abruptly aware of her reasons for questioning me. She'd seen others.

"How many?" I asked, cutting through the shit. Did she have any idea of the dangerous path she walked? Self-preservation was a powerful instinct. Those others might have slaughtered her just for looking too close. Very few of my kind had the restraint I possessed, and even I had killed.

She flinched at my tone but didn't retreat or ask me to clarify, confirming my suspicion. Vampires had been feeding in the area, and I couldn't help wondering what game these demons were playing.

"A man," she said plainly. "It was hard to tell, but he looked older than us. He approached me early this morning when I was closing up."

"Really?" I raised my eyebrows in surprise.

She sat back then, and her eyes flickered around us nervously, almost as if she expected him to be here watching her now. If he was, I couldn't sense him.

"He asked my name. There was something about him." She stopped, and her whole body shivered. When Ari looked down, I noted the blush across her collarbone, blossoming up to her cheeks. "He reminded me of you. Except, you've never made me feel that way. I'm not scared of you."

"You should be." I stood, compelling myself to do it at a speed that wouldn't attract undue attention.

"But you haven't had your coffee yet," she argued, standing too. A couple at the next table turned to look at us. I wanted to know I could return and take care of this situation if I needed to. Openly having a spat with Ari in front of customers would make that difficult.

"Please," she went on. "It's on the house. Forget I said anything." She reached out, planting her hand on my lukewarm forearm. It was an intimate gesture, too intimate for strangers. Far too intimate for a human to purposely initiate.

I tensed at the contact. I may have led them to her. If I weren't such a creature of habit, I wouldn't have come here night after night. It was the most likely reason she had caught the interest of one of us and lived to tell. Now it was my responsibility to take care of this.

Revulsion at the situation I'd landed myself in and anger at this unknown vampire coiled in the pit of my stomach.

The other girl came to the door, watching us. I gestured to Ari by inclining my head and led her away from prying ears. She knew something, but I highly doubted she had any idea of what it was she knew. Like most humans encountering the supernatural, she wanted a reason not to believe the truth. She wanted a reason not to be afraid of the boogeyman.

I lowered my head and kept my voice down. "As you so astutely pointed out, I neither eat pastries nor drink coffee."

"Is there something else you drink?" she asked calmly, keeping her voice at a similar volume.

I almost laughed at her audacity. For an instant, I pretended paranoia had gotten the better of me and her questions were nothing more than an awkward attempt at conversation. She was clearly attracted to me. I could smell the sweet scent of the pheromones she gave off in my presence and the adrenaline in her blood.

She was still ferreting for the words that would put her mind at rest, like a child seeking comfort from a parent at bedtime. She wanted reassurance there was no monster in the closet waiting to leap out at her.

The bizarre thing was, it would have been so easy for me to give her what she wanted. I could have told her lies, said exactly what she wanted to hear. I could have made the whole thing seem like just a bad dream or her imagination. I'd done it before with others. It'd been over a century since I'd killed a human who came too close to my secret, ending my devilish reign over London as the infamous Jack the Ripper.

"I think you already know."

Her eyes widened slightly, perhaps taken aback by my candor, and her heart pounded beneath the white cotton of her top. She blinked several times before her eyes flashed to my hand holding onto her bare arm. I released it quickly, rubbing my hand on my thigh to rid myself of the sudden pins and needle shooting over my palm.

"I'm sorry," I said. Why couldn't I tell a simple lie? Lies were second nature to me. Even my name was a lie. I turned to leave.

"Wait…please." She moved in front of me again, almost slamming into an unsuspecting tourist dressed head-to-toe in green when I kept walking. "You can't just leave." There was a strange pleading in her voice, and for the first time I heard the barely-there rise in the pitch. "What should I do if he comes back?"

I stopped. So did she, almost falling over one of the slabs of concrete that made up the pavement and had come loose. I caught her upper arms and held her. She was so close, yet she seemed utterly oblivious to the temperature of my skin when she looked up to meet my eyes. Ari's palms pressed against my chest, and her eyes narrowed. Her fingers twitched over my heart, beating far too slow and strong for a human heart, but she didn't pull away.

"What can I do if he comes back?" she asked again.

I sighed heavily, aware it wouldn't instill confidence. I didn't intend to be cruel or scare her, nor did I seem capable of lying to her. Maybe that was a good thing. If someone had been honest with me all those years ago about the real dangers of the city streets, about the beasts that roamed at night inflicting a terrible fate on the city's inhabitants, maybe I would have been more careful.

"Nothing. If he comes back for you, there is nothing you can do."

Ari's eyes searched mine. She swallowed and carefully pushed away from me. I wasn't sure what reaction I expected from her. Maybe to scream or run? I had just done something incredibly stupid. I had revealed myself out in the open where I could do nothing if she chose to shout or scream or cry hysterically. She did none of those things. Ari simply nodded, indicating she understood, and stepped away from me.

"Thank you," she said, almost as an afterthought.

It caused another twinge of guilt, and I had no idea why. It didn't make sense. "Are you okay?" My arms hung from my body as if still holding her or reaching for her.

She stared into space, trying to wrap her head around the revelation of monsters and demons in the real world. Finally, Ari chuckled darkly, and her lips pulled up into a half-smile as she turned to leave. "No."

I stepped forward, and her head spun in my direction. For the first time, she flinched away when I reached out.

"I have to get back to work. I'm sorry I bothered you." A veil had come down. It happened when the human mind didn't want to admit something to itself. I had seen it before. "What's your name?"

"Clay Black." It was as if my brain had short-circuited. I had just handed her my name. It wasn't my real name, but that didn't matter. It was the name I went by. Undiluted panic welled in my chest. My actions were forcing me into a corner. She could easily tell her friend who I was.

She smiled, taking another step away. "Thank you, Mr. Black."

My throat wrenched into a sudden knot at the sound of her voice, as though a million tiny razors shot through my blood.

"Ari," I called after her.

Her body turned halfway, and she peeked over her shoulder. Her eyes narrowed curiously.

"Henry." The knot in my stomach instantly eased. "My name, it's Henry Clayton."

Chapter 3

I had been living a short distance north of the city for three months, in the same Georgian townhouse I had once shared with my family. The houses in the semi-circle row faced onto the small, green space populated by trees and thick shrubbery, providing much needed privacy. Most of the houses had been converted into apartments, and the neighbors kept to themselves. Regardless, I had little interest in parting with the property. Call it sentimental reasons, a reminder of past transgressions. Guilt.

The curtains behind one of the paned windows had been disturbed, and a dim light glowed from the drawing room. An intruder would be more aware of accidentally exposing himself, if he managed to get past my home security without triggering it.

I entered the dimly lit room. My guest didn't react or even move from the leather wing-back chair facing the fire hearth. Like all the rooms in the house, the drawing room had been updated in the last few years. What remained wasn't even vaguely similar to how it had been in my youth. I didn't want to forget, but I wasn't a masochist, either. I wanted to remember who I was then and what *she* stole from me, but I was under no illusions about what I had become.

The room was square, not accounting for the two deep alcoves that housed tall, mahogany bookshelves filled with the reference material I preferred reading these days. I found reality to be far more terrifying than fiction. The entire house was modern with a touch of Old World to it. The limestone hearth in this room was real, as were the Palladio moldings on the ceiling, although rescued from another property. I chose mostly antique furniture or quality reproductions, from the red leather, studded couch against the wall to the Queen Anne cabinet where I kept my alcohol. My considerable affluence prevailed thanks to my investments, allowing my continued material comfort.

Judging by the hand holding a tumbler half-filled with my Glenmorangie whisky, my guest seated in the wingback by the fire had already helped himself.

"I see you haven't managed to rid yourself of that nasty breaking and entering habit." I tossed my keys in a crystal bowl on one of the side tables.

His head appeared around the leather, and he smiled broadly, his shaggy, dark blond hair unkempt as ever and his bright green eyes crinkling with mirth. "Brother, your fascination with home security always did amuse me. How unfortunate it would be for any human who disturbs you in the dead of night." His voice still held a hint of his Scottish accent after three hundred years.

I went to the cabinet and poured a tumbler for myself, shaking the bottle to offer a refill. He held his glass out.

"It's *any* intrusions I am eager to avoid, Dougal." I raised an eyebrow. Just as he never understood why I surrounded myself with human protection, I could never understand why he didn't. It wasn't as if we were indestructible.

"Your paranoia is astounding, Henry." He shook his head in disbelief, taking a large mouthful of whisky and puffing out his cheeks before swallowing. "I can always rely on you for the good stuff." He grinned in appreciation. "And it's Doug now."

Instinct should have kept humans from straying too close to a predator, but many humans were completely oblivious under the right circumstances. They were too tied up in their own lives or consumed by modern life to recognize a dark angel in their midst.

I took a seat in the other chair, inspecting the half-emptied bottle. I gathered Dougal — Doug — had been here awhile. Vampires tended to drink hard and fast, but rarely got drunk. Our bodies processed the alcohol too quickly. Whisky wasn't as easily absorbed in our bodies as clear alcohol like gin or vodka, but I enjoyed the woody taste better.

"And I go by Clay now. I don't consider it paranoia, more like self-preservation. I prefer not to take the chance."

My recent interaction with Ari only went to further prove I was right to be careful. Humans were losing the instincts that kept them from danger. They rushed to it like moths fluttering blindly to a flame. More than that, they found legends of our kind alluring, fascinating.

"When did you arrive in Dublin?" I asked. Had he been the vampire sniffing around Ari?

"This evening. I came straight here. I've been up north for a few weeks and Paris before that."

I took a drink and enjoyed the warming alcohol slipping down my throat. "So, *Doug*, what are your plans?" I asked casually, leaning forward to rest my elbows on my knees and rolling the smooth glass between my palms.

Doug smirked and stretched out his long legs in front of him. He'd been a Highlander once and retained the body of one. His muscled arms and shoulders under his black shirt came from years of sword training, and his hard stomach was honed from fistfights while still human.

He'd returned to the Highlands only once after his infection. His people had banished him when he reappeared two weeks after his apparent death during a raid. They believed him a devil...and he was. His people paid the devil his due with their lives. All of them. Doug had never made it to his twenty-first birthday, and like me, his introduction to this existence had been brutal and bloody.

He knew me well, and I didn't have to speak my real question out loud. With him being older, it wasn't at all likely it was Doug being sloppy when feeding, but his sudden appearance after fifteen years indicated something was up.

"I'm getting out of Dodge," he said. He took another drink. "You should do the same."

I narrowed my eyes curiously, sensing his worry. It was very unlike him to worry about much.

"It's Abhartach."

I snorted, almost choking on a mouthful of whisky. "This again? You can't be serious."

"Aye, I am deadly serious, and if you didn't cut yourself off from everyone and everything around you, you would have heard too. The news is rampant. What do you think it is that's attracting the crazies?" He swallowed thickly, the tight muscles of his jaw twitching.

"How?" I asked, humoring him. It would make sense, if there was a group of foolish vampires intent on the notion of waking Abhartach, that there would be others waiting in the wings to welcome the father of all vampires back, hoping for favor.

"No idea." He picked up the bottle I had left on the floor between us and poured his glass almost to the brim, then did the same to mine. "I just know this can't be good. There was a reason he was put in the ground, and believe me, if they do manage to raise him, he will not be happy. We are talking mayhem, slaughter, a blood war… the end of life as we know it. I am not going to be sitting at ground zero when it strikes."

He paused a moment, gauging my reaction, but I wasn't sure what my reaction should be. I only knew about Abhartach from legends and the stories Doug had told me. He was the monster in the nightmares of monsters, a pure demon that ravaged the land and survived on blood offerings until he had been trapped by a Druid and buried in Northern Ireland thousands of years ago. Surely if there was a way to wake the original vampire, someone would have found it before now?

On the other hand, Doug had taken me under his wing when others would have walked away and left me to rot. I owed him my trust. If he said this was going to happen, I had to at least take him seriously.

"Come with me, brother," he said. "She hasn't evaded you for all this time by being stupid. Constance is long gone from here."

I frowned into my glass, watching the liquid ripple from the tiny movements of my hands. I was shaking. He was right, of course. Three months and I had had no indication she was still here. So, why did I feel a strange tugging in my stomach at the idea of leaving? I should go. I should go tonight. There was nothing left for me here in Dublin.

Still, I hesitated. I tipped the glass back, draining the last drop, and returned to staring, this time into the empty glass.

Doug laughed, breaking into my thoughts, and I turned my head to see him scrutinizing me with interest. His smile was wide, his teeth gleaming white in the darkened room.

"I know that look," he accused, shaking his finger at me. "I've seen it in my own stupid reflection. Who is she?" He leaned forward, sniffing at the air.

I sat back, dismissing him with a wave of my hand. "What? There is no one."

"Really?" His eyebrows rose, disappearing into the disheveled hair that fell across his forehead. "By your pallor, I would say you haven't fed in at least several days, but you reek of human."

"I've come from the city." I stood and moved away to pull a fresh bottle from the drinks cabinet, suddenly feeling the need for more alcohol.

"Aye." He chuckled, but I got the distinct impression he wasn't agreeing with me at all.

I opened the bottle and poured more whisky, glowering at him, which seemed to amuse him further. He tilted his head back, closed his eyes, and inhaled deeply as if tasting the air around him. I returned to my chair and sat in a stony silence for a moment. Finally, he smacked his lips and smiled again.

"A tasty wee morsel, brother."

I flinched, and as if of their own accord, the fingers of my free hand curved in, my nails biting into my palm. There were several scents trapped in the fibers of my clothing, but I was well aware the strongest was of cocoa, coffee grounds, and adrenaline—Ari.

Doug's eyes flashed to my fist and instantly darkened on reflex.

"You've been alone far too long, Clay," he started, showing the edges of his white teeth. "Believe me, there is nothing I would rather see than you happy."

"I would never consider a relationship with one of them." I looked away and shook out my hand, releasing the tension.

"I did."

"Yes, and look what happened," I said bitterly. "She died." Why were we even having this conversation? It was irrelevant.

When I looked back to Doug, his shoulders had relaxed, and his green eyes glistened in the lamplight. They tightened, pulling his eyebrows together as he regarded me with an almost fatherly concern.

"Aye, she died, and I would do it all again in a heartbeat for just one more second with her in my life." He sighed deeply. "Regardless, now is not the time. We need to leave."

I pursed my lips, tossing the full bottle in my hands. I still couldn't make myself move. "You are wrong. She is not a potential companion. She has figured out what I am, and I couldn't lie to her. Once she finishes work, I'm going to follow her home and clean up my mess. I'm going to kill her." The words felt like barbed wire dragged through my throat, and the alcohol did nothing to relax me.

Doug abruptly snatched the bottle from my hands, and less than a half-second later was standing in front of me pouring into his glass.

"No you won't," he said earnestly, "but if you want my advice…" He tipped the bottle toward me, and the amber liquid swished around inside.

"I don't. Not on this."

He shrugged, apparently unaffected by my bluntness, and then smiled. "You know you're going to get it anyway. You're not going to kill this girl. We both know it. My advice is to take the girl and get the hell out of here before it's too late."

A few hours later, I was hiding out on a rooftop in Temple Bar, watching Ari lock up for the night. It had passed four a.m. Inebriated men and women still filled the square, prancing around as though participating in some bizarre group mating ritual.

I dropped down from my perch and rounded the corner as two young men approached her. She smiled before turning away and making a point of politely ignoring them. By the slump of her shoulders and the way her movements lacked the determination they had had earlier in the day, I deduced she was tired, distracted…too distracted to notice me trailing her in the shadows through the city streets. I maintained as much distance as possible while holding her just within my sights.

She kept her head down as she walked, every now and then hiking the backpack she carried on her shoulder. She crossed the river toward a twenty-four-hour, multi-story parking garage, I presumed to collect a car, meaning she probably didn't live in the city. It was almost too easy. There would be no need to go any further. A dark, lonely multi-story was the perfect place to finish this.

However, we weren't alone. I caught his scent long before I spotted the boy. His clothes were matted in dirt and crusted with brown, dried blood.

"Well, isn't this a fortunate coincidence."

The vampire's ungainly movements gave him away as newly made, and his own living blood still burned inside his body. I could smell it on him. My throat ached at the thought of his thirst. I suspected he had yet to feed and had set his sights on Ari as his first meal. He would tear her apart, devour her in a despicable fashion, and the thought made me sick to my stomach.

The young vampire crouched behind a car a short distance away from me on a deserted side street. He watched her check over her shoulder before pulling open a door to the stairs and disappearing inside. I could have walked away and allowed him to deal with my little problem…but I didn't.

I kept to the shadows, my stomach twisting with fury. This vampire was too young, too wild to be the same one who had approached her before. His nose lifted, sniffing at the air, and his lips drew back, revealing his fangs in a snarl. The vampire's growl vibrated in the night air as he turned his sights on me. I launched at him, slamming us both into a metal Dumpster. His strength couldn't match mine, but he was a scrapper, throwing wild punches and kicking at my legs.

"Calm down," I snapped, rolling my lips back over my exposed teeth. He couldn't be much older than I had been. "You have a choice."

He bucked, attempting to throw me off, but I slammed him into the Dumpster again, clasping his wrists to hold him steady.

"Run or die."

He heard me. He blinked and narrowed his dark eyes. For a split second, I thought he'd run, so I loosened my grip. He drew his arm back with blinding force and smashed a fist into my face. Pain exploded across my jaw and rocketed down my neck. I stumbled back and received a jab to my gut. Maybe I'd underestimated his strength. He crouched, ready to pounce at me. I didn't give him the chance. I spun away from him — his knuckles missing my chin by an arm's length — and reached into the Dumpster, wrapping my fingers around a panel of a wooden crate. I yanked the strip free. He came at me like an animal, devoid of logic or reason, and drove himself onto the pointed shard of wood.

The boy's eyes widened in horror at what he'd done. His jaw slackened, and his human features returned. The crackle began at the point of impact as it always does. His clothes blackened and smoldered around the makeshift stake piercing his heart. It spread quickly, taking only seconds for charred flesh to turn to dust, leaving me standing alone in the side street.

I tossed the wood aside and rubbed my throbbing jaw.

With the other vampire out of the way, I quickly made my way inside the multi-story. I kept my distance and evaded the sparse security cameras dotted around the building. The air smelled stale with pollution from the river combined with gas fumes and the stench of human urine. I knew I had to act quickly once I heard the beep of a car unlocking. I knocked out the camera directed toward Ari, who was standing with her hand on the door handle, ready to climb inside the small red car. Her head turned swiftly in the direction of the shattering glass, but she was too late. I was gone.

"Hello?" she called nervously. I didn't answer. "Is there anyone there?"

I moved again and allowed the predator in me to take over, circling her—my prey. The scent of her blood invaded my head. Instantly, my fangs pressed into the flesh at the back of my lips. The thirst burned down my throat and through my entire body, cooled only by the increased saliva. My mouth watered for her. My fingers twitched by my side, wanting to reach out. The hunt awakened every nerve in my body, and my skin crackled as if electricity passed over the surface. I stood stock still in an unlit corner, the muscles in my legs flexing, ready to pounce.

It is no different from any other hunt.

She looked around uneasily and frowned, yet I made no move in her direction. I held back. It was unfathomable. Everything in my body told me to take her, but I didn't. It felt as if some unseen force kept me there against my will. I wanted to attack, but I couldn't bring myself to act.

Ari shook her head and chuckled quietly, perhaps thinking she imagined the presence and that the monster in the closet wasn't there.

I steeled myself, thinking about Doug's earlier assumptions. He seemed to think I was attracted to the girl. There was no doubting her quiet, reserved beauty, but she had an air of sadness that seemed to linger around her. It was this sadness and my curiosity that drew me to her. I wondered what she had lost...she *had* lost. If there was one thing I recognized, it was torment. Strange that I never took the time to see her before, as she saw me. Her inquisitive blue eyes had seen straight through my carefully constructed façade. If I had taken the time to notice this young woman, maybe it would have prepared me for her questions. Perhaps I could have kept my world from tainting her.

Doug's hypothesis was ludicrous. Other vampires took humans as lovers—often ending in a bloody death—but that was something that had never appealed to me. I no longer saw them that way. Their fragile bodies were far too easily worn out, and I had no desire to form attachments and watch the object of my affections wither and die before my eyes. There were no exceptions for me.

It was merely the power of suggestion. Doug had told me I couldn't kill her, so I doubted myself. I could kill. *I have killed.* Savagery was my special vampire gift. I braced and took a rattled breath. *Coffee and cocoa.* My thirst escalated until everything else disappeared except the delectable flavor of Ari's body. Hunger ripped at my insides…yet I remained hidden in the darkness.

I didn't need to breathe. It was a latent reflex left over from human life. Blood provided everything I needed for my body to function, the luscious blood that happened to be pumping through a moist, straining heart just feet from where I stood.

I moved swiftly, determined to make this as painless as possible. After all, it was my fault. I'd told her things against my better judgment. The least I could do was offer her a quick death.

Her hand gripped the door handle and, in the very instant I moved, Ari called my name. I brushed past her. The only evidence of my presence was her hair fluttering in the whoosh of breeze my movement created.

"Henry," she called again, a detectable tremor in her soft voice, "are you here?"

I closed my eyes and laid my head back against a van, out of sight. As an alternative to taking her life, I pressed my hands to the cool paintwork, listening to her elevated heartbeat drumming so loud it felt almost as if it was beating inside my own chest. Without another word from her, I heard the car door open. Moments later the engine turned over, and the car pulled out.

I stood there concentrating on the sound until it faded into the murmur of the other sporadic traffic on the street outside, paralyzed by my indecision and with no idea what had just transpired between us. What about this girl that I had never before taken heed of was suddenly squirming itself so far into my mind? Why didn't I act?

Something about her made me weak, as if she had bewitched me. I couldn't lie to her. I evidently couldn't kill her. Ari was nothing special from what I could see, and yet, even now, I found myself wanting to track her down. I wanted to discover the source of this influence. If I could discover that, then I could do what needed to be done.

Chapter 4

1868

My entire body felt as if my skin was being flayed slowly and tortuously, leaving every nerve exposed and raw.

"I'm sorry, Mr. Clayton, we've done all we can do." Dr. Boyle's voice rang out in my head, loud and booming as thunder, although I was sure he wasn't even in the same room. In fact, I was positive my father had excused himself and the doctor to discuss my fate in the study, away from my wailing mother and my young sister.

"Is there nothing to be done?" my father pleaded. "Money is no object."

I writhed again, hit by another convulsion. The bed linen was too heavy and far too coarse. Every fiber irritated my skin as if it were shards of glass scraping at me. The tendons in my neck stretched so rigid that one part of me feared they would snap. Another part wished they would. I wanted this over. My blood burned a path like molten rock running through my body, consuming me from the inside out. Soon, there would be nothing left but ashes.

"I'm sorry, Mr. Clayton," Dr. Boyle said. "Your son is in the hands of the Lord now."

"Anything," my father begged. I had never heard him beg.

My back arched off the bed as another surge of agony ripped through my body.

"I was recently introduced to a man named William Alexander while attending a lecture at the College of Surgeons. His knowledge of anatomy and obscure illnesses is unsurpassed. Perhaps he may be able to help. I will send for him immediately."

The agony surged up again. As a child, I had traveled to Paris. The journey had been perilous, by land and sea, fraught with unexpected bad weather. To a child's eyes, the waves were monstrous and the storm raging. I had cried when my father had told me to be brave, terrified the black water would swallow us whole.

Tears slipped from my eyes, my bravery faltering once more. My heart galloped unnaturally. Pain licked at my body and crackled over my skin like lashes from a flaming whip.

The last sound I heard, before pain swept me into oblivion, was the sound of my father weeping alone in his study.

I had no idea how much time had passed when I became aware of my surroundings once more. I twisted in my bed, experiencing the most excruciating pain I had ever known in my life. It thundered through me until I feared I had died. Only the flames of hell could torment so. Everything constricted, and my body spasmed over and over, the pain squeezing inward toward my chest and my galloping heart. I screamed, but no one came to my aid. Had I spoken aloud at all? White-hot agony blazed in the center of my chest, and my body locked down. My throat burned as if someone had ignited the flesh inside. I pressed my hands to my ears in an attempt to drown out the voices of my father and mother arguing. What was the origin of the soft, wet thumping that drummed inside my skull?

Thump, thump, thump…

"It's a miracle, Henry." My mother's voice rang in my ears as I twisted and turned, keeping my eyes shut to the blinding light overhead.

"A miracle?" my father echoed, mocking her.

The clink of crystal pierced through my eardrums, followed by a thunderous downpour that sounded like the loudest rainstorm I had ever heard.

Thump, thump, thump…

I heard humming nearby, outside, but as though inside my head. My stomach convulsed, and my brain tried to wrap around what was happening to me. I had no idea how I had gotten here. I needed water. I needed to quench this terrible thirst ripping me apart.

"He should be dead," my father said. "He *was* dead, I tell you. Yet he isn't dead and grows stronger by the moment. It's the devil's work, Esther."

I knew my father, and I could clearly hear the strain and exhaustion in his voice, and the way he spoke a beat too slow after consuming several brandies.

His words made no sense to me. Nothing made sense to me. All I knew was the thirst and the relentless thumping.

And the smell, dear God, the smell. Rich and luscious, with the faintest metallic undertone, like cool well water, except I knew instinctively it was thick and would slide over the thirst, soothing and quenching. I needed it.

Thump, thump, thump…

The humming was familiar to me. Lottie always hummed when she played alone in her room. No doubt playing with her dollhouse, make believe lady of the house. Yes, I could clearly hear the swish and crinkle of the stiff fabric my mother dressed her in. She hated when I called Charlotte *Lottie*, but still it always made my little sister smile.

Thump, thump, thump…

Another wave of agony burned through me, and I gritted my teeth against it. The bed sheets ripped from the force of my hold.

"You are mistaken, Henry," Mother pleaded with my father. Why plead?

"No." He sighed with an edge of defeat.

It was no use fighting, I needed to drink. I threw the cover back, squinting against the brightness. I became aware of the strangest sensation of dust being disturbed where it then settled on my skin as the hairs rose on my arms. My body was slick with sweat; my bed shirt clung to my chest, and my hair matted against my forehead.

Thump, thump, thump…

I stumbled blindly; my limbs didn't feel like my own. They were stronger, more powerful, beyond my control. How long I had been lying in bed? Perhaps this was a side effect of my treatment, maybe why this ravenous thirst consumed me. I held on to the end of my bed as I fumbled into my trousers, startled when the obviously mite-ridden wood crumbled beneath my fingertips. I didn't bother with a clean shirt or shoes. That could wait. My plan was to find the source of the scent.

The most potent of it emanated from Lottie's room, so that was where I headed, and then I could reassure my weeping mother.

Thump, thump, thump…

The sound grew louder as my feet moved over the ground, stumbling toward it. The pain scalded my body and my skin, as if every nerve was stroked like a bow across the strings of a violin. The pain was only enhanced by the lyrical humming. My nails dragged along the walls, tearing away the expensive wall cover my mother had had shipped from London. I peered through my eyelashes, unable to open my eyes against the artificial light of the modern gas lamps. An oval mirror reflected ghostly, pale skin, white almost to the point of being gray against my dark hair. My eyes looked sunken and hollow, bloodied. It was a mask of death. The memory of my attacker returned to me with the force of a blade slicing through my very being, cutting me off from everything I once was.

Thump, thump, thump…

Every other sound disappeared. Everything but the thumping. In the very moment I realized it was Lottie's heart, I realized my own heart pounded too slow and with inhuman force. I closed my eyes tightly. I wanted to scream, but my dehydrated throat closed in. The thumping in my ears grew ever louder. My body twisted in on itself, seizing against the abrupt agony as I was immersed in the sour, metallic scent and the stab of unnatural sharpness against the back of my lips. Fangs, just like the woman that attacked me in the dark alley. *No,* my mind roared. *No!*

"Henry?" Lottie's small voice called as the door to her bedroom continued to creak open.

Thump, thump, thump, thump…

It came faster. "Stay back," I choked out, but my voice was lyrical and more comforting than I intended. It didn't sound like me at all. I didn't feel like me. I was overwhelmed with an insatiable hunger, and my body battled against me to move. I imagined myself a lone man standing in the face of raging waters crashing toward a shore. There was simply no way for me to stop it.

"Henry? Are you still poorly?" she asked, clearly confused.

Thump, thump, thump, thump…

The walls pulsated, and I licked my lips, my will crumbling. Everything happened very fast or very slow, depending on how it was perceived. For me, the heinous nature of my actions seemed to stop time in its tracks. It was as if the world fell away, leaving nothing but a red veil cursing everything in that hallway. Yet, I was sure, for my family, what happened next was over in what must have been the worst, blackest, most vile and gruesome seconds imaginable.

My head snapped up, and my lips pulled back in a hungry snarl. I felt the sting of pointed fangs piercing my own skin. She smelled delicious. I saw only red, as though through glass that had been washed with scarlet. She stood on the other side, looking on at me aghast, both hands pressed firmly against her open mouth. My precious little sister, whom I had vowed to love and protect, with her perfect dark brown hair in ringlets and ribbons down her back, and her hot blood pumping so very close to the surface of her porcelain skin.

Thump, thump, thump, thump…

A door downstairs swung open, and the stomping of my father's shoes crossed the floor, followed by the gentler patter of my mother's. Both were frantic, no doubt knowing they left a dearly loved child at the mouth of the beast. My head swiveled to the sound, but they were too late.

"Henry," Lottie called my attention back to her. She looked at me with wide blue eyes, the artery below her ear pounding invitingly.

Hardly a second had passed. Fire exploded throughout my body, and thirst strangled me. I acted on pure instinct; my body needed blood, and Lottie was nothing more than prey. I pounced. The sound of bones crushing to pulp and flesh ripped open drowned her cries.

The first sip caressed my tongue, and I was overtaken with sheer bliss. It was the most natural thing in the world to feel the smooth, velvety wetness slip down my throat. The metallic taste was still apparent, but didn't dissuade me as my lips closed over warm, ragged muscle and skin. I drank deeply from the limp body.

All too soon, my father reached the top of the stairs. His collar was undone and his shirt crumpled. A layer of dark stubble speckled with gray covered his jawline and neck. He stopped, frozen in horror at the sight before him, but I didn't care. All I cared for was the blood.

I would not allow him to take it from me. I bared my teeth, hissing out a breath, feeling the warm liquid drip from my chin.

My mother forced him forward, pressing into his back because she couldn't see past his petrified form to the atrocity he was witnessing. Color drained from her delicate features. Her hand flew to her mouth, and her eyes opened wide.

It was the defining moment of my existence—the very instant I knew I was lost forever. My mother wasn't looking at me; her gaze fell lower. I looked down to the battered, mangled corpse of the seven-year-old in my arms—my darling Lottie. Her head hung unnaturally over my forearm, exposing her mangled throat. Her eyes were vacant and staring at nothing, and her tongue dangled from her lips. In her outstretched hand, she still gripped the tiny figurine she had been holding when she came to investigate the noise outside her room.

I watched as her tiny, blood-soaked hand opened and the specially made porcelain replica of her brother—whom she adored as much as he adored her—slipped, broken into two pieces, from her palm to the floor.

Chapter 5

2010

"I knew you couldn't do it," Doug stated, with more than a little I told you so in his voice. He had swapped whisky for blood from one of the same crystal tumblers.

My supply came from a local hospital, although I consumed only as much as necessary. I considered it better than the alternative and the madness that accompanied abstaining. I'd found over the years money could buy most things.

"I expected you to be gone," I retorted, removing my jacket and throwing it on the couch.

"So did I." He raised his eyebrows. "I decided I should stick around for a bit, keep an eye on you."

I poured myself a whisky and turned back to him. "You don't have to do that. I can take care of myself—"

I cut myself short when I spotted what he was holding in his latex-gloved hand. Clamped between his index and middle finger, a small, rectangular piece of silver caught the light from a lamp outside and reflected back into my eyes.

"Aye, I do. It seems I may have jumped the gun in thinking Constance was gone."

I gulped down the remainder of my drink and approached him tentatively, keeping my eyes on the inoffensive lump of metal as if it might explode at any moment.

"Where did you get that?" I demanded coldly.

"So, it is yours, then?"

I nodded stiffly.

"I remembered you described it, but I still wasn't sure."

"Where?" I repeated. I moved directly in front of him, forcing my hands to remain by my side. I wanted to hold the money clip, a piece of tangible evidence that my life before that night wasn't a figment of my imagination…that I hadn't always been this way.

The clip had been a gift from my father on my first day at university. "To hold all the bank notes you will earn," he had told me. It had been a talisman of his unreachable expectations.

"This little beauty was sitting on the stoop outside your door," Doug said. "I caught a vague scent of a vampire, but by the time I got there, whoever it was, was gone."

"It was her. It had to be."

"Clay, think about it. It could have been anyone. You don't know it was her."

I knew he was trying to rationalize, trying to see it from all angles because he still wanted me to go with him, but I didn't want to hear it. Any scent left by the vampire had long faded, so there was really no way to know for sure, but I did, regardless. Who else could have possibly come across my clip and known to find me here? I pulled my T-shirt over my head and used it to take the piece of metal from his hands, turning away to examine it closer.

It was mine. The silver was engraved with my initials woven through elaborate swirls. *H.C.*, Henry Clayton. Someone had taken care of it. I would have expected it to tarnish long ago. Why would she contact me like this after all this time? Surely she had to know I had been looking for her. I thought of Ari. How I'd lost the trail near her place of work, how the vampire had questioned her and the other vampire had stalked her. My instinct caught me off guard once again, as it had a number of times concerning Ari. I wanted to protect her, even though I knew she should fear me.

Those things had to be a coincidence and nothing more.

"What is it?" Doug pulled the gloves from his hands. "I can see the cogs of your mind spinning, and that never leads to anything good. Usually, it means you're looking for trouble, and I'm going to end up right in the middle of it."

He sounded more than a little eager for whatever trouble I might find.

"I don't understand the connection."

"Why does there have to be one? You think far too much for any sane man to bear." Doug walked around to stand in front of me again. Before I could stop him, he touched the tip of his finger to the silver and retracted it sharply, his face scrunching up in pain. He stuck his finger between his lips. A small circle blackened on the metal and then burned off, disappearing to nothing.

"Damn it man," I scolded him, "you're like a lab rat that never knows when it's had enough."

He quirked an eyebrow, pulling his finger from his mouth. "Really? Sorry, I was under the misapprehension that I was the one who wanted to get out of here and away from whatever discord is brewing." He sucked on his finger for another moment and then frowned as he looked at the small burn that was already healing. "How about you let me take care of the girl—"

"No."

Doug held his two hands up and took a step back. "I wasn't going to kill her, just sort her so she doesn't talk."

"I don't need you to clean up after me anymore. I'll take care of the girl tonight." I stared straight into his eyes, showing him my determination to handle this situation myself. I didn't want to admit that I liked the fact that she wasn't scared of me, even though she should be. However, now the idea of another drinking from her, or placing their hands on her smooth skin, caused a tremor of rage.

I wanted her gone and couldn't quite bring myself to analyze my reasons further. The rage morphed to a tingling panic in the pit of my stomach. Thirst roared in my throat at the idea of her body in my arms and her blood pulsing into my mouth. I desperately needed to feed.

I went toward the living room door. "It's almost fully daylight. I'm going to rest. Make yourself at home if you're staying. You know where everything is."

The next evening, I returned to Temple Bar with the determined intention of ridding myself of this festering obsession. Ari had somehow crawled under my skin and inside my subconscious. Her face, her voice, the sensation of her fingers on my skin, and how it prickled at her touch invaded my thoughts and allowed me no rest. When I should have been thinking about *her*—the demon who had left the money clip at my house, I was fixated on a human girl I hardly knew.

The square felt more crowded than a usual Saturday, although I knew it wasn't. It was me feeling boxed in, confined by my failure to act earlier, the failure to take control. I was unable to move on and deal with the real issues at hand until I removed Ari from the equation. So, I was very much vexed when I took my seat at the aluminum table and realized she wasn't there.

The other girl, who had been working the day before, nodded to me, letting me know she would be with me soon, but something about her eyes held an accusation. The air was thick and heavy with the scent of tobacco, beer, and food. It lacked the scent I had begun to associate with this place, and it struck me quite brutally that, in fact, I had noticed Ari before.

She had wormed her way into my head when I wasn't looking. How did she do that? I wondered if she even meant to. I knew nothing about her besides the scent of her flesh and blood, the sound of the tremor in her voice when she was frightened, and the heat of her body. Then I'd made the mistake of opening myself to the hunt.

"She's not here," the girl said in a thick north Dublin accent. She was younger than Ari and wore too much makeup. It made her skin take on an unnatural orange pallor. I never did understand the need for women to paint their faces.

"I'm sorry?" I took out my newspaper with the illusion of casualness.

"Ari. She called and asked me to come in today. It was my day off," she stated coolly, avoiding my eyes as she wiped the table down.

I shuffled my newspaper in front of my face and pointedly ignored her.

"Ari is a nice girl. A bit weird." She paused and shrugged. "She's had enough grief and doesn't need to be messed around, so whatever it is you want or whatever you are doing to her, you should stop it," she prattled on, reprimanding me as she cleaned up the table, never once lifting her eyes, as I was now waiting for with my newspaper lowered. "She moons about the place waiting for you to show up every single day, and one conversation sends her into a tailspin. I know your type—"

She cut off when she looked up into my eyes and froze with her index finger of one hand pointing at me and a cup and cloth in the other. The girl looked little older than a child. Her skinny fingers were adorned with several rings, including a Claddagh ring on her wedding finger with the small crown over the heart turned out, indicating she was taken and therefore would be missed.

I was shocked, although I didn't let it show. Ari had apparently been watching me closely for months. I didn't like that it made a sudden adrenaline-like feeling rush through my body. I didn't like that it bothered me that I had upset her. Why should I care in the slightest about one human girl? If Abhartach rose, or the group of crazies that believed he would rise descended upon the city, they would be nothing more than dinner.

The girl stood frozen in my gaze. I held her there intentionally. It was a few seconds, but it allowed me the knowledge that I hadn't lost my touch. I still possessed the ability to terrify. It was only by the grace of fate that she had a husband or lover at home. Otherwise, she would find herself another statistic in the growing rate of unsolved murders in the city, simply for the way she dared to speak to me. Little did she know she was gazing into the face of death.

The blunt kick of a heavy boot landed against my shin, and I caught myself still looking deeply into the blackness of the young waitress's eyes. Doug wrapped his long fingers around her upper arm as I sat back, slightly disoriented by my recent discovery about Ari. Doug's smile was dazzling and charming. The girl smiled back at him, her cheeks slightly flushed. I glanced around quickly, but no one seemed to notice our exchange. They were all too busy leading their own lives.

"How's about you bring me and my friend here some coffee, all right, Petal?" he asked. His face was right up in hers, hardly an inch between them.

She nodded silently. Doug then leaned in toward her shoulder casually, still holding her arm as if they were old friends. She swallowed tightly. He was so close that his nose brushed one of the tendrils of hair framing her face. It had come loose from the knot at the back of her head. He inhaled deeply, catching the scent at the curve of her neck, and his jaw clenched before he smiled again, this time the smile of a devil. Doug never did know when to stop.

"As soon as we leave, you will decide to lock up early," he whispered seductively next to her ear. I knew no one else could hear him. "You won't remember us being here. You'll make love to your man." I watched as the smile turned the edges of his lips upward. "Maybe you could try something new, something you've always wanted to do and never felt brave enough to. You'll enjoy it."

She nodded her head, her heart rate picking up a beat, and I rolled my eyes. Some had abilities beyond the norm. For Doug it was manipulation, although it only appeared to affect humans. He could spot a human's weakness with little difficulty and influence their mind to turn their vulnerability to his advantage. Sometimes, like now, he simply used it to amuse himself. Doug pulled back, talking at a normal volume again.

"Now off with you, wench, and fetch us some sustenance." He swatted her ass a little harder than playfully, making her jump, and yet she smiled at him.

An older woman at the next table glared at Doug, then huffed with second-hand indignation for the girl and turned away.

He slumped heavily into the seat opposite me, letting out a satisfied gush of air and smirking like a child that had just gotten away with unspeakable mischief.

"That was uncalled for," I told him sternly.

"Of course it was called for." Doug shook his head in disbelief and his gangly legs stretched out below the table. He eyed up a young woman that walked by. It wasn't hard for him to catch their attention either. Females flocked to him despite their residual instinct to stay away. He winked, earning an excited giggle. "Sex is always called for. I did her a favor."

I envied Doug for that, the casual way he could interact with human women. It was an unnatural coupling, and still he managed it as naturally as human breathing. I envied the illusion of humanity he still managed to retain, all these years later. He hunted and drank from them on occasion. He had killed. There was no doubt in my mind Doug could be an untamed animal if he wished it. But he loved life; he lived it. It had brought him heartache, but he traveled and experienced the world regardless, unlike me. I simply watched from the sidelines.

I leaned forward to avoid speaking loudly. Just because no one was paying attention didn't mean I should invite it. "How do you know her boyfriend will want sex?"

He snorted and did a double take, seeing I was completely serious, before he laughed incredulously. "Spoken like a man who has abstained for one hundred and forty years."

The girl returned and placed two cups of coffee on the table. She certainly appeared to be of a brighter disposition than moments ago, but she didn't glance at either of us.

Doug smirked his signature *I told you so* face and picked up a coffee, taking a mouthful. His face immediately contorted and creased up. He opened his mouth, his tongue protruding into the air as he attempted to rid himself of the taste.

"How do you drink this? It tastes like dirt."

"I don't, and what are you doing eating dirt?" I asked innocently, amused at his reaction.

He narrowed his eyes and tilted his head suspiciously. "Well, if you aren't coming here for the coffee, what brings you here, I wonder?" He looked over his shoulder to the girl and back to me, then back to the girl. "Nah, not her."

I rolled my eyes dramatically.

"Really, Clay, we don't have time for whatever this old-man courting is that you have going on."

"I'm taking care of it."

"It doesn't look like it."

"Tonight," I said simply.

Doug's hand shot into the air snapping his fingers to alert our young waitress to our table. She came rushing over straight away, practically panting. "What's her name?" He directed the question to me.

"Ari."

"Be a love, Petal, and fire off Ari's address."

Without hesitation, she did, while I fixed my gaze on Doug. I was beginning to feel cornered by him, pushed into leaving. What I couldn't figure out was why I needed to be pushed.

"I could have tracked her myself," I told him after the girl walked away again.

"But you didn't."

Chapter 6

I told Doug I could handle one human and came alone despite his protests. I didn't want to listen to him pushing and prodding. It was *my* mistake. I was the one who had revealed myself, and I could deal with the repercussions.

I broke the lock to her back door with little effort. It was a myth vampires couldn't cross a threshold without an invitation, something humans told themselves to feel safe.

The house was a rundown, slightly isolated, one-story property in the suburb of Howth, north of the city. Despite the disrepair of the building, I was surprised she lived in a considerably affluent area of Dublin. Her house was on high ground and far inland from the harbor. Down below, the promenade with its boutique shops and eateries lay silent and empty. The scent of salt water and fish from the fishmongers at the end of the pier burned in my nostrils.

I had been here a good portion of an hour, and still Ari was alive, sleeping uneasily in the bedroom I had yet to enter. The interior of the house was equally as dilapidated as the exterior, seeming like it had lacked care and attention for several years. I made my way through her living room, trailing my fingers lightly over her possessions. It was cramped, with a small couch and one armchair in a flowery fabric more suited to the seventies. A DIY chrome and glass bookshelf, almost as tall as my chest, looked utterly out of place in a room with lace curtains and vinyl wallpaper. It housed an eclectic collection, stacked rather than standing.

Finally, I examined the brown tiled mantel, where picture frames cluttered together haphazardly. They consisted of an array of shapes and sizes, from a black and white image of a bride and groom inside an expensive looking glass frame to a faded picture of a scruffy, small dog rolling in the dirt. The dog's frame appeared to be made of cardboard covered in string and dried pasta. I concluded someone had loved the animal dearly.

I would have thought the room's intentional disorganization some form of design statement, except the stack of packing boxes sitting in the corner indicated Ari was anything but organized or didn't care to be.

Her small kitchen was practically devoid of food and seemed more suited to an old person, someone who never managed to move with the times. The cupboards were freestanding, and the appliances included an ancient ceramic-coated stove with an eye-level grill. It shone as if scrubbed regularly. The air held a faint hint of chemicals — detergent and mild bleach.

Ari was proving to be a conundrum. I wanted to hear the story behind every item I touched. I was inexplicably drawn to her and irrationally reluctant to admit it aloud. I wanted to know more about her life, about the people in the pictures, and why she kept clean a kitchen she didn't even appear to use.

Her sleepy murmurs grew louder, floating through the warm air of the house until tangible, as if they became real tethers wrapping around me and dragging me forward. *It had to be the pictures. I should never have looked at the pictures.*

Ari became an individual with a history, a family, and behavioral quirks and bizarre little habits I didn't understand. It made it so much harder to see her as collateral damage. She had piqued my interest. The idea of killing her now disturbed me, but the reasons why I felt so powerless against her disturbed me even more.

I thought of another night long ago when I'd entered another woman's house and had picked up an envelope from a small table, the night Jack the Ripper had claimed his last victim. I shook off the memory for now.

Ari's bedroom represented the final boundary into her private space. The threshold was the invisible line I was loath to cross and yet compelled to. It taunted my weakness. Walk to the end of a short corridor, through an open door, and I would be there among all her secrets.

My stomach cramped, and I swallowed thickly, unintentionally tasting her in the air. It stirred something inside of me that I couldn't put my finger on. It wasn't only the hunt; it was more of a lead weight sitting on my chest. Something felt out of kilter, out of control and rotting, like old dead leaves, curling up and desiccating. I didn't understand why.

I hesitated for a moment. The walls seemed to sway, and when I attempted to take a step forward, my legs shook, then refused to move. The sensations felt too familiar to ignore. I had walked a corridor to my downfall once before. *This is all wrong.* I looked down and saw my feet sinking into the old carpet as far as my ankles, like treading a river of molasses. My mind was playing tricks to keep me from her.

I am a vampire, God damn it! I took a step and then another, and another, contemplating whether my intended actions were out of necessity or served another purpose entirely. I wanted this confusion gone. What was it about this young woman that had invaded my psyche over the last thirty-six hours and left me both shaken and enthralled?

I held my hand up and flattened my palm in empty air when I reached the open door, as if there was some invisible barrier I needed to push through.

Ari tossed and turned, knotting the bed sheet around her waist. She wore a flimsy little tank made out of some silky material that rode up over a taut midriff. The fingers of my free hand twitched by my side, and I wanted to reach out, to touch the soft fabric. Were her nightmares part of her regular resting state or instigated by our recent encounters? I imagined they would worsen astronomically if she knew about the demons stalking her in the shadows and creeping around her home. Thirst burned through me, and I licked my lips in response. It was more of a struggle to keep it at bay now that I had allowed the hunter in me to seek her out.

Her room, like the other rooms, was a mishmash of new and old. Most noticeable was the high-tech treadmill facing onto the large picture window and a punching bag hanging from the ceiling. A set of wraps lay discarded on the floor. I moved silently and pushed aside the lace curtain. Most of what I could see past the small, simple-lawned garden were trees and the tops of the neighboring houses. In the distance, to the right of the view, I glimpsed the smallest area of moving water, rippling like black ink in the darkness.

Something else caught my eye—an open book at the edge of the bed by her leg, inching closer to toppling off the side every time she moved. *Shakespeare's Love Sonnets.* It appeared Ari was a romantic.

On top of the dresser, a larger book, this one about mystical Celtic creatures, lay half-hidden under a discarded silk scarf. I made out the words *The Veil* on the cover. It smelled of old, disintegrating paper and too many humans, suggesting a library book.

I moved closer, intent on solving the mystery of Ari before destroying her. My hand reached out, my fingers a hair's breadth away, when I heard a change in the fluttering of her heartbeat. I spun on my heels to see her stretching out, her eyelids moving quickly, her body fighting sleep. Maybe she sensed danger nearby.

I held still and inhaled, knowing I should end this now and move on. The air in the room smelled strongly of the scent I had come to associate with her…cocoa and coffee, laced thickly with the slightly musty smell of a house left closed for some time, and the sea. I needed answers. I couldn't stand the idea of the torment that awaited me if I ended this young woman. The idea of never knowing the answers I craved was beyond chilling.

She turned over again, flopping onto her back, and her fingers dragged slowly across the top of her breasts in an act that was unintentionally incredibly sensual, before her hand fell by her side. The movement trapped her hair below her head. It exposed her neck and the tendon protruded when her face turned toward me. Ari's lips pouted, clearly unsettled by her dreams.

As for me, she had stirred the warm air in the room further, and my stomach trembled. I had an overwhelming desire to touch the soft, pale, golden skin where her throat met the curve of her shoulder and blood throbbed, making the skin there pound rhythmically.

It was foolish to resist. She would never know. My touch could be as light as a feather and fast as the wind. More importantly, Ari had invited a fiend into her life the moment she sat down at the table with me, a fiend who had thought of nothing but killing her since. Why should I feel remorse for wanting to touch her?

I crossed the narrow space between us and stood by her bed, observing her for a moment before I knelt. Her lips continued to move in the steady murmurs, yet even from this distance I couldn't make out the words. Before I could stop myself, I stroked her cheek tenderly with the back of my fingers and skimmed down her throat to where her blood pumped under her jaw. Tingles pricked at my fingers. I closed my eyes, concentrating on the tremors of the living pulse under her delicate skin. Her throat was smooth and soft as velvet, but as easily ripped as tissue paper. My mouth watered.

Inexplicably, even though I knew my touch had to be too fast for her to feel, she sighed, and her face turned ever so slightly, seeking something. It was almost as if she immediately felt the absence.

I blinked several times. An alien rage spread through my chest, sending a fiery heat flashing down my spine and crackling over my skin. I didn't want to feel for her, because I didn't want to feel anything. This girl had plagued my life. She had watched me, sought out my company. She had ensnared me, and like any caged beast, I was enraged. The sharp sting on my teeth was instantaneous. This would end tonight. Hunger I hadn't known in decades tore through me as I finally allowed the hunt to take over.

As if she could read the devil's mind, she whimpered, and a single tear escaped from her closed eyelid, running down her temple and into her hairline. The book teetering on the edge of the bed finally fell, hitting the wooden floor with a quiet thump. In the next instant, she opened her eyes.

She hadn't seen me, but it did nothing to alleviate my sense of failure. I panted, clenching and unclenching my fists. How could I go home and admit to Doug that I couldn't handle one human? The girl was nothing to me. Absolutely nothing.

I walked toward home, keeping my pace slow, forcing myself to appear human. The action gave my mind something to distract it as I reeled over leaving Ari alive. I didn't want to admit to Doug that I wanted something from her other than blood. There had been the ever-present niggling in the back of my mind from the first time she touched me. Damn, I desperately wanted her to touch me again. Perhaps Doug was right; perhaps I'd been alone far too long, and this was the result.

I was so close I could practically taste my revenge on the one who cursed me into this life, and all I could think about was Ari. In my frantic, pathetic state, I needed to think of anything but her. Added to that, there was the other situation—those intent on waking Abhartach? What kind of future would be left for any of us if they succeeded?

I walked blindly along the Howth Road in the direction of my home, concentrating intensely on each staggered footfall. I itched all over; I wanted to rip the flesh from my body. The agony was blinding, and all I could see behind my eyelids was blood bubbling and flowing, pumping a slow, steady beat. For an instant, I was almost convinced my heart had begun to speed up, although I knew it to be impossible. I was hanging on the edge of a precipice, sickeningly close to falling off and returning to her. I wanted to fall at Ari's feet and beg her to release me from this escalating torture. She had to be some sort of enchantress sent to tempt me. Just one conversation and I was lost in her.

The pounding grew exponentially louder, and the metallic scent of blood burned in my nostrils along with the fresh salty human flesh and coffee. There wasn't a soul in sight, and the vast majority of houses and apartment blocks I passed along the road were in darkness. Still, the pounding tormented me, telling me she was near.

My muscles twitched under my flesh, jerking and flexing, needing to bound after my prey. The rich, pounding blood came closer, and the air stirred with each contraction of the body's heart and tightening of its chest. Rain began to fall, lightly splattering the ground and soaking through the light cotton of my shirt. Then, she was there.

She wasn't Ari, but I imagined this unfortunate girl as her. The girl jogged toward me with purpose and destination, her brown hair swinging from a ponytail and already beginning to dampen in the rain. The sky lightened as morning grew near, pale blue inching over the horizon.

My stomach knotted into a tight ball. Excitement crept outward like vines around my muscles. I had to have her. She didn't look up as she passed, puffing out labored breaths and listening to pumping tracks on her iPod. I swiftly turned to follow her, refusing to be denied again. Before the sun rose fully in the sky, I would have her blood.

In a flash of speed and with the wind and damp whipping against my face, I spun us both into the car park of an industrial retailer, just below a raised stone wall. No one would see us there.

She fought uselessly and struggled to cry against my hand, flat over her mouth, muffling the sound. The girl's blue eyes looked up at me, terrified for an instant, but it was only an instant. Why would she fear an angel? I had learned a long time ago that death came in many forms. I could send them on their way easily unlike the monster who took me. I didn't need to kill to drink. A bite alone didn't infect a human. Also, it happened too fast for them ever to get a good look at me. Ordinary people didn't believe in real vampires.

The small muscle at the side of her eye twitched once before she stopped fighting. I took my hand away slowly, all too aware of the shortcut in my head. I didn't want this. I knew somewhere inside me that this girl wasn't Ari, and yet it was *her* challenging eyes that gazed back at me and *her* dark brown hair that shook loose, falling across creamy shoulders and over my hands. It was *her* lips I saw parted a little, and *her* breath I tasted in the air.

"What are you?" she asked, a single tear rolling over her cheek. Too terrified to scream, perhaps believing this a dream.

I held her close with one hand and with the other gently wiped away her tear with the pad of my thumb. "You know what I am."

"You're death."

My hands trembled, and my tongue peeked out to roll across my bottom lip.

"I don't want to die." Her lips quivered, and she attempted to inch back.

"This won't hurt," I whispered against her ear, treading my fingers upward through her hair, twisting the strands and gripping it firmly, wanting to experience it just once in my fingers. It was damp from rain and perspiration.

"Am I dreaming?" she asked as I ducked my head.

"Yes," I murmured against flesh.

She sighed deeply, and her head fell to the side, allowing me more access to trail my lips down her throat. Her blood pumped hot and heavy under her fragile skin. I groaned, darting my tongue out to swirl over a small area of salty skin, and pressed my body against her.

I didn't intend to. Taking blood could be considered erotic; there was some form of base desire quenched for other vampires, but not for me. I had never taken such perverse satisfaction at the idea of taking a human life, and drinking blood had always been simply a part of this existence. Something I did because it was what I was. I thought of drinking blood no differently than a human might sit down to a supper of lamb or beef.

Reason stabbed an accusing finger into my brain, telling me I knew why this was different, but I didn't want to listen. My insides liquefied, leaving me too weak to fight this all-encompassing desire to possess. I toyed with my teeth, my tongue slipping over one sharp point. I grazed my open mouth below her ear.

She whimpered, and her hands pressed against my chest, curling with the pressure. I traced the contours of her breast, stopping where I could feel the pressure of the luscious, thick liquid through her rapid heart. The same hand circled her waist and locked her against me as my other hand covered her mouth to smother her cries.

I dissolved into the languid ecstasy of drinking human blood, only vaguely aware of what I was doing, sinking deeper and deeper into the void again. I only thought of Ari, grappling uselessly as I settled myself at *her* throat, the feeling of my fangs slicing through *her* flesh, muscle, and sinew, and the fresh meat and salt taste of the succulent liquid as it slipped down my throat. The sound of a heartbeat sped to a dizzying crescendo in my ears and ceased abruptly.

Chapter 7

1869

My rampage didn't end with my family. It extended to the entire household. In total, seven souls were lost, not including mine.

I lay curled in a ball, covered in blood, in the corner of my room. The scent of death permeated every breath I took. I quickly learned I didn't need to breathe, and if I didn't, it became easier to block out the scents. I didn't know if I stayed there for hours, days, or weeks. The concept of time meant nothing when hell stretched before me. I slipped in and out of consciousness. The thirst was constant, and my limbs grew weary and ached. It could have been the illusion of a devastated mind.

I didn't move when I heard the hall door open. One part of me feared moving would add another soul to the list of my victims. As long as I remained perfectly still, didn't breathe or open my eyes, I could continue to exist in the blackness. Another part of me refused to stir because I hoped whoever had just broken the lock to gain entry was also strong enough to put me out of my misery.

"Too late," the male voice said quietly.

I expected screaming, shrieks of terror, when this stranger discovered the body of Emily, our chambermaid. She had tried to run, begging for life. The attack was so vicious, her head had become separated from her neck and the hallway painted crimson with her blood. It took seconds.

Scarcely more than the time than it took to establish that this visitor wasn't tempting the raging thirst and his heart beat as slow and strong as my own.

"Henry. Henry Clayton," he called out.

I didn't inhale, didn't move, didn't blink. I did nothing to alert him to my presence. It was animal instinct, nothing more. A struggle raged inside me, I craved survival although another weaker part wanted to die.

"Henry, I'm not here to hurt you."

I wanted him to destroy me. Even though he spoke at a normal volume from some distance away, I heard his smooth voice as if we stood in a room together.

Footsteps on the stairs, more quiet sighs, and then a tapping on the door. It pushed in slowly. The hinges screeched in protest, although I couldn't recall it ever happening before. I may have been mistaken; all my memory had become obscured by a red mist with only a few coming through strongly.

I wondered why my mind selected that small number to retain. Lottie, my father's face, my mother's smile, and only a few others.

My fingers clenched around the shard of mirror, and blood seeped across my knuckles. I opened my arms to him revealing the sealed wounds at my wrists. Nothing remained of the deep gashes but raised pink scares.

"Henry, my name is William Alexander. I apologize for not getting here sooner. I'm so sorry I was too late."

I turned on him. My mind thought the action, and I was already there lunging at the devil, snarling like a deranged dog. *Too late? Too late for what? Too late to curse me himself, too late to assist me in destroying everything that mattered to me?*

I crashed into the wall, demolishing it, dust and fragments swirling in the air. He had easily swiped me out of his way with the back of his hand. Pain sliced across my shoulder. It knocked the wind out of me, and I inhaled on reflex. *Blood,* my mind screamed, and my throat roared in protest. It was old, dead blood, not holding near the attraction of what I had already consumed, not nearly so succulent. In one swift movement, I was on my feet, crouching and ready to fire myself at him again.

Dried sweat covered my skin, and the rancid smell disgusted me. Who knew how long I'd been lying in my own filth. My fingers and toes twitched, wanting to lash out.

"You did this to me," I accused in the voice that was no longer mine, but that of an animal. "You cursed me."

"No," the man insisted. He split his stance but made no other attempt to protect himself. "No, Henry."

A deep growl rumbled through my chest and ripped through me, loud as a clap of thunder. He raised his hands, and his expression only bestowed pity, but I was already away from the wall. This time he didn't touch me. He simply stepped aside. Everything was so fast, and yet I could clearly see every ripple of his clothing as he moved. I crashed head first into the mirror. The sound was blades in my ears. *Too loud...too loud.*

He stood in the rubble at the wall where I had been a half-second before. "I can deflect you for as long as I need to. Your human blood is making you strong, but your rage makes you impulsive and careless. I don't wish to fight you. Neither of us is immune to pain. I am only here to help you understand."

Anger flowed out of me like water from a cracked glass. I slumped to the ground among the splinters of shattered mirror and curled in on myself, wrapping my arms around my head. Their blood covered me and made my clothes stiff. The fabric irritated my sensitive skin. I would have removed them, shredded them. I knew the action would leave me naked. Clothing was my link to civilization. Without it, I would be nothing more than a wild beast.

My mother and father had been strict regarding my manners. As a boy, she called me her "little gentleman." I adored my mother, yet her face as she used the term of affection was lost to me now, never to be seen again, a painting that had been smudged.

Just like my body, my emotions were beyond my control, desperation, sorrow, anger, fear...all magnified inside me. They ricocheted around my head, making it impossible to hold onto any one of them for a significant length of time.

"Help me," I sobbed. "I beg you, help me." My eyes burned, but no tears came. I had lost the basic human ability to weep. *Human...I am no longer human.* "Destroy me. Take pity and send me on my way."

"If that's what you wish, Henry, I will...with one stipulation."

I pulled my arms away and peeked up at him. He had not attempted to move from the wall, and I scrutinized his appearance for the first time. We were a similar height, but he wasn't as slender. His shoulders were wide, and his posture straight. He seemed older than me, and handsome. The kind of man that ladies swooned over. He looked like a human man but clearly wasn't. His skin was pale, and his black hair reached past his collar, a little long for current fashion. He dressed as a gentleman in a dark sack coat, a pale gray waist jacket, and trousers. His wide tie fastened at the loose knot with a gold stickpin.

Doctor…even my inflamed mind remembered he was a doctor, and English by his slight accent. The memory of my father begging for hope, begging for me to be saved, returned to me. He couldn't have known the creature he summoned was the same as the creature who attacked me.

I stared at his impossibly chiseled features and his gray eyes, searching for honesty.

Like the woman I encountered in the alley, this man was clearly a creature of affluence, which meant he existed in society. From that, I deduced he must possess some ability to control the craving for blood tearing my insides apart.

It took all of three seconds for me to come to my conclusion.

"What is your stipulation?" I said.

"You wish me to destroy you?"

"Yes."

He pressed his lips together into a straight line and sighed again. "Listen to me first, Henry."

William made all the arrangements. The authorities would believe he had moved me at my father's request and bandits later attacked the house, leaving no one alive. Doctor Boyle had examined me; no one would believe me capable of such devastation.

We took a carriage and traveled west through the night to a deserted hunting lodge high up in the Dublin mountains. The building itself was almost a ruin—nothing remained but stone walls. I had heard of this place; rumors of debauchery and devils abounded. It was once the meeting place of the Hell Fire Club, surrounded by forest and land. I had never believed in the devil any more than I believed in God. I knew different now.

William explained that I didn't require oxygen but still needed to force breath through my vocal cords to speak. Therefore, if I didn't inhale, I could make the journey without smelling blood and so taking a life, but it also meant we couldn't speak. It did nothing to alleviate the excruciating agony of the thirst. I suffered in silence, reliving the final moments of my family. The scene repeated in my head with crystal clarity. I began to suspect that, like everything else about me, my memory was changed. Every detail of my life, however long that might be, from here on out would be etched behind my eyes.

"I was thirty-two when I was turned," William explained in what was once a reception room of the building. We had to jump to the second floor, something I did with ease. "I once felt as you do. I wanted to take my own life."

"What am I?" I dragged my nails down my throat, scratching at the burn. My voice echoed around the walls with each word, and despite the cold night, no vapor escaped my lips. I was as cold as night; my body, no longer able to produce its own heat, took on the ambient temperature. "I died."

"No." William dismissed the suggestion with a wave of his hand. "But you are different now."

"Then, what am I?"

He turned to a window that was nothing more than an empty frame and looked out across the vista. In the blackness of night, past where he stood, I shouldn't have been able to see anything, and yet I could. The sky, the grass, trees, everything was clear but in shades of purple, violet, and silver. I wanted to say it wasn't beautiful. How could beauty and darkness exist together?

William placed one pale hand on the wall, and his shoulders slumped a little. "You've been infected, Henry." He moved at blinding speed, a glint of light flashed by his side, but before I registered it, a blade sliced through my palm.

My eyes widened, and I attempted to pull away from his grip. It was pointless. I may as well have tried to remove my hand from stone. William held my hand flat, and scarlet liquid pooled until it dripped to the floor, forming a small puddle before soaking in.

"This infection, this wicked blood has twisted your very being and changed your nature. You are a creature of blood now, but the question remains—what will you hunt?"

I slid down the wall and pulled my knees up to my chest the moment he released me. I did not need to. I could have stood forever. My limbs were weary, but I had no desire to sleep.

William returned to his position by the window as though he had never moved.

"You promised," I reminded him gruffly. I didn't want this existence, whatever it was. I didn't want to drink blood. I wanted to be a gentleman, a doctor. I wanted to finally make my father proud. It all seemed so distant now, like a wisp of smoke I would never grasp.

William spun lithely, so fast I was sure my human eyes would never have seen it. "And you promised too, Henry. You promised to hear me out."

I nodded stiffly, finally conceding to one of my habits and rubbing my fingers across my forehead. The movement felt unnatural now, and I dropped my hand. "I will not live as a murderer."

"You don't have to. There are other ways," he began. "I was turned by my fiancée against my will. She had a perverse notion of us spending eternity together and sought out a creature of the night. She slaughtered her family and mine. The thirst took hold of me as it holds you now."

As if his words were heat to kindling, the vicious fire ignited once more. *Blood*, my mind screamed. I tightened my eyes, but blocking out one sense seemed to increase the others tenfold. I heard the hearts of birds and other small wild creatures in the distance, none near. Then I caught the scent of a larger animal. It was faint, very faint, and not as appealing as human. My mouth watered at the thought of draining another body, and my eyes flashed open.

"You can control it, Henry."

"No. I can't. It's too strong." I twisted to the wall and dragged my fingers down the stonework, leaving long, deep gouges. "Please, end it now. Don't make me suffer this any longer."

"Henry," he said softly. "You don't know what you are asking. It is a terrible, gruesome end. I would save you that—"

"Save me this," I snarled at him, bunching my hair in my hands.

"I attempted many ways to end my existence in the beginning. Drowning, hanging, a pistol, bleeding myself, but nothing worked.

We heal much faster than humans, and since we don't require oxygen, asphyxiation is out of question. We starve if we don't feed, but starving will not kill us. You don't want what starving will do to you. Eventually I discovered that I don't need to kill to survive."

"The thirst, how can you stand it?"

"I said I don't kill, but I must feed. When reborn to this life, human blood lingers in the veins. It makes you strong but unable to focus. It also inflames the desire for blood. In a few days, the thirst will become…muted. You will always crave blood; however, you can feed without killing."

I lifted my gaze to him; his expression spoke of nothing but sincerity. A monster but not a monster. A gentleman devil.

"You are a creature of darkness now, but you may choose to live in the light, metaphorically."

I allowed his words to sink into my addled consciousness as he continued to share the tale of his life.

"Henry, in my calling as a physician and surgeon, I have saved many who would have otherwise perished. My hands are more precise, my instincts sharper, my reactions faster. I see better; I smell better. I have reminded myself of that many times. This is the reason I continue to exist."

I swallowed, although the action did nothing to ease the constant thirst. The image of William standing over my bleeding family flashed through my mind.

"The thirst, how can you stand to be so near their blood?" I asked, each word slicing through me.

He chuckled darkly. "Each moment of every day is about temptation. Over time, it gets easier. We grow stronger. We all must find our purpose. Mine is science. What is your purpose, Henry? Before you choose to die, search inside yourself and find your reason to live."

Instantaneously, black eyes and a vow flickered in my memory. I had to concentrate to clear my thoughts and recall the creature that attacked me, yet thirst made the memory cloudy.

I will find you again. I will find a way back to this life and I will destroy you.

Chapter 8

2010

By the time the sun rose, I had concealed the evidence of my feeding frenzy in a local wooded area, deep below the ground where no one would discover it. I locked myself in my study. I didn't want to run into Doug. I didn't want to explain the reasons why Ari was still alive and another now lay rotting in the earth. I had no doubt he'd find me soon enough. Guilt plagued my thoughts over the girl's death, and the blood I'd taken from her seemed to congeal in my guts. I sat for hours unable to function to the smallest degree or rationalize my actions. It hadn't been hunting, although I took a fair crack at convincing myself otherwise. It had been cold-blooded murder, a needless death. I couldn't align my guilt with my knowledge of self. What did one human life mean in the grand scheme of terrible things I'd done? And yet, it meant everything.

I spent the day researching, attempting to get my mind back on track. Every time I closed my eyes, the girl was there to haunt me, glaring up from her unmarked grave, a vengeful wraith.

I contacted a private investigator, a vampire who knew how to retrieve information and I knew to be discreet for the right price. I asked him to find out everything he could about Ari and supplied her address, although not how I came about it.

How likely could it be that the one who changed me decided to make contact at a time of such deep unrest in the vampire world? I couldn't shake the feeling that the two were connected and that Ari had some part to play. Regardless, it was becoming more apparent that I wanted her around for my own desires.

By late afternoon, I was no nearer to answers. I contemplated phoning William, but I couldn't bring myself to do so. Not yet. It had been such a long time.

The radio had been issuing reports about a missing girl all day, almost lost amongst several other brutal attacks around the city. She'd been a nurse and had gone running before her shift, as was her normal routine. She'd never shown up to work after, and her roommate insisted she had never returned. I felt sick to my stomach. An unwelcome sensation.

Doug hovered outside the door, waiting for me to emerge so he would have his opportunity for confrontation. I didn't want to hear it. Surely, he would be the first to understand there could be no logic derived from matters of the heart, if that was the root of my problem.

A nauseated shiver rocked my body even contemplating it. *Matters of the heart—my heart.* I had always been so careful in completely avoiding any situation that would lead to unnecessary emotional entanglements. We existed against the laws of nature, and as such, things like the requirement for companionship, comfort, and romantic love should not apply to us. It was how I had endured all this time. It was the reason I had resisted friendship.

When I was a young human, there were plenty of women. I was no stranger to places where ladies of loose morals frequented. As a student of means, I thought myself beyond reproach and capable of anything. I thought life was there for the taking, and I truly believed I would live forever. How ironic.

I remained in my study until the day began to fade, remaining vigilant about my conscience. I tried not to think of the girl in the woods, but the more I tried, the more I failed abysmally. It wasn't simple remorse; this dug deeper and warped my insides, throwing up old memories of a young man with revenge hot in his blood, tempered with hope of a cure for this affliction. I feared the monster, feared my corruption was at last complete.

Fear was an emotion I wanted to believe was foreign, something I hadn't experienced since the early days of my immortal existence.

It wasn't entirely true. Now that I recognized it, I felt it everywhere. It was all around me. I was practically drowning in it. I had been afraid of so many things for so long, the emotion had begun to feel natural to me.

What happened with my latest victim was an emotional response. It was animalistic and brutal, a savage attack on an innocent. I allowed my vampire nature to completely overtake my logical mind. I didn't need to feed from her. I could have gone longer; I had in the past. That wasn't the reason I attacked. I needed an outlet for my feelings toward Ari—anger, frustration, desire, fear, and insatiable hunger, a hunger for possession, so violent and basic, I couldn't make sense of it. She had reached inside me and brought them all out.

The full horror of the attack was that I allowed the young woman to experience some of it. I took a demented solace in the idea she was aware a demon was slaughtering her, because in my mind I only saw Ari, and I wanted her to fear me. I wanted to be safe from her, but I wanted her safe from me too.

My actions in the early hours of the morning were repugnant. I had once, long ago, asked myself if a demon could repent. I knew now it was possible.

My mind seemed torn apart, split in two by opposing cravings. I wanted to know Ari, I wanted her to know me, and I was beginning to hate her for it. I also wanted to protect her but feared I was the greatest danger. I wanted to punish her for *my* lack of restraint. I had spent almost my entire existence as a vampire practicing self-control. I controlled the blood; it did not control me. I had lost control twice before in all that time, when I turned and the night I was forced to flee London. Thanks to Ari, my resolve had dissolved like a sandcastle in the rain for the third time.

I battled with myself, presenting reasons I should stay away, go to her, let her live, and end her life. However, by the end, my curiosity won.

I found Doug and his long legs sprawled on the floor outside my study when I emerged. He didn't stand, just pulled one leg up and draped his elbow across his knee, observing me with challenging green eyes.

"What's the play here?" he asked. "How long do we sit at the mouth of hell waiting for it to chow down?"

"I've told you to go. This isn't your fight."

Doug leaped to his feet and stopped inches from my face with an angry scowl. "Aye, and we both know it's that simple, right?"

I met his fierce eyes with equal determination not to back down.

"What's the play here, Clay?" he repeated, his words emerging with a rumble.

I backed away first. Doug wouldn't walk away. Giving in wasn't in his nature. It was the reason I owed him my life and the reason love had shattered him fifteen years before.

I placed my hand on the wall, jerking away when a vision of the hallway under lamplight shot across my sight and my mother's scream rang out in my mind. "I need you to put your ear to the ground, call in favors, contacts, whatever you need to do find out what the hell is going on."

"While you go to the girl," he said tonelessly. "I know you didn't kill her. It's not her blood I smell on you."

I made no response.

"Clay—" he hedged the one word carefully "—this isn't you. I need to ask, are you losing control again? Because…it didn't end well the last time."

I looked at him over my shoulder. "The day is fading, and I know she must have something to do with what's going on in the vampire world."

Doug took a couple of measured steps toward me. "Or, just an inkling, you're telling yourself that so you can be around her. Because it doesn't make any sense."

"Just find out what you can."

"I was wrong. This isn't love, Clay. It's obsession," he called after me as I walked away. "And it will get one of you dead."

Ari wasn't at the cafe. This time I didn't bother with sitting or any pretense. I walked to the nearest train station and took the commuter train for the short trip to Howth. I planned to watch her home from a distance, but as unfortunate circumstance would have it, she was there on the street when I emerged from the station at Howth. She didn't see me, and I quickly retreated into the late evening shadows.

The harbor front thronged with people enjoying the bars and restaurants, or some walking where a wide grassy verge met the concrete walls, keeping the sea back. Cars squeezed along the narrow two-way road that led to the pier and sloping walkway up a steep hill overlooking boats bobbing on the ripping water. The aroma of food and liquor hung thick in the salt air.

Ari's stoic expression gave nothing away about her frame of mind. I hung back and watched her walking until she found a secluded spot on the West Pier, away from the main thoroughfare, where strategically placed boulders prevented cars from driving off a steep dip onto the bay.

She sat on top of one of the boulders, gazing out as the tide dipped and flowed beneath her. At a glance, her pallor appeared healthy enough, and she seemed in no discomfort. She closed her eyes and tilted her face to the sky. There was nothing to see there anyway. Rolling clouds blocked out the stars, but I wasn't looking up. The action had exposed her long throat. I froze, fixated on the tremor of her flesh when she swallowed.

My knees unexpectedly trembled at the memory of my feeding the night before. No, it hadn't been a feeding. It had been some sort of twisted exorcism to rid myself of Ari, and it had failed.

She stayed over an hour, until night settled in and the air chilled. Despite my own recent murderous intentions, my irritation rose. Didn't she know now there were nasty things hiding in the dark? I intended to protect her from them. The irony wasn't lost on me.

A couple emerged from a nearby restaurant, their voices raised in an argument over the bill. Both had been drinking, I could smell it on them, tainting their blood. I paid them no further attention as they continued their squabbling on the way to their car.

Ari turned to make her way back along the pier. I wondered what she was thinking about so deeply. Could it be me?

I retreated into a doorway, waiting for her to pass. She appeared so lost in thought she probably wouldn't have seen me had I been standing in front of her.

She looked up, catching her foot on a crack. She teetered, attempting to regain her balance. When her hands lifted, I realized momentum had her, and she knew she was about to topple into the sharp rocks at the water's edge. I acted on impulse to lunge out of the shadows and catch her. We tumbled from the force, and I did my best to cushion her fall against the concrete. Breath left Ari's chest in a loud whoosh, and blurring pain raced up my arm. I felt skin shred. The scent of my own blood caused my nostrils to flare. But at least I was the only one bleeding.

I pushed myself up first and held my hand out. Ari lifted her hand to her head and blinked, disoriented. I crouched and listened to her rushing heartbeat. Adrenaline perfumed the air around her.

"Are you okay?"

She shook her head and tilted her chin up so she could meet my eyes, although I wasn't entirely sure she registered my presence. I was sure she hadn't hit her head. I would have heard, and my concern felt all wrong.

Ari ignored my hand and scrambled to her feet, brushing off her knees and elbows before peering up and down the street. Her lips pressed together tightly in annoyance.

"What the hell are you doing?" She scowled at me as though I was an irritation to swat away.

"Saving your life, apparently."

"I don't need saving."

I dragged my hand across the nap of my neck where the hairs bristled. "I'll try to remember that for the next time you want to dive in rocks."

"Aren't you a drama queen? I wasn't diving anywhere."

"Because I caught you."

She scrunched her eyes closed and inhaled. When she looked at me again, her heart quickened. "You're hurt."

I remembered my elbow and poked my fingers through the torn hole in my jacket sleeve. A hot sting throbbed, and I winced when I touched the four inch rectangle spot where a few layers of skin had ripped away.

"It's nothing. It will heal."

Ari ignored me and tugged my injured arm until I followed her into a triangle of radiance cast by one of the street lamps. Her strength surprised me.

"No, there's debris in there. It should be cleaned."

"It will heal," I repeated, wondering if she'd entirely forgotten our talk in the city or forced it from her mind.

"I don't want to owe you anything," she said without meeting my eyes. "Let me clean it."

A frown creased my forehead. This girl was twisting me in knots. I couldn't begin to decipher her reasoning.

"Please," she added.

We walked in silence. I allowed Ari to lead the way since I wasn't supposed to know where she lived. I had almost convinced myself she'd forgotten about our earlier conversation when we reached the house. She fumbled with a set of keys and glanced back at me uneasily.

Inside the door, she paused. "I have to invite you in, right? You can't enter without an invitation?"

The edges of my lips quirked up in an expression that I hoped would reassure her, and I stepped across the threshold.

"Oh," she uttered in a low annoyed voice. "Okay, so, no invitation required."

She ushered me through the narrow hallway to the living room I'd been in the night before. "You probably think that's pretty lame, believing things I see in the movies."

"No."

She shrugged off her sweatshirt and tossed it on top of the packing boxes in the corner. "Wait here, and I'll grab the first aid kit."

I nodded, perturbed and more than a little surprised by this unexpected twist.

The room was exactly as I remembered it, except this time the overhead light cast the room in a bright artificial glow. I approached the mantle, using the opportunity to take a second look at the photographs, relieved Ari's presence had brought out the thirst but not the monster in me this time. A student ID dated from 2009 lay beside the photographs, and I wasn't sure if I'd missed it the night before.

"Harvard — impressive, Arianna Caulfield."

"Med school," she replied on coming back into the room. "Not all that impressive since I dropped out almost immediately." She inclined her head to the couch and sat down on the coffee table in front of it. She opened up the small green box and bit her lip. "Take your jacket off."

"I told you it will heal."

She smiled tightly. "Then it won't be a big deal to humor me, will it?"

I shook my head. I didn't understand my own motives. The wound stung when I removed my jacket, but I'd had much worse. I wasn't lying; it would heal in a matter of hours.

"How does someone become…"

"A vampire?" I arched an eyebrow, and she nodded. "It's an exchange of blood. A lot of blood. A vampire drinks from a human, and then the human drinks from the vampire."

Ari's lips puckered.

"Why did you drop out of med school?" I asked.

Her heart thudded faster, indicating something she didn't want to talk about. She kept her gaze anywhere but my face, busying herself with taking out antiseptic wipes and gauze.

"Forgive me, I didn't mean to intrude."

Her lips curved up. "I like how you speak." She peeked up. "Your shirt is in the way."

I pulled the shirt over my head.

Ari did a double take and swallowed stiffly. "I meant for you to roll up your sleeve, but this will work too."

"Oh." I shifted closer to her but didn't attempt to cover up. I'd lost any notion of fake bashfulness long ago.

She set to work cleaning out the wound with steady hands. Muted pins and needles shot over the surface of my skin, every nerve inside me sparked to life and reached for the static her touch created. I forced myself to remain calm, fearing my actions if the hunter in me emerged.

Ari's eyelashes fluttered, and she forced out a breath. "It's a long and boring story. It wouldn't interest you."

I tilted my head in question and caught a flash of her blue eyes.

"My life wouldn't interest you," she insisted.

"You'd be surprised," I said. "How long have you lived here?"

"Six months, give or take a few days."

I glanced around at the packing boxes. She noticed and shrugged.

"Same boring story. I think you could use a couple of stitches."

"No, I won't."

"What were you doing out there? Were you following me?"

"Of course not," I lied without hesitation. "I was eating."

She tensed, and her hands stilled for a fraction of a second. Someone other than a vampire wouldn't have detected it. Her reaction amused me.

"I eat," I said.

"I presumed."

"Food," I added with a chuckle. "Regular food."

Her cheeks flushed, and she smiled at me. "I thought you didn't."

"I don't enjoy pastries," I explained. "I don't need to eat, but sometimes the mood takes me."

Ari nodded quickly, indicating she understood.

"So, Harvard?" I pushed when curiosity got the better of me. It provided a distraction from the building thirst. Another vampire wouldn't be thirsty at all so soon after feeding.

"My folks died in a house fire nine months ago. Only, as it turned out…" She trailed off, and her brow wrinkled. "It turned out they weren't my folks. Not the most pleasant way to discover you're adopted. After a couple of months, I was getting nowhere on my birth family, so I hired a private investigator who didn't mind digging where I couldn't." She taped a bandage over my arm. "He found I had a distant relative from Ireland, except when I got here, I found out she'd died almost a year before I was even born. This house was hers, and it was for rent, so I took it."

"I'm sorry." I meant it.

She shrugged. "I never knew her. I didn't consider her family." She checked over her work. Ari lightly traced the tape and skimmed along my arm. A stream of heat flowed beneath her fingertips.

The spicy hint of excitement spiked in her blood, and my mouth watered. The path of her touch continued over my shoulder and stroked down my chest toward where my heart should speed but didn't. Static itched beneath my flesh.

"You look like a man," she breathed.

My fingers wrapped around hers and removed them from my chest. However, I didn't release her. I cradled her hand in one of mine and scrutinized it, looking for the source of the energy that zinged in the air around her. She turned her hand over and flattened our palms. Her blood pulsed, and a rushing liquid sound thundered in my ears. When I looked up, she was staring at our hands in utter fascination. I realized it affected her too, like magnetic poles pushing away from each other. She didn't want to let go and maneuvered to thread her fingers through mine.

The sensation intensified, becoming painful, and trickled down my arm like scaling water. Red tinted my vision. The scent of warm dirt filled the room, the rumble of it cascading into a fresh dug grave. Hunger roared, and I saw the face of the girl I'd killed. I jerked back and flopped against the couch.

"Is that a vampire thing?" she asked plainly. "Pins and needles?"

The heightened sensations vanished as soon as the contact broke.

"I don't know what *that* is."

Ari pressed her fingertips to her temple and turned her attention to putting the first aid pack back together in the pretense of casualness, as though I couldn't read her every physical reaction. Her fear, her excitement, and curiosity.

"How did you know?" I asked. "About what I am?"

She shrugged, not answering. "So, how does this work? You bleed. I didn't expect you to bleed."

I picked up my shirt and put it back on, careful not to disturb the bandage. "I bleed, I feel pain, and I sleep. I do everything a man does."

"You eat," she added.

"I don't need to."

"But you do need to feed," she hedged and immediately held up her hands. "That's as much as I want to know about that."

The box clicked closed, and she stood, wrapping her arms around herself and walking to the bookcase. "What about sunlight, stakes, and garlic?"

I smiled indulgently. "Garlic is a myth. I've never been particularly fond of the taste, but it won't kill me. Stakes are true enough if they destroy the heart. Direct sunlight burns, although after about a hundred years or so, we can walk round outside in day, if we keep to the shade."

Ari kept her back to me and combed her fingers through her hair.

"I know the mirror thing is a myth. I've seen your reflection."

"It came from the old belief that mirrors reflected the soul and we don't possess souls and so cast no reflection. Of course it's nonsense."

Her head turned slightly, enough to show her profile. "That you don't have a soul?" she asked.

"That we cast no reflection. Our dislike of the more modern variety reinforced the idea we feared seeing the evidence of our monstrous nature."

"You don't like mirrors?"

"It's the silver nitrate used to coat the glass. We don't like silver."

She released a nervous chuckle. "I suppose this is no use either." She spun on her heels with a wooden crucifix clasped in her hand.

My stomach knotted, but I made no outward reaction, unsure if she meant to test me. The religious symbolism meant nothing, but someone had carved the crucifix from mountain ash, a wood long used in the protection against darkness. I rose to my feet slowly, keeping my eyes locked on hers. The room was small, leaving little distance between us. For this, there needed to be less. I approached her with care and stopped inches away. Her blood pounded at an alarming rate. She'd be exhausted as soon as all that extra adrenaline left her system. With her hair pushed over her shoulder, it left her throat exposed and reminded me of how easy it would be to remove her from the equation.

She didn't blink or flinch, not even when I slid my fingers over the crucifix and clasped it the way she'd clasped my hand earlier.

The pain was immediate, white hot and blinding. I forced it down and resisted the instinct to pull away. My flesh sizzled like meat tossed on a grill. I gritted my teeth, and every muscle in my body locked down.

Ari's lips slackened. Smoke and the aroma of burning meat thickened. She held her breath.

"The demon blood inside me burned my soul to ashes long ago. I am a monster who once dreamed he was a man. Never mistake me again."

Her eyes widened, and her cheeks paled. Her hand began to tremble, and the vibration passed through the wood. When I was sure my little display had gotten through to her, I removed my scorched hand, leaving a black mark behind. It smoldered and faded in seconds. The pain remained, pulsing through me like a heartbeat.

Chapter 9

1886

The lilting music of the piano danced around me as I forced my mind away from beating hearts. What kind of thirsty fool dipped his parched tongue in the most clear, fresh water imaginable? I did it to prove I could, to prove I controlled the blood and it did not control me.

So many hearts.

Years of practice had allowed me to pick out the ones who genuinely loved the music, those who lost their soul to it, as opposed to those who tolerated it for appearances. A love of the arts when London positively buzzed with creative energy showed character and refinement. The duplicity of the city astounded me.

Behind closed doors, those same ladies indulged in wicked romance novels and graphic photographic images. Extra marital affairs were rampant. Wives were no longer beholden to their husbands now that they could retain their own wealth after marriage. Gentlemen's pleasures took place in houses of ill-repute, and alcohol, drugs, sex, indulgences of senses were available in private clubs that were no more than cesspits of immorality. Tonight, many would trawl the slums in their white ties and tails, seeking excitement and a mug of gin before passing out between some unfortunate's warm, pink thighs.

Of course, none of that was of consequence. At the end of the nineteenth century, London had become a place where it didn't matter what you were as much as what you appeared to be.

It suited me just fine.

Time moved on all around me, not as it did for others. For me, time wasn't something linear that took me from A to B. My life wasn't a journey, as I had so often heard it described. I existed outside of time. I was a mere observer, studying humans as if they were nothing more than ants scurrying about, and so quickly and easily crushed.

I had become a patron of the arts, literature, the theater, sculptors, painters. I funded them all with my father's money, and as hard as I tried, my knowledge of investments meant my accounts never diminished. Music was my preference, violin in particular. On William's suggestion, I had learned to play. It was another means of perfecting focus with a mind that could now spin in a million different directions at once. So, I lost myself in music instead of the bloodlust. I became a gentleman vampire just like William, and then I surpassed him.

I had evolved beyond other vampires and drank only animal blood, a situation inspired by my savior that first night when he asked me what I would hunt, although he had meant the caliber of man.

In many respects, humans were becoming inconsequential. The zoological gardens had lost two of its larger animals recently. Ironically, society lauded my sizable donation to replace them. I had grown tired of hunting deer in the parks of London after dusk.

I spent more and more time locked away with my research and felt my own humanity slip through my grasp a little each day, despite my best attempts to remain part of society.

The music finished, and the warm bodies that surrounded me began to shuffle through the doorway. I waited until all but the last few had left. I had no desire to be part of the crush. Eventually I did make my way through the doors and down the ornate, sweeping stairs to the gallery where fine people bided their time until they could safely leave to their evening pursuits without causing a scandal. Oh, how London did love scandals.

Ladies in evening costumes sat rigidly straight on delicate brocade seating, whispering gossip while their escorts put the world to rights. Both were pointless and frivolous activities.

"A striking image," a gentleman standing next to me commented on the portrait hanging before us.

I wasn't actually looking at it, although I appeared to be. My vampire eyes had taken it in nonetheless, and I answered without taking a beat to consider. "I suppose so, but isn't that the purpose of all art, to catch our breath?"

"Many would say art is nothing but folly," he responded, raising his eyebrows.

I glanced at him sideways. He was almost as tall as me, but a little older in appearance, with a knowing reserved smile. His accent almost gave him away as English, except that my enhanced hearing picked out the tones and syllables of an Irish dialect—somewhere north. I didn't know him at all, and yet he didn't seem perturbed by my company, merely curious, although he kept a respectable space between us.

"Not at all," I said, somehow knowing he had made a statement he didn't agree with in the slightest. "Art serves a purpose. It expands our horizons, frees our minds, and opens us up to new experiences. It opens the imagination. All these great discoveries of our time—without the desire to reach beyond our boundaries, we would be forever stagnant. The folly is in closing one's eyes and not recognizing it."

"Well said." In my peripheral view, I saw his closed lips pull up on the side nearest to me. After what might have seemed an impolite but easy pause in conversation, he asked, "And what do you think of our friend in the painting?"

I hadn't thought much of him. It was somewhere to look, a painting to the side of the large room, almost a hidden corner where natural light never touched no matter if the sun might glance off the large paned windows. A place where I could be present and remain remote, be seen and keep my distance until I appeared to have spent the allotted time in company, so as not to be considered a mad scientist. I'd heard the rumors—people were curious about me, and it wasn't good to draw too much attention.

I studied the portrait while the man watched me, and I observed him further too, examining the information I had collected without intention. One advantage of my affliction.

The gentleman's heartbeat remained steady, and he waited expectantly, truly interested in my opinion. His fingers were stained with ink—a writer with an unhealthy curiosity. Not a journalist, though. He was too well attired, and by his robust frame, he clearly enjoyed a comfortable lifestyle. I had thought, at first, he might have been the artist of the piece before us.

The subject in the painting was nothing unusual for the time—a young man of obvious wealth, gazing into the distance. The work was a different matter, with careful measured strokes shown in the texture of the surface and great care taken to get the colors just right. The backdrop was vibrant red velvet I imagined I could almost reach in and touch. No detail was missed, even down to the specks of dust floating across gentle rays of light. Clearly the artist cared about the subject enough to catch even the slightest hair out of place on his head, and his face…I closed my eyes briefly, not wishing to see his eyes, the color of lush forest leaves in summer, watching me as I watched him.

"I see darkness," I said, opening my eyes but subtly averting my gaze from the painting.

"But such beauty and youth, ivory and roses…"

Suddenly, every heartbeat grew louder, and the sound of blood rushing like water flooded my ears. My mouth watered at the metallic aroma, the taste of life across my tongue. I wanted it and struggled to keep my hands from clenching and giving away my discomfort. This was what happened when I had let my guard down. Flames curled around my organs and rose up to engulf my senses in a searing inferno. The result of denying my body the human blood it craved. I swallowed again—the temptation, always followed by the resistance.

He was still talking, about art and the poetry of images, words and colors. How the people around us only recognized price and not value. He had lost me to my own demons. The young man in the portrait could so easily have been me, once so young and filled to overflowing with promise of a bright future.

"Sir," I cut him off more brusquely than I meant to.

His brows lifted at my tone, and I thought I heard his heart quickening, drowned out by those around him. William had warned me about this if I chose to forgo human blood. He said the thirst, the all-encompassing hunger, could strike the moment I let my guard down. Laughter around us increased in volume, and faces flashed in and out of my line of vision, grotesque, bloated and mocking. But oh, the taste…the taste would be divine.

Temptation and resistance.

"I'm sorry, but you must excuse me."

"Please, my good man," he began, a forced wit now barely concealing his desire to understand. He had no idea how close he was to dancing with the devil himself. "You must share your insight with me before you leave. It would be so unfortunate to spend what could otherwise be a perfectly dull evening pondering."

I paused, measuring the air in my lungs. I would not take another breath while surrounded by the fragrant pulsing blood. I would not breathe until I escaped to a place where I could satisfy it.

"The painting is a reflection, a mask, never changing, always beautiful. You must ask yourself what it hides of the subject. Perhaps now a decrepit monster, ugly and corrupted by flesh and blood and sin. Perhaps he is death. Even so, now he will always be this, too." I waved my hand dismissively at the young man in the painting. "This perfect creation."

He stepped back, finally listening to his instincts and sensing danger from the demon who merely dreamed he was a man once, a long time ago.

Someone called his name, distracting him, and in that moment, I fled, keeping my pace as slow as possible. Still, I moved faster than prudent, with the scent of blood in my nostrils and moisture pooling at the back of my tongue. I clung onto my last shard of humanity like a man skirting a great cavernous valley. One slip and I would lose my tentative footing. An image of the raven-haired woman played behind my eyes.

I will find a cure. I will take back what she has stolen from me.

I moved swiftly, thinking of the deer in Regent Park and swearing to move forward in my experiments. Animals would no longer suffice. I would have to find human subjects to work with.

Chapter 10

2010

I had told Ari I was leaving, but I didn't go far. I watched over her small house as long as I could, until the sky lightened enough to sting my skin.

She had taken to her treadmill. I listened to her pounding a steady pace for almost two hours. Her level of physical fitness explained her strong heart. I had been so sure she would fall into exhaustion after our encounter. Her stamina proved worthy of note. When I thought she must be worn out, the thumping began. It wasn't an even beat. She punished the punching bag with a rhythmic series of punches and kicks as though she was dancing with it.

Several times I came close to going back inside. My imagination had tormented me with what I couldn't see. I pictured her muscles glistening and her long limbs in motion. Finally the shower had started, along with images of warm water sluicing salt from smooth skin and curves.

I considered the possibility Doug was right and I was skirting closer to a precipice than I wanted to admit to myself.

Doug didn't return to the house during daylight hours, and I left as soon as it was safe. Temple Bar buzzed with partygoers, despite the heavy rain that had begun to fall. I watched from the rooftop of a nearby hotel until Ari closed up for the night and followed her home. Soon after, I headed back to the city.

During the day, it had occurred to me that maybe the first vampire that approached Ari wasn't looking for her but something else. Maybe he wanted something within the building. I was clutching at straws but wanted to rule it out. I ignored the fact that that unlikely theory did not account for the presence of multiple vampire stalkers in Ari's life.

The building itself was several stories tall, and it didn't take me long to get inside through a window on an upper floor. The alarm hadn't been set. I really didn't know what I expected to find as I made my way down the stairs. Some sort of proof that the Abhartach crowd was interested in her, I supposed.

At first, I thought the noise I heard underlying the consistent and steady pelting of rain on the roof emanated from the buildings on either side of the shop. It was only as I silently descended that I realized the sound was coming from inside. At the exact same instant, I caught the scent of other vampires wafting upward. I froze and waited until I was sure I hadn't accidently alerted them to my presence. Finally, I made my way down further; a silent fury began to prickle at the back of my eyes until a red veil fell across my vision.

The bitter scent of death twisted at the back of my tongue, and my fingers curled by my sides. Every nerve shuddered and bristled. There were two of them and one of me. In the light of recent events, perhaps they were not here to feed but for some other unknown mission. After all, Ari had encountered more than one vampire and been left alive. How unfortunate would one human have to be to attract another two, this time purely intent on feeding?

The hairs on the back of my neck stood on end, and an angry chill raced over my skin. *What if they are here to feed?* The mere thought of it set off a chain of rage I couldn't comprehend but was powerless to stop.

If nothing else, at base level, vampires survived on instincts: the instinct to feed and to live. We were natural predators, feral, territorial. These encroachers threatened Ari. I had been inside her home, inside her world. Reason told me I should be more worried that they *weren't* here to feed. Reason told me the sensations I experienced around Ari weren't natural, but instinct declared that she somehow was mixed up in an unthinkable plot to raise the original vampire from his grave.

I had the element of surprise, but I also had only a matter of moments before they discovered me. I no longer cared why they were here. It sounded as if they were meticulously searching through every space in the small area, secure in the knowledge that a rolling shutter hid the front of the shop and no one would be aware of their intrusion.

Flying forward at full speed, I leaped over the guardrail, intending to take the stairs a flight at a time. I landed on the first painted concrete step with a hollow thump and heard their heads snap up and their angry snarls at the intrusion.

I slammed my shoulder against the door at the bottom of the stairs and felt it creak on its hinges at the force of the blow. One of the vampires assaulted the door in that same moment and ended up smashed against the wall on the other side, obviously dazed since he didn't present much resistance.

"You really don't want to do this," I warned.

The other dived at me, and I jumped aside out of his path when I recognized them both as new vampires. They were strong, but their lack of coordination and restraint indicated they weren't yet used to their new bodies.

"Or maybe you really do."

They weren't only young in the vampire sense. When the other one slid from behind the door, snarling like a rabid animal, I estimated that they couldn't have been more than fifteen or sixteen when turned. Three new vampires in as many nights suggested someone was using them to do their dirty work. I lashed out, catching the one I'd already stunned with the back of my hand with a brutal swipe and sending him flying back into the hallway. At the same time, I leaped, bounced off the wall, and somersaulted over the head of the other one. I caught him off guard and easily seized him in a headlock. I felt the bones in his neck snap before his body went limp, twitching and juddering as he collapsed to the ground in a heap. He would heal.

The other one came at me from behind and tried to grab me around the shoulders, hissing in my ear. He, who I swiftly realized was a she from the small mounds pressed against my back, clearly didn't know when the game was lost.

I gripped her head and doubled over, pulling her with me. This time I made sure to fully remove her head from her shoulders. It was easy, like twisting a cork from a bottle. Her body dissolved to ashes and smoke before it hit the ground and disintegrated to nothing.

An arm wrapped around my throat. Fury pulsed inside me like a heartbeat. I drew my elbow back, catching the monster in the gut and giving myself room to pivot. I caught him by the waist and smashed him backward into the wall. I was only vaguely aware of the humans nearby beyond the shutters.

My fangs sank into his neck below his jaw, ripping his flesh rather than piercing. Blood spurted from the open gash, and my head fell back. A low agonized growl rattled my entire body, despite my best efforts to remain silent. I hated it, the raw metallic tang of the blood coating my tongue, and still my mouth clamped down on his skin repeatedly, tearing at his flesh, devouring every drop. My attacker had long since ceased fighting, and his body was already well on its way to becoming a withered husk. He had fed on fresh blood recently…young blood. It hadn't yet been absorbed fully and still lingered in his veins.

A blinding flash cast the small shop in unnatural glaring light, and my head snapped to the sound of a luscious thumping. I was still only vaguely aware of my surroundings, but now my only thought was the scent of adrenaline-rich blood in the human who had interrupted my assault. I tore the head from the vampire in my arms and spun in a cloud of ashes. I leaped over the small counter in one quick, lithe bound and pinned the intruding human to the wall, my body pressing firmly against hers before she even had a chance to gasp at my appearance. Ari's rapid heart and wide, terrified eyes only enraged me further.

I am a monster, I am a vampire…and I am thirsty.

Chapter 11

I held Ari by her arms, tighter than safe for a frail human, tight enough to break blood vessels below her delicate flesh and leave imprints of my fingers. My lips touched her skin, settled at the gentle curve to her shoulder. She didn't cry out, didn't beg for her life or scream like the ones I scared so senseless they became convinced I couldn't have been more than a nightmare.

Instead, her fingers tightened on the fabric at my waist, almost as though she were clinging to me. I ran my lips up and down her neck, savoring her fragrance and feeling the throbbing blood below her tantalizing skin. *Blood*, my mind roared. Her heart thundered against my chest, beating out erratic thumps and racing to a dizzying crescendo.

Her heat and electricity were everywhere, cocooning me in flames that battled with the inferno raging through me — the bloodlust at full force. The anticipation made it so much sweeter, and adrenaline spiking in her body intensified her scent, pushing against me like a tidal wave.

My lips parted. My tongue swirled over the throbbing vein below her ear, and my fangs touched flesh, barely grazing. Only enough to release a bead of ruby liquid, and that dried almost immediately, so close and so delicious. Goose bumps rose on the skin under my mouth, and her sweet, warm breath ruffled my hair. Still no fighting, no whispered plea, only those long, slender fingers twisting into the fabric of my shirt as if to keep me there forever. They wouldn't…they couldn't.

My tongue peeked out and tasted the salt of her skin, felt the zing of the charge, dimmer now than it had been. My lips pressed down, shielding the sharp edge of my teeth for the kiss I placed at her shoulder. Her body shivered against me, stirring the air with the aroma of cocoa and coffee. Her fingers loosened and skimmed over my hips, falling by her sides.

Blood, my instincts demanded, but my body refused to comply with the order. Ari's head tilted, giving in to me, exposing more flesh, but I didn't bite. I wanted to. The monster was out of his cage, eager to be satisfied.

When my mouth next pressed to her skin, a different hunger abruptly consumed me — one I fought against harder than the thirst. I wanted this human with everything in me. I wanted her in more ways than I should have. My insides warped and roiled violently.

Human desires flared as her heart slowed, taunting me with my own weakness.

In that moment, I wanted Ari alive more than I wanted her blood. *Impossible.*

I trailed the tip of my nose to her jaw. Why didn't she fight? A strange calm crept inside me, cooling the ravenous thirst. The desire to kill receded slowly, fought back by the desire to protect. A relative calm returned to my mind as I continued to hold her, keeping very still, my face buried in the crook of her neck.

She was limp in my arms. Ari hadn't given in to me while I fought myself. She'd passed out cold.

What am I doing?

Ari was still unconscious. I'd listened for injury and found nothing out of place. Had the shock of seeing my true face been too much for her? She'd been in a bed at my home for the last two hours. I'd spent the entire time watching her, waiting for any change at all, a flutter in her steady heartbeat or a shift in her breathing. Not so much as a twitch. It was as if she were merely sleeping peacefully.

I didn't dare move for worry I would lose control. The vampire in me still desired to finish what I'd started. It held on to the prospect of tasting her like a prize just outside its grasp. The scent of Ari's blood filled the entire house, and it itched at my throat. Fortunately, the vampire I'd drained muted the thirst for now. It was the only thing that brought me back from the brink, that and Ari. The newly awakened male in me craved other things from her body, other tastes and dark desires just as heinous. I didn't dare move.

This had once been my parents' room. Just about the only thing that remained was the ornately carved bedframe, although a new luxurious mattress replaced the old horsehair one. The ugly, dark geometric pattern wallpaper was also gone, the walls now a simple cream. My father's dressing room had been converted to a bathroom with marbled tiles and a roll top bath. My specially installed shutters kept the room dark. They had the added advantage of keeping the windows secure when locked.

She looked so tiny, mostly hidden under the plush comforter, and her lovely hair splayed out over the pillows. I wanted to move closer but was wary. In this place where the scent of human blood rarely invaded, her presence was almost overpowering.

"It's done." Doug appeared by my side, shirtless with a towel around his neck and his damp hair ruffled. "There wasn't much damage."

"Thank you. It's the last time."

"Aye." Doug snorted, drawing my eyes to his smirk. "Please, Clay, let's not go there again. It's not the first time nor the last I'll clean up after you."

"Thank you."

Doug leaned casually against the doorframe, crossing his arms, and then stood on his toes for a closer look at Ari. He hummed thoughtfully once, and then again, clearly indicating I should ask what was on his mind.

"What?" I kept my voice low.

"We're kidnapping humans now?"

"I didn't kidnap her."

He paused for a moment. "Well, I was wondering exactly what it is you think you are doing?"

"Waiting for the girl to wake."

He hummed again. "You're watching her sleep, brother. A vampire watching a human sleep, in your home. Asleep…in your home… a human…a vampire."

I darted a cold glare in his direction, cutting him off before he went through his cycle of passive aggressive comments again. Doug shrugged, lifting a hand to show he meant no harm.

"Just pointing out it's a wee bit creepy. You've migrated from stalking your prey to just stalking." He slapped his hand on my shoulder. "Come on, I'll buy you a drink while you're waiting for Sleeping Beauty to wake."

I chuckled quietly, "Now, that would be a first." I was more comfortable now I wasn't alone with Ari. "What have you learned?"

"Nothing good. I'll fill you in downstairs."

I pulled the door closed and followed Doug, barely making it to the second step when we both heard her stir.

Ari's heart remained steady for a moment or two; perhaps she was taking in her unknown surroundings in those few brief waking seconds when real life remained in soft focus and the truth existed between darkness and shadow. All too soon, the beats became erratic and loud, pumping fresh blood through her veins and her scent through my home. I swallowed thickly and clenched my fists, resisting the urge to return to her.

Doug frowned and looked up to me. "She'll be scared, but she *is not* going anywhere. Let's go get that drink." His words were both advice and warning. My actions had placed us both in danger.

I followed him into the kitchen two floors down, where he proceeded to pour us two large tumblers of whisky. I knocked mine straight back, placing the empty glass on the counter for a refill before he put the lid back.

This was the darkest room in the house, with only high narrow windows providing any natural light during the day. The kitchen had been refitted with sharp contemporary beech cabinets and thick black quartz worktops. The shelves were stocked with every cooking utensil a modern kitchen should have — everything was about the illusion — but nothing had ever been used, apart from the dishwasher and glassware.

The sun hadn't risen yet, and harsh artificial light illuminated the room, bouncing off the defined hard lines of Doug's face and body.

"So, tell me?"

Doug tilted his glass back and swallowed loud. "It wasn't easy to get this. I had to crack a few heads." His eyebrow quirked up. "I mean that literally."

I pressed my palms flat on the surface of worktop. "And?"

"The new ones that attacked you were from some sort of loony vampire doomsday cult. They call themselves The Circle. End of the world sort."

"I got that from 'doomsday cult.'"

Doug raised his glass to his pursed his lips. "Now, now, no need for snip."

"What else?"

"Bunch of nasties intent on ending the world as we know not enough for you?"

Neither of us acknowledged what we could hear from above us. Ari tiptoed across the floor, moving stealthily — or so she thought — from window to window, trying for escape. I slipped my hand into my pocket and pulled out her powered-off phone. There were no other phones lying around in the house for her to call for help. No way out of the shuttered windows or locked doors. I'd had the house sound-proofed during the latest renovations to dampen external noise. If she screamed, no one would hear her.

It seemed to take quite a while for Ari to attempt every window. She persisted, slowly and methodically, until she'd finished with the upper floors.

"The nasties, they're all about blood prophecies in the vampire line and sacred rituals, something about Cailleach — a crone from Celtic mythology."

"Do you think Ari's some kind of sacrifice?"

Doug shrugged. "I think you're clutching at vapors and assigning importance where there is none. How could she possibly be con-nected? The vampires you killed were young and stupid and probably just got hungry. Looks like a random attack to me."

"I can't shake the feeling I'm missing something."

"Maybe now's not the time."

"You've changed your tune. You came to me with a scenario much like this. Remember Abhartach?"

He scratched his fingers through his hair and ground out a hard breath. "So you'd leave here."

"Is this Circle connected to the Abhartach crowd? Because it sounds like the same sort of thing."

"Aye," Doug said grimly. "It's a bit of a stretch that there are two cults trying to raise long-dead mythological figures at the same time, isn't it?"

Ari lost patience at the main floor's front door, pulling on the lock and slapping her palm hard against the unyielding wood. She huffed out several deep breaths at her failure to make it budge.

I winced at the damage she might have inflicted on her delicate hands. The scent of adrenaline was intoxicating. Turning off the hunter hadn't been a problem for many years, yet her blood inflamed my thirst.

Doug and I waited patiently. Well, I waited patiently. Doug paced the length of the kitchen, flicking switches, opening doors, and sliding drawers back and forth. I stopped him in his tracks with a glare. An excited smile trembled at the corner of his mouth, like a child on Christmas Eve listening for the sound of sleigh bells overhead.

Finally, a bare foot touched the first step of the stairs leading to the ground floor and the kitchen. I sensed her trepidation as she held her breath, listening carefully for sounds of life. Finding none, Ari slowly descended the stairs.

Neither Doug nor I moved. I stood by the stove while he waited by the doorway at the base of the steps. He flashed me a full grin — I hoped it wasn't a warning of mischief to follow. To him, she was just another human to play with. I needed to take the situation in hand quickly.

I narrowed my eyes in his direction, a silent warning for him to behave…a fruitless warning.

The moment Ari's bare toes became visible around the doorway, Doug tugged her inside by her arm so fast she had no time to react. Her long hair whipped around, mostly hiding her startled face for an instant before she stopped, pressed against the wall beside the door. Her wide eyes fixed on Doug.

Her heart drummed so quickly I feared she would pass out again. I swallowed, seeing the furious blush across her cheeks and rapid movement of her chest. Ari inched away from him, her fingers dragging along the plaster, tiny particles no human could sense gathering under her nails.

"Stay the hell away from me," she warned Doug.

He frowned and moved in a blur when she lunged for the door. "Not a good idea, Petal." He rested his large hand on the frame, towering over her, still bare-chested and his hair still damp. His other hand opened and closed a couple of times, stretching out his fingers. "I thought you said she knew about us."

Doug's eyes met mine over Ari's head, and she whipped around, finally noticing someone across the room. The moment her terrified gaze landed on me, I felt the rumble of a growl building in my chest. My fingers twitched by my sides and balled into fists. Thirst ravaged my throat, and the memory of her hot blood filled my head. I instinctively licked my lips. Bringing her here was a mistake, anywhere but here. The memory of events in this house combined with allowing myself to taste her made for a bad combination.

Ari spotted the knife block on the island between us and darted toward it. Doug didn't try to stop her.

She rolled lithely onto the island. The screeching metal as the knife drew from the holder made me wince, and I closed my eyes, seeing nothing but red blood cells bouncing around behind my eyelids.

Thump, thump, thump… just like a night in this very house long ago.

She tumbled off the other side, catching her foot on the foot bar of one of the high stools. At first I thought fear made her reckless, but when the wooden spoke gave way and Ari grabbed it in her free hand, I saw I had underestimated her.

"Well, aren't you just the secret surprise in the cereal box," Doug said with a short laugh.

She glared at him. The food analogy wasn't at all helpful.

"I do know what you are, and I know how to end you. He told me." She turned her attention to me. "You tried to kill me."

"No."

Thump, thump, thump, thump…

"Aye, Petal," Doug answered. "You're looking at the would-be hero of the piece. He was after the ones after you." I heard the careful undertone of his words. He answered for me, so I could concentrate on reeling in my scattered emotions.

I leaned on the stovetop and willed away the thirst just as I had done so many times before. Blood would not control me.

In truth, it had been a long time since I truly had to resist the temptation of blood. I told myself control was the basis of my existence, but now I realized it was more about power, delayed gratification. I flirted with the temptation, denied myself blood until my every sense heightened impossibly, and then I gave in. Over and over, I had given into the bloodlust without even realizing the extent of its power over me.

"What's wrong with him?" Ari asked. The fear was slipping, replaced by something else. The same note of pity I felt from her the first day we talked seeped into her words.

"Ah, well, that would be him trying not to kill you now."

"Dougal," I ground out. The iron grid of the stove creaked and strained against my grip before I released it.

"He only calls me Dougal when I'm in trouble." He chuckled darkly.

"Dougal! Give me a moment. Thump, thump, thump," I mumbled in time to her heart. The thirst receded, leaving a dull ache, a need that would never truly go away. "Thump, thump…"

"What's he doing now?"

A light footstep in my direction brought the beating closer. Dust particles swirled through the air, and tiny droplets of moisture from her breath settled on my skin, prickling like needles.

"It's a sort of meditation. Like you would count sheep until you relax enough to fall asleep," Doug explained.

"I don't count sheep."

"Of course you don't," he said dryly. "I bet *you* count little pointy sticks."

"He never had to do that around me before." She took another step, her voice significantly less scared and her heart calming.

"Once we taste, it makes it about a thousand times harder for us to resist that particular blood until it's out of our system. Our boy came pretty close to a full on taste test tonight. He'll move past it soon."

"Blood…oh God," she murmured, fear spiking in her body once more.

"Plus," Doug added brightly, "he's never been in this house with a human since—"

"Doug," I roared, flashing my eyes open and cutting him off mid-sentence. My history was my story to share, or not. In this case, I chose not.

Ari gasped and took a step backward, raising the chair spoke.

"I'm sorry," I told her honestly. I didn't mean to scare her. "This is difficult."

"Why don't you give me that knife, Petal, before you hurt yourself?" Doug's eyebrow disappeared into the disheveled mess of hair hanging loose over his brow.

I had regained control. The thirst was there, but I could disregard it for the most part, the way I usually did. Still, I was more aware of Ari than I usually would have been this close to a human. Every sense tingled, my nerves oscillated below my flesh, stimulated and eager for more of her.

"Where am I? Why am I here?" she demanded in a strong voice. The blade shook in her grip. Her body betrayed her.

"This is my home. I brought you here."

"Let me go." Again the blade trembled. She knew I wouldn't let her go.

"I can't do that," I said.

Her eyes darted from me to Doug, still blocking her only way out and wearing a smug grin.

"Why?"

No tears. She showed courage, even in the face of her fear, and her heart had finally found its balance. It pumped slow and steady. Her body gave off a sweet musky aroma—excitement.

Doug made a show of sniffing the air, demonstrating he smelled it too. Her fear mingled with elation. How confused her human mind must have been, to want to be here and not.

I told her the truth. "I don't know why."

Her jaw slackened, clearly not expecting that response. Her scrutiny drifted over me like the warm tides of the Mediterranean Sea, as if she was picking me apart piece by piece, stripping me bare, seeing me and not the charade.

I didn't have to turn to Doug to know his surprise at my admission. I wanted to find out why the other vampires wanted her. But mostly, I liked how she looked at me. I liked how she spoke my name. I liked *her*.

"You said you weren't scared of me," I reminded her.

"And you said I shouldn't have said that," she countered sharply. Her blue eyes locked with mine, making everything else in the room seem to disappear. The wood wavered in her hand, lowering almost imperceptibly.

I couldn't hold her here against her will. Killing was one thing. We could cover our tracks easily, but kidnapping was sloppy. Kidnapping risked exposure, and now it wasn't just me or even Ari. I had involved Doug too.

"Did you hunt me?" Ari asked. There was a strange note of disbelief in her eyes. She blinked twice, her long eyelashes fluttering.

I nodded. I didn't tell her that her disturbing me at the coffee shop while I was feeding brought her nearer to death than my hunting her ever did.

"Are you going to kill me?" Her voice was eerily calm suddenly. She swallowed, bringing my attention to the delicate slope of her neck where my mouth had been just hours ago. The slim graze had dried over.

I licked my lips, but not from thirst. A burst of excitement caught me completely off guard. I wanted to place my mouth on her skin again. I wanted to taste that chocolate flavor that clung to her warm flesh. No, I certainly would not kill her. However, that didn't make me any less lethal.

"Doug." I said it calmly in his direction but kept my eyes unblinking on hers. She didn't look away. "Swear you will stop me by any means necessary if I attempt to attack Ari. By any means."

He sucked in a deep irritated breath and blew it out loudly before pulling in another. "Now I'm protecting humans too?"

"Dougal—"

"And how do I trust him?" Ari's head tilted in his direction, clearly unaware that the fact that she was still alive meant she could trust us both to some extent.

"Doug, swear on Sarah's soul."

Ari blinked, and her lips parted. She appeared to sense the gravity of my request immediately. Her breath hitched and then held.

"Hen—" He started, unsure and standing straight, his usual swagger evaporating into the fragrant air.

"Please, Doug. I won't make you regret it."

Everything was abruptly still and silent, all except for Ari's heart beating loud in my ears. Doug had to know I would never ask this promise of him if I thought even for the smallest measurement of time I would betray it. For me, the oath would be binding.

"I—" He heaved a breath and finally circled his arm before him and bowed his head in a flurry of propriety, fitting the magnitude of the occasion, and his own love of the dramatic. "I swear on Sarah's soul."

Ari closed her eyes for a fleeting moment and opened them again.

"Thank you." Her lips twitched in one corner. I thought she might smile at him in gratitude for his gift of peace of mind, but she seemed to quickly remember herself and straightened her back defiantly.

"I don't need your protection. I'll go to the police, or I'll leave here and go home to America."

"That won't help you," Doug said. "Even if you could find someone to believe you, we're everywhere—military, police, government, and business. You may as well present yourself at your local cop shop with a wee sprig of thyme between your lips. You'd be dinner before you could blink."

"So, I'm stuck here?"

"No," I told her, hoping she would be reasonable. "You can choose to go and die, or stay and live until we can figure out why they want you."

She took one step and then another, bringing her to the island that separated us. The knife pinged against the shiny quartz surface. Another step and another, all the while her heart remained steady and her breathing even. Either the girl was incredibly brave or had a penchant for life-threatening situations. Even with a vow as solemn as Doug's, most humans would still cower in terror, but not her.

We were less than a foot apart, and I remained perfectly still as I had done during most of our exchange.

"You won't hurt me." Her fierce eyes narrowed, measuring me, and softened for the briefest instant. Her hand trembled. She stretched out her fingers until I heard the quiet clicking of her joints.

"I might try," I said. "I am a predator. It's my nature to devour blood, and I want you."

I stiffened further, although it seemed impossible. Her pupils dilated, and her heart skipped along for five quick beats. If I inhaled, I knew I would smell her excitement thick in the air between us as her eyes focused firmly on my mouth.

"You won't hurt me," she said again, her fingers adjusting on the wooden spoke. Not a question at all—an instruction.

"I won't."

As soon as the words left my lips, Ari's trembling hand lifted and drew back. It came flying at my face in the same instant I realized she didn't tremble from fear, but from restraint.

Chapter 12

1888

"Another?"

I raised my eyes to the proprietor. Gas light sliced across my face, and I watched with satisfaction as he swallowed harshly before I receded back into the shadows of my corner bench. The man was clearly eager for my custom but not so eager for my presence in his establishment. Such as it was — a low-lit, public house in Whitechapel playing host to both the better off and the scoundrels of the east end.

I nodded once in confirmation, and he placed a slightly dusty bottle of gin on the table. At least the man had the good sense to serve me from his older store. I fished him out a coin from my pocket and slid it across the rickety table with the tip of my gloved index finger. He wasn't long about scooping it up.

"Anything else you want?"

The corner of my mouth twitched upward. There were many things I wanted, none of which could be obtained at The Princess Alice.

"No."

The grimy landlord turned, leaving the pungent fragrance of week-old sweat in his wake. The public house overflowed with what he offered. Drink I could buy myself, women too, if I was so inclined. But I came here to watch them — to study what made them human.

My research in London had stalled when I had gotten word of a mysterious woman in white slaughtering men in the rainforests of South America. To my vexation, Constance had eluded me again, but I'd stayed there longer than I intended. The air there had been clean and the wild hunting plentiful. Returning to the pollution of London had been difficult but necessary if I was to continue my research.

I poured another glass, mindful of a woman watching me from a nearby table. I had seen her earlier in conversation with a reporter. She'd been plainly using him for gin—he was an easy target. In exchange for keeping her glass filled, he got the information he wanted, even if none of it was the truth. Although, the woman did possess a secret, one she hadn't held close enough to her ample bosom.

"Read it," she'd demanded, indicating the notes he'd shown her. "You know the likes of me don't read." Her accent wasn't proper to London, despite her attempts to sound it. I'd recognized the lyrical tones of Welsh.

He had read as she had watched, her eyes following the script and her lips silently mouthing the words on the page. She had lied; the woman was educated.

The city reeked of death, and the savages that resided within its imposing starkness existed in fear of their lives. They had been shocked by the recent bloody Whitechapel murders, as if starvation, disease, moral degradation, and perpetual smog drowning all color in gray wasn't enough to bring home the pathetic reality of their miserable existence.

The police were no nearer to capturing the monster that lurked in the crevices, and London seemed stiller in the dark, the streets devoid of hope.

The woman's eyes shifted in my direction again with some trepidation, though I was sure she couldn't see more than shadow and outline. Her glass and table were both empty now. She would be turned out soon and was probably on the hunt, desperately seeking prey. I empathized with that predicament.

The scent of sex floated in a cloud of vapor around her. Educated or not, she was clearly an unfortunate. Her heart pounded rapidly, and her chest heaved, almost spilling out of the meager fabric of her dress, though she was relatively clean with a white apron over her skirt and her reddish-blond hair combed into submission.

She, like the landlord, didn't desire my company, but she had yet to consume her fill of gin, and her grumbling stomach was perhaps driving her to do something more despicable than she would normally consider. She ignored her preservation instincts and good sense for the sake of something as vulgar as money.

I lifted my hand into the light and crooked a finger, indicating for the woman to join me. She stood immediately, like an obedient hound, and brushed down her skirts. The woman crossed the small distance with her arms pressing her bosoms together, perhaps in an attempt to make herself more appealing to me. I almost laughed.

After a small curtsey, she sat and placed her glass on the table, though its contents were long gone, leaving nothing but sticky residue. A blush colored in her cheeks, a dusty rose color against her pale skin, and extended down her throat. Hunger coursed through me at the sight of the warmth below her flesh. I inhaled the coppery scent of her blood and the musk of her body.

I knew she would be able to see me better from her present position, though not clearly, not enough to know she shared air with a monster.

"Would you like a drink, my lady?" I asked kindly.

She snorted a quick laugh. "I ain't yours, I ain't no lady, and I ain't no lush neither, sir," she retorted quickly, biting down on her cracked lip, as if she could bite back the words that had already escaped.

I tilted my head forward in the pretense of contrition. Once she sat down at my table, she was mine...mine to possess, mine to use at my liberty. "Forgive me. I meant it as nothing more but a term of esteem." With that, I flashed an impressive smile.

The woman's blush deepened and spread down her long, slender throat. I could tell she was once very beautiful, and much of her beauty remained, although half-used up by a world that showed her no kindness or pity. Her eyes were striking blue, and her features fine, with high cheekbones and a delicate nose that turned up slightly at the tip. I estimated her age to be somewhere not far past twenty, although her profession made it hard to tell. Maybe she wasn't a lady, but the way she held her shoulders and back gave indication she had been taught manners well beyond the rough urchins raised on the streets of London. I found her mildly interesting.

I poured her a glass of gin, and she knocked it back in one mouthful. Her chin lifted right up in the air and gave me full view of the muscles, veins and arteries under her milky flesh. For a moment, I relished the sight of the blood moving beneath skin so pale as to be almost translucent…and so fragile.

A flash of a vision cut to my brain like a straight razor — me with this woman in my arms, her back to my chest, the scene washed with rivers of crimson as I feasted. I licked my lips, saliva flooding my mouth. I hadn't tasted blood in several days, and my parched body craved it. It would be so easy to take her from here and act on the rudimentary impulse.

"I'm sorry," she said. "I must've been thirstier than I thought."

I laughed at her unintentional empathy. "Have another." I smiled, but not so much as to scare her. "Have as much as you care to. I doubt that this fine establishment will run out."

No one paid us any heed. I was just another gent passing time with an undesirable to reaffirm my position in my own mind as a master of the world. The men of London liked to prove to themselves how far up the ladder of society they had climbed by treading all over the lives and dreams of those lower down. In all areas of life, in all animal kingdoms, there was a chain, and each beast was a link in that chain, whether it was the wealthy and the desolate, or vampires and their victims.

"Oh, no, sir. I ain't got no money, you see."

Ah, yes, the negotiation begins. It was not enough for this young woman to have drink in her belly and a respite from the street. No, she wanted coins in her hand. A business transaction.

I pulled several coins from my pocket and slapped them on the table. I noted a bedraggled man nearby look up at the sound, even with the ambient noise to muffle it. His eyes went wide at the sight of the money, and he dragged his hand across his stubbly chin. The back of his knuckles were crisscrossed with thin white scars. The man quickly returned to his drink when I leaned forward and our eyes met.

Making no attempt to hide her glee, the woman scooped up the excessive number of coins — I had no desire to haggle — and stuffed them inside her dress. With them safely tucked away, she settled herself more comfortably on her stool.

"I'm —"

"Your name is of no consequence to me, madam."

"You don't want me name?"

"Should I?" I asked. "If I hadn't paid you, would you want mine?"

Her eyes went to her glass and the liquid swirling around inside as she dipped it first one way and then the other, no doubt contemplating how to frame the obvious answer. No, she wouldn't care. Not as long as it led to food, shelter, and payment to the protection gangs who owned these streets.

"Tonight, I desire your company and nothing more."

"Nothing?" Her heart stuttered, and she looked up at me, her eyes glassy from a combination of too much gin and not enough food.

I made no answer.

"You're a funny ole sort." She smiled wryly. "We don't normally get the likes of you round 'ere."

"Round 'ere?" I prompted for clarification, mimicking her accent perfectly.

"You know, a gentlemen-like."

"Really?" I smirked. If only she knew the crucible of thirst and rage, the wanton lust for blood, the jealously bubbling inside of me every moment. *A gentleman devil.*

She blushed again. "Well, we get plenty of 'em with money, but they ain't gentlemen. None of them are."

"Appearances can be most deceptive," I said.

"I'll drink to that." She grinned widely, revealing a missing tooth at the rear of her jaw, oblivious to the fact I had disagreed with her assessment of me.

We clinked glasses, and she drank slower this time, eased into relaxing in my company by the alcohol.

It was then that I smelled it. Hidden among the pungent orders of the hodge podge of customers, a vampire had entered.

I held perfectly still, judging the position and distance of the creature by scent alone. It wasn't one I recognized, but as sure as I knew it was here, the other vampire must have picked up my scent, too. Possibly, it followed me in.

"What's the matter?" my companion inquired as I surveyed the crowd, perhaps worried another female had garnered my attention.

"You are mistaken." I leaned in and spoke without emotion or tone. "I am no gentleman. You have caught the eye of the devil himself."

Her eyes widened to saucers, and fear piqued in the warm coppery scent of her blood. Her breath caught in a gasp, sending a wave of foul air my way. Suddenly, I wanted her gone from my sight. What was I thinking, inviting this human to my table? I didn't want her company, only her blood.

"May God forgive you, sir, for saying such things." As she said the words, a terrified tear escaped and rolled over her ruddy cheek uncorrected.

"Aye. Aye, Petal," the other vampire chimed in with a Scottish accent, sliding across the bench beside me and placing his arm around my shoulder. "You will have to excuse my friend…" His eyebrow rose to nudge a name I hadn't sought from the woman. When she didn't answer, he waved his hand in a wide arc toward her.

"Emma," she finally shared.

"Ah." He grinned easily and sat back, releasing me from his strong grip. "Fair Emma. The fairest of the fairest in the whole of London."

I certainly got an inkling from his proclamation that this vampire had an overdeveloped sense of humor.

Like me, he was dressed well, although his clothes were from several years prior. His hair set him apart most of all—longer than fashionable, blond, and unkempt. Some of it was falling loose across his face, and he positively reeked of whisky.

I relaxed some, thinking this creature would be no match for me in a fight. I was fast and strong. Strong enough to dispatch one Scot, should I need to.

Extraordinarily, the woman didn't bolt as most would, face to face with not one, but two predators. He was fresh from a feeding, the scent of human blood remained on his breath.

In fact, Emma appeared utterly transfixed and unable to draw her eyes away from my strange new friend. He, in turn, captured her attention and devoured it with relish, almost preening for her.

He reached into the coin pocket of his waist jacket and pulled out several, more than I had already parted with, and stacked them neatly in a low pile right in the center of the table where she would have to reach for them. I suspected his latest victim had been relieved of the bounty.

I watched in barely concealed fascination as he tilted his head, first to the right and then to the left. The woman remained spellbound, leaning her head as he did. A wicked mischievous grin widened on his handsome face, and his eyes darkened to black—he made no attempt to hide his nature, and yet the woman remained oblivious to it. *Intriguing.*

"Now, Petal, I want you to have these and go home. Stop to buy food, but nothing else, and don't talk to anyone. It's time for a rest, fair Emma. The devil will take your soul soon enough." He spoke in a low, steady voice without giving any hint of the inevitable danger he referred to.

I had thought the mischief he meant to cause involved the girl. I understood too late it was me he was playing the fool. Still, I was curious.

The woman nodded once and swiped the coins off the table in a heartbeat. Very soon, she was gone, taking with her the combination of musk, salt, and sex unique only to her, swallowed up by the crowd unconsciously keeping a safe distance. No matter. I could find her again easily.

"How did you do that?" I asked.

He smiled again. "A simple parlor trick."

"Like no parlor trick I've ever seen."

He raised an eyebrow, and it disappeared under a clump of straggled hair. "Surely you know some of our kind are blessed with certain useful qualities?"

"'Blessed' is an assertion we shall have to agree to disagree on," I retorted.

"Blessed, afflicted, cursed, bestowed…What's the difference? One word doesn't alter how we are perceived in this world." He took a deep drink and grimaced, scrunching his face up in disgust. "Hog piss," he spat, sticking out his tongue as if the air might rid him of the taste.

"If you say so," I said calmly, naturally wondering about his basis for comparison. "Tell me more about this ability. I've never met someone who could influence that way."

"Now you have," he replied simply. He refilled the woman's glass.

Against my better judgment, the scientist in me came to the fore. "How does it work?"

"I don't know." He shrugged, shaking the bottle in front of his face to measure the diminishing content. "How does a rainbow appear in the sky?"

I began without missing a beat. "According to Sir Newton—"

"Magic, brother," he cut me off, laughing. "The entire world is a magic show, and we are nothing but a turn of illusion." The vampire's hand waved downward in a flurry of circular motion, and his head dipped in a bow.

I began to suspect he had no idea how he did what he did and that I was squandering my time with this conversation. I got to my feet, followed immediately by my companion.

"What do you presume you are doing?" I asked him.

His shoulders sank in mock distress, and he held both his hands out as if to show me he meant no harm. His intentions were irrelevant. I had dallied enough for one evening. Over the years, I had found I needed to pace myself at all times, not because I rushed anything, but because when time stretched out as an endless road, it was easy to get distracted from the journey. I knew my journey and my purpose. It was two-fold: revenge and deliverance.

"Come, brother, it's been weeks since I've last encountered one of our kind, and I'm new to London."

I tugged my gloves at the wrist and fastened my black cloak around my shoulders. "I take pleasure in the solitude of my home, and I hunt alone." Without another glance, I swept from the public house out onto Commercial Street and toward Whitechapel road, away from the scent of the woman, Emma.

Mid-September had at least cooled the weather some and lessened the human stench that permeated the air in warmer months. Although, cool air brought with it the layer of fog that seemed to settle across the ground like gray snow, except this snow moved and slithered around the legs of those walking through it.

Sometimes when I wandered through this part of town, I became lost in the smell of musk, human waste, rotted food, and decay, but I came here nonetheless. At other times, the meaty, metallic fragrance of their blood and the beating of so many hearts became almost unbearable, almost too much to resist. Humans often met messy ends in this part of London, and it rarely caused a stir. Until recently. They had worked themselves up into a frenzy over these so-called Leather Apron murders. At least two, they believed, with speculation on another.

As if to remind me, I passed several posters calling for information and offering a lofty reward of one hundred pounds. Astonishing, when it was considered the victims were nothing but unfortunate prostitutes who would never have dreamed of seeing so much money in their entire miserable existence.

I had heard the whistle of the bobby sounding out across The Chapel after the last body was found. The Chapel—that was what the locals called Whitechapel. I considered myself one of them now in some ways. After all, I was the very fiend who haunted their nightmares, despite the wholly inaccurate description of the last man to see a previous victim, Annie Chapman, alive. I was now as much a part of The Chapel as any of them. There were more victims, many more, but it was only recently they'd begun to pay attention to my activities. There would be others, although they didn't know it. My research was not yet complete.

I was careful in my choices. I waited and watched from a distance, then came the final test. They accepted payment and were only too happy to venture down dark alleys or behind walls where they freely lifted their skirts to show me they were shaved — a necessity in their line of work to prove themselves free of parasites. That was my test, and they had all failed miserably.

"It's not very inventive." The Scot caught up to me.

"I beg your pardon."

"No need for begging, brother; I give it freely." He chuckled at his own ridiculous joke. "The name, the Leather Apron." He rolled his eyes and waved his fingers by his head in a gesture I felt sure meant to insinuate fright, but came nearer to emulating a fit of some sort. "Well, aprons don't exactly instill terror, eh?"

I noticed that the intensity of his accent fluctuated, indicating he had probably traveled extensively outside his homeland.

"How about The Ripper — Jack the Ripper?"

I spared him a sidelong glance in question, and he scratched his temple.

"I knew a man named Jamie once. Well, hardly more than a boy, really, but a big bugger. Legs as thick as tree trunks and a face that looked like his mother dropped him a few times. Anyway, when he swung a sword, sure it'd nearly cut men in two. They called him The Ripper."

"So, why not Jamie the Ripper?"

"Och, we're in England. A good English name for an English madman."

I flinched at his insult, but he didn't appear to notice. "So, what happened to The Ripper?"

"I killed him."

I hummed thoughtfully. "The Ripper got ripped."

"So, where are we going?" inquired my new acquaintance, appearing suddenly anxious for a shift in the direction of our conversation.

"*We* are going nowhere," I answered flatly.

A weathered preacher stood at the junction of the Whitechapel high street, half-crazed and hollering at the top of his lungs to a ragtag captive audience. He called on them to repent and return to God, lest they be struck down for their sins.

I chuckled darkly. Now I was doing God's work.

The preacher's glassy eyes grazed across the two mysterious, beautiful gentlemen passing by his improvised pulpit. He heart stuttered out an uneven beat. By the sound of it, the man would be dead before the week was out—a blockage of some sort, preventing steady blood flow.

"Keep your pretty speeches, old man," I murmured, too low for the preacher to hear. "Own the salvation of your soul before mine. He has already struck me down, and I will rage against His damnation until the heavens burn and He feels the heat of the fire He cast me into."

The vision of a tiny child's hand dripping blood fortified my whispered vow.

"How do you move?" the other vampire asked curiously, his eyes narrowed briefly, all joviality suddenly gone.

"I beg your pardon, sir?"

"With that weight you wear around your neck like chains."

I pursed my lips and continued walking. He was persistent—I had to give him that—and almost childlike in his enthusiasm, albeit a naughty child. I couldn't help wondering what his story was.

With no warning or explanation, I experienced a pressure at my breastbone, as though a hand pressed over my chest. My own covered the curious warmth. I experienced the strangest sensation of being observed, of someone staring at the back of my head. I turned, searching. However, as quickly as it manifested, the sensation vanished, and the only thing I felt was the London chill settling deep into my bones.

"I live a good distance west," I told the vampire. "Keep up, or I will leave you behind."

"Nae problem. I'm Dougal, by the way."

Chapter 13

2010

Ari was in the bathtub overhead. Every time she disturbed the water, I could pinpoint the most miniscule of her actions. I could smell the powdery scent of steam laced with soap. The fragrance of cocoa, coffee, and that other scent that lingered around her was gone, replaced by honey. It was wrong somehow. I liked the way she'd smelled before. Her heart pulsed slow and steady, surprisingly relaxed. My desire for her blood had settled for now, driven down by years of practice in ignoring the thirst. Yet, I still desired her company. At first, I savored each breath that reminded me she was here, only very slightly out of reach.

It was so much harder to reel myself in now. I knew it would be a long time before I could ever get back to not being tempted to drink from Ari. Of course, I was aware of other temptations. I was attracted to her as a female, and I had no idea what to do about it. I knew what Doug would suggest. Besides the other obvious complications of our situation, I had no notion of how I would begin to seduce a woman. I had not sought a woman out since my youth.

Doug was gone to her home to collect some of her belongings. She didn't know, but I hoped she'd be even a little grateful to be surrounded by the familiar while here. So far, she was being very uncooperative, refusing to provide me with any information that might help discover her part in what was going on, which immediately made me suspect she had something to hide.

This brought me to my current position, sitting in my study, at the desk I had rescued from a dilapidated building in Paris. The builders had thought it was junk, while I had recognized it as unloved nineteenth century art nouveau. The substantial curved shape restored beautifully, the fluid lines and uncluttered design helped me think. It was one of only a few pieces that moved with me whenever I stayed somewhere for a longer period of time.

I hit the power button and leaned back, lacing my fingers behind my head. The leather and wood beneath me creaked while I waited for my computer to boot up. It did nothing to cover the sound of water draining away from the tub upstairs or keep my mind away from the thought that Ari, with her silky wet skin and toned body, was naked in my house.

Conflicting sensations rushed through me, and I pressed my fingers together tighter to keep from destroying my furniture. The thirst returned, and I closed my eyes, biting down on my bottom lip, waiting for the distraction of the sting. The other sensation occurred lower where I felt the beginnings of sexual arousal like electrical pulses shooting down through my stomach and tensing the muscles in my thighs. It was wrong on so many levels to want her, and yet my body reacted anyway. I avoided breathing. I didn't need to speak for the moment, and I was tormenting myself with her scent needlessly.

The screen flickered to life and flashed colors across my closed eyelids. After briefly clenching my fists, I tapped in my passwords and opened my inbox. Danvers, my private investigator, had left a voice mail to say the information I requested had been sent. Danvers was efficient—that was one of the reasons I used him. The other reason was that his silence and loyalty could be bought.

Something told me that if Ari had any idea what I was doing, she would do more than slap me across the face for the unwanted intrusion on her life. She would see this as another gross invasion of her privacy, but it was necessary, and I decided I might as well be hung for a sheep as a lamb. I had committed myself to protecting her, and I couldn't protect her in the future without learning about her past.

Birth and death certificates flashed before my eyes. Many death certificates: her adoptive parents and birth parents, and the latest family death, the woman who had resided in Howth.

Ari had lost, just as the girl in the coffee shop had said. It went some way toward explaining the almost palpable loneliness and sadness that seemed to shimmer around her like heat rising from asphalt on a summer day.

Gentle footfalls alerted me to her moving from the en suite to the bedroom. I imagined dark hair sticking to the slick skin of her naked back and unconsciously lifted my eyes to the ceiling.

"Enough," I huffed out under my breath and forced my attention back to the screen.

She was book smart and popular in school, but it had been like she'd dropped off the face of the earth around the time her parents had died. There was nothing I could use in her file. I entered *Cailleach* into the search and hit return.

Cailleach was a crone, a demon with power over life. Also known as The Veiled One—the subtitle of the book that had been sitting on Ari's dresser.

A mostly unfruitful twenty minutes later, I heard Ari making her way down to the kitchen. I expected she was probably hungry and in search of food. Since I fortunately remembered humans liked to eat, I had called a local delicatessen earlier and had some delivered. I could have left her to rummage through the basket sitting on the counter but decided this might be a good time to get some answers. There were practicalities to take care of too.

I shut the screen down and stood, steeling myself for the onslaught of thirst. I was more prepared now, able to keep it at bay. I followed her scent to the kitchen, hoping Doug remembered to pick up her toiletries, whatever it was that made her smell of winter, and then quickly chastised myself for considering it any of my concern what she chose to bath in.

I leaned casually against the doorframe, crossing my arms over my chest and making extra effort to cause some noise so as not to surprise her. Although, I suspected nothing I could do really would.

Ari, wearing jeans and a tank top, stood with her back to me. She'd tied her long hair in a single braid that fell down her back and left patches of darker fabric along her spine. Scarlet nail polish on her bare feet caught my eye, and I swallowed thickly when I imagined placing my hands on them, smoothing my palms over her slim ankles and toned calves.

She made no acknowledgment to my presence, yet her body gave her away, her quick heart and deep breath. She unloaded the square wicker basket, usually meant for gifts, and carefully examined each item before placing it on the counter.

"Was there something you wanted?" she asked in a low challenging tone.

"There are many things I want."

She paused a beat with a loaf of white bread in her hand before pulling it to her and inhaling deeply.

"Something specific right now?"

"You lied. I can usually tell when a human lies. I can usually read humans quite well, but I couldn't tell with you. You lied straight to my face." The book in her room couldn't be a coincidence in all this.

She walked around the counter to the opposite side, trailing her index finger over the surface, leaving a shadow of a fingerprint that quickly faded to nothing. Ari's expression was completely devoid of any emotion, unreadable for a moment before she seemed to settle on feigned innocence.

"I have no idea what you're talking about." She spread her arms wide, looking me directly in the eyes as she lied again. "But then, you're the expert in untruths, aren't you, Clay? Or is it Henry?"

I uncrossed my arms and approached her, more and more aware of Doug's absence with each step and testing my control continuously. Having her here would be draining. I would have to feed sooner rather than later if I wanted to keep my cravings in check.

"My name is Henry Stephen Clayton. I was named after my father. My mother was Esther Clayton, and this was once their home. Is that enough honesty for you?"

I mirrored her stance on the opposite side of the island. Her eyelashes fluttered, and her gaze flickered in an involuntary motion, as if she expected my parents to disturb us. Of course, I knew they wouldn't.

"At the moment, I go by the name Clay Black."

"Oh," she uttered casually, but her blood moved faster, and she blinked several times.

"What do you know of Cailleach?"

"I've never heard of Cailleach."

If I didn't know she'd had that book in her room, I might have written it off as nerves. "Are you sure?"

There. She looked away, caught in the lie.

"Is this for me?" she asked, gesturing to the basket.

"Yes."

She turned away and continued sorting through it. Clearly, that particular conversation wasn't going to proceed for now.

Once Ari had found what she needed, she set about breaking eggs into a bowl. I moved around the counter, aware of her eyes following me and the delicious heated fragrance she gave off when I got too close. Just like our earlier encounter, I recognized physical desire. What was wrong with this girl? What was wrong with me that I ignored how every muscle in my body tightened the closer I got to her?

She continued to beat eggs and kept her breathing steady while I stood directly behind her. *I could break her so easily*, I thought, imagining how it would feel to press my chest against her back and allow her pounding heart to echo through me.

The beater moved faster, and Ari's excitement escalated. I inhaled deeply, dipping my head to the crook of her neck. She smelled wrong, but something inside me roared out because I recognized the scent all over her now. Me—she smelled like me. Suddenly, I noticed how my jeans had tightened over my erection. Fierce thirst caused me to dart my tongue out over my lips. The sight of her throbbing artery was so close.

Her body stilled, her hand frozen over the bowl of beaten eggs, waiting for my next move. What would that be? So many needs and desires rushed forward in my mind. All the things I could do to this human whose blood and arousal drove my own body in so many different directions. I closed my eyes, inhaling again, and slid my hand gently from her elbow to her wrist. Static prickled at my fingertips. Goose bumps raised along her warm skin, the fine downy hairs lifted as if calling out to my touch.

The beater clattered against the bowl, and I guided Ari's wrist to my mouth. My other hand slipped around her waist, pulling her back to me. She had to know the power she held over me.

"So fragile," I whispered against the silken skin across the inside of her wrist. Her pulse throbbed invitingly against my mouth. My tongue swirled a circle over the delicate flesh.

"No."

The word she murmured was barely a breath, hardly loud enough to drown out the thumping inside my skull. Her body flinched, and her hand tried to tug away. Pointless, it only made me want to hold her tighter…and so I did.

"Stop," she roared, pushing back against me with all her strength.

I came to my senses with a bang and flew backward away from the human girl I'd almost feasted on, smashing into the fridge door and buckling the chrome as if it were simply foil. I turned from her, clutching the dented appliance and unable to look into her eyes. I didn't want to see the disgust and fear she had to feel. It was humiliating, my inability to control myself around her. Not only had I almost killed her again—my libido was suddenly that of a schoolboy.

Her heart raced, and each breath she took was quick and sharp as a blade.

"I don't want to hurt you," I said into the metal.

Ari sighed. "You won't."

"I mean it."

"So do I."

I turned from the fridge to look at her. She stood watching me, rubbing the heel of her hand over her pounding heart. A red ring wrapped around her wrist, and I was sure the mark would match my fingers. A wave of guilt rushed up from my belly. Her eyebrows pulled down in that same way they did the first day we spoke. A soft breath left her lips, and she turned her back to me. I'd kidnapped her and tried to kill her more than once, yet she still felt sorry for me.

"I need my phone back if I'm going to stay here. I have people who will worry. My job, my landlord." She sliced bread as if nothing had just happened. "You will need to learn to keep your distance."

"Fine." Not touching her would be almost as hard as not killing her. "You can't tell anyone where you are." This was one of the practicalities.

"Fine."

I stepped away from the fridge, and because I didn't know what else to do, I began to wipe down the countertop, working around Ari but keeping my distance as she asked. I still needed to approach the subject of her family.

"One more thing," Ari hedged as she dipped a slice of bread in egg. "I want you to destroy whatever it is that's after me. I think it killed my family."

The sudden viciousness in her voice caught me off guard. I glanced at her out of the corner of my eye. Anger radiated from her, although she appeared calm.

"Don't do that. You don't want to hold onto hate, Ari. You don't want to live that way."

"Wow."

"What?"

"You are judging me. That's rich."

"I'm not sure I understand," I said lightly. I moved around the counter, diligently removing every trace of food, every crumb. Unlike a human, I would notice even the tiniest morsel left behind to rot.

"You're a murderer. You've fed on innocent human beings." Her voice held the flat observational tone of a scientist watching an experiment, even though the temperature in the room heated simply from the rise in her body temperature. "Yet, you can stand there and criticize me. You scold me for wanting to see monsters dead."

My fingers tightened on the sponge, and droplets of water sloshed out onto the quartz counter top. I wanted to admit the truth that I couldn't bear the idea of her becoming like me. I wanted to make her understand that I didn't want her to have the vile longing that possessed my every waking hour and tormented me during rest. Nevertheless, I forced myself to slacken my grip before I met her eyes.

"I am a monster. I am a predator," I told her coldly. "I am simply higher up the food chain. You and your kind are little more than cattle to us."

She refused to shift her eyes and met mine with a steely determination. Her heart thrummed like a butterfly's wings inside her chest, forcing blood through the artery in her throat. My mouth watered as the scent of her blood grew more intense, flushing her creamy skin.

"Then this gilded prison you're keeping me in is nothing more than a fancy abattoir." The tenor of her voice remained steady despite her physical reaction.

Neither of us blinked, staring at each other in a battle of wills to see who would crack first. Of course, I had the added advantage of none of the human frailties. I could go on staring at her for hours, days, even years if I chose to.

She growled out a breath through her clenched teeth when she finally folded. What could I say? The cards were stacked in my favor. The flat of her palm crashed down on the counter before she stormed from the kitchen indignantly, abandoning her food. She left the scent of her excitement lingering thickly in the air behind her. Her anger smelled of sweet vanilla.

"Hmm." Doug sniffed the air as he entered the kitchen moments after she had left. His eyes flickered toward the mangled fridge door. "Something's been cookin' in here."

"French toast," I responded, rinsing the sponge again.

"Is that what the kids are calling it these days?"

I scowled over my shoulder at him, but he just chuckled.

Chapter 14

1888

Dougal had no trouble keeping up, leading me to suspect he was a good deal older and possibly stronger than I had credited. We arrived at my home near the west end a time later and were greeted by Thomas, my manservant, in the two-story entrance hall. Dougal's shoes echoed across the marble tile as he walked in a wide circle, taking it in. I lived comfortably with a small household staff of three who all respectfully kept their distance until required. They asked no questions. It wasn't unusual for a gentleman to dine out a lot.

Dougal stopped by the curving stairs and followed them upward with his eyes, pausing for a beat on each of the paintings. There were no portraits, nothing to tell my history.

"Prepare a room for our guest, Thomas. We will be in my laboratory and don't wish to be disturbed until further notice."

"Of course, sir." He nodded and left, taking my top hat and cloak with him.

"Don't you risk exposure by having humans around?" Dougal asked, clearly heeding the other heartbeats nearby and smoothing his fingers down one of the decorative pillars at the entrance to my reception room.

I noted how tactile he was. He seemed to have an uncontrollable desire to touch everything he passed.

"More so if I lived alone without a staff to care for the house. I've listened in on them, of course. They consider me an oddity, eccentric, but they are oblivious to my nature." I spoke in a volume consistent to his, so low no human would hear from distance. "I wish to be clear. I'm allowing you to stay here so I can keep an eye on you, nothing more. My research is important. If you get in my way, I will squash you like a bug. Are we clear?"

He smiled widely. "You like me already. I can tell."

I pushed my hair away from my face. It was slightly unkempt from my hat and running over London rooftops. "I need to work now."

"Your laboratory?"

"I'm a scientist."

Dougal's eyebrows rose, and a small indent curved at the corner of his lips as he once again smiled. He appeared fixed in a perpetual state of happiness. Annoyingly so.

"Follow me." I turned to the panel below the stairs and lifted the molding to expose the lock. I always carried the only key on my person.

Once inside the narrow hallway, I locked the door again and led him down the winding stairs to the basement. There was no need for light as we could both see well enough through the blackness. At the bottom, I pulled out another key and pushed the heavy door open. Dougal eyed it curiously.

"Solid iron, several inches of it. I value my privacy," I said, lighting a gas lamp. I preferred not to work in darkness.

Dougal immediately stepped into the cavernous room hidden in the bowels of my home. The ceilings were low, and the walls were covered by roughly finished wood, which had begun to darken from a combination of chemicals in the air and age. His shoes clicked on the dark gray slate at he moved around, running his fingers along the long counter tops and over the array of scientific equipment.

I pretended to busy myself, adjusting glass jars inside one of the many cabinets that lined the walls. He peered into the microscope and pulled back, blinking. It was a little disconcerting the first time, especially with our already enhanced vision. He tapped bottles of liquid and shook a bowl of lancets with a mystified narrowing of his eyes.

The moment I turned my back, I heard a popping of a cork. In a flash of movement, I swiped the bottle from beneath his nose.

"Highly concentrated silver nitrate. You don't want to inhale that. Sufficient quantity in the body, and it can kill our kind." I pushed the cork back in and stored the bottle away.

I watched Dougal with crossed arms as he turned his attention to the rows of specimen jars on shelves along the opposite walls. He moved sideways, slowly examining the animal organs, fetuses, and some smaller mammals.

"What is it you study, brother?"

"Hematology," I responded.

Dougal shook his head and continued to tap glass jars as if it might bring the contents back to life. "I don't pretend to understand."

"Blood. I'm using the sciences to establish what it is that contaminates us," I explained casually. It felt strange. I hadn't spoken to anyone about this since William.

Dougal spun to face me. His eyes widened. "Some of these organs are human."

"Yes. I've been adding to my catalogue."

"Are ye cracked, man?" he exclaimed. "You're him. You're the Ripper."

"Do not call me by that name, sir."

"You're killing humans to steal their parts?"

Now it was my turn to smile. At last, something affected my strange companion. The muscles in my cheeks tightened, and my lips pulled back over my teeth, revealing fangs. To a human it would be terrifying.

"The humans believe one of their own is responsible. I seek a cure. The deaths were *necessary*, unlike those killed to feed."

"Even that is enough to get you wiped off the face of the world." His eyes narrowed, and the green seemed to intensify, tumbling like storm clouds. Dougal moved at lightning speed to my side. "What makes you imagine any of us wants a cure?"

Rage ignited in my veins and twitched in every muscle. My hand darted out at blinding speed and gripped his throat, pushing him back onto the counter. I felt the tremor of the straining wood beneath his body and held him with just enough strength so as not to cause damage to my laboratory.

"What makes you imagine I care what a monster wants?"

I released him and stepped back, my body tense and ready for his retaliation. It didn't come. Instead, Dougal straightened himself and chuckled, a sound so low and dark, and it reverberated through the underground space like a specter haunting it.

"Brother, from one monster to another, I think you need me more than you know."

Chapter 15

2010

It had been two weeks since Ari's arrival, and we hadn't exchanged a single word since she stormed from the kitchen. We'd had no further progress on The Circle. I sat at my desk, listening to her and Doug talking in the drawing room, an encroacher in my own house, an unwelcome ear in their conversation.

She seemed more at ease with Doug, and since I denied her liberty, I couldn't deny her company. Doug, for his part, warmed to Ari quickly. Why wouldn't he? She possessed qualities he valued in a female — intelligence, bravery, and a quick wit to rival his own. Irrational jealously jabbed at me constantly.

They watched old movies and modern humorous features I found crass. Other times they played Scrabble, at which Ari proved a worthy opponent and Doug a terrible cheat. On a few occasions, like tonight, Ari idly flicked though pages of a book while they chatted.

As a vampire, I had come to believe in God. Too little, too late did I realize that demons existed and walked the Earth — and if there was hell, surely there must have been heaven. I hoped my family found peace there even if I would never see it. I suspected Ari was an angel sent to torment me for my sins. What other reason could there be for such a creature? So delicate and beautiful, so near and yet so far beyond the grasp of a monster like myself.

"Who is Sarah?" she asked in a whisper. A page turned in the book she was browsing, perhaps the Shakespeare I'd seen her with earlier.

I heard the tinkle of glassware and the gentle glugging of pouring liquid. "The one that got away," Doug lamented sadly.

Her heart fluttered, and surely, he must have noted it too.

"I'm sorry," she told him with genuine sadness in her voice, emitting a strange little sound I didn't understand. It was almost as though she caught her breath. "Eh…" Nothing followed.

I drew circles on a notepad with a pencil in my other hand. Perfect circles, or as near as possible with human materials. That was the contradiction of being a vampire. We were so far beyond the capabilities of humans, yet limited by a human world. Perfectly imperfect.

Doug chuckled after a moment, and the sound grew to raucous laughter. Skin made contact with leather. It sounded like Doug slapping the arm of the chair. "I do mean 'got away' in the traditional sense, Petal."

I smiled despite myself at Ari's confusion. Clearly, she had briefly wondered in hindsight if Sarah had been some prize hunt Doug had failed to capture. Why wouldn't she? What did she really know of Doug and me? Sarah had been a prize, all right.

"Was she like you?" Ari asked, shifting on the sofa.

Almost inaudible swish of movement followed the thump of a book dropping on the rug, then the groan of leather as Doug moved from his seat to retrieve it. The friction of the fabric in his clothing and the furniture and flicking pages gave away his movements. Although not always as fast as other vampires, Doug was often silent as the grave. Not tonight, so I assumed he knew I was listening.

"No."

"You don't have to tell me. I didn't mean to pry."

"Tell me, Petal, do you think creatures like us are capable of love?"

"Of course," she answered with surprising determination.

Doug chuckled. "Clay believes we are damned. He believes the blood that infects us burns away our souls. Without souls, how can we love? How can we be anything but monsters?"

"No," Ari said brusquely. "No, I can't believe that."

"Because you feel something for Clay and you think, since you are still breathing and all, he might actually return those feelings?" Doug suggested lightly. "Maybe it's exciting to you not knowing the truth?"

The pencil snapped in my hand. When I looked down, it was nothing but a pile of wood splinters and crushed graphite. Part of me wanted to rush in there and cut the discussion short. Another part of me froze, desperate to know the answer. I was fascinated by the possibility of a peek inside this strange young woman's head.

Her breath hitched despite her best attempts to control it, and the house flooded with the scent of her adrenaline. "The truth?"

"About who you are and why you're here. Maybe you're just a little enthralled by his fascination with you."

She said nothing.

"He doesn't know how to love. He's been too long without it," Doug said, pushing on regardless. As ever, never knowing when he had said enough. "Clay wants everything and nothing from you at the same time. That's not love. That's not anything at all."

I could have slaughtered him there and then for putting her in that position. What did one say when confronted with the possibility they had caught the eye of a monster?

"He doesn't know me, and I don't know him," she said simply. It was a swift kick to my gut, sounding more like a prediction than a statement. She didn't want to know me. "I don't want to talk about it."

"He's a blood addict, Petal."

I tilted my head back and closed my eyes. My fingers locked around the armrests. I wanted to stop the conversation. I didn't, because I couldn't deny the sense of relief in not having to say the words myself. She needed to know the dangers of staying in my home.

Ari laughed at his statement. "Aren't all vampires blood addicts? I mean, isn't it part of the job description?"

"Not the way it is for him. Usually, blood addicts don't last long. When vampires are turned, we are overcome with bloodlust. You can't imagine the thirst. It's like you're wrung inside out and set above a fire. Most adjust to the craving within a few days. But there have been some who wake up isolated, too far from human blood. They essentially starve. Starving dries out the insides, messes with the head, makes them crazy. They never really come back from it. Most are killed off quick by other vampires. Runts of a litter. Evolution, she's a bitch."

"Is that what happened to Clay?"

"No, Petal. Clay did this to himself. He wanted a cure, so he experimented. He lived on animal blood and contaminated the only human blood he drank with silver."

"Silver?"

"Poison to us."

"Jesus." Ari's voice came low and strained with shock, laced with pity.

"When the dark takes a man like it took Clay…very few come back. He still fights it, but he must have human blood, or the crazy comes back. And he might fancy you, but it's all mixed up with the craving for what's in your veins. When he said he might try to kill you, he wasn't lying."

She stood then, her feet padded softly across the rug. "Thank you for getting my things from the house. Even if you did break and enter."

"Nae bother."

"Good night."

"Petal," Doug called softly.

Her movement ceased.

"Sarah was my wife. Till death do us part, which it did after forty-nine years. She saw right through me from the very beginning, just like you see Clay." His brief pause left me wondering what her reaction was to that statement. "You know exactly what I mean. Anyway, when I met Sarah in nineteen forty-five, she was little more than a girl with her whole life ahead of her. She didn't stand a chance, really. I'm quite the crumpet in uniform."

"You fought in the war?"

"For the Allies. Two weeks I knew her, and then I left her for her own good." He choked on a pitiful laugh. "Well, I copped onto myself pretty quick and went back."

Doug's voice faded, and I knew he must have been recalling what happened next as only a vampire can, in crystal clarity, as though it was playing out before him right now. Sights, sounds, scents…they didn't fade over time for us.

"What happened to her?" Ari prompted when his silence dragged on.

Doug sighed deeply. "She passed, Petal, as humans do. She never wanted to be what I am, and time took her from me."

"I'm sorry," Ari said.

"Don't be. I wouldn't take back a second of our life together. I loved that woman fierce, loved the bones of her. Do you want to know how I know my soul hasn't burned away?"

She must have nodded, because he continued.

"When we lay together, she showed me her soul, and I showed her mine, and they were the same. As you can imagine, mine was battered and bruised, tarnished like ancient metal. She scrubbed it clean. I cannot deny my own soul any more than I can deny she held it in her hands for a time."

More liquid sloshed into a glass after she left the room, and I listened until I heard the click of the lock on her bedroom door. As if a simple piece of metal could keep one of our kind out if we wanted in. My fingers trembled. I swiped a hand across my desk and carefully brushed the remains of the pencil into a wastepaper basket. I shuffled papers, tapped keys on the keyboard, opened and closed drawers repeatedly.

I needed to feed, and there was no blood in the house. I'd removed any stocked in the fridge since Ari's arrival. Perhaps that hadn't been smart.

Doug had made decent headway into my stock of whisky and was just about to open another when I entered the room. He waved the bottle, offering me some.

"I need to go out."

He nodded once. I had already put in a call to the man who provided me with human blood.

"Doesn't it make your skin twitch?" Doug asked. His brow furrowed deep in concentration.

"What?"

"A girl like that just rolling over and accepting fate. It's not normal. She's not normal."

I took the bottle from his hand, essentially cutting him off. "She knows I can protect her."

"If you don't kill her first. There's an energy around that one, and it's nothing like I've ever felt before. My gut is starting to agree with yours. It says whatever fire's coming, she's the spark that going to blow us all to kingdom come."

On an instinct I couldn't pinpoint, I went to the window and pulled back the drape to peer into the violet darkness. There was nothing amiss. I picked up Doug's scent and Ari's, no one else. Blood rushed through my veins as my protective feelings came to the fore. I swallowed.

"You've always had a flare for the dramatic."

Doug grabbed my arm, standing before I had a chance to register his movement. "I mean it."

I tugged my arm free. "I'll be back soon."

"That's the other thing. She seems to be under the impression we're murderers."

"We are."

Doug rolled his eyes and snorted a laugh. "I haven't killed a human in almost two hundred years. You haven't killed in —"

"It doesn't matter how long it's been."

He took the bottle back and walked away. "Aye, you're right. A few days or a few centuries, every moment is an eternity when fighting against your nature. And we fight it anyway."

He knew about the girl buried in the woods, though he'd never said what had given me away. I wasn't sure if he guessed or if he somehow smelled the death lingering on my skin. Shame pinched my chest. I had given into the bloodlust too easily. I should have been able to resist. I should have fought harder.

Instead of making excuses, I walked away and left the room. Doug followed me out into the entrance hall intent on finishing our conversation. He never knew when to let things rest, but I wasn't in the mood to spill my emotions out on the rug. I opened the door.

Doug's large hand clapped my shoulder when a breeze blew inside. I took in the sweet fragrance of plumier, a bloom I'd come to associate with my maker. It was a heady combination of tropical heat and pungent floral notes with just a hint of ripe peach. Ice slithered down my spine.

"Not now."

"Clay." Doug's sharp voice cut into my thoughts, holding a warning.

"Go. Keep the girl safe."

"Clay —" he began again.

"Keep Ari safe," I growled at him. "She is all that matters."

He nodded, and I stepped out into the night, closing the door after me.

She waited beneath a tree, half in shadow some distance from the house. Her short white leather jacket and pants gleamed silver under the half-moon, and her hair rippled in torrents of raven waves around her shoulders. She strode toward me with liquid movements, her long limbs willowy.

Constance smiled. She possessed the face of a goddess, so beautiful my impeccable memory did her no justice, and my blood burned with a sudden desire to touch her. My maker was no ordinary vampire. I'd followed her trail of destruction long enough to understand her to a degree. She was a succubus, a creature who existed by seducing and draining men. The high heels of her boots clicked on flagstones and made her hips sway—a snake coiling through grass.

"Henry Clayton, as I live and breathe, you are the very picture of perfection." She stopped, her hip popping to one side casually and her arms crossing. She showed no fear. Her voice filtered through the air like smoke, something so insubstantial I could almost convince myself I had imagined it.

But I hadn't. She was here at last, right in front of me after almost a century and a half hunting her across the globe, and the only thing I wanted from her was her absence. I'd waited so long. I'd craved this reunion so deeply that I was sure if my flesh was torn from my body, her name would be found carved into my bones.

"You don't live," I spat. My fingers twitched by my side, my body and every instinct eager to make good on my vow to destroy her. If I failed, I wouldn't only risk my own life. So, as much as it disgusted me, I forced my hunger for revenge far down.

A small curve formed at the edge of her lips. "True, there are opposing opinions on the matter."

"What do you want, Constance?"

"All this time and no kiss?" She advanced with inhuman grace and paused several feet away.

How could anyone mistake this demon for a woman?

"I seem to recall you made me a promise the last time we were together."

"I haven't forgotten." My jaw clenched.

"And yet you don't act." Elegant fingers stroked the rough bark of a nearby tree.

My stomach roiled fiercely. I refused her the satisfaction of show-ing her.

"We have much to talk about."

I chuckled, and vibrations of the bitter sound itched at my throat. "We have nothing to talk about other than your leaving here."

"Our world is on the threshold of a great evolution. I know how you love to brood, Henry, but you are mine, and Mummy has come to tell you a bedtime story."

"I think you mistake me, Constance, for someone who gives a damn about the vampire world."

She flashed me a viper's smile. "And that, my darling, is the sticky wicket. All your books and you know so little of our world, our legends, our religion."

"Enlighten me."

"You'll enjoy this story. This is about a young girl under the spell of a wicked witch. One day, she meets a handsome prince, only the prince doesn't seem to notice her at all. She goes about her pitiful life as a serving girl, hoping one day he'll see her as she sees him." Constance pressed her palms together and lifted her eyes to the sky as though praying with mock desperation. Her expression turned deadly, and her hands fell by her side. "The serving girl doesn't know the spell had been fading. Soon her prince would finally notice her, but then so would all the other beasts creeping in the darkness."

"What is this lunacy?" I pushed with a nervous knot twisting like a knife in my chest.

She shrugged. "Okay, maybe the witch wasn't wicked, or a witch. I suppose it all depends on your perspective. I'm talking of the Druid priestess who protected your little serving girl." Constance tilted her chin up and sniffed at the air. "You reek of the girl, but you were mine first. You were always mine."

I crossed my arms and stood firm. "Is that what you think? That I've chased you across continents because I belong to you?"

Constance threw her head back and laughed. "She's been bitten, Henry. And the girl has tasted blood and lived. The only known human in existence to possess a natural immunity to the virus, the closest you've ever come to purification of your blood, and she's been right under your nose for months."

My arms dropped. "You lie."

"It was my bite. My blood. She is the one we've been waiting for, but the old Druid bitch hid her. Made it so we'd keep losing sight of her. Until now."

"You're one of The Circle."

She didn't respond.

"I won't let you kill her," I warned blackly.

"Darling, if I wanted to kill her, she'd be dead. Did you hear me—my bite, my blood? Make this easy on yourself. Join us and hand her over."

"If I don't?"

"The hocus pocus is slipping, and soon it will be gone. You know that some have already found her. Others will come soon. I've kept them away as long as I care to."

I glanced up at the house. Was Doug listening? "Why would you do that?"

Constance closed the distance between us and enveloped me in the sweet fragrance of her body and the coppery scent of blood on her breath. Hazel eyes framed in long, curling black lashes captured me as though held there by a physical force. Thirst made my mouth water, and unwanted desire tightened my thighs. Her nails scrapped along my jaw and my neck, popping the buttons of my shirt as they trailed down my chest. My heart thudded against her palm.

"I can help you. Don't let's fight, my darling."

I laughed in her face, narrowing my eyes. "You're jealous. You see me with another woman, and you can't stand it. If I'd known taking a lover would bring you out of the woodwork, I would have done it decades ago."

She snapped her hand back as though burned, her seductive, hooded gaze replaced by fury. "You petulant fool, Henry. You have no idea what you are playing with." She flicked her hair, and it swished down her back, a curtain of silken black waves.

I saw her now for the first time, how her beauty was nothing but a clever construct, a façade. She needed the chase more than I needed revenge. Her curved eyebrows puckered into a confused scowl. All this time wasted in hatred when I should have pitied her.

"I see it now," I said. "I've been clinging to an imagined villain. You are nothing to me."

Her hand whipped out and lashed across my face. White hot pain exploded behind my eye. My head snapped to the side, and I came back swinging an equally fierce blow. She wasn't prepared, presuming I wouldn't strike a woman. She didn't know me as well as she claimed. Besides, she had never been a woman in my eyes.

Constance collapsed against the tree, clutching her face and whimpering. I'd fallen for her game once before and stepped back, watching for the tiniest of movements. When she swung again — this time at my gut — I stepped aside, and she missed completely. She spun and plowed her fist into the tree. It shuddered to its roots, showering us in a confetti of drying leaves.

I lashed out with a kick and knocked her off her feet.

"Stay down," I growled at her, experiencing a bizarre calm. I'd imagined this moment so many times, and never once had I allowed her to live. Now, faced with the moment, I wanted no more death if I could help it.

Of course she ignored me. She leaned back on her hands and bounced, planting her feet on the ground, her features in transition. Veins slithered like worms beneath her porcelain skin, and the whites of her eyes vanished. She meant business and retaliated with a kick to my lower ribs. The force sent me flying backward into another tree, this one more resilient. My skull cracked against the thick stump.

I pushed off the tree for momentum and fell into a crouch before somersaulting backward into the air. The toe of my boot caught her viciously on the base of her chin, sending her stumbling, with an ear-splitting grunt. My other boot narrowly missed the same spot. She grabbed my ankle, snapping it like a dehydrated twig in her fingers. Pain caused me a moment's hesitation, and Constance used it to smash me into the hard earth.

"I never imagined you'd be such a disappointment. You are not who I thought you would be, Henry Clayton. At least, not yet. I'll be taking the girl and leaving now."

"No," I roared, ignoring the fiery throbbing to get to my feet. I twisted her hair around my fist, using it like a rope to tie her to me.

She howled when I smashed her face into the tree, again and again. Her laughter rang out despite her face becoming a mass of scarlet flesh and bone. The aroma of peaches mingled with dirt and blood.

"You. Will. Never. Hurt. Her." I punctuated each word with a slam.

Her demented cackle pierced the air when I discarded her in a heap.

"What's so funny?" I demanded, my hands fisted and my nails splitting my palms. My knuckles were shredded, and only my anger prevented me from falling to my knees.

"That you think it's me who will hurt the girl. Silly, silly boy. This is nothing but misdirection." Red and brown streaked her white leather, and she spat blood on the grass. "We already have her."

She laughed again as the fog cleared from my brain and I understood. A tidal wave of emotions threatened to drown out rational thought. My ankle gave way twice, but I ignored it and rushed toward the house. I picked up the foreign scent almost immediately and nearly choked on the dank aroma of warm wet stone and salt. It didn't belong in my home.

"Ari," I called out. "Doug." I thundered through the rooms, too disorientated to think straight. My thoughts smashed together, twisting and overlapping.

I found him in the kitchen, slumped over the island with a carving knife sticking out of his back. I pulled the blade out, and he straightened with a shriek. His face had been sliced from his temple to his chin, pouring blood down his shirt.

"What the hell happened?" I asked, tossing the knife aside.

"Damn buggers got me, didn't they. Swarmed in out of nowhere."

"How many?"

"Four, maybe five. Young wildlings. I told Ari to hide because someone tried to drive a knife into my skull." He rolled his shoulders back and winced. "They got my heart. Idiots, don't they know it has to be wood?"

"Is she here?" I pulled him to his feet, ignoring the groan of protest. "Constance, her perfume is clouding my head. I can't, I can't…"

Doug grabbed my arms, his fingers pushing into muscle and flesh. "She's here. Listen."

I stopped for a couple of seconds and picked out the rapid beating heart and stilted breath. Then, a second, slower beat followed by a crash of glass.

"She's not alone."

Chapter 16

Both Doug and I barreled up the stairs, desperate to catch the final act of whatever show Constance had decided to put on for us. It wasn't a graceful maneuver; I stumbled on my damaged ankle, and Doug's head injury affected his balance so he had to hold the wall, dragging a ruby stripe along the paint.

I froze at the door while momentum propelled Doug several inches along the corridor. His long fingers hooked the doorframe, and it creaked under the strain.

A cloaked figure lay crumpled on the threshold between the main room and the bathroom. I guessed a male, given the size and form of the body, but it was difficult to tell beneath the abundant fabric of the brown sackcloth robe. Ari stood over him, slamming the door against his head repeatedly, crushing his skull. Shards of shattered mirror covered the rug, glistening in the low light, reflecting patterns on the wall and causing Ari's damp skin to sparkle. She seemed a woman possessed by unearthly rage. Sweat dribbled down her ruddy cheeks, and her lips were drawn back, baring her teeth. The hair that had come loose from her braid clung to her skin. She released a furious grunt with each slam, and my throat constricted at the sound of the accompanying crunch.

Ari didn't appear to notice us, and neither of us made any attempt to go to her. I had no notion of Doug's thinking, but I wasn't convinced for a second that she required assistance in dispatching her would-be kidnapper. My initial thought was it could have been me. Why had she not unleashed this level of violence to defend herself against me?

She stepped back, panting wildly, and her face screwed up with determination. She pulled in a swift breath before delivering the final blow. The sole of her boot met the edge of the door with enough force to separate the head from the body. The figure faded to ash and smoke before disappearing. Ari had beheaded a vampire.

Her shoulders softened, and a tiny satisfied smile curled her lips.

"Did you see—" Doug began, his voice creeping over the words as though he couldn't believe he was speaking them.

"I saw," I broke in.

Finally recognizing our presence, Ari turned her attention our way, and her smile widened. She laughed with a shill edge of hysteria. "I got one."

An instant later, the color drained from her face, and her eyes rolled. Doug was there to catch her before I even thought of moving. She didn't lose consciousness, but he swept her up in his arms regardless and placed her on the bed, still a little off balance himself.

"Clay." His voice snapped me back to the present. "Make sure they're all gone and get the alarm."

I hadn't noticed the alarm still ringing throughout the house. I nodded and moved as an automaton, switching off the alarm and checking each room to be sure the intruders were gone. I still possessed the wherewithal to test the doors and windows, and discovered a window on the second floor to the back of the house broken, the shutter hanging askew. *So much for security.*

Apprehension muted my relief they didn't take Ari. I had to confirm if there was any truth behind Constance's assertions. A few moments later, I stood at the door to my bedroom watching Doug wipe Ari's face with a wet cloth. My feet froze as though trapped in a block of stone and took me no further into the room.

"Is it true?" There was no inflection in my tone, my voice as numb as my body.

"What?" Doug asked while Ari made no acknowledgment, although her eyes were open.

"Is it true that you were bitten? And that you drank blood?"

"What the hell are you talking about?" Doug demanded.

"Not you. Her." My words took on a dark nuance, and fangs pinched my skin. I cursed my heart for maintaining its slow and steady pace. A human heart would pound, just as Ari's began to. "She's immune to the virus."

Dough chuckled darkly. "You're cracked, man. No one's immune."

Her head fell to the side, and her eyes widened. She crept over the covers toward Doug, no doubt seeking his promised protection. The movement sent heated waves of her cocoa smell into the air. My throat closed up, making it impossible to swallow my anger. Blood seeped over my knuckles from my curled fists and dripped to the wooden floor.

Doug walked around the end of the bed slowly, with no sign of his earlier unsteadiness. I was sure it took great effort. His muscles tensed as he came to stand between us, his eyes darkened, and blue veins wormed inward under the skin on his face.

"When were you planning to tell us the truth?"

"I suggest you take the situation down a notch," Doug warned. "Nice and calmly does it."

Her lips parted as though to speak, but only a small breath of air emerged when she pushed herself up to sitting.

"I know," I said, surprised by the hurt her deception caused.

Doug frowned, and his eyes flickered to her. A silent exchange passed between them and compounded the sting in my chest. She trusted him more than me.

"I didn't know anything until after I came to Ireland. How could I? Who the hell believes in vampires?"

"Did you seek me out?" I asked.

"Not intentionally." She edged to the nearside of the bed hurriedly, giving no physical indication her answer was a lie. "I didn't even know what you were at first. I didn't know if I believed any of it. I thought you were a random, hot, slightly odd guy so I noticed you. There was a fight one time, and I saw—"

"I recall," I interrupted. Tension slipped from my body once the truth started flowing. I remained vigilant in case the intruders returned.

She dipped her head and went on. "You know what happened after. The other vampire came, and then I talked to you."

"What about before you realized Clay was a vampire?" Doug's face eased back to his human appearance; blood streaked his cheek and matted his hair. Dark stains spilled over his shoulder and down the front of his shirt. "You said you didn't believe any of it, but what's 'it'? When were you were bitten?"

"A letter," she said and swiped her hand across her forehead. "I was sent a letter soon after I arrived in Ireland saying vampires had killed my birth family but that I'd survived. I threw it out. I thought it was a prank."

Doug dragged his fingers through his hair and winced. "This isn't good, brother. Not good at all. I need a drink."

I bent my neck to one side and then the other, stretching out tight muscles as the thirst returned, scorching up my throat. I needed something to dull the craving. "We could probably all use one. I could use several."

"It might be a better idea to get out of here," Doug suggested. He watched me warily for signs of my mind fracturing. It gave me a strange comfort knowing he intended to keep his promise.

"According to Constance, the old woman who Ari came here to find was a Druid priestess. She went to great lengths to keep Ari protected. If they want her, it doesn't matter where we go. They'll find us. Was there anything else, a talisman of some kind, a stone?"

Ari shook her head and absently pulled the band from her braid, redoing it to a sloppy topknot. "I don't think so. It said the vampires were looking for someone, but the name meant nothing to me."

"Yes, Cailleach."

"How did you—" Her eyes narrowed, probably recalling the library book at her house, and she slid off the bed to stand beside Doug. She smirked and huffed out a breath. "I get it. I knew you weren't just out taking a stroll that night."

"Maybe we can talk personal space after the end of the world as we know it?" Doug suggested with a scowl. "I'm going to get that drink now, and there wouldn't be a talisman. Contrary to popular belief, Druids didn't go in for them, or write stuff down. Like everything else in this place, real Druid magic is tied to the blood." He yanked the waistband of his jeans, adjusting them at his hips and nudged passed me, heading downstairs.

Ari and I followed.

"What does this Cailleach have to do with it?" she asked, following Doug into the basement.

"Cailleach, also known as The Veiled One, is of particular interest to The Circle. Best we can figure it, that's the name of a vampire sect that's been around a long time. Last I heard of them, they were using Nazi prison camps as their all you can eat buffet and entertainment during the forties, except I didn't know what they were called back then. There were experiments—"

Ari swallowed hard. "Stop. Nazi vampires is gruesome enough."

"I thought you weren't convinced it's the same group after Ari." I pushed when we reached the kitchen.

Doug pointed to his head wound and winced when he tried to raise his eyebrow to mock me. "Color me convinced, brother. I'm ready to accept anything right now."

"What does this mean for us?" Ari said.

Doug lifted three glasses and a bottle of whisky from the counter and placed them on the island. "It means we are up to our arses in shite."

"Is that right?" she said caustically, taking a filled glass from him. "Can you be any more vague?"

"Aye, I could try." He grinned wryly. "But I might be better when I'm drunk off my arse."

"That's not helpful," I reprimanded him.

Doug's glass clinked on the quartz counter. He picked up a dishtowel from near the sink and ran the cold water.

"Let me do that," Ari offered, attempting to take the cloth from him.

"Thanks, Petal, I got it." He wiped drying blood from his face, where the slash was already healing. "When the old woman brewed up an abracadabra, she had to know there was an expiration date and the creepy crawlers would come crawling."

"What if she didn't know?" Ari asked. "What if it was something I did that caused the protection to fail. Perhaps I was never meant to come to Ireland."

"It's possible." Doug shrugged.

Ari held her hands out, palm up, and stared at them. A red oval mark on her upper arm had begun to turn pale purple. It would soon bruise. She had other marks too, a few scratches and a mottle coloring on her jaw.

"It's a leftover from the protection, that static you feel. I imagine it's fading too," Doug said to her.

I pulled out a handful of ice from the freezer. "That explains it." I grabbed a plastic bag from a drawer and wrapped the bag of ice in another towel.

"What?" she asked.

I hadn't forgotten Ari's warning. She'd told me in no uncertain terms that physical contact wasn't welcome. So, I walked toward her cautiously, holding the makeshift ice pack out.

"It explains why I didn't see you then, and now, you're all I see."

Ari paused and released an unintentional low sound from her throat. She cleared her expression to hide her surprise, but she couldn't hide her heartbeat or the rush of cocoa fragrance. The sweet aroma mingled with vanilla. It seemed my honesty made her angry too. She reached for the ice without breaking eye contact. Her index finger skimmed mine, but the static was barely noticeable. Instead, a sharp blast of energy exploded in my chest. Her pupils dilated, and I realized the touch was intentional.

"Stop," Doug snapped, drawing attention from both of us.

Ari pressed the pack to her skin and winced at the contact of the cold on her bruised upper arm.

"This—" he waggled his finger between Ari and me "—is no good. Whatever it is, you have to stop it right now. This situation is going nowhere fortunate. Think about it for a minute."

I stepped back from her and downed another full glass of whisky, hoping to drown the thirst.

"Use your head, brother." He slapped the heel of his hand to his temple and flinched. "Send some blood rushing upstairs for a minute."

I glowered at him and moved further away from Ari.

"She was pushed here…to you. They found her and sent her looking for an old woman who was already dead. Probably created just enough mystery to pique her interest and keep her here. Constance led you straight to her."

"Me?" I chuckled blackly. "What do I have to do with it?"

"Och, I don't know, but I do know it's no coincidence Constance's scent went right to the door of the only person with a natural immunity. She's been driving you two together. She's playing you for a fool."

"With a girl I hardly noticed for months?" I laughed it off. I wasn't ready to face what her immunity could mean for me. My drive to solve that puzzle had almost destroyed me once.

Ari's tinkling giggle interrupted Doug's rant. She backed up to the wall and slid down to the floor cross-legged, as though she'd been waging a war with gravity and it'd defeated her. Her laughter deepened and grew in volume, her cheeks turning pink. Doug's eyebrows bunched together over his nose, and his eyes flickered toward me, but I had no explanation for her reaction. I wasn't entirely sure I understood anything about her. Her heart jackhammered; she pulled her knees up and discarded the ice pack to bury her face in her hands.

"Ari?" I said in a low voice.

She dropped her hands and looked up, her expression unreadable. A full smile contradicted her frightened, searching eyes. She stared at me with a sort of new recognition I couldn't quite understand, as though seeing me for the first time.

"This is not my life. I'm not who I thought I was at all," she replied. Neither of us responded to her; our non-reaction prompted her to stand and begin pacing. "Let them take me."

"You're not talking sense, Petal."

"Why not? I should have died years ago, and it's not like there's much else left to take. I had a family, a plan, friends, a boyfriend, but none of it was reality."

A rumble crawled up from my chest at this first mention of a boyfriend, too low for her to pick up on in her distressed state. Doug noticed, though, and cut me a disgruntled glare.

"I opened Pandora's box, didn't I? I can't ever go back to that life. The reality is vampires and darkness and death and blood. So, what's the point? I don't fit in here, and I don't fit in there, in my old life. Let them take me and choke on me."

"No," I told her honestly. "You can't go back."

She stopped and swallowed, my eyes fixed on the movement of tendons and straining vessels beneath golden flesh.

"Tell me what to do." Her voice strained with pleading. "I won't be a pawn in anyone's game."

My foot shifted forward without a conscious decision. I was only vaguely aware of the change in my stance and not at all in control of what my next actions would have been if Doug hadn't acted.

His right palm pushed solidly against my left shoulder. His lips twitched, but he remained tightlipped, although I guessed his instinct was to snarl or bare his fangs. I knew because it was also mine.

"You need to go see that man now, Clay. I'll take care of Ari."

Thirst itched, and my throat and my tongue seemed to swell and stick to the roof of my mouth as though made of Velcro. My eyes pinched shut, and I forced down the quick and brutal urge to fling him across the room for coming between us. There wasn't a part of me that disagreed with Doug in theory.

"It isn't safe to leave," I whispered through gritted teeth.

"It isn't safe to stay." His lips hardly moved, but his chest puffed out, almost touching mine. I imagined his body swelling, becoming an immovable wall between me and the sweet, liquid silk I craved, despite my best intentions.

I slid one foot back an inch and then a second.

"I think we might've been more than the match they were expecting. Constance is a smart girl. She'll pull back and regroup. She'll come back hitting swifter and harder, so we need to regroup too." Doug darted a glance over his shoulder, including Ari in the conversation before he redirected to me. "When you get back, you'll make *that* call. If we're buckling down here, we're going to need back up. I might be fast-talking and good-looking, but I'm far from invincible."

He meant for me to contact William, the very thing I'd been avoiding. I hadn't seen him in person for almost a century. I had no desire to face him with everything so out of control. My friendly associations in the vampire world were limited to two, and one already resided in my home. Ari pushed up on her toes and peeked over Doug's shoulder. Tendrils of hair had come loose from the messy bun that had replaced her braid and twisted down her neck. Her gaze moved over my face, not resting on any particular point, as though she wanted to avoid meeting my eyes but wanted to see my expression.

I nodded and inched back further, interlocking my fingers at my nape where my hair tickled skin. I dragged my hands upward over my scalp and back again, not caring that I'd look a mess. Anything to distract myself, to keep my thoughts pinned in one spot and away from Ari's blood and the secrets it might hold.

"I'll be back inside an hour," I assured them both.

Chapter 17

1888

I glanced up from *The Times* when my guest sauntered into the dining room. Deep frown lines creased above the bridge of his nose as he quickly took in his surroundings. I returned to reading theories about the identity of the Leather Apron Killer.

Wood screeched on wood, and I winced at the intrusive noise, not accustomed to company in my home. Dougal threw himself into the high backed chair at the opposite end of the polished table, his motion so boisterous he left me in no doubt of his intention to irritate.

My servants knew well of my preference for keeping the curtains drawn on bright days elsewhere in the house. Due to the proximity of other properties, this room had been designed without wall windows. Fragments of colored glass partially made up the sloping ceiling. Although a magnificent piece of art, the glass and lead structure allowed only passive daylight at this hour.

Thomas emerged through the service door to set another place for breakfast. Dougal's eyes widened at the sight of the glittering metal before waving him off.

"No…thank you," he tacked on as an obvious afterthought, at least feigning manners.

The vampire was loud and brash and unkempt. His hair refused to stay within the confines of its tie at the back of his head. His every uncultured gesture caused my toes to curl in my boots. Yet against my better judgment, I welcomed the distraction of his company.

"Steel," I commented.

"What?"

"The cutlery, it's polished steel. With progress moving so swiftly these days I expect one day soon steel will generally replace silver for everyday use. For now, it's still too hard to keep clean to be convenient or fashionable, but more suited to those of a certain disposition."

"Disposition?" He scowled. "What is this, Henry?"

"Breakfast," I responded, shaking the paper, although we both knew he wasn't referring to the remnant of bloody steak before me.

"This charade, surely you see the madness of it? You could expose us all." The dark, smooth texture of his voice hinted at genuine concern, and he glared at my plate.

I added it to the things I couldn't fathom about the Scot. A grin tugged at my lips. "I imagine, despite whatever years you may set claim to, that you recall the concept of food."

He blinked, and his back straightened. "Aye, I do. Do you?"

Thomas returned to usher my plates away, and Dougal watched him curiously. Perhaps he thought I might lose control, but I never would. Never again in my own home.

As soon as Thomas left, I said, "This is the only sustenance I require these days."

"Animals? Who led you to believe that was a good idea?" Dougal slid forward on his seat and rested his elbows on the table. "You must know you can't live on them. It's as much as starving." One hand waved in the newspaper now settled on the table with lurid headlines of death in London. "How did you come to be this abomination?"

I narrowed my eyes, daring him to expand on his question.

He pressed his lips together when it became clear to him I wouldn't explain how I came to my experiments. "A doctor, then, how did you come to be a doctor?"

"A scientist," I corrected him. "I studied in Dublin, and after—" I paused, allowing the word to linger between us "—I was fortunate to be discovered by the man who became my mentor. William arranged the cover for my crimes and took me away. I continued my studies as his apprentice. William is a foremost authority on rare blood disorders."

"Where is the great man now, then?"

"One man may live in the shadow of another for only so long."

He scratched at his temple, once again drawing attention to how naturally human he appeared. "You were fortunate to have someone… anyone with you."

I nodded, acknowledging this truth. "And you, what is your tale of woe?"

He drew in a long breath, puffing out his cheeks. "There is none, at least none I wish to revisit. The sun turned to blood, and death took me. My people are ash now, blowing through highland winds."

I could relate.

"Stay as long as you will. I may one day find myself lacking for company."

"I am grateful for your hospitality, brother."

I nodded and stood to leave. I had preparations I wished to attend to before continuing my explorations.

"Don't make me regret inviting you into my home."

Chapter 18

2010

It took forty-nine minutes to collect my package from my contact at the hospital and return to the house. I'd called ahead to let Doug know I'd already consumed two pouches of the ten I'd collected. The rest were safely packed away inside a cool box, but they needed refrigeration quickly. I wasn't at all pleased when I found Ari in the kitchen, sitting on one of the remaining unbroken chairs at the island, drinking whisky. I could hear Doug fixing a temporary covering on the broken window upstairs. I had no idea where he found the wood he was in the process of hammering.

I didn't bother with the overhead lights. I didn't need them to see, and Ari appeared happy to remain in the muted glow of the ambient under-counter lighting. The amber liquid in the crystal tumbler sent ripples of gold flickering over her features.

I continued with the necessity of transferring the pouches to the fridge, but self-consciousness about her presence made my movements sluggish. At least the thirst had abated for now.

"I'm sorry," I said. Why did I feel the need to excuse my actions?

"You didn't choose to be what you are." She continued to swirl the glass. "I know you need to drink, and I'm not squeamish about blood."

"I'm still sorry."

She'd showered recently and skipped toweling dry. Clean water and soap evaporated from her warm skin, and a single strap had slipped from her bruised shoulder. The dark wet tank clung tantalizingly to every curve, and I chastised myself for noticing.

"I know," she breathed against the lip of the glass.

The fridge door clinked closed, the seal flush despite the damage to the exterior, and I twisted slowly, ready to slip quietly from the room.

"How do you do it?" Ari asked without turning to me. She freshened her glass with the open bottle on the table.

I shifted uncomfortably, recalling our last conversation about feeding. Doug was right that I had deliberately led her to believe in my ambivalence to it. "If I don't feed, I change. I become everything I detest."

"You wanted to die once." Her blue eyes fixed on mine, determined to delve in and scoop the truth from my head. "Didn't you, when you killed your family?"

"How did you..." My words trailed off. "Doug."

"I worked it out for myself. How do you do it—live, knowing you're responsible for their deaths?"

I finally grasped her line of thinking. It wasn't about feeding. "Your parents' deaths aren't your responsibility."

"Sure they are." She tipped her glass again. "I'm trying to make sense of it. You know, fix all the pieces in my head so they fit. I'm not embarrassed to say I'm struggling. I feel like I'm slipping down a hole, and every time I find a foothold, the walls disintegrate."

I'd never seen her consume so much alcohol and wondered about her tolerance for hard drinking. Pain glazed her eyes, and red crowded the white, pushing in toward her irises. It was another swift kick to the gut. I couldn't give her the answers she wanted.

I leaned my elbows on the island and interlaced my fingers. "William, the vampire who discovered me with my family, told me I needed to find a reason to go on living."

"You chase after what you can't have, and you call it a reason." Her eyes lifted and pierced right through me, seeing the truth and all my ugliness right down to my core. "Isn't that why you almost destroyed yourself looking for a cure? Why you've been pretending to follow this woman all over the world?"

"I did follow her."

She laughed, spun on the seat, and hopped down with her drink in her hand. "Oh, please, you could have found her years ago." Her plump lips pouted, and she rolled her eyes. Some whisky sloshed from the glass and dribbled over her fingers to the floor. "Am I just another excuse not to die?"

"No." I kept my voice level and remained motionless as she wandered around me stirring up the air with her scent.

"Redemption, then?"

My jaw slackened, and my lips parted. Words wouldn't come.

"Don't lie," Ari said. "Not to me." A tremor shook her hand when she pointed at me. "Don't say it hasn't crossed your mind that saving me will ease your conscience."

Light and shadow slid over the contours of her body as she swayed on her tiptoes and spun again. Her hair whipped out, and the combination of damp clothes and cool air rose gooseflesh on her skin. My fingers clawed against the quartz. She was so beautiful, even when her confusion eclipsed her bravery. A tight ball of frustration constricted in my chest. I wanted to reach out, but her warning to stay away kept me restrained.

Ari almost fell next to the counter with a giggle, and then she hiccupped and covered her mouth, giggling again. The next hiccup stole her smile, and the dance ended abruptly. Her lips turned down at the edges.

"Why are you doing this?"

"I don't know."

Her watery eyes filled, and one tear brimmed over, sliding down her cheek. She sniffled and swiped it away. Glass clinked against quartz, and Ari rubbed her eyes with both hands.

"Urgh, I'm sorry." The delicate skin had turned pink and swollen when she relented. "I'm having a pity party right now, and I didn't mean to drag you in. I'm feeling a little sorry for myself tonight."

"It's okay."

She picked up the glass and tossed the remaining whisky into the sink, keeping her back to me. "I thought this might help, but it just makes things more foggy and complicated. It's ridiculous because I've always known I was different. I'm just that little bit faster and stronger than everyone else. I knew, I knew…"

Her head dipped, and she gripped onto the edge of the sink as though it was the only thing holding her up. "Do you think they can do this thing? Bring this monster—this Abhartach—back?"

I stood straight and pulled in a deep breath. "What I think is irrelevant. The Circle believes they can."

"Do you think you might find your cure in my blood?"

It occurred to me to lie and say I hadn't thought about it. "There is no cure. It's like you so elegantly pointed out, I've spent my existence chasing what I can't have so I could avoid the truth."

She pushed back from the sink and turned, tilting her head in observation. "You never truly wanted to die."

"I never truly wanted to die," I repeated her words, each one a razorblade, shredding me from the inside and ripping apart what I believed I knew about myself.

Her bottom lip quivered. "Does it make me a monster too? My parents loved me. My mom, she had this habit of mouthing the words when she read a book. I used to just sit there and pretend to watch the TV, but I'd be watching her. My dad, I think he secretly always wanted a son, but I never doubted for one second of my life that he loved me. We used to go fishing sometimes."

She chuckled, and the red around her eyes deepened at the memory. Her lips pulled down further as she attempted to continue the story without breaking down.

"I know Mom hated whenever we brought something home and insisted on cooking it for dinner. She hated the smell of fish cooking. They raised me to be a good person, and they'd be alive today if I never existed. It's my fault, and all I can think is I'm glad it wasn't me."

I straightened, and even from several feet apart, I towered over her. She seemed so small, almost folded in on herself.

"It's not the same. Not the same at all. I've done terrible things, some you couldn't understand and some I don't ever want you to think about."

"Do you feel remorse? Can you?" Her eyelashes fluttered, shadowing the pale blue for a moment. She squeezed her eyes shut and opened them again, refocusing with a penetrating gaze.

I allowed myself one step nearer. Blood whooshed in my ears, the poison forcing a white hot path through my bloodstream. "I think I do. I want to believe I do. Honestly, it's been so long since

I've been human, I'm not sure how to define my emotions, but I believe I feel remorse."

Ari's teeth came down on the edge of her lip, and I tasted salt in the charged air between us. "I don't know what I believe anymore. I guess that's why I'm trying so hard to understand why I'm here."

"I wish I could explain what it is that captivates me." My brow furrowed into a scowl. "Yeats said the world is full of magic things, patiently waiting for our senses to grow sharper. To be truthful, sometimes I feel as though the world came into focus that day in the square, and other times I'm not sure you are real. I wonder if the madness has finally taken me, and you're a figment of a fractured psyche. Maybe none of this is happening."

Ari laughed. She licked her lips and smiled forlornly. A couple more tears overflowed, and she brushed them away. "What a pair we are," she said, and she closed the space separating us.

I locked my arms by my side. My throat closed as I attempted to choke down the sudden explosion of thirst seizing my senses. It was nothing compared to earlier, so I knew she wasn't in any immediate danger. My leg muscles tensed and trembled regardless.

She raised one hand hesitantly, her fingers closed and opened as doubt flickered across her expression. Vanilla and chocolate sweetened the salt air and swirled like ribbons binding us together. I couldn't walk away if I wanted to. Perhaps she had a little of the witch in her too.

Ari's fingers softened, and her warm breath washed over my face. Every nerve came alive, raw and aching. As though she breathed life back into my chest and punched clear through my ribcage, my heart constricted.

Pheromones flooded the kitchen. Her excitement intensified and tested the limits of my restraint. My arousal surged in response, and my jeans tightened despite my best efforts to keep my libido at bay. Ari's fingertips touched my cheek near my ear and skimmed down my jaw, trailing a line of scorching heat.

"I am real." Her voice trembled over each word. Her lip color deepened a shade, and her pupils dilated.

A growl vibrated at the back of my throat. My erection throbbed, and the sensation of pleasurable cramping in my groin and upper thighs eclipsed the thirst. This confused me. It'd been so long since I'd allowed myself to explore sexual desire apart from thirst.

I hoped she'd linger close, but she retreated to the sink, stumbling backward and lowering her gaze. "Or maybe you are crazy. Maybe I'm crazy. The hell if I know." Her cheeks flushed, and she forced a smile. "I know I'm very drunk, and I'm exhausted."

She filled her discarded glass with water from the tap and headed to the door, leaving without throwing so much as a glance toward me. "Night."

I turned and leaned my hands against the sink.

"Wilde said the optimist sees the donut, the pessimist sees the hole," Doug informed me a moment later with a wry half-grin. He walked into the kitchen, cleaning his hands on a rag. He wore sweatpants from my wardrobe and no shoes, and smelled of sawdust and metal. The warm, dry odor irritated my nose.

"You were listening." I adjusted my jeans and swiped the whisky from the counter, not bothering with a glass.

"Hard not to, but damn it, brother, if you don't half-make a stone heart bleed."

I snorted a laugh at his word choice given my predicament. Doug took the bottle from my hand and downed the remaining two fingers of amber liquid at the bottom, placing the empty bottle on the counter.

"The window will hold for now, although you'll be needing a new door on the wardrobe of that room I've been using."

Diminishing furniture was the least of my worries. "Thank you."

Doug spread his arms and flattened his palms on the opposite side of the island. The hard corded muscles of his torso and arms tensed, and the overheard lights picked out the gold in his hair where it shaded his eyes. A tiny pinch of jealousy stung my temples at the thought of him walking around the house displaying his chiseled abs. I wasn't oblivious to the world around me. Doug's looks rivaled any of the Hollywood leads who made young women of the day swoon. *Do women still swoon?* I pinched the bridge of my nose hoping Doug didn't notice the instant I glowered at him.

"Are you sure about staying put? It's not too late to go. You know Ari'd follow you in a blink."

I matched his stance. "I thought you didn't like what's happening. You called it obsession." I rolled my eyes. "Oh, wait…no, you said it was nothing at all."

Doug hung his head, and his shoulder blades narrowed. He raised his eyes just enough to peer at me from under his eyelashes.

His nostrils flared, and he forced out a hard breath. "You want me to take it back? Fine. This love story you've got going has the makings of Shakespeare—*Romeo and Juliet*."

I chuckled at his reference to Ari's favorite reading material, resigned to his judgment. "Romeo and Juliet was a tragedy."

Doug straightened and threw his hands in the air. "You got me." He dragged his fingers through his hair and scratched roughly at his scalp. "This is a mess. Just tell me you have some sort of a plan."

I eased back, comfortable now that the physical evidence of my excitement had was no longer visible. Soft snores filtered down from upstairs and provided a melodic backdrop to the creaking and groaning of the old house settling. I dragged the stool Ari had used earlier over the tiled floor and took a seat.

"Maybe we should go. After all, if someone went to a lot of trouble to get Ari here, it must be for a reason."

Doug threw his hands up a second time, and a wide grin lit up his face. "Hallelujah, brother, you've seen sense."

"Except," I pushed on, interrupting his celebration, "it must be for a reason."

"What?"

"I don't know."

"Gah, you're impossible."

Our conversation appeared to be churning in circles, which meant it was time to take my leave. I stood and put my stool back. "I have a call to make."

After Doug left to do whatever he did when he wasn't around, I picked up the mobile phone from my desk.

"*Ahoj?*" the female voice answered. *Hello?* William had been living in Prague for several years.

I didn't recognize her. I knew he'd been living with a female vampire and had readied myself for someone other than him to pick up the call.

"Hello," I began. "May I speak with Alex Williams?" I used the name he currently went by, though in my head I found it difficult to think of my mentor as anything other than William. I was sure he'd know this wasn't a courtesy call since his home phone number was not at all easy to procure. However, not much was unobtainable with enough money. There was a long pause at the other end of the line before she spoke again.

"Henry? It's Henry, isn't it? He has been hoping to hear from you for so long," she prattled on excitedly. This female I didn't know and who didn't know me. Yet, she spoke as if we were long separated friends. My fingers tightened on the phone. My impatience grew as though a ball of elastic pinged repeatedly in the pit of my stomach.

I leaned back in the chair and listened to the wood and leather creaking, giving way to my weight. The fingers of my free hand found their way into my hair, tugging it from the roots and scratching at the back of my neck. I focused on these little things to ignore the acid heat in my veins. Anticipation of hearing William's voice after so long caught in my chest. It would be easier for both of us if I hung up and didn't disturb the status quo of our estrangement.

I had to speak to him before I lost my nerve. "Excuse me," I broke into her ramble, "is he home?"

Without another word, she harrumphed and the phone clicked, and I was placed on hold. It took no more than a few seconds for the next click.

"Son."

That one word from William caused my throat to constrict almost painfully and my lungs to seize up as though transformed to solid lead. So much regret and guilt I'd been holding back for decades rushed forward in great angry torrents. It felt almost like a punishment that he should still use the term of endearment. If I was his son, I was surely the most wayward of children.

I swallowed stiffly, giving myself a moment to erect the barriers once more.

"I —"

He broke in before I could continue. "I presumed you would be in touch when you heard the news. Are you safe?" He asked it with the same fatherly concern I had quickly come to know in him, as though the last ninety years hadn't passed in estrangement despite his repeated attempted to connect.

"Safe?" I asked, confused by his question but presuming he meant the renegades and their plans.

"The vampire community is in chaos, and I suspect things will get much worse—"

"Wait," I stopped him. "What are you talking about?"

An abrupt wall of silence met my question. I had called to figure out what, if any, information he could provide, but I got the distinct impression the chaos he indicated to was more than a deluded cult.

"You haven't heard?" he asked.

"Heard?"

"Henry, the most influential vampires of each continent have been wiped out—assassinated. The most powerful links in business and politics are gone. It appears someone is intent on separating us from the human world."

"What?" I demanded.

"It was calculated and precise," William went on. "The most important leaders of our kind were gathered at the vampire World Council, and someone injected silver nitrate into the bloodstream of the humans presented as nourishment at the feast. The vampires' frenzy meant many had already consumed enough contaminated blood to kill them before the discovery of the poison. Word leaking out says those who didn't succumb were slaughtered as they tried to flee." He paused and inhaled deeply. "Have you heard of The Circle?"

"Yes." I didn't elaborate, not by conscious decision, more because this flood of new information caused me to revert to stoic responses. It all seemed so fantastic, even to me.

"It would appear a new world order is on the horizon for all of us. I always believed The Circle would someday put plans into action."

He'd never mentioned them to me in our time together.

Ari was in grave danger, much more than I had given credence to. The idea made every cell inside my body oscillate, and my brain automatically began to envisage the ways I'd kill anyone who would attempt to cause her harm.

"Henry." William called me back into the moment, but the red veil that had descended across my vision faded only a little.

It was as though the world had suddenly been drenched with blood. Maybe it soon would be.

"If that's not the reason you called, then why?" His tone was carefully remote, almost shielding something—hope? "Maybe it's something better discussed in person," he suggested. "Henry, I'm coming to Ireland on the first flight I can catch out."

I sighed, holding the phone tighter. The plastic began to crack along the seam.

Chapter 19

1888

The remaining weeks of September provided no respite from my new friend. He was everywhere, forever by my side insisting on "saving me from myself." He fed from humans, but only ever enough to sustain himself and often relieving them of enough money for his other needs at the same time.

I intended to select another subject for use in my experiments this night. Although, I had refuted as much to Dougal when leaving my laboratory.

My steps on the footpath were impossibly loud in my ears. The knife in my pocket weighed more than it should, almost unbalancing me, but I walked on. Rain had ceased, leaving the midnight air uncommonly clean. A malevolent cloud draped over the city, and its inhabitants remained ill at ease, seeking shelter where they could and traveling in groups whenever possible.

Thirst had a firm grasp on my body, which bayed for sustenance I already knew I would deny it. I felt myself drying from the inside out, my mind gasping for answers.

Failure, always failure.

I had no choice but to kill for my experiments. I needed the blood from the reproductive organs of those women. I had rationalized it to myself many times over and only used the lowest dregs of society, those who would never make any other meaningful contribution. I combined the dead matter and blood with a solution based on a silver extract and my own contaminated blood sample. Using electric pulses, I was able to reanimate the human cells while destroying the vampiric virus. It worked, however briefly. I was on the very edge of discovering how to fight this disease.

However, every time I tested the serum on myself, it had the opposite effect. It seemed to rip the life right from my veins. I could only hypothesize it worked on the virus, accelerating it temporarily, leaving me ravenous with hunger and stealing the last shards of my humanity. In these moments after I'd consumed the serum, the demon inside me unleashed, desperate to be sated with blood.

An experiment earlier in the day had left me physically weakened, and draining a horse did little to clear my mind or dull my thirst. I wasn't in the correct frame of mind for my work. Good sense should have driven me home, but instead I found myself walking the streets of Whitechapel, driven on by a wild compulsion to end the misery of this affliction.

I walked along Commercial Road, keeping to the shadows and avoiding a number of working men in high spirits. They were coming from Berner Street, and without intending to, I headed in the direction they came from. Music floated through the air, along with horse hooves clattering on the ground in the distance. A piercing hiss of gas lamps played on my ears, slicing through every thought and allowing me no peace to think.

The tendons in my neck strained with each hollow thump of my heart, reinforcing my revulsion at its constant unnatural slowness. A relentless urge to howl into the night for release from my frustration swelled. It would make me little more than an animal, a dog in the street. So, I pushed on without relief.

I stumbled into a wall when one leg almost gave way and steadied myself on a gate. A tingling numbness inched a path through my limbs. Time meant nothing, and I had no idea if one hour had passed or several when I caught the familiar scent of sex and gin behind me.

"Are you ill, sir? Should I fetch help?"

I turned on her. The woman screamed and began to stagger away. Fangs dug into the flesh inside my lips as I stared into wide gray eyes. I grabbed for her, but my movements were sluggish and heavy, and she slipped away. I had a method for choosing my subjects, careful controls. Despite her shabby but proper appearance, I was sure of her profession. Still, I wasn't ready. The darkness inside me was forcing its way to the surface, and she'd seen my true face. All the houses around us were populated, and singing coming from the club on the corner meant witnesses would arrive on the scene in minutes.

My gaze fell on a posy in the lapel of her black coat, scarlet roses set against green. The petals rippled as though liquid, melting over the dark fabric. This was all wrong.

I reached for her a second time and pulled her into the alley by the shoulders. She screamed again when I spun her around and a third time when I pushed her to the ground.

A stone scuttled across the cobbled street. I turned and bared my fangs at a passing man. A tall, bedraggled man in worn clothes and a peaked cap. He ducked his head as if to pretend he didn't see me or my altercation with the woman, which he couldn't have missed. Even if he hadn't seen my fangs, he could easily give my description to the police.

Just in the same moment, Dougal appeared out of the shadows. He'd been following me. My senses were all askew, and I'd failed to notice him there.

"Dougal!" I called out, and the bedraggled man took off running.

Dougal dipped his head in acknowledgment and dashed after the man, allowing me to return my attentions to the woman.

She floundered, only half-conscious. Perhaps she'd fainted. Her blood had slowed, a state I usually achieved by strangulation. It made dissection less messy. She smelled so good, and I shook with need. The wanton darkness coiled through my body. My desire to abstain from human prey was overshadowed, and my own spark of humanity almost faded to nothing. I wanted to drink from her. Just one taste and then I could think straight. Just one taste and then I would stop.

I whirled away and slammed my fist against the wall. *I won't be a savage.* Swallowing harshly, my fingers curled over the handle of the knife in my pocket. The woman at my feet moaned and attempted to crawl away. I yanked her onto her back and sliced her throat. I would have her blood for my work if nothing else.

When I found Dougal a few minutes later in another alley nearby, I had already wiped the blade clean and stored the bloody handkerchief in my pocket.

"I took care of him, altered his recollection. He won't remember anything of use," he said, leaning back against a wall and crossing his arms. "It was the darndest thing—I could have sworn I saw a woman on the roof, just over there." He pointed out into the street. "Then she was gone, no scent, no nothing. Did you see?"

Icy fingers walked up my spine with the recollection of feeling watched after leaving The Princess Alice the first night I met Dougal. The same curious warmth bloomed in my chest, and the powdery, metallic smell of London fog tickled my nose. I pressed my hand against my sternum and heard the preacher's ravings about damnation as though a window to the past had opened. It was a mere instant of distraction, and more immediate matters returned my attention to the present.

I lunged at Dougal, an action he clearly didn't expect because he didn't act to prevent it. The wall clunked and trembled on impact, showering us both with dust.

"What is the meaning of this? Why are you following me? What do you want?" I raged at him, spraying spittle into his blinking eyes.

He bared his fangs, his gaze flashing to where his coat lapel bunched in the grip of my fingers. "I am trying to help you."

"I haven't solicited nor do I require your *help*, Highlander." I released him with a grunt and turned my back, taking a deep breath to alleviate my anger. My fingers trembled. Dougal wasn't to know my strength had temporarily deserted me. I couldn't have held him there against his will, even if I wished it. "You have no conception of what you have done."

I spared him a look over my shoulder. His fangs had already retracted into his gums. This vampire had more self-control than I.

He shook his head when I turned, a grave stoop to his shoulders. "You don't see it, do you?" His features creased at my lack of response, and he tapped his finger against his temple. "You poor, wretched creature, starvation has warped your mind. Surely the great *William* warned you."

"This has nothing to do with him," I ground out though gritted teeth. William may have planted the seed, but it was my decision. Mine. "I must kill again tonight."

"You need not kill at all! It has become sport for you."

"No, not sport." I laughed bitterly. "Never sport. You fail to comprehend me, sir. This thirst is a stain on my heart. It is a stain on the memory of a most beloved sister. It has corrupted every part of me, and one day soon I will forget I was ever human and become only the animal. I feel it." I clutched at my breast as through I could rip out my charred soul and present it to him. "I feel this monstrous sickness poisoning every thought, craving death and blood like a wild, senseless beast. I must complete my work and find a cure."

Dougal stepped forward, his countenance somewhat softened toward me. "I am too late, and you are insane, brother. You happily play with fire and risk exposure, and by extension, may expose us all."

"Then, take your leave. I won't attempt to detain you. You have no business here."

Dougal threw his hand up in frustration, and a listless smile curled at the edges of his mouth. "My business is you. No man is an island, Henry. No man. I would be your friend, if you'd only allow it."

"I am not a man," I said coldly.

Dougal stepped forward so there were only inches between us. "We are all exactly what we choose to be."

We glared at each other in an awkward, protracted silence until I inched back first. My legs shook, and I needed support. Short of leaning on Dougal, my only other option was a wall. I dragged the back of my hand across my parched lips and caught the lingering scent of human blood on my fingers.

"You are wrong," I said.

Chapter 20

2010

The following day, the sun remained hidden behind undulating storm clouds, as though even the weather reacted to the turbulence in the vampire hierarchy. Rain fell in sheets, pushed askew by the biting wind all morning, turning the pathway to the front of the house black, stripping rocking branches of leaves, and forming puddles in the grass. By late afternoon, the rain had eased, but the day brightened only marginally, leaving every room dark and gloomy.

Dull gray light cast long shadows through the high windows in the kitchen. I stood by the refrigerator door, sipping blood from a crystal tumbler. The low humming acted as a buffer of sorts, helping to drown out the constant rush of Ari's bloodstream. Like a badly tuned radio mixing static and music. I focused on the glass of water I'd left on the island beside two painkillers, in anticipation of Ari coming downstairs. Droplets of moisture rolled down the side of the glass, creating patterns and shapes in the condensation. I watched the way someone might watch clouds forming patterns in the sky, seeing hooded figures and dead bodies.

I expected William to arrive later. His travel itinerary had been arranged to allow him to avoid direct sunlight. He was anxious to meet Ari but unconvinced of Constance's claims regarding her. He knew more about The Circle than either Doug or me, although Doug had spent most the night and morning before he'd left trawling though books on Celtic legends and researching on the Internet. I wasn't sure what he hoped to find; luck alone couldn't sort endless threads of false information from the truth.

Ari'd been awake at least an hour, at first tossing and turning with the occasional groan. Eventually she bounded from bed to the bathroom to vomit. That was when I settled myself against the refrigerator. I was aware of the intrusion to her privacy. It stirred a foreign remorse.

It seemed Ari struggled with guilt too. She appeared at the door to the kitchen, freshly showered and pale, wearing a sheepish expression and one of my hooded sweatshirts over yoga pants. She peeked up at me from under bare eyelashes and pushed her clenched fists deeper into the pocket at the front.

"I was kind of cold. I hope you don't mind?"

My pulse vibrated through every part of my body, and blood rushed in my ears at the sight of her in my clothes. *It doesn't mean anything*, I told myself. *She was cold, that's all*. I forced down the primal possession rising inside. I cursed my mind when it called up a vivid image of Ari wearing one of my shirts and nothing else, the smooth flesh over her toned thighs exposed as she crossed the floor to my bed.

"Not at all." I kept the glass in my hand hidden as best I could and placed it in the sink under a running tap. "Take whatever you need. Take it all."

Her lips turned up at one side, and she scooped damp hair behind her ears. Some pink returned to her cheeks. "I don't think *all* will be necessary." She inhaled and pressed her lips together. "But I will have some of that coffee."

I'd brewed a fresh pot while she showered, guessing she might need it. The rich, bitter aroma mingled with her cocoa lotion and her personal heated scent.

I pointed to the island and the glass of water.

Ari's forehead pinched, puckering over her nose, and her chin quivered. Her eyes darted back to me for an instant and returned to the glass. "Thank you, Henry." Her voice cracked over my name and disappeared to a croaked whisper.

She bit down on her lip and sniffled, sliding onto the tall stool I'd left pulled out for her, while I filled a mug of coffee. It wasn't a blend they used at the coffee shop, but the young man who had sold it to me at the delicatessen assured me it was their most popular. Ari had swallowed the pills and downed half the water before I placed the mug in front of her. She didn't meet my gaze directly, although I noted her glassy, bloodshot eyes. Purple shadows circled beneath, as though someone had pressed their thumbs too harshly against the tender flesh.

"A friend is arriving from Prague later," I told her. "He may be of some assistance to us."

"Someone you trust?"

"Implicitly."

Ari nodded once. "I'm sorry," she said, picking up the mug and cradling it between her hands.

I went to retrieve the plate of pancakes I'd left warming in the oven, presuming she'd be hungry but not inclined to cook. "For?" I prompted when she didn't continue.

Her eyes widened at the stack of golden pancakes and small jug of maple syrup. "Oh my God, you cooked for me?"

I waved a hand dismissively. "Nothing worth blasphemy."

"Sorry."

"It was joke." I flashed a smile and retreated to the refrigerator, giving her space.

"Not for the pancakes, for last night. I'm not normally the self-pity type. I seem to have a lot on my mind all of a sudden." Ari poured syrup over the pancakes and sliced off a piece with the edge of her fork. Her lips bunched up as she slid a fluffy piece into her mouth and hummed in satisfaction. "This is really good," she mumbled around a mouthful of food.

Her reaction and brightened mood pleased me. "I told you, some-times I eat, and I've had time to practice."

She nodded, munching her way through another piece.

"I meant what I said," I told her when she'd almost finished.

She gave me a questioning sidelong glance. "I'm a little fuzzy on the details."

"You shouldn't feel guilty for what happened to your family."

Her fork clattered a little too loud on the edge of the plate and slipped off, hitting the quartz with a sharp ping and splashing syrup.

She sipped coffee and stared ahead, the slight twitch in her eye and the scent of vanilla gave away the anger she tried to hide.

"I can smell your anger," I said.

Ari's jaw clenched, and her eyes widened with the mug grazing her bottom lip. She placed it back on the counter. Vanilla intensified. "That is so intrusive, and it's…icky." She shuddered. "I don't want you smelling me like that."

I shifted and crossed my arms over my chest. "It's unavoidable. If I don't inhale, I won't smell, but I also won't be able to speak."

"Double win."

I frowned, and Ari let out a loud breath. She leaned forward on her elbows. "Apparently I suck at apologies."

"I'm inclined to agree," I said.

Her smile was genuine this time, and she met my eyes directly, still tired but with more color in her face. "I know you can't help your senses any more than I can stop breathing. I'm still getting used to it." She waggled a finger toward me. "But you don't get to corner the market on grief and self-loathing."

I groaned and rubbed at the back of my neck. "Ari, it's different. I brutally murdered my family. My mother, my father, and —" I stopped. It'd been so long since I'd said her name aloud that I struggle to force the word out.

"Charlotte," Ari whispered, almost reverently. I stared at her.

I blinked away the stinging sensation at the back of my eyes. A ball of sorrow welled in my chest and made it hard to inhale the breath I needed. I followed her line of vision to where the heel of my hand rubbed a rough circle over my heart. I dropped my hand by my side and flexed my fingers, ridding myself of the tension.

"Lottie. I called her Lottie."

"That's pretty."

"She was very precious to me."

"I can see that." Ari swallowed a mouthful of coffee. "Though it doesn't change the fact you had no control over your actions. Pain is pain is pain. My pain, yours, it's not a freaking competition."

I gestured to the plate and the remains of the pancakes with my hand. She nodded and I removed it to the sink. I'd tidy up later. I didn't want Ari to comment on my obsessive cleaning again.

"I've killed others."

"When you were out of control. When you acted true to your nature."

Her scent filled my head, and her heart pumped invitingly. I knew I was strong enough to resist for the moment. Since she'd finished eating, I came to the counter, not worrying about personal space this time. My fingers spread wide on the cold quartz, and I pursed my lips, narrowing my eyes. Ari held my gaze for a few moments. Her eyes tightened too, reflecting my expression, and moved over my face.

"You don't know what I've done. You have no comprehension of how far down the dark goes." My voice came out low and dangerous because what I had to say would scare her.

She closed her eyes, and her nostrils flared. Ari's head tilted back, and her lips parted enough for her warm breath to stir the faint musky excitement mingling with the other fragrances in the air around us. Her tongue peeked out and swept over plump pink flesh. A tingle of anticipation rushed under my skin. I retreated, but only an inch or two.

"There's a part of me afraid it's the dark that's drawing me in. Have you considered maybe that's what drew me to you?" Her heart skipped along, betraying her nerves regarding the admission.

I waited patiently for her to open her eyes and then watched her fathomless black pupils adjust to the light.

"You've heard of Jack the Ripper?" I asked.

Confusion screwed her features, and she nodded. I remained silent, hoping the penny would drop. After a moment, her eyebrows rose.

"Hold up," Ari exclaimed, amused. Her lips curled up in a wide smile. It wasn't the reaction I'd expected. "You're not saying—"

My jaw clicked from my clenched teeth. I dipped my head to indicate I was saying exactly what she was thinking.

Her smile lessened, betraying more shock than amusement now, and she dragged her hands through her hair. "I didn't know that."

"Why would you? I didn't ask to be this, but I am a vampire. Sometimes the darkness rises up and takes over. It makes no difference if I'm in control or not; I did these things. I can't atone for the past, and it's possible I'll kill again because I will always be at the mercy of my thirst."

Ari shook her head and scrubbed her hands over her face. I imagined she was attempting to make sense of this new information. I wasn't sure what I'd wanted to achieve with the truth.

She sucked in a loud breath through pursed lips and winced. "Everything in me tells me I should be disgusted by you. I know it. I should hate you, and I should want you dead." She tilted her head and gazed at me with penetrating blue eyes.

My skin prickled in response, not from the faint magic lingering on her but from the awareness of this human seeing me for everything I was, even in the midst of everything going on around us. Should she finish by telling me she could never care for a demon, a cold killer, I could accept her decision. But, damn me to hell, I wanted her to care.

Whatever her thought, she didn't finish it. "Tell me something… something good about you. A memory from before."

My shoulders slumped, and my head fell forward so far I felt the strain at the back of my neck. It seemed I'd spent an eternity blocking out the good. I wasn't sure there was anything to remember until, out of nowhere, the aroma of cinnamon and citrus sprang from my memory, of sherry and brandy, combining with the sharp tang of fresh pine. I heard the crackling of a fire and a child's laughter. These were memories of Christmas, my last as a human.

"I remember a party," I began. I closed my eyes and immersed myself in the memory. "A small gathering. It was Christmas Eve, and my parents had invited several friends to dine. It wasn't company for a child, and Lottie had been dismissed to her room." I smiled as the ghostly tinkling of her laughter enveloped me, followed by the first notes of a musical piece. "After dinner, the young lady my parents hoped I'd one day wed graced us with a musical selection. Although she was beautiful—I think, I can't recall her name—I was young and foolish, and the world seemed to hold the promise of wild adventure. The last thing on my mind was marriage."

A stab of pain sliced at my heart, although it continued at its ever-constant pace. I opened my eyes, unable to stand watching the scene as it played out in the blackness behind my lids.

Ari focused intently, and her elbows rested on the counter, her chin propped in her closed fists. "Please keep going."

My eyebrows drew together harshly. "I excused myself, much to my father's consternation, and made my way upstairs." A flash of memory invaded, and I heard my father's footfalls racing up the steps the night I turned. I scratched my fingers through my hair and shook off the thought.

Ari's hands flopped to the counter, obviously sensing my discomfort. "I'm sorry. I'm being intrusive. You don't have to tell—"

Without thinking, my hand shot out and stopped, hovering above one of hers. I caught myself before they touched and drew back. Ari's heart punched out a quick pace, and her body temperature elevated.

"I want to," I assured her, not confident whether I referred more to the story or touching her. I wanted both so badly it caused a physical ache.

She exhaled, and her lips curved up, warming her expression and her gaze.

"I found Lottie sitting on the top step with tears in her eyes. She said one day she'd go to glamorous parties and dine with beautiful people. Music filtered up through the house, piano notes curling like smoke and ribbons." I chuckled briefly, recalling what I did next. "I scooped her up and stood her on the toes of my shoes. Then we danced. She laughed and laughed as I spun her around…"

My voice trailed off with a sharp edge of pain, as though ice shards had slipped down my throat. I scrubbed the heels of my hands into my eyes but nothing could remove the image of her tiny broken body, limp in my embrace.

"She must have been so afraid and confused." Each word tasted like acid on my tongue. I choked back an unexpected sob of grief.

Ari's stool creaked from her shifting weight, and she cupped my elbow. I opened my eyes to see her standing on the foot-spoke and leaning over the counter to reach me.

Silence hummed in the charged air, and my skin prickled as though a million mosquitos attacked at once. My hand lowered, and Ari's fingers slid down my arm to my wrist, her touch burned as though ripping through my flesh and cauterizing the wound in one stroke. She had the power to break me apart, to make me want to climb out of my skin.

"I could lie," she whispered softly, "but you'd know, wouldn't you?"

I don't know. I remained silent, guessing the question was rhetorical, and threaded my fingers through hers, both ecstatic and terrified at this unspoken permission to touch her. It was a strange sensation, and a sense of peace followed.

The last thing I wanted was to break our moment. Unfortunately, I had things to attend to before William's arrival. Doug had taken on the task of retrieving the scientific equipment he required. I needed to prepare a room, and as time passed, I became increasingly concerned about another attempt to abduct Ari from my protection.

"I need to see to a guest room for William," I said, releasing her hand. "Don't bother with the dishes. I'll get to them after."

To my continued fascination, she struggled to conceal her surprise behind a mask of indifference. I supposed that meant, even though she believed she couldn't lie to me, old habits wouldn't be so readily broken.

"I could come with you," she suggested, hopping down off the chair. All trace of her hangover seemed to have cleared, although her body still gave off the vaguest woodsy aroma.

"If you'd like."

"I would like." Her words broke off, and sensing she meant to say more, I snapped a look over my shoulder. "I would like us to talk more too." A pink flush colored her cheeks. Ari laughed. "I can feel my cheeks burning, and my heart is racing. I don't know why. I've never been what could be described as shy." A touch of adrenaline spiked in her blood, and her direct scrutiny waivered. She swallowed hard. "I know what you are, and I think I'm starting to figure out who you are. I see you clearer now than I did before, and I would like us to be friends, Henry Clayton."

Perhaps she feared a rejection. Instead, I smiled and offered her my hand.

Chapter 21

1888

"This is out of hand." Dougal dropped a newspaper on the counter, only barely missing a glass bottle of silver nitrate. His hand flattened over the page. "Did you know there's a whole bucket load of lunatics who want to be you?"

I picked it up, folded it neatly, and slapped it against his chest. "Not me, some grotesque caricature. This is your doing, not mine."

He grunted and turned away, dragging long fingers through his unkempt hair. It was free from its tie and, together with his crushed open-neck shirt and rolled back sleeves, gave him a wild appearance. With his quick, changeable temperament, I had begun to wonder if Dougal didn't model himself on Byronic style heroes from the romance novels he enjoyed so much. He considered himself two sides of one coin, dark and dangerous but capable of great depths of feeling. A devil with good intent.

Since the night of the double killing, now dubbed The Double Event, newspapers had been filled with reports of letters said to come from the pen of the now infamous Jack the Ripper, one of which also contained a human kidney.

"Your exasperation is hardly justified, Dougal. You came up with the name and are almost certainly partly to blame for this hysteria."

A small guilty smile lit his face, and he chuckled. "That reporter from *The Star* almost wet himself when I whispered in his ear 'bout it. I'm sure at least one is from him."

I incinerated the parts I had taken from the bodies when they had served their purpose. I was not culpable for what they called the "From Hell" letter. I initially suspected Dougal's hand but decided there was a limit to his meddling. He intended his interference to lead the police astray, and only a little to amuse himself. Sending a human kidney through the postal service would serve neither purpose for him.

"Let's leave London to its folly and seek entertainment elsewhere."

"My work—" I began, waving my hand over the counter.

"Och!" Dougal broke in. "You're work is going nowhere." His brow creased, and his eyebrows disappeared beneath his tousled hair. "You said yourself that science is advancing by knots. Give it ten years…fifty, even. You're immortal, man. Don't destroy yourself in this madness here and now."

Before I had an opportunity to answer, the doorbell chimed. I wasn't accustomed to receiving visitors, and deliveries came to the servants' entrance. I arched an eyebrow at Dougal.

"What? Now, who would be callin' on me?"

The mystery was solved in no time at all. Upstairs, Inspector Abberline from H Division of the Metropolitan Police requested to speak with me. Thomas attempted to make excuses, saying I couldn't be disturbed while working, but the inspector wouldn't be dissuaded from his task. I knew him by reputation, of course. A man respected among his colleagues, seconded from Scotland Yard because of his extensive knowledge of Whitechapel and the surrounding area. His name had become synonymous with The Ripper investigations.

I rolled down my sleeves and reached for my waist jacket.

"I'm coming with you," Dougal said, straightening his clothes.

"If you insist. Just let me do the talking," I warned him.

Upstairs, Thomas had shown the inspector and the uniformed officer accompanying him into the library. Double doors opened into a grand room with floor to ceiling bookshelves, rich rosewood inlaid pillars, and a grand marble fire hearth. Red velvet curtains had been drawn against the late evening light, and gas lamps cast the room in a warm golden glow. The room smelled heavily of leather, polish, and the slow degradation of paper in the many books held there.

The man I presumed to be the inspector rose from the couch when we entered, walking past the uniformed officer. He was an unassuming type of fellow with an abundance of wiry facial hair. He wore a suit, not the latest fashion, but it was clean and well kept. A bowler hat lay discarded beside his seat. Under other circumstances I might have taken him for a banker or office worker, except that he carried the distinct scent of rot and blood with him. Here was a man who'd seen more than his share of violence.

"Dr. Clayton, I'm Inspector Fred Abberline." He offered his hand, as was the custom.

I glanced down before gripping it firmly and meeting his eyes again. His eyes flickered down too, perhaps noticing the coolness of my skin. I was confident that the ambient temperature had warmed my hand sufficiently so as not to seem unnatural.

"Inspector, this is Mr. Dougal Gunn."

Both Dougal and Inspector Abberline nodded an acknowledgment, and Dougal moved toward the back of the room.

"Please, take a seat. How may I assist you, sir?"

He sat back down, his gaze lingering on me a beat more than polite and his expression curious. "Forgive me, Dr. Clayton. I was given to believe you were older."

I smiled. "Life has been kind to me."

"Not always, sir."

The forced, polite bluntness of his comment left me in no doubt that he knew of my family. His steady heart picked up for a handful of beats, expectantly. I narrowed my eyes but kept my expression guarded, despite the bubbling resentment making my chest tight.

"No, not always, but I presume you aren't here to question me on a robbery which happened twenty years ago."

"It was a little more than a robbery, as I believe. You were the only survivor after your family was murdered in a savage attack on the household."

I felt Dougal's eyes on me, and my back straightened. I had yet to share the details of my history with him. A vampire of half his intelligence could read between the lines and work out it had been my doing. My fingers tensed, but I resisted the urge to curl them into a fist. Instead, I stood and went to the drinks cabinet, pouring myself a goblet of wine from a decanter.

"I am acutely aware. As you are no doubt aware that I wasn't there. Drink?"

He raised a hand. "Thank you. Not for me while on duty."

I gave Dougal a glass without asking since he never said no, and took a seat on the couch opposite the inspector. "May I ask why my tragic history is of interest?"

"Surely a great man like yourself is aware our history makes us who we are," he said matter-of-factly.

"I am a scientist."

"That you are, sir." His mustache twitched. "That you are. I'm here about The Ripper case. May I ask your whereabouts the early hours of September thirtieth between midnight and two a.m.?"

I screwed up my face, allowing my genuine surprise to show, and smiled, raising my hand to Dougal so quickly Abberline and the officer wouldn't have seen. The vampire was ready to silence them using his particular talent, but there was no need…yet.

"Am I a suspect in your case, Inspector?"

"Please indulge me."

"I was here all night, working in my laboratory."

"And someone can confirm that?"

"My household and my house guest, Mr. Gunn."

Abberline nodded to the uniformed officer, and he left the room, presumably to verify my words. I had complete confidence they would. He smiled, but his clinical gaze gave it away as insincere. The man had an acute insight, but he apparently couldn't pinpoint what made him suspicious of me. The knowledge that he would never solve these crimes gave me a grim sense of satisfaction.

We sat in silence for a few moments. I measured time by his heartbeats and became increasing agitated by his presence and the slow gurgling slurp of blood moving through his body. The embers of thirst ignited, steadily building. I concentrated on the movement of my chest and shoulders to give the impression of breathing. It didn't take long for the officer to return and lean down to whisper.

"They were both here, sir," he said.

Abberline dipped his head and stood, taking his hat from the seat and perching it on top of his thinning hair. "Well, it seems I've detained you gentleman long enough."

"Not at all," I replied, using the remnants of air in my lungs. "These killings are nasty business. It's not so long ago murder was rare in London." I was toying with him, goading his inability to unravel the truth of the fiend before him. "I hope you catch the monster responsible."

Dougal glared at me from behind him.

"Indeed," Inspector Abberline said and pressed his lips together.

Thomas appeared at the door to let them out.

"Good day, sir." He tipped his hat to me and to Dougal before leaving.

Dougal was in front of me in an instant. "There was a woman. I told you there was." He spoke too low and fast for anyone to hear but me.

"There was no woman." I refilled my glass with wine almost to the brim and gulped its contents down. Wine did almost nothing to dull the constant ache in my body.

"Och, you see nothing till it slaps you in the face."

I downed another glass before sinking onto the couch. "There was no woman. I wonder sometimes if you actually read those newspapers you pore over every day, or if you only look at the pictures."

Dougal took the seat recently vacated by Abberline and squirmed about before he settled. "That man has an oddly warm arse."

"Abberline is looking into every man in London with any knowledge of anatomy. He's desperate. He has nothing on me. He knows nothing."

"But surely you won't want to continue—"

"Want?" I spat, bounding to my feet. "None of this is about want. I *need* to continue my work. I'm so close." I dragged my hand across the back of my neck and undid my shirtsleeves to roll them back to my elbows. "It's as if the answer is sitting on the opposite side of a glass pane. It's just right there." I stretched my hand out in frustration, touching thin air. "Right in front of me, but I can't grab it."

"You are insane, Henry." He shook his head.

Chapter 22

2010

Ari had been staying in my room since the first night, while I stayed in a guest room. The other bedrooms in the house were functional, if not designed to be aesthetically appealing. I'd been utilizing the last unused room—Lottie's room—for storage, but I transferred the paintings and instruments I kept there to my study before she woke up. What remained of Lottie's bedroom was a square box containing a small carved bed and nothing else. The bathroom was situated across the narrow hall. I hoped William would be comfortable enough, although I also hoped his visit would be short, given the circumstances.

The awkwardness with Ari, which had evaporated when I took her hand downstairs, had reemerged. Ari worked silently at snapping freshly laundered sheets flat on the bed while I stuffed a duvet inside a cover. She held tension across the top of her back, making her movements stilted, and her heart rushed at an uneasy pace. She tilted her head to one shoulder and then the other, a small hushed moan leaving her body with the relief. I sensed she wanted to ask something, maybe to begin getting to know each other better.

I pressed my lips together, measuring my responses to her. Losing control was the last thing I wanted now we'd planted the seeds of a tentative understanding. The air held a note of anticipation, like a winter morning before the sun appears on the horizon, stealing the remnants of night, equal measures of anticipation and invigoration.

"Do you remember being in love?" she asked, startling me from my thoughts. A large white sheet billowed above her head like a cloud and obscured her face for a moment before settling on the bed. She didn't stop to look at me.

I paused. For some reason I'd presumed we'd begin with easy questions like what music we liked or our favorite color. I should have known better. I should have suspected she'd jump in with abandon and want to delve deep.

A warm heat spread across her cheeks, and her lip lifted on one side causing a tiny curve at the corner of her mouth. She knew she'd caught me off guard, and it seemed all at once my heart pounded everywhere in my body. Her smile was both beautiful and terribly twisted. I grinned in response.

I dropped the duvet on the floor and picked up a pillow. "I've never been in love."

"I can't imagine never having been in love," she said wistfully and crooked her fingers to indicate it was time for the next layer of bed coverings.

"Your boyfriend." It wasn't a question as such, more a prod in the right direction. I would've been lying if I said the subject hadn't crossed my mind since she'd mentioned him.

She helped me adjust the duvet on the bed, running her fingers over the expensive cotton fabric and smoothing it down over the edges. She smiled again, perhaps deliberately tormenting me.

"Yes, I think I loved him." She paused and shrugged. "Or, at least I think I could have if we'd had more time. It was very new. He was sweet, protective, smart, and so good-looking." Her head tipped back, and her eyes rolled to the ceiling as though remembering. "I mean, smoking hot—"

"I get it," I broke in, and she laughed at my blatant jealously.

"First kiss?"

"Marie. She was a young French serving girl of fifteen, and I was twelve." I tossed a pillow to her. "You?"

Ari hugged the pillow, and her breath hitched. She looked away before I could catch her expression. "He was a local boy, and we were seven. I was insanely in love and thought we'd be together forever. He grew up to be a good man, and if things had been different, maybe we would have been."

"Where is he now?" I asked, really wondering why it ended, because her elevated adrenaline and sentiment indicated it had been more than a child's kiss.

She fluffed the pillow and placed it at the head of the bed. "He went away."

"Do you miss him?"

She peeked up. "I used to. Why can't you accept what you are?"

"I have accepted it."

"You fight your nature with everything you can muster." She smirked, unconvinced. "That's not acceptance."

I turned and sat down on the side of the bed and lay back so my feet were still on the floor. The bed shifted, and air filled with Ari's cocoa scent. She lay down too, from the opposite side so I was looking at her upside down face only inches away when I turned my head to her. Ari's focus moved to the ceiling.

I skimmed my index finger along her cheekbone to her chin to draw her full attention back. She bit down on the tender plump flesh of her lower lip. Heat clawed up my thighs, and desire swelled in my chest. It wasn't a physical desire, although that settled in my stomach and crept outward, like ivy weaving through me, coiling around my organs. I craved her love, a yearning so painful and eerily exquisite, my life before her seemed shrouded and set in darkness.

"I want to be a good man."

As I said the words, I knew they were true. Despite my actions, they always had been.

Her eyes narrowed curiously. "I believe you."

She didn't look away, and neither did I. The only movement in the room was the warm breath leaving her. Ari tilted her chin, keeping me trapped, and inched up until we shared the same air, and I tasted her sweetness on my tongue. I didn't dare move when her lips skimmed over mine. I closed my eyes and inhaled deeply when she pulled away. The kiss had been comfort, not passion, but I relished it nonetheless, lifting my fingers to touch the warmth that lingered.

Ari beamed, all tension gone from her posture. "What's your favorite flavor ice cream? Do you have one?"

"Ice cream?" I frowned.

"What?" She smirked and rolled onto her side, propping herself up on her elbow to look down on me. Her hair fell forward and brushed my shoulder. "You can tell a lot about a person from their favorite ice cream."

I interlaced my fingers over my stomach and puckered my lips, attempting to appear stern. Something I wouldn't have attempted if Ari showed any indication she feared me. "Aren't you afraid I'll say—" I shrugged innocently "—you know—blood?"

"Really?" Her nose scrunched up.

"No. It's vanilla."

She slapped my shoulder playfully.

"Okay, then," I teased. "What can you tell from that?"

"You prefer when your life is simple, uncomplicated. You don't like change much. You see things a certain way, and it's hard for you to change your mind, but it can make you impulsive and prone to regret. Beneath it all, you can't help being an idealist. You hope when everything advises against it."

"Wow, you can tell all that from ice cream?"

She laughed a little.

"I'm not sure about the last assertion. I don't want to hope. It so often leads to disappointment."

Ari's expression became guarded at my words, blocking me from whatever she was thinking. "It must be tricky to keep expectations so low."

"It's easier than hoping. Not knowing how things will turn out is harder, I think."

Her eyes tightened. She hummed, considering what I said and tilted her head to her shoulder as though conceding. "But it's not real, is it?"

"Excuse me?"

"I find that hope is like a river. It's fluid, always moving and being fed from what's around it. We make dams, build walls to block it out. When we think we've filled up all the gaps, along comes hope, and it flows into the tiniest spaces. Before we know it, happiness creeps in and bursts our safe little bubble of illusion and misery."

My stomach flip-flopped. This wonderful creature had come from nowhere and toppled my world. I loved how she saw it. I loved how she saw me and the things she said. As much as I attempted to batter it back down, the optimism accompanying these other sensations continued to rise up.

"What about yours?" I asked, a quiver of giddiness making my blood rush. A number of conflicting desires skirmished inside my head and my body. I eased up onto my elbow, ignoring the voice that whispered to drain her dry. When I drifted nearer to Ari, settling my attention on her mouth, other passions took precedence, holding the seductive temptation to drink at bay.

"Vanilla," Ari murmured.

We had such a normal thing in common. It took another moment for panic to set in at what she meant. I drew back. She considered herself impulsive and prone to regret. Her penetrating blue eyes looked deeply into mine. Her chest heaved with each breath, and her excited heart fluttered against her ribcage. Ari's tongue glided across her smiling lower lip leaving it glistening with moisture.

"I need you to kiss me so badly right now. I've been waiting too long." Ari inhaled a slow breath and watched me expectantly.

"What?" She'd kissed me a few minutes ago. I'd kissed her back. The awareness of the soft pressure was imprinted in my mind, but she'd started it.

"Kiss me."

I moved back an inch on each word and froze, because she said it again and again. Each time the intensity of her words seemed to soak through my skin and made my insides liquefy. Her lips turned up in a sexy grin, and her eyes glimmered like sapphires reflecting light. I tilted my head sideways remembering her mouth slipping over mine. It wasn't enough; I hadn't had nearly enough of her yet. I wanted to touch and explore her skin and thread my fingers through her silken hair. The heat and adrenaline emanating from her body were intoxicating, distracting…

She waited. A small crease appeared above her nose when she frowned at my silence. "Are you okay?" Her honeyed voice and warm breath fanned across my cheek, igniting flames beneath my skin.

I wanted her to know how much her kiss had meant to me but also how much pleasure it gave me simply being close to her. Talking and laughing, sharing ourselves was much more than I'd imagined possible. She had to know I wanted her, that I needed her, and that she was fast becoming everything important to me. I didn't want her to regret any of it.

"It doesn't have to mean anything," Ari assured me in a low, unsteady voice. "I can't explain why, but I need—"

"No," I interrupted before she completed her sentence.

Her expression was hard to read, although I recognized shades of anger and disappointment in her scent. Her eyes slid away, concealing a flash of hurt. In the silence that followed, I feared I might have missed my chance, and sharp pain stabbed at my chest. Perhaps she would never open the door again, now she believed I'd slammed it shut in her face.

I had to do something, take a leap of faith, regardless of the outcome. "It does have to mean something. A huge part of me is terrified of what it could mean. One way or another, I can't keep you, and I want to so badly it's like lava in my veins. It's like I've been stripped clean down to my bones and remade for you only."

She lifted her watery eyes and salt mingled with the other scents already creating a heady concoction in the air.

"You have me now," she said.

I leaned in without allowing myself another moment to change my mind and covered her mouth with mine. My tongue darted out and lapped gently at her top lip, and sucked it firmly between mine. She reciprocated, moving her lips with mine, exploring my mouth. I savored the sweet taste of her, the smell of her hair, her warm breath, and her moan vibrating against my tongue. Pressure in my lower stomach built in waves. The muscles in my thighs constricted, and my fingers found their way onto her hair, holding her there. The usual tingles I felt from being near her were lost in a haze of pulsing tremors raising gooseflesh everywhere on my skin.

I longed to climb on the bed and shift our position, to feel her body yielding beneath me. It took all my restraint to hold back, to absorb this intimate moment without going too far. I wasn't ready to lose myself in Ari. I couldn't forget who I was, even for a moment. Bloodlust continually simmered under my arousal.

To Ari's groaning protest, I stopped when the aroma of warm dirt and blood registered. My nostrils flared, and muscles twitched, already itching for the fight I knew was coming. The alien scent contained under notes of an exotic perfume. Constance had sent more of her lackeys into my home.

I pressed my index finger to Ari's lips and met her hooded eyes with a stern glare. Her breath sucked in with a hiss, but she appeared to understand we weren't alone.

A flurry of muffled footfalls indicated there were four of them, one quieter, perhaps older, than the others.

Ari wasted no time, skittered across the bed, and hunched down. I fell to the floor beside her.

"No matter what happens, stay down. Do you understand?" I whispered as low as possible for her human ears. Heat radiated from her flushed skin, and her blood pulsed a hypnotic rushed pace. I was glad a finite number of beats didn't measure human life since she appeared to be racing through hers of late.

For a fraction of a second, I thought she might refuse, but then she nodded stiffly.

"What are you going to do?"

My fangs bit into the flesh at the back of my lips as scarlet tinged the edge of my vision. "I'm going to do what I have to."

Ari's fingers locked around my forearm, preventing me from leaping to my feet. Her nails dug into skin, and the warmth of her touch penetrated the sleeve of my cotton shirt. I bristled.

"No, wait," she said.

I unwrapped her fingers, forcing myself to be gentle. "Ari, they are here to take you. I won't allow—"

"I know, but maybe they know what she plans to do."

"What are you suggesting?"

"Just don't kill them all, okay? I have to know what she knows."

Footstep grew closer, and I was eager to keep them as far from her as possible. Ari had a point. Maybe one of these vampires knew Constance's next move. I doubted she'd be so witless as to send one of her inner circle straight to my door, but maybe one of them unwittingly picked up a nugget of information we could use. I pulled my phone from my back pocket.

"Call Doug. If they overpower me…"

What? My words trailed off, and my jaw cracked under the strain of the frustration and rage ignited in my veins. A million things I wanted her to know rushed through my head. There were things to say after the moment we'd just shared, and my lips still buzzed with the phantom pressure of her lips.

I took the recollection with me as motivation to beat the invaders back and bounded across the bed.

Chapter 23

I dashed down the narrow hallway to see the intruders scurrying and clambering over each other to reach the top of the closed-in stairwell first. They were less than halfway there. The space was too small for four grown adults, two of them large males, and they mostly succeeded in getting in their own way. Despite clean street clothes, there was nothing civilized about their movements or livid, hungry expressions. There was nothing human about their faces — black eyes tinged with red and cracked lips straining over fangs.

"You're really going to make me do this?" I snarled angrily, bending to crouch at the knees. Blood roared in my ears, and a door slammed behind me, the mechanism of a lock resisted turning but clicked into place after a couple of tries.

"We're here for the girl," the one in most control of his movements growled. I suspected he was the oldest, and no ordinary door lock would keep him away from her.

One of the others, a smartly dressed woman with coiffed golden hair, lashed out, and her elbow landed square on the bridge of his nose, knocking him back a step.

"It's never going to happen," I spat and lunged forward, bulleting straight into the neck of Goldilocks with the crook of my arm and twisting upward under her chin. I separated her head from her shoulders with a grunt, showering the rest of us in a cloud of ash.

This left the two large men and the smaller, older one. However, now I was a part of the scrambling group. I could hear Ari rushing out words, telling Doug to hurry. As though the sound of her voice invigorated the remaining three, they all pounced for a higher stair at the same time. The darker of the large men lunged into the side of the other vampire, pummeling his jaw with a fist the size of a sledgehammer. His head drooped side to side like a dashboard bobblehead doll.

A hand wrenched my shoulder back, but I couldn't be sure who it belonged to. I jerked out of the way and kicked out, hoping to catch at least one of them. The force of the blow rippled up my leg. My teeth gouged through flesh and tendons as I hopped on the back of the already dazed large man and tore at his neck. Velvet smooth blood coated my tongue. I had no desire to drink from him and spat it out. My fingers clawed into his eyes, and he released a hideous cry, but he didn't fight me off. Not even in self-defense. *What in hell is going on here?*

The only rational explanation I could come up with was that each wanted to be the first to reach Ari, as though she were some sort of prize ring to claim. Constance must have offered a strong incentive for them to covet Ari enough for this brawl.

The momentum of the skirmish drove us all forward. However, as much as they struck blows at each other, none of them intentionally hit out at me. Had they been instructed not to engage me? I released the sagging, injured vampire to test my theory and smacked the palm of my hand flat into the older vampire's nose. He laughed, lines crinkling the area around his eyes. Two streams of bright red gushed over his top lip and dribbled down his chin. He swiped it away with the back of his hand, but instead of launching a counter assault, he turned on the weaker of the other two, reached into his chest, and withdrew his pulsating heart in his fist, blood spilling over his fingers. The heart stopped and turned to ashes, along with the body it had once belonged to.

This left a dilemma. Although only two vampires remained, it also meant ample room for them to climb the remaining steps to the top floor of the house. I could stop one before they reached Ari, but not both. The larger vampire would take more strength to pull down, but the smaller one was more cunning, older. If either of them held any knowledge of The Circle and Constance, it would be him.

"Ari," I called at the top of my lungs. There was no way out of the room for her. I expected her instincts to kick in — the ones I'd seen her display when she broke the stool for a stake or fought off the other vampire attacker. As much as I wanted to protect Ari, I couldn't do it alone, and I didn't have to. Ari didn't need to defeat him, just hold him back for even a few seconds until I could get to them. She wouldn't die at his hand.

My chest burned as I stepped aside and allowed the cunning vampire to spring past. I pitched forward, the sound of his scrambling feet thunderous in my ears.

The large vampire snarled. Pink spittle dribbled from his bloody mouth. His shovel-like hands shot out and cupped my neck; he'd have to fight me or give up on his target. I slid my arms between his and jerked them wide, knocking his hands away. I gripped his ears, grunting through clenched teeth, and took advantage of his momentary shock to pull his head forward, meeting his face with my knee twice.

Ari screeched as the cunning vampire slammed into the thick bedroom door.

Scarlet spray streaked the walls of the stairwell in wide arcs as the goliath before me stumbled back. He reached for my waist, failed to find purchase on the step, and wobbled on his unfamiliar powerful legs. I slammed my shin into his groin. The hulking beast's eyes rolled in his head as his knees gave way and he toppled back. I was on him in a fraction of a second, locking my jaw around his throat in midair. I ripped his spine out before we hit the ground. He splayed out, twitching with wide terrified eyes gaping at the ceiling. My hand scrambled for the nearest weapon, a small hallway table. It didn't take much effort to crack one of the wooden legs and drive it through his chest.

I didn't wait for his body to turn to dust. Ari needed my help. I stormed up the stairwell and hauled the heavy door open but froze at the sight. The cunning vampire was sprawled out against the wall by the door. His shoulders and head hung sideways at an unnatural angle toward his chest, and one foot twisted the wrong way.

"Ari," I yelled. Her scent hung thick as molasses in the room — cocoa and coffee, strongly laced with vanilla and adrenaline. Something was different. It was too strong and tainted with copper and salt.

She moaned from the other side of the bed. "I'm here."

Ari sat, propped at the wall, clutching her upper arm. Crimson liquid seeped from between her fingers and soaked the sleeve of the sweatshirt. She peered up to me, hesitant and wary, perspiration glistening over her brow.

"I'm sorry."

Conflicting instincts battled for control of my body, and my mouth watered. The room spun in a dizzying haze of scarlet. I rooted my feet to the floorboards, curling my toes inside my shoes and my fingers into fists. The aroma of fresh human blood flowed over me. I wanted to go to her, but feared what I might do. An angry growl clawed up my throat. My back stiffened as though the vertebrae were welded tight.

Ari must have observed my struggle in my expression and fixed stance. She shrank back, wincing in pain, and tears sprang to her eyes, spilling down pale cheeks. "Please. I don't want to hurt you."

Hurt me? As though her words broke a spell, the hunger died down enough for me to regain control. I swallowed hard and flicked a glance at the broken body at the door. How had she fought him off? I had no desire to end up like a discarded ragdoll too. Tentatively, I tested my resolve and relaxed a little, allowing my lungs to draw in air. My fangs retracted, and my face shifted back to its human appearance.

Ari choked out a sound somewhere between a sob and a hiccup. She closed her eyes, and her head drooped forward. I scooped her up before my next heartbeat and settled her on my lap. Pieces of metal, plastic, and glass covered the floor where my phone had been shattered.

"It's okay," I said into her damp hair. I kissed her head, rocking her gently. "You're safe now."

Ari shifted, still holding her injured arm, and turned her face into my shirt, stifling another sob. Her lips moved soundlessly over words I couldn't understand, but I expected shock prevented her from thinking rationally.

"Let's get you out of here." I pushed up, taking Ari with me, and stood her on her feet. My gut said she wouldn't want to be carried downstairs.

"What about him?" She nodded in the direction of the prone body.

We'd have to discuss the cunning vampire. I needed to know how she'd put down a second monster. I couldn't shift the niggling suspicion she was still lying to me. But I had to take care of her wound first.

"His neck is broken. He'll be down for a while."

I helped her downstairs to the drawing room and sat her down in one of the armchairs before going to retrieve the small first aid kit, a glass of water, a bowl with warm water, and towels. I struggled to balance my bounty with unsteady hands and paused at the threshold, steeling my resolve before going in.

Ari watched me with careful eyes as I dragged the low table toward her to sit down. The weight of her scrutiny bore down on me.

"Are you sure?"

"Yes." I held the glass to her lips. "Sip."

She did and then shook her head indicating she'd had enough. I placed the glass on the table and moved her bloodied hand away from her arm. Time seemed to freeze and then expand. A hollow silence enveloped the room, and even my heart ceased beating. If he'd bitten her…But the skin was merely cut, not torn. It was hard enough not to rush back up the stairs and slaughter the beast who'd hurt her. I wasn't sure I would hold back if he'd drunk from her.

Time charged back in, and I tasted wet copper on my tongue. The smell made my nose twitch. My shoulders stiffened. It would have been easier not to breathe, but if I stopped talking, she'd be suspicious about my restraint. In the back of my mind I measured the thumping of her heart in the hope it would stop my mind from wandering.

Cradling the wrist of her injured arm, I removed a pair of scissors from the first aid kit and slipped one of the blades inside the sleeve.

"I'm sorry about your sweatshirt," she said as I made the first cut.

"Do you think I really care?"

"Still…" She shrugged and hissed under her breath. "It stings."

I smiled without lifting my head, afraid if she met my eyes she'd know I was faking my calm. "I'll have you fixed up soon enough."

Once the sleeve was clear, I got a better view of the long laceration stretching from below her already-bruised shoulder halfway to her elbow along the front of her arm. The voice counting her heartbeats in my mind grew more insistent.

"It would be easier to remove the sweatshirt," I said and swallowed.

Ari chuckled quietly, and I peeked up to her, catching a glimpse of her smile through the shadow of my eyelashes.

"What?"

"There's something oddly familiar about this situation. I seem to remember getting a flash of some impressive pecs and abs when our positions were reversed."

"Oh." The scissors wavered in my hand. I didn't want to admit I needed to clean her up and get rid of the blood.

"Unless you're trying to get me naked," she joked. My fingers twitched around her wrist.

"I'll just cut the sleeve away," I suggested. There were flecks on the other sleeve, and the front was already turning brown and crusting.

Ari sighed. "I'm sorry. I shouldn't make jokes. I guess I'm a little scared of what happens next. Laughing's easier than crying, right?"

The muscles in my jaw jumped, and I looked at her, doing my best to keep my expression neutral. "Let's get this done, and then we can deal with what comes next, okay?"

Her brow puckered almost imperceptibly, and she nodded. She sat up straighter and tugged the bottom of the sweater out with the stained fingers of her free hand. I cut up to her armpit and then to her neckline, then peeled the destroyed garment away, leaving her in a black tank. It was hard not to notice the shapely firm mounds of her breasts through the light fabric. A twinge of inappropriate desire ignited in my belly. I tamped it back down. I had enough temptation to handle.

I cleared away the dried blood on her hand and arm and cleaned up as much of the still-seeping wound as I could before applying waterproof paper stitches to hold the gash closed.

"This could probably use proper stitches and an antibiotic." I scowled, cleaning off some red liquid that had leaked out while I worked.

"You're doing great."

The front door opened, slamming against the wall with force that rattled my teeth before rebounding with a crack.

"Ari? Clay?" Doug roared. He came flying into the room. "What the hell?" He froze, his eyes falling on the bloody pile of fabric and wipes as Ari spoke.

"More of them came, but we got them."

A beat later, his stormy green gaze settled on Ari's arm and then me.

"You need to back up, brother." His warning shook with a threatening growl.

I stood…or at least I attempted to. The instant I budged, Doug was on me. He forced his full weight down on me, smashing my spine into the hard floor. Pain lanced outward through every nerve ending. An impulse to throw him off trembled through my fingertips. Veins threaded below Doug's pale skin, while his dark eyes, golden halo of hair, and fangs gave him the appearance of a furious, otherworldly lion.

"Doug!"

Ari's startled cry made no impression. He slammed me a second time. The scent of blood and my predatory instincts bombarded my resolve. The sharp points of my fangs pricked against the back of my lips.

"Get off me," I snarled up at his face. "I didn't do this."

His grip loosened on my shirt.

"Doug." Ari's fingers slid over his shoulder and wrenched him backward with so much force his eyes went wide and he landed on his backside at my feet.

She stood over us, glowering like a schoolteacher at naughty children. Doug's features settled, and the whites of his eyes returned to normal.

He perched back on his hands and whistled, a smirk pulling his lips up at one side. "Whoa, Petal, you been working out?"

Ari looked down to her hand, her heart thrumming furiously. Her breath whooshed out in gasps that caused her chest to rise and fall with exaggerated motions. Her fingers flexed out straight, and she blinked several times. Neither of us moved until she stumbled back and fell heavily into the chair.

"I'm sorry," she whispered, her eyes darting from Doug to me.

He sat up, scratched his jaw, and rolled the shoulder she'd grabbed. "I'm made of mean stuff. I can handle it." He exchanged a worried look with me when she closed her eyes, rubbing her temple.

He got to his feet first and extended a hand for me without apology. It wasn't necessary. We both knew he was making good on his promise to protect Ari.

"Is it safe to ask?" He kept his back to her and his voice low enough she may not have heard.

I shook my head. "These things need to be burned." I indicated the sweater pile and polluted water with a flick of my head. "Then we should work out a way of restraining a vampire. I want it done before he wakes."

Doug's eyes tightened, and his nostrils flared when he finally caught the cunning vampire's scent, dim beneath the luscious blood aroma. His face tipped back as though he could see through the floors above.

He hesitated, indecision written all over his expression. His gaze slid over his shoulder to Ari, who still needed a bandage over the paper stitches. She hadn't opened her eyes, but her cheeks now flushed a deep pink, and exhaustion weighed heavy in the way she sank into the chair. Her actions with Doug and apparent strength went some way to explaining how she could put down two vampires. It was fortunate she actually liked Doug. We could have been waiting for him to wake up too…or worse.

"Dougal," I prompted sternly, knowing his real name would garner his attention faster. His mouth gaped like a fish caught on a hook for a moment. "Dougal."

He shook his head to clear his thoughts, set about gathering the items, and then headed outside. I sat again and licked my dry lips. Thirst prickled my throat, and my tongue stuck to the roof of my mouth.

Ari opened her eyes, reached across me, and pulled a tube of skin glue from the first aid kit.

"Make sure it's sealed," she instructed, handing the glue to me. "Please," she added. Her hand brushed mine. Her skin was hot, and the hair at the back of my neck stood on end. The energy I'd felt from her skin whenever we'd touched before was gone. "If the cure is in my blood—"

I opened my mouth to stop whatever she was going to say. More experiments were out of the question. I wouldn't go back to the monster I had been in London.

"Let me finish," she said. "Perhaps William might find something."

I set about removing the paper stitches and applying the glue. "None of this is coincidence, is it?"

The tendons in her neck strained, and my eyes fixed on the pulsating artery just below her ear as her blood raced faster.

"Some of it is," she sighed.

I leaned forward, blowing on the glue to help it set. Ari shivered, and her heart rate spiked.

"If you've been hiding something, now is the time to say."

She leaned an elbow on the arm of the seat and tapped her temple absently with her index finger as I wrapped her other arm.

"There're things in here, stuff I can't make sense of. Memories, I think."

"If you tell me, perhaps we can figure it out together."

"No." Her answer was resolute, inviting no argument or additional questions. "I have to speak to that vampire."

I cupped her chin, forcing her to meet my eyes, and slid my palm to her neck. She tried to look away again, but I added a second hand to the other side, using enough pressure to illustrate the intensity of my request. She bit down on her lip and wrapped hot fingers around one of my wrists. Her touch scorched through my flesh and bone, turning my entire being to jelly. Desperation surged through me.

"I never *wanted* to feel for you. I fought it, but you are in my blood now. You're in my heart and my mind. I feel you everywhere. I don't know if I can stand to go back to not having you here with me. Let me help you, Ari."

Her chin wobbled, and her eyelashes fluttered, casting long shadows over her cheeks. A frantic sadness crept into her eyes. Something snapped in my subconscious, like an elastic band pulled beyond its limits. A ball of grief lodged in my throat until I thought I might split apart from the pain of it. This was more than anticipation of losing a girl I'd hardly known and met only a short time ago. This was a marrow-deep agony, a sensation of loss so violent my hands rattled from it.

Something must have shown on my face. Ari pressed forward, and her lips crashed against mine, smothering my mouth with fraught passion. She pulled back, and her fingers pressed tight enough they would have bruised a human man.

"That's just it." She breathed out the words. Their warmth drifted over my face, soft as dandelion seeds floating away on a breeze. "*You* aren't meant to help me."

Chapter 24

1888

M y closed fist slammed down onto the counter, then through it. A large chunk of wood clattered against the floor of my laboratory, leaving splinters and dust particles floating in the air when I opened my eyes.

"It should have worked this time," I growled through gritted teeth.

Dougal, sitting crossed-legged in a high-backed chair in a darkened corner, shuffled his broadsheet and peered over the top of the curling pages. "This is a fool's endeavor, and you know it. Why are you surprised at your failure every single time?"

I laid my burning palms on the wooden surface, my shoulders slumped in defeat, and unmerciful heat charged a path through my body. It seemed almost audible, as if I could hear the cells crashing again each other. My ears rang, and I swallowed, hoping it would dull the sensation. The side effects were worse than ever this time.

"Because I'm Henry Clayton, and Claytons don't fail." *I sound just like Father.*

"Clearly," Dougal muttered under his breath.

I moved in an instant, despite my shaking legs, and whipped the broadsheet away, leaving only triangular remnants in his fingers. He rolled his eyes and opened his hands like a magician performing a prestige at the end of a magic act, as though he had made the paper vanish from his hands. The small triangles fluttered to the ground like delicate butterflies on a breeze.

"You are not helping," I scolded him.

He sat forward, leaning his forearms on his thighs. "I'm not here to help you solve your riddles or to support you using yourself like some damned science experiment."

"Then why are you here—besides drinking my wine cellar dry and meddling in my affairs?" I slapped the backs of my tingling fingers against the headline.

Jack the Ripper Remains At Large

"Och, even a dry shite like you has to admit the name has a certain ring to it." Dougal's lips curved upward, and a mischievous twinkle in his eye caught the lamplight, making them gleam like a cat's on a moonless night.

I crumpled the paper and fired it at him. He easily swept it aside. The tingle in my fingers was subsiding, leaving an uncomfortable numbness.

His forehead creased. "You need to feed. And not on that animal swill. This one really took it out of you. Your eyes are black pits in your face."

"I'm fine," I lied. I didn't feel fine at all. "I won't kill humans to feed." I turned away. "I was so sure I had it this time."

"You don't have to kill."

"I do. I've never learned the skill of leaving them alive after. I won't drink human blood."

Dougal stood. "You've been drinking human blood for weeks."

"That's different."

"How?"

"It's different," I roared over my shoulder.

Dougal sat down and leaned back, away from my rage, hands aloft and palms out. "Aye, you slice and dice them first."

I turned from him again, wringing my numb hands. No, it wasn't the same thing at all. I had no choice.

Even now I imagined I could taste the velvety wetness flowing through the bodies of my household and feel the pulse of their hearts inside my head like the steady clattering of a train relentlessly pushing forward on a track.

"What is wrong with this life, anyway?" Dougal asked. "Do you think the shark feels guilty? It's the natural order."

"Don't," I warned him. "Just don't."

Dougal had already given me this speech on how we were higher up the food chain than any other creature. The ultimate predator. He believed we were a creation of heaven, just like all other life. A philosophy easily maintained by a vampire who fed without killing because he could.

But we weren't created. We were made. Made of death, and darkness, and despicable hunger.

I stepped forward tentatively to assess my balance. It had been temporarily compromised by my experiments in the past. The scientist in me knew that noting every effect was beneficial for future study, but the animal only cared it could delay my hunt. The hollow inside me needed to be filled.

Holding my breath, I tugged on the rope near the door and stormed from my laboratory.

Thomas appeared in the foyer with my coat, and I saw my reflection in his eyes, the wild desperation and deathly pallor of my skin. My hair was a disheveled mess from running my fingers through it, and my eyes perfectly rounded circles of coal black against white, threaded heavily with veins. With the addition of my black cloak, the interior of which was made of expensive scarlet silk, I appeared as Death himself.

His pulse escalated to dizzying speed, and beads of perspiration formed at his temple. His blood would be laced with adrenaline, and the scent of boot lacquer would linger on his skin as always. *Do. Not. Inhale,* I warned myself at the sight of the slim vein throbbing beneath his skin. Not only would Thomas be missed among my own staff, but it would bring undue attention on my home from local authorities, perhaps Inspector Abberline.

That's not the reason. I forced my hands to move at a human pace so as not to startle him. *I will not steal his life to feed, and I cannot feed without killing tonight.*

He said nothing. It wasn't his place, after all. He simply lowered his gaze and handed over my gloves and top hat.

I left on foot, as was my usual practice. My staff presumed I preferred walking. In truth, I could travel anywhere in London faster on foot than I could in a hansom.

November had set a chill upon the night, and thick fog coated the ground, almost sentient in its movement, as though it had purpose and destination when slithering over the cobblestones and coiling around anything that got in its path.

This time was so much worse than any of the other times I had experimented on myself. Fire raged inside me as I moved over rooftops, concealed in the darkness and shadow by cloud cover across the moon—nothing more than a specter in the night. I imagined my insides drying out, the serum stealing any remnants of blood and charring my organs until they blackened, becoming insubstantial as a log in a hearth. One touch and it would dissolve to ashes…I would dissolve. I was disappearing inside the hunger. The vampire infection raged, pushing through, contorting my being to its vile nature. *Feed*, it demanded. *Feed*.

I had meant to find the zoological gardens and to feast on the great beasts contained there. I was horrified to find myself in the East End, in the vicinity of Spitalfields. Below, door chimes rang out at Ten Bells public house as two patrons fell out the door. A man and a woman, his fingers and threadbare clothes black with coal dust, startling even again her grubby cloak. White streaks of hair, aged by hardship and the misery of poverty and malnourishment, hung limp and tangled over her shoulders.

I remained in my crouch by a chimney, hugging the shingled roof like a cat on the prowl, and watched them turn left, heading toward the entrance of a dark alley. I had begun to fear myself. Desire for my own death had long since faded, replaced by a passion for retribution and vindication for the crimes committed against me and by me. That part of me considered drinking the blood of these humans a necessary evil.

I stood, my cloak flapping in the wind behind my back. I was a demon ready to raise hell. An angel of darkness with scarlet wings splayed wide behind me, ready to burn down the world. What did it matter if anyone saw? The prospect of their fear sent shivers of pleasure rushing over my skin. I salivated for it. The monster in me had never felt so strong, and I never in less control of it.

I tilted my head back, inhaling the putrescent stink of the night air along with the aroma of blood rising from below me like heat off stone. The street reeked of ammonia from the unwashed humans making their way to and fro, nothing but rotting meat sacks. Still, I thirsted for what they contained and prepared to hunt—if I could call catching such easy prey hunting.

It was then I caught the other scent. Something cloying and familiar. I inhaled again, sex and blood, tinged with gin and desperation. Ignoring the gnawing in my gut and my parched, aching body, I turned from the maggots below and chased the scent across the rooftops.

I didn't have to travel far. Tucked in the shadows created by a nearby streetlamp, Emma, the woman who had drunk with me the night I first encountered Dougal, was locked in a verbal exchange with a man. At first, I suspected a business transaction in process. However, no, Emma was begging, and none too happy when the bedraggled gent refused, claiming he possessed nothing himself. A lie. Even from my position twenty feet above, I could sniff out the metal hidden in the lining of his jacket.

I dropped from my perch the very moment he walked away. It was the woman I wanted, the one Dougal had allowed to walk away from me before I had dismissed her from my company.

She spun on her heel, hand pressed to her heaving bosom, and faced me. Her rapid heart sent blood coursing through her body and flushed her cheeks a delicate rose color. Musk, salt, and sex, underlain with a lush coppery tang.

"It's you," she exclaimed, adrenaline rising in her blood. I couldn't be sure whether it was from the surprise or the prospect of a customer. "My, sir, but you didn't half-give me a fright."

My fingers trembled to grab her, and my teeth pressed sharply against the inside of my lip. I felt hollow and as cold as a statue in a chapel. However, unexpectedly and to my horror, as thirst roared anew like a great jungle beast, I hesitated. I heard William inside my mind, telling me I had a choice about what I wanted to be, and Dougal telling me I didn't have to kill. I could choose to be different from other vampires. How could they be right? How could I be different when I craved death?

Behind me, I sensed the other man pause and heard the crunch of stone under leather as he twisted to take a look at me, believing himself safely sheltered by darkness away from the streetlamp.

I did my best to smile charmingly. My lips quivered. "Well, I believe my companion promised you the devil would take you. I'm here to fulfill that promise."

Her body temperature elevated, and the scent of musk intensified. She feared me, and yet pushed that fear down to return my smile. Clearly as before, her desire for liquor and coin overrode her other basic instinct to run. Her hands lifted to push her hair back, her fingerless gloves drawing down her neck where her lifeblood pulsated below pale flesh.

"I'm such mess." She smiled, so wide that I spied the missing tooth at the back of her mouth. "And I can't find my 'chief." Emma patted her skirts, worn under the flimsy cloak around her shoulders, as if search for something. The cloak couldn't have retained much heat against the chilled night, and yet her blood seemed to boil so hotly I could taste its fragrance in air.

"Allow me." I whipped out a square of red silk from my shirt sleeve with an impressive flourish.

Emma's eyes widened at the sight of the expensive cloth, and she hurriedly held her hand out to receive it. I draped it carefully across her fingers. She stared—at it, at me, and then at the handkerchief again.

"I don't think I've ever seen anything as beautiful," she mused with awe, drawing her fingers over the fabric and then pressing it to her flushed cheek.

The sight of her blood tinting her skin pink inflamed my thirst, and her pulse rushed in my ears along with that of the man, who was still watching us from the corner. "Keep it," I said graciously. "I have many others."

"Oh, but I couldn't," she said, attempting to hand it back, but not really. Offering and holding on tightly in the same instance.

"I insist," I replied. Not fully comprehending why I continued resisting her blood, even now, when I could take both her and the man so easily. I supposed somewhere inside me a grain of humanity existed after all; something not-yet-altogether lost held the vampire at bay. Whomever I drank from tonight would die, and I had already chosen this woman.

Emma looked up to me, narrowing her eyes, and swallowed thickly, taking one small step back. I suspected my hat and the dimness made it difficult for her to see my eyes clearly. She glanced over her shoulder and then back to me thoughtfully, thinking something over. Her gaze darted around again before she took a breath and spoke.

"My home is just back there in the court, if you'd like to stop awhile." She paused and then added quickly, "I'm sure it ain't much to the likes of you—"

"I would like that, thank you." How much longer would I delay?

"Oh." She seemed to expect a different response. After another quick look around, maybe for the man, she turned to lead me away. Perhaps the man was her pimp. I was confident he hadn't seen my face, and so he was of no concern.

I made to follow Emma. On my first step, my balance faltered. The numbness I had experienced in my hands had spread to my legs. A dead sensation, as though I no longer controlled the movement. I imagined myself desiccating from the inside out. Of course, I caught myself before she noticed.

She led us to the doorway of a small room inside Miller's Court, glancing back repeatedly as if I might wander away along the short distance. I considered the predatory nature to Emma that I had noted before. In her mind, I was sure, she presumed herself the huntress, leading her prey into a lair. Nature wasn't always so simple.

She removed one of her gloves and slipped her hand inside through a small broken windowpane to the side of the door. I heard the quiet click of it unlatching before she pulled her hand back. There were scratches over the back of her knuckles where she had clearly been entering this way for a while.

Emma pushed the door in and then held it, waiting for me to follow her inside. I did. Our encounter felt almost part of my experiment at this point. How long could I restrain this violent thirst before it became unbearable? How much restraint did I truly possess? Was it possible I could hold off, take my leave, and sate myself with an animal after all? Or perhaps I could feed and leave this woman alive. The gnawing ache told me it was unlikely; the heat thundering through my veins, begging to be quenched, told me it wouldn't happen tonight. All I was doing was holding off the inevitable and prolonging my own torture. If I left it too long, I could fall into near frenzy as I almost did on the rooftop earlier. I could lose control and expose myself.

Still, standing in the single room lodging of this unfortunate with her meager personal possessions, I couldn't help seeing her as more than an animal, more than one of my experiments. That placed me in a certain moral predicament.

The room was cold, smelling of mold and damp mortar. Breath formed small puffs of smoke as it left her lips. She either didn't observe or care that mine didn't as she removed her cloak and bent to light the small fire in the hearth.

It flickered to light, bringing an orange glow to the sparsely furnished room. A candleholder and framed portrait sat on the bedside table, further enforcing my first impression that this woman hadn't always been poor but instead had fallen on hard times.

A bed cover had been recently hand washed using lavender soap. An expense I hardly expected from someone of Emma's means and profession. Perhaps pilfered from the shopping of a more affluent London lady. It brought to mind a memory I hadn't thought of in so long, a memory of my own mother's embrace and the lavender perfume she always wore.

A letter lay open on a table beside me. The page was bleached and crisp, relatively expensive, and covered with elegant script. A torn envelope lay beside it.

"Your name isn't really Emma, is it?" I asked, dragging my eyes from the perfect swirls of the address.

"No," she replied, standing up and approaching. She edged past, keeping a small distance between us, lifting the letter from the table and gazing at it for a moment before turning away. "But Emma does me just fine for our business."

After retrieving the envelope, she walked over to the bed and raised up the edge of the mattress to push the envelope deep inside.

I closed my eyes for a moment, leaning on the tiny unpolished wood, suddenly feeling I had made a grave error in judgment. Maybe I had been making errors all along since I left William. What would he say if he knew how far I had strayed from his ideals in my attempts to continue his work? I had become a murderer. Slaughtering humans, and not as a means of survival. I had been playing God, deciding who was worthy of life and who should die. What if during my experiments I had chosen wrong? In my divorce from my humanity, was it possible my judgment of guilt was flawed? Perhaps those unfortunates had simply fallen on hard times like this woman and had no other choice.

I did have a choice. These experiments had to stop. I swallowed down the thirst and tested my limbs. I still likely needed to feed from a human to regain my strength, but not like this. I would quietly take my leave and return to my original plan—drinking animal blood until I could consume no more. Perhaps I could obtain blood from the hospital.

I reached into my pocket for coins.

"Ouch!" The woman jerked her hand away from the bed and stuck her finger in her mouth. "Damn splinters," she swore, mumbling against her hand.

Too late. Coppery sweetness leaked across her tongue where a loose splinter of wood had sliced through the skin of her finger. I was too thirsty to resist.

Against my will, my body took over, sucking down the scent, fanning the desire to taste. Scarlet tinged the edge of my vision. Thirst raged upward like a forest fire, ready to obliterate anything in its path.

"Run," I growled, tearing the clasp that held my cloak and tossing it to the ground. My hat too.

"Sir?" she uttered, barely above a whisper.

Or it could have been screamed—the syllables were almost lost beyond her thundering heart.

I lifted my chin and met her eyes in the glow of the fire for the first time, my fangs bared angrily. "I said, run!"

She stepped back several times, mindless, like a rat scurrying in a sewer. "You're 'im. You're The Ripper." Her voice again sounded like a whisper, although I was sure it couldn't be from the movements of her lips.

I grasped the table, planting my feet on the bare floor. Wood crumbled away, and red seeped further across my line of sight. The room seemed dripped in blood. *Blood*, my insides screamed. *Blood, blood, blood…*

"I don't want to kill you."

Her heart raced, her bosoms heaving so violently I imagined I could see each beat clear through flesh and bone. Her pupils dilated, and tears of shock and terror rolled quickly over her flushed cheeks. Yet again, she stepped back, her injured hand swinging limply by her side.

I took a step, involuntarily lowering into a crouch with a growl rumbling in my chest. My lips stung where my fang had already split the flesh.

"Murderer," she mouthed, no more than a breath. "Murderer." Louder this time as gravity allowed a single drop of blood to slide over her knuckle.

It was as though time slowed in that one instant when the shining red liquid fell to the ground. It splashed, spreading outward over the parched wooden board and accompanied by a noise that seemed impossibly loud. A part of me knew there would be nothing I could do to prevent my vile actions. As with the night I awakened as a vampire, in that moment, the human in me had disappeared.

It was hours later when Dougal found me, drenched in blood and curled in a fetal position in the corner of the crimson-washed room. Had he been a human, I still wouldn't have acted. I would have allowed them take me and faced the consequences.

I had fed savagely, tearing at the woman's body like a wild animal let loose. I couldn't get to the blood fast enough. By the time I had finished, her mangled corpse barely resembled a human.

"Henry, good God." Dougal's voice sounded foreign to me. An underlying disgust laced his words.

I curled in on myself further, shaking violently as flashes repeated behind my closed eyes. A hand, bloody and lifeless. A torso ripped to shreds to reach the beating heart tormenting my thirst. Arcs of scarlet spraying across the room, sizzling on the dying embers of the fire. I was still ravenous. In my fury, so much had been wasted.

A hand touched my arm. "Henry, we must get out of here. We must leave London. Now. This morning. Before the sun rises, we must be gone from this city."

"No," I snapped, shoving his hand away. "Leave me."

"I'll not leave you to this, brother."

Slowly I lifted the arm covering my head and looked up, focusing only on Dougal. I didn't need to see the blood turning brown, or the exposed bones contorted into hideous angles. I could smell it. Smell the decay, the excrement and urine her body released when I ripped her throat out.

Dougal watched me as though I were a nervous stallion ready to bolt, both caution and fear in his green eyes.

"I ate her heart," I said simply. When I couldn't drain it, I tore into it with my teeth, allowing the meaty chunks to slide down my throat. "I'm a monster."

"Aye." Dougal nodded, his blond hair falling across his eyes. "And we'll both be dead monsters if we don't get out of here. The humans will have your head…and mine."

"Leave me. Let them have me. I can't exist like this."

Dougal groaned. "It's the serum and the animal blood. It's driven you half-out of your mind. I'll not leave you here, man. Come with me."

"No." I closed my eyes again and dragged my hands over my scalp, the tangled strands sticky and matted with blood.

"And what about Constance, eh? You stay here, and it's not just a cure you're giving up on. You'll never see her. Come with me, Henry. I *can* help you."

Chapter 25

2010

Doug came from the back yard, carrying an armload of thick chains. The aroma of smoke and lighter fluid permeated the air, blown in by the sharp breeze. He glanced down at his bounty and raised an eyebrow.

"Look what I found in your shed. Do I want to know what you were planning to do with these? Something fun, I hope."

"I picked them up while I was out the other night. I thought you might want to use them on me at some point."

He chuckled. "Aye, you're a fine looking man, Clay, but not my type."

"In the event I lost control," I clarified. "I don't want to hurt Ari."

He scowled, his lips pinching up in disapproval. The chains clanked against the quartz countertop of the island. "Well, at least it's convenient. Will you please reconsider leaving now?"

"I can't."

He rolled his eyes.

I took a blood bag from the fridge and poured it into a large glass. "It's hard to explain it. I can't leave."

"How long do we have before—" his eyes flickered upward "—wakes up?"

"He looks like he went a few rounds with a truck, so a while yet."

Doug dragged his fingers through his hair. "I wish I didn't have to ask…"

"It was Ari."

He huffed out a breath. "What happened while I was gone?"

"Four of them came in as soon as daylight faded. I fought off three, and the fourth got to Ari."

Doug began to pace slowly and shook his head as though trying to work something out. He tilted his head sideways, and an eyebrow arched into his ruffled fringe. "And she took care of him?"

I dipped my head once.

"I knew it wasn't normal how she just took everything." He rolled his hand toward himself, illustrating his point.

"I really don't need an 'I told you so.'"

Doug stopped across from me. "I wasn't going to offer one." He tapped the counter with his knuckle, his knowing green eyes piercing through me. "What else?"

I took a swig of blood, biding some time. "We talked, and we kissed."

He waited a moment while I finished the glass and rinsed it. However, I wasn't inclined to share the details.

"Just a wee kiss, eh? Anyone ever tell you that you've a gift for bad timing and understatement, Henry Clayton?" A moment later, his expression hardened. "I want this to be a good thing. I want to believe it's real, but you have to admit the timing is all screwed up."

"You don't have to tell me. When I kissed her, it was like the end of the world."

He laughed. "Exactly how a good canoodle should be."

"No." I wasn't sure how to make him understand. He didn't believe whatever I felt with Ari was real.

"Yes," he asserted again, that stupid knowing smirk plastered on his face. "A lover's first kiss should be like a dying breath, a last terrifying gasp before the inevitable. It should also be a glimpse of something so beautiful, so brilliant and inescapable, that whatever comes next, you've already lost yourself to it."

It might be easier than I thought to make him understand.

"I get it, Clay. I do. I've been there, remember? The problem is that it twists the mind." He slapped his palm against his temple. "It makes it so you can't see what's in front of you."

I thundered around the counter, bringing us inches apart. Icy frustration slithered into my veins. "What do you want from me?" I demanded.

Doug tugged on the collar of my shirt. I flinched away, and he grappled to hang onto me and force me to remain facing him. "You are my friend. My only friend. You gave me back my life—twice."

I paused on hearing his words. I'd always known how close Doug came to giving up after Sarah died. Regardless, his will to live had always been stronger than the pull of death.

Sensing my curiosity, he went on. "You asked me if I ever considered giving in. When we met in London, I wasn't in a good place. I hadn't spoken to another vampire in fifty years. The ones I met, they were little more than animals. The prospect of being alone for eternity isn't appealing. I said you needed me, but the nasty truth was I needed you as much, brother."

He released me with a grunt, and I stumbled back a step, dazed by his confession. Doug scratched at his scalp.

"I know you think of this life as a curse. If it is and I could lift it for you, I would. This situation is getting hairy. I just want you to live long enough to give me the opportunity. Okay?"

"Okay," I conceded, clapping a hand on his shoulder.

He did the same. "Okay. I'm going to go truss me up a vampire." He pulled back and kicked at the base of the island. "This thing go deep?" he asked.

"How long does this usually take?" Ari stomped around the kitchen, wearing another of my hooded sweatshirts and radiating nervous energy. Doug and I stayed out of her way.

The cunning vampire was sprawled on the top of the island, wrapped in as many chains and ropes as we could find. The room seemed extra bright with every light switched on to benefit Ari. I had never bothered much with them before she came to stay. I saw adequately regardless.

"It takes as long as it takes, Petal. With injuries this bad, the body shuts down to repair." Doug's eyes followed her as though waiting for her to sprout wings. "It should be any minute."

She rattled a chain holding the captive's ankle down. "And you're sure this will hold him?"

"Long enough," I assured her. I didn't intend to set him free when we were done.

His body began to twitch, coming out of the self-imposed hibernation state. We still had time. Every vampire healed at a different rate. This one took longer than most.

"Why don't you tell us exactly how you inflicted these injuries while we wait?" Doug crossed his arms and leaned back against the wall by the door. "I don't mean to be overly particular, but it would be nice to know in case you decide to go postal on one of us."

"I won't hurt you. Either of you." Her blue eyes sparked with determination and slid over both of us before coming to rest on the chained vampire.

"All the same, I don't think you're being entirely honest, Petal."

"He came at me with a knife, and I pushed him a couple of times," she said, seeming only half-tuned into the conversation.

Doug's nose wrinkled in puzzlement. "Why would a vampire come at you with a knife?" I could almost hear the cogs turning in his head, playing out what happened in the room.

Ari shot him a disgruntled glare. "I don't know. How about we ask him when nap time is over?" She shoved the prone vampire's shoulder as she passed by.

I stepped forward and tentatively took her hands in mine and held them between us to halt her constant trudging across the floor. If she kept it up, she'd wear a trench in the tile. Her eyes met mine, and irritation flickered through them before she released a breath and her body softened. I saw my reflection in her pupils, my tensed jaw and the tightness in my expression. Without the nettled static, her hands were soft and warm and small in mine. Pain welled in my chest at the idea of letting her go.

Despite what she'd said about not being able to return to her life, we existed in different worlds. Neither of us could live in the other's.

The burden of this truth weighed heavy on my heart. At least the thirst remained muted. This came in handy when Ari threw herself against my chest and clenched her arms around my waist. I laid my cheek on top of her head and hushed her while committing her scent to memory. Ari's heart raced, and her lungs worked overtime, taking in only shallow breaths. Dread curled like ribbons around my organs because of what this was doing to her. This situation was stripping bits of her away, leaving her exposed and weakened like a raw nerve. None of it was fair.

Doug clicked his fingers and whistled. "People, people, I'm still here."

Ari attempted to shift away, but I tightened my hold on her, careful to avoid her wounded arm.

"I don't think they wanted us dead, which begs the question, what do they want with us?"

"They believe my immunity makes me the key to bringing back your vampire god," Ari said harshly.

"So, why not kill me to get to you?" I pondered aloud. "I mean, it was four against one today. They weren't even trying. It was almost as if they wanted me alive."

Ari's heartbeat accelerated, and she pushed away, avoiding meeting my eyes. She filled an empty glass with tap water and chugged it down. The overflow poured over her chin and down her neck. I tried not to notice the movements of her long throat tipped back, tendons and muscles working as she swallowed repeatedly. It was a pointless exercise in restraint. Blood bags curbed my thirst, but I couldn't deny its existence.

"We're wasting time," Ari spat with panic lancing each syllable. She spun on her heel, and her arm lashed out, throwing cold water in a high arc.

It rained down on the barely-animate vampire lying like a carcass on a butcher's block.

"That won't work." Doug swiped droplets from the front of his T-shirt where she'd gotten him too.

For good measure, she slapped the vampire's face too. "Wake the hell up."

"It won't—" Doug's words cut off when the vampire hissed and strained against the chains holding him down. "Maybe it will work." He shrugged.

I clamped my hand around Ari's arm and tugged her back to my chest when the vampire's fangs snapped centimeters from her wrist. She struggled to get back to him, her hair swishing cocoa scent into my face. I groaned at the effort that it took not to hurt her.

"Who are you?" she demanded.

The vampire appeared more creature than man and not fully aware of his surroundings other than his captivity. He jerked, testing the tension of his restraints to their limits, but they held fast. He wore a sharp striped suit and shirt, and could have passed for someone from the business world. However, the blue veins threading under his skin and his black marble eyes chipped with red gave him away as a monster, not to mention the spittle dripping from his snarling fangs.

"Answer me," she roared. She had every right to be upset, but I didn't expect this. Ari had always shown resolve and moderation in her behavior. She seemed so much more put together than anyone else I'd ever known. This girl was a stranger and might harm herself if I let her go.

"Calm down," I pleaded with her.

Doug's cool eyes flashed from Ari to me and tightened. His head jerked to the door, indicating I should take her from the room. As angry as she was, after seeing the result of confrontations between Ari and other vampires, I wasn't all that inclined to become another statistic in her growing list. A peculiar leeriness sizzled through me, a faint whisper of self-preservation murmured in the back of my mind, telling me to give her space.

I shook my head, and Doug's lips pressed into a flat line. He tugged his fingers through the tangle of his blond hair and stepped up to the side of the island. His hand covered the vampire's chin, locking his head in place, and fixed his eyes on the monster.

"Now, I'm going to ask you a few questions," he said, black ice coating each word, "and you're going to answer." Lethal danger wrapped around Doug like a cloak of fury, and a shiver rushed down my spine.

No wonder he'd lasted so long in the world. I'd never seen him so terrifying. The vampire would be crazy to test his resolve. Apparently, he was.

The chains wrenched, and Doug pressed down harder on the vampire's jaw. A thin lightning-bolt tear rushed out from the edge of his ruby lips, spilling blood on his cheek. Doug was ready to rip his jaw away.

"Ah, ah," Doug admonished with an eerie calm.

The monster ceased his struggle, and at the same time, Ari calmed too, perhaps sensing he might answer her questions after all.

"What do they call you?" Doug asked. He eased the pressure so the creature could speak.

"Cyrus," he ground out, licking dark blood from the corner of his lip.

Doug looked up with a raised eyebrow and flashed Ari a dazzling grin. "Now, we're getting somewhere."

I allowed my hand to slip down Ari's arm and linked my fingers through hers, half-hoping she wouldn't rip my arm off to get at the vampire again. Her fingers squeezed mine, and her blood pressure calmed somewhat.

"What were you doing here?" Doug asked.

The vampire clenched his teeth and rattled the chains. "We came for her." His black eyes landed on Ari with blind hatred. "For Cailleach," he screamed to the ceiling, wrenching the chains again.

Doug's knuckles met his jaw so hard the force of the blow vibrated through the captive's body, but he only laughed. It was the high-pitched raving of a lunatic. I already knew we weren't going to get much from him.

Doug continued the interrogation. "Where is Constance?"

"Where you won't find her."

"Why does this Cailleach want Ari? Why do you want Ari dead?" I questioned, hoping to get at the root of one thing.

He made no response.

"And me?" I pushed.

He laughed again, cackling so loud the noise bounced off the walls and cupboards.

Ari wrangled her hand free from my fingers and approached the island. "How do I stop it?" Her voice climbed on each word. A heady combination of fear and anger lingered in the air surrounding her.

The creature eyed her with loathing. He opened his mouth wide, ignoring the broken skin, and ran a bulbous tongue down the length of one fang. He pressed against the tip until a bead of scarlet swelled on the dark pink flesh.

"Tell me!" Ari seethed. She shuddered all over, her cheeks flushing red.

He lifted, endeavoring to bring his face nearer to hers, but only managing an inch or so. "You can't." The words were cold, dripping in venom.

Ari released a whimpered cry somewhere between resignation and devastation. It was as though I could hear her heart breaking in the sound. She shook her head and staggered back. Doug's jaw slackened, and his eyes opened wide, probably mirroring my expression.

The doorbell chimed, shattering the tension in the kitchen.

"I'll get it," Doug offered.

I nodded, thankful for a few moments to prepare for seeing William, especially under these circumstances.

Ari took advantage of our distraction. The first thing I knew of it was the screeching of metal setting my teeth on edge. It happened at extraordinary speed. Too fast. A glint of light on metal stung my eyes. Doug and I both lunged forward for Ari, but we were too late to stop the cleaver she'd pulled from a knife block on the counter coming down on the captive vampire under his chin. It separated his head clean from his body, and an instant later, the chains clunked against quartz and rattled to the floor.

Doug held his hands wide, his mouth opening and closing. The cleaver clattered to the floor at Ari's feet. She panted, staring at the island as though she couldn't understand where the vampire had gone.

"She's bloody flipped," he exclaimed, aghast.

The sudden burst of adrenaline in her body made my muscles twitch, and my stomach ache for blood. I swallowed around the lump in my throat and stepped away from her.

"He was useless. I don't need a puppet. I need answers."

My jaw clenched, and my nails bit into the palm of my hand. I concentrated on the sting to distract from how my mouth salivated. When sure I was in control, I grabbed Ari by her uninjured arm and swung her around to face me. My fingers locked on her bicep, ready to control her if she lashed out. Her unreasonable emotional state was kindling for an already combustible situation.

"Answers to what, Ari?" An uncomfortable frown creased my features as I continued to fire questions at her. "What are you not telling us? What answers?"

Ari's mouth opened and snapped shut. She shook her head, her eyebrows knitting over bleary eyes. The doorbell rang out again in several continuous lengths, but Doug appeared reluctant to budge.

I shook her, tempted to use firmer force and grappling with my thirst. Ari wriggled, her expression fraught with misery. I refused to give an inch. Letting her run and hide from this now would be worse than anything she could do to me.

"Tell me," I ordered.

Ari ceased fighting me and stared up at me, her chest heaving. "Who I am."

Chapter 26

I drew my bow across the stings of my violin. It wasn't music in any sense of the word. It was barely noise, which failed to buffer Ari's heartbeat coming through the walls from my office. She'd been in there with William for several hours, only emerging to grab a bowl of pasta she threw together. Even then, she'd refused to talk to me when I casually leaned against the doorframe with folded arms. She had thrown up an impenetrable wall of silence between us, refusing to meet my eyes or acknowledge my presence. I wanted to be patient. She'd thrown me with her actions and words in the kitchen. I'd convinced myself we'd shared a moment earlier, that we'd broken a barrier. Her reticence stung like a knife in my back.

My reunion with William—the visitor at the door—had been brief and less painful than I'd anticipated. He appeared more interested in Ari than in our long estrangement. I'd built the moment up so much in my mind that I felt foolish for keeping him at a distance for so long.

Together, he and Ari were testing her blood using the laboratory equipment Doug had procured. Besides an introduction and directions while William extracted blood, she hadn't spoken. It appeared he would fare no better than I would at getting answers. This led me to believe her location had more to do with avoiding me than assisting him. I didn't know what to do about that, or if I should do anything at all.

Doug entered the drawing room and closed the door with a quiet click. He poured two glasses of whisky and left on one the small table beside my chair. The other he took with him when he sagged noiselessly into my seat, leaving me standing over him. He said nothing, and I continued to play. I was sure he intended his stoic presence to be comforting, but it grated on my nerve endings and made me restless. I played faster and harder, clenching my teeth at the sound of Doug slurping a mouthful of the amber liquid from his glass. A string snapped with a ping and sprang back against the back of my bow hand, splitting the skin on the knuckle above my index finger. I put the cut to my mouth, tasting sour metal on my tongue.

"Ouch," Doug commented, sipping again.

"It doesn't hurt." I laid the violin and bow on a side table and shooed Doug from my chair, taking his place. He pulled another seat over, and I took the glass Doug had poured. I leaned forward on my elbows, rolling the glass between my palms. A ruby bead streaked over my knuckle and dripped to the rug unhindered.

A moment after, a box of tissues landed at my feet. I plucked out a couple and dabbed at the cut.

"They're not for your hand, you big weeping haggis. They're to wipe your baby browns."

I scowled up at him from under my eyelashes. He pursed his lips and arched a brow in mock innocence.

"Pull yourself together, man."

I knocked the whisky back in one long gulp and held the glass out for a refill before the heat of the alcohol had reached my stomach. Doug obliged and topped off his own while he was at it.

"I know as much as you," I said.

"Which is that that girl is not who she says she is." He leaned forward when he spoke, keeping his voice hushed and rapid, settling one elbow on the arm of his chair. "Or *what*, for that matter."

I rolled my eyes. "Ari can't hear you."

"How do you know? Did you know she's some kind of humanoid anti-vampire killing machine?"

"Have you lost your marbles completely?"

"Fine," he snapped. "I like Ari, you know I like her, more than a lot, but she as much as admitted she doesn't know who she is, and what was all that 'stopping' nonsense? Do you think she meant Abhartach?"

"What do you mean, more than a lot?"

"That's what you picked up on?" He glared, released a breath, and sank back into his seat. "I'm not trying to be cryptic, Clay. She's a fine woman, but that fine woman is carrying a bagful of crazy."

"I'm lost, Doug. I don't know what's going on, why they want her, how she does what she does."

"You have to find those answers, sooner rather than later."

"How can I find the answers when I don't even know how to ask the questions?"

The sun came up behind a curtain of gray cloud on another dark and gloomy day with Ari and William still hidden away in my office. Doug had gone to rest, leaving me stewing in the drawing room.

They eventually emerged after midday. Ari thanked William for his assistance before I heard them parting, him heading outside and her descending into the kitchen.

"We should talk," I said from the doorway, watching her tip a glass of orange juice to her lips.

She drank the glassful down and swiped the back of her hand across her lips, leaving the sticky residue to glint in the dull natural light coming in through the high windows.

"I want to help you."

She cut a glare to me, and I tensed at conflicting emotions rolling off her in waves of spicy heat. There was sadness there, in the dark circles under her tired eyes, and a resigned fury, as though she had reached her capacity to fight and despair dragged her down. At the same time, her expression blazed with longing. She pulled in several deep breaths and rubbed the back of her neck, calming herself. She'd twisted her hair in a messy knot leaving tendrils of warm brown silk framing her face.

"I don't know where to start," she whispered, scooping strands behind her ear. The whisper failed to hide the sharpness in her tone.

I pushed off from the doorframe and entered the room as if I'd been waiting for an invitation to cross the threshold.

Ari's eyes traced the cleaned island and lingered at the new crack in the quartz and the chips from the paintwork where the vampire, Cyrus, had battled with his restraints. She had to be thinking about the body she'd destroyed. I was. She approached and touched the crack, retracting her fingers sharply.

"My blood doesn't hold a cure." Disappointment laced her tone.

"It doesn't matter."

Ari snorted a laughed. "How can you of all people say that?"

"I'm lying so you won't feel bad. It matters. I should have said it's not your fault." I wished away the pang in my chest. I hadn't realized I'd been clinging to a secret expectation until she'd said the words. Deep inside, the last wisps of ever escaping this curse and living to tell the tale dissipated to nothing.

She smiled weakly. "That's the crux of it. It is my fault. All of it."

I made to move to her, thinking I could offer some form of comfort. Ari's glower stopped me in my tracks, and she backed up, replacing the distance I'd erased. She turned her back, showing she still trusted me regardless of whatever weighed on her. I held onto that thought when her shiver ran the length of her body.

"I'm leaving with William tonight."

"No."

She glance over her shoulder, revealing her face in profile, but didn't meet my eyes. "I don't have a choice. I have to leave you."

"You can't just walk away from this. You have a choice. You can stay! Do you believe I invited him into my home so he could take you away? I won't hurt you." Anger flared, stamping down the sense of betrayal by William.

She looked away again. "But *I* might hurt *you*. I wanted to go now, but he said I should rest. I think he wanted me to tell you the truth. I think he knew…something. He'll know the rest soon, one way or another."

"The truth?" I pushed.

Ari spun toward me, intense blue eyes boring through my cool façade. On the inside, I was losing it. My confusion and anxiety fueled a ravenous thirst that felt like molten rock forging a relentless path through my veins. I pitched back on my heels, straightened my shoulders, and stood tall.

"The truth that I'm the real monster," she said.

"You're making no sense."

"Memory isn't always reliable. It's not like I woke up one morning, blinked, and remembered who I was…the other me, I mean. It's not like everything just slid into place. It took time to fit it all together. The last few days have been like trying to figure out a puzzle where all the pieces keep shifting. I honestly couldn't remember."

"The other you?" I rolled my tongue over each word, wondering if the stress had caused her to have some kind of mental break.

"Every story has a beginning. Mine started with a boy."

"The boy who grew into a good man, the one who left you?" I interrupted and stuffed my curled fists into my pockets.

Her lips stretched into a smile. "I said he went away. He died, and it ripped my heart out. I was so sure I couldn't live without him."

"But you did."

She moved her head from side to side so slowly I wondered if she even realized she'd answered before verbalizing. "It was said the people of my family were special. We had abilities beyond normal. The people of my village honored us for maintaining the order of the seasons. They said death and rebirth flowed in our very blood. But there were rules. Things I'd been warned about all my life. I didn't listen.

"When the man I loved died, I fed him my blood. I took a knife, opened a vein, and poured it down the gullet of his lifeless body. I dragged him back from the other side and made the first vampire."

"No." I shook. This was crazy. "It's not possible."

"It is possible. It happened."

"No." I pulled a hand from my pocket and yanked it through my hair, swallowing around the lump in my throat.

"Yes."

"No." I recognized I sounded like a spoiled child stamping my feet and didn't much care.

She closed the space between us. I'd wanted her to do that a short time before, but my body acted without instruction and flinched away when she reached for my hand. She hesitated and dropped her arm down by her side.

"Who are you?"

Her head tilted softly to the side. Long eyelashes fluttered when she blinked, registering my question. "I'm Arianna Caulfield. I'm still me, the girl with a crush on the lonely guy who doesn't like coffee. The girl who likes the smell of bleach, whose dad brought her fishing, and whose favorite ice cream is vanilla."

I searched her expression for something different, something that would help me to accept what she was saying. There was nothing, nothing that set her apart from the girl who'd been staying here for the last few weeks, except for one thing. A shadow of something aged and knowing lingered in her eyes. I'd seen the same shadow in the eyes of the older vampires I'd encountered over the years.

"But you are someone else too, aren't you?"

"Yes, I have lived many lifetimes."

I swore under my breath, raging at the inhuman heart in my chest and its inability to react to Ari's declaration. It taunted me with a slow, unaffected thumping. "How?" Bitterness crept into my voice. It sounded hollow, even to my ears.

Ari backed away and turned from me to walk, attempting to place the island between us. "It doesn't matter now. I'm so sorry for the pain I've caused you. I'm going away, and I hope you'll never have to see me again."

I went the opposite way around the rectangle counter and wrapped my fingers around the tops of her arms. She winced at the pressure where the knife had cut her. I bent enough to bring my face inches from hers while only vaguely conscious I was hurting her. The reality of losing her paralyzed my limbs and left me unable to release my hold. Ire thundered, made terrible by my desire to drink and the artery pulsing invitingly below her ear. The defeat in her expression incensed me further. I wanted to shake her.

The hairs across the back of my neck prickled. *Ari never showed defeat*, I thought, suddenly panicked at the notion of never seeing her again, that this woman in front of me was someone else. Her cocoa scent and her heart beating furiously assured me this woman was Ari. I couldn't make sense of the yearning and grief surging up and hauling my mind and body in different directions. It felt as though she'd already been taken from me. I needed to understand. In that moment, it felt more crucial to my existence than the thirst constricting my parched throat.

"Tell me," I shouted so loudly my breath disturbed the fine hair around her face. A vein throbbed painfully at my temple, agonizing, as if my head might split in two and my mind fracture from this torment. "You owe me that, at least. Make me understand."

"Let go of me, Henry," she demanded, her voice rising to match the volume of mine.

Determination and exasperation flickered across her flushed face. She glared, showing no fear. For an instant, I saw Ari…only Ari. It was enough to snap me back to my senses, and my hands softened enough for her to shrug them off.

"What is going on down here?" Doug asked. He rubbed his eyes with the heels of his hands and dragged them through his hair. Gold strands fell back in place across his forehead. He sniffed at the air as he took in the room, his concerned eyes zipping from me to Ari and back again.

I presumed by his rigid stance he hadn't listened to enough of our conversation to get the full picture. Hell, I'd been here the entire time and didn't have the full picture.

Ari broke away from me and went to him. Doug cupped her chin between his thumb and finger. He lowered his face a few inches to peer into her eyes, much as I'd done moments before, except there was no malice when Doug looked at her, no fear or judgment.

"You okay, Petal?"

She smiled at him, winding her fingers around his wrist to lower his hand. "I'm okay."

His eyebrows quirked up, wordlessly seeking reassurance.

"I promise. Thank you for taking care of me, Doug. Can you give us a minute?"

His lips parted to answer. Green eyes flickered to me hesitantly.

"Please," Ari said. "I know you deserve an explanation for what's going on too, but I need you to give us some privacy right now."

His tongue clucked as he considered her request.

"I've got this," she assured him, and part of me was embarrassed because he wanted to protect her from me. I'd almost lost control.

Finally, Doug heaved a breath and nodded, although not entirely appeased. He looked up to the windows where dark clouds tumbled ominously, threatening a storm on the horizon and blocking any direct sunlight. "I'm going to take a walk. If I stay, curiosity will get the better of me." His full attention slid to me. "You made me swear to protect her, and I'm giving you two space to sort the wheat from the chaff. Don't make me regret either decision."

His lips pressed into a line, and with a last challenging look, he left us alone.

Chapter 27

Neither of us budged until long after we heard the front door close. "Make me understand," I repeated my words, almost pleading with her. "Who are you?"

Her head drooped forward, and her shoulders rose and fell with each staggered inhale. "Now, I'm Ari, but before, in the beginning, my name was Cailleach."

"Cailleach?" The name sounded like an obscenity on my tongue.

Ari turned to face me, her mouth tight as she scrutinized my startled expression. No. I couldn't accept this. No.

"The boy's name." She paused and smiled wistfully. "His name was Eógan. I was young, naïve, and distraught at his death. I didn't heed my mother when she warned my actions would carry a terrible price, and when I ripped him from the underworld, I cursed us both."

She took a couple of tentative steps, her bare feet padding on the tile, and dipped her head to see my downturned face. "When he came back, his blood was tainted, corrupted. The darkness took him and made him something else—a terrible soulless thing that needed blood to survive. He wasn't Eógan. He slaughtered his family and then mine when they tried to keep him from me. He wiped out our village and moved onto others. Some tried to placate him, offering animals as sacrifices. It didn't work. Death followed him, and the countryside ran red with blood. The people gave him the name Abhartach."

She stopped and rubbed at her forehead until a pink mark bloomed over her eyebrow. I knew I should have allowed her rest, but we had no time.

"There's more, isn't there?"

Ari leaned her hands on the counter and pressed down, placing her forehead against the cool worktop.

"Ari," I pushed, and she straightened.

"They tried everything to kill him, but nothing did. A Druid priest said he should be buried alive. Even that didn't work. He was too strong. He climbed right out. I knew it had to be me. I had made him, and I had to kill him, so I did. I had to. I put a wooden stake made from mountain ash through his heart and cut off his head. There was nothing left of him but dust. The body they buried wasn't Abhartach; it was some poor wanderer who'd died at the side of the road. The people needed some kind of closure, and I thought it was over. Until years later when found myself a young girl again with the memories of a past life.

"And I'm not the only one who is reborn. It's an endless cycle for both of us. Eógan's new incarnation is turned, he becomes a monster, and I kill him. It's my punishment."

"And I'm just supposed to accept this crazy story?" I yelled.

"Why is it crazy?" she snapped. "Because reincarnation is so much harder to swallow than vampires?"

"Yes!"

Ari laughed blackly. "I would rather be insane, trust me."

"How can I trust you when you've been lying to me? Why didn't you tell me this before? Why pretend you didn't know anything about what's going on?"

"I didn't know."

I shook my head and dismissed her.

"I didn't remember. It was different for this incarnation. The last time, I lived to be an old woman, but The Circle got close. I used magic to conceal myself and tried to make it so they could never find me again. I guess I never learned my lesson. It backfired, and when I was reborn, I couldn't remember who *I* was. The Circle found me anyway as a child and then as an adult. Both times they slaughtered my family. I suppose the magic worked to a point, and they lost me in between. I believe they've been watching me since they killed my adoptive parents. The Irish relative, the letter…It was all a ruse to lead me to exactly where they wanted me to be."

"To me?"

She made no reaction, and I scowled.

"They want Abhartach back. He's a god to them. They believe if he kills me before I kill him that the cycle will be broken, that I won't come back to kill him again."

"That's why they want you alive. So Abhartach can kill you."

She nodded, and I didn't want to ask my next question, but she stared at me expectantly, as if she knew where my mind was headed before I got there. The bizarre connection between us…the draw I felt to her and couldn't escape. They believed I was the reincarnation of Eógan and that Abhartach existed in me as Cailleach existed in Ari.

"That's why Constance thought I would roll over and join The Circle. That's why the vampire Cyrus didn't want me dead."

She nodded again. "I'm so sorry. If they hadn't led me to you, I think I would have found you anyway at some point. I always find you. Apparently even when I don't remember you, I still find you. The Circle was already keeping track of you, and when we connected, they must have thought it was time to make their move."

I thought of the killings in the vampire world and realized they were meant to make way for Abhartach. The Circle killed any vampires with power, anyone who might resist giving up that power. Anyone who might resist Abhartach. Was it to win favor, or did they actually believe they had some control over any of this? I slammed my fist down on the countertop. The shining black surface crumpled under the force and sent splinters of quartz into the air. Ari shrank back, but not out of fear. She looked on me with sorrow and pity, her eyes red rimmed and her brow puckered. My skin itched as if maggots crawled over the surface. It felt too tight to contain the blood roaring in my ears. My vision swam, and my mind buzzed with unintelligible questions.

The unquenchable thirst crept into every cell, draining my strength and will power. It would have been easy to test The Circle's theory. My eyes fixed on Ari. My sweatshirt was too big on her, falling below her hips but exposing flushed skin at the neckline. I watched how light bent over the gentle dips and slopes of her collarbone and the sweet spot where her shoulder met her throat. I knew how creamy smooth that skin felt pressed beneath my mouth and how adrenaline intensified her scent there.

I licked my lips, wanting to drown in her, to drown out the questions and the truth I felt deep within me. The truth I'd always known, that something dark and heinous dwelled there, just waiting for an opportunity to take me over.

"Why don't I remember any of it?" I stumbled back, away from her and temptation, toward the fridge. I opened the door and plunged my hand in, grabbing one of the blood bags. I didn't bother with a glass this time; instead, I tore into it and slurped the blood until the plastic collapsed.

"You've never remembered. Each life, you're born completely new, with no memory of me or Abhartach." She choked down a sob. "Perhaps it's part of my punishment that you don't know who I am until it's too late. So many people have died, and I'm to blame. What you are was never your fault. It's mine. I'm sorry. I'm so very sorry."

"Stop saying that!" I wanted answers, not apologies that wouldn't solve anything. Lottie's face flashed through my mind. I knew I should think of the others, all those I'd dispatched, but I only saw her. I saw Lottie's curls and peachy skin, heard her delighted giggles and then her cry when my teeth sank into her flesh. In my mind's eye, she stood before me alive, until her flesh turned blue and rotted from the bone, sliding away and taking clumps of her lovely hair. Her pretty dress blackened and disintegrated, turning to ashes with the rest of her.

An agonized growl ripped free from my chest, and I scrunched my eyes until nothing existed in the darkness but dancing stars. My knees hit the tile, and I collapsed forward, bunching my fists into my hair. Air rushed into my lungs, and I forced it out again just as hard, concentrating on the pain seizing my chest to slow my impulses.

"Why couldn't you have killed me a century ago? Before I killed all those people." I clenched my teeth until it hurt and my fangs stabbed at my lips.

"It doesn't change anything, Henry. It would just start all over, and you wouldn't remember. I couldn't take that chance."

"Why?"

"You're different this time, the only incarnation who has ever fought the darkness. You even sought out a cure. What if you kept fighting? I don't know how to destroy Abhartach, but what if you could contain him? This is my third lifetime watching you hold him back."

My head snapped up to her standing over me. I looked away, unable to see Ari and hear these things. "But I've killed."

"Not nearly as many as Abhartach would have."

"How do we stop it for good?" I asked and snorted at my unintentional use of words. *Good*, there was nothing good in any of this.

"I told you, I don't know," she admitted in a whisper. "William was my last hope. I thought if we could end vampirism, Abhartach would be gone too."

"So, you're going to run?"

"I've been running forever, and I've always stayed one step ahead of The Circle before. I'll hide better this time. You have to stay alive. You are the cage that keeps the darkness locked up."

"Everything was a lie."

"No." She dropped down beside me, her pulsating heart forcing luscious blood through her body. The metallic taste of the bag I'd consumed still persisted to remind me of how Ari's blood would taste on my tongue and sliding down my throat.

Her hands settled on my back, and the slow thumping vibrated through her palms. I was hyper-aware of the heat rising from her, her scent and touch, the muscles twitching beneath her skin. My insides coiled in excruciating anguish.

"When I saw you at the coffee shop, I had a weird déjà vu. I didn't understand the draw I felt to you, but it doesn't mean it wasn't real. It was real. When my memories started returning after I killed that vampire, I thought…I thought if I could find a way to save you, maybe we could try…I hoped you'd never have to know that all this was my fault. I hate what you might become because of me, what all your previous incarnations became. I hate the thing inside you, but I can't hate you, Henry."

"You were the woman, or some version of you. The women I felt watching me all those times."

She nodded. "For well over a hundred years, I've made your life a living hell because I didn't know any other way. You have to believe this is real. I lo—"

I bolted upright, taking Ari with me, and slammed her back against the dented fridge door. Air left her lungs in a whoosh, and her eyes opened wide.

"Don't say it!" I bellowed in her face. I must have appeared terrifying to her. "Don't even think it."

She gave me no warning when she retaliated. It happened faster than I could react, and our positions reversed. The contents of the fridge rattled at my back, and Ari had my shirt bunched in her hands, tackling me as she leaned in. At least it explained how she could overcome two vampires.

"I love you," she said slowly.

I swung her around, shoving her back until she met the plaster wall beside the fridge with a yelp. Dust swirled in the air and sparkled in the light, raining down on us like glitter. Every nerve in my body exploded with heat rolling through me. My nostrils flared as the scent of fresh blood wafted upward from her arm. The wound had opened, taunting me. If she experienced pain, she didn't acknowledge it. Ari was on her tiptoes, her back flat against the wall, compensating for our height difference. Her chest heaved, pushing into mine with each breath. Her hands came up to my wrists, and she circled her thumbs over sensitive skin, perhaps in an attempt to sooth my rage, to hold the monster back. She cleared her throat of the lump preventing her words.

"I don't want to hurt you," she murmured, more pleading than warning. Her pupils dilated, and she looked up to me with dark, heavy-lidded eyes.

I slammed her again, and she blinked back tears from the sudden, jarring force. The shock of my own actions made me pause, and I forced my fangs to retract. Ari hated her weakness, her inability to affect the curse she'd brought down. That much we had in common. A part of me hated her too in that moment. Even through the haze of jumbled emotions and stimulation, I couldn't say I loved her.

Regardless, there was something there in my gut, a connection that tethered us and kept her alive when I should have killed her several times over. I couldn't reconcile this young woman with another unknown version of her who had caused me so much pain. The idea that everything originated from Ari stretching backward through time seemed abstract in the extreme. I had to take responsibility for my own actions, for the decisions I had made in my lifetime. If I denied the bad, I also denied the good. I would be denying the battle I'd waged with darkness and my own strength each time I'd turned from it.

Love. My baseline of experience was non-existent. I couldn't say if I loved her or if one word could adequately convey these alien emotions. If I didn't know who I was anymore, how could I trust how I felt?

"Don't go." I challenged her to push me away, running my thumb over her flushed bottom lip.

A slow-building, visceral desire smoldered in my chest. It lit my skin on fire, and every nerve ending screamed for stimulation. I kissed her gently but deeply, exploring her mouth and seeking her tongue in a slow torturous dance. She tasted faintly of orange juice and the blood I'd taken earlier. The metallic, sweet combination caused a hunger to shiver through me. Gooseflesh raised along my arms; somehow the temptation and restraint heightening my sexual desire.

Ari's hands moved down my forearms and up over my shoulders. Her fingers slipped into the short hair at the nape of my neck and urged me on. A lilting moan sent her breath into my mouth, and my thumb traced a line under her chin and down her throat, absorbing the vibrations of the sound. She pushed up higher on her toes, and I leaned into her.

A sound like a gasp whistled passed my ears when our bodies connected. I wasn't sure if it was Ari, or me, or both of us. Every sensation and sound tangled, and the tightness in my stomach and thighs increased unbearably. Her heat was everywhere, raging in my veins, molten.

This was our precipice, the place from which there was no return if we took this final step. I drew back enough to meet her passionate gaze, searching her expression for any hesitation. Her heart jackhammered inside her ribs, and her eyes darted to my mouth. Her tongue peeked out, the grainy pink flesh swiping across her kiss-swollen lips, leaving a shimmering trail of moisture.

An unwelcome thought of Eógan flickered in the forefront of my mind, and I surprised myself when I hesitated. Did I look like him? Had they been intimate? Was she Ari now, or Cailleach, or any one of her countless incarnations, and was I simply a poor substitute for the man she'd lost so long ago? It seemed ridiculous to be jealous of him if I believed we were in some way the same person, and yet, jealously scorched.

Ari's expression softened, and her head tilted a little. Her fingers twitched at my neck and fell away. I ached all over at the loss of the contact.

"Henry?" The word was hushed and rasping, but it effectively released me from my doubt.

I came down on her again with more vigor, covering her mouth with mine, exploring her skin, her cheek, her jaw. I stretched the thick fabric of the sweatshirt aside to taste the delicately perfumed skin over the hardness of her collarbone. My kisses conveyed promises of something far beyond these stolen moments. Promises that I couldn't possibly hope to fulfill.

Ari's hands fumbled at my shirt, tugging it from my jeans, and she slipped her hand under to my lower back. Her fingertips dipped inside the band and squeezed. I hooked the bottom of the sweatshirt, trailing my knuckles up her sides. She sucked in a sharp breath at the contact. The sweatshirt caught the elastic holding her hair up as I lifted it over her head, and long, silken waves fell messily over her shoulders.

She worked on the buttons of my shirt while I continued to kiss and touch her anywhere I could reach. She was too slow; I pulled and the last button popped with a yank and pinged on the tile. Ari dipped her head, placing her mouth over my heart. She feathered a kiss that dragged her bottom lip against my skin, her teeth grazing and pinching sensitive flesh. My erection throbbed.

I couldn't get close enough. My palm flattened over the base of her skull and dragged down each vertebra, memorizing the curve of her spine. Her back arched, bringing us together. My hand continued over a firm mound and pulled her even closer. I relished my name on her lips.

The rest of our clothes followed quickly. Her hands gripped tighter each time she found new skin to explore. I hooked my hands under her thighs and lifted Ari from the ground. Her lips curved into a smile when her legs tightened and I pushed inside her heat.

Ari moved her hips to meet mine on each thrust, and my pelvic bone skimmed her delicate pink flesh. She gasped, and her nails dragged down my back. A delicious rush of pleasure caused my legs to shake.

Ari moaned against my tongue. I grunted again as I met her hips carefully and allowed one hand to travel to her breast. She slid her calf down the back of my leg and changed the pressure between our bodies. Her heart thundered, and I swallowed each breath she gave me, cherishing her taste in my mouth and her tongue stroking mine as our bodies worked together, grinding, plunging, arching. I concentrated on the energy forming a tight ball of flames, the euphoria of it pulling and pushing, making me want to take her harder. Making the thirst and desire meld into one. Ari's head dipped to my shoulder, and she let out a high-pitched whimper. She went so still, fighting the escalating, agonizing euphoria. We reached an apex and became two bodies clinging together, accepting the fast approaching, inevitable tumble into pure, vivid pleasure. Her fingernails clawed into skin below where her forehead rested. I felt her shudder again, and I grew harder inside her. The sensation was overwhelming, unbearably beautiful. She threw her head back, knocking the wall, but she didn't appear to notice. Her whole body bowed toward me.

"Henry," she cried out as heat like newly forged metal twisted around my insides and exploded outward. Blast after blast pulsed into her.

The waves abated to shudders, and my trembling body began to calm. Ari, pliant and exhausted, sagged against me, lacking the strength to stand. Her quivering form was damp with perspiration, and she was still whispering my name over and over against my neck. Her vulnerability made my heart clench.

If I attacked now, she wouldn't fight back.

A terrifying voice in my mind whispered dark thoughts and spurred me on. I tamped them down, reminding myself of Ari's faith. She didn't intend to kill me as she'd done to my previous incarnations because she believed I could resist.

My fingers splayed out on her cheek, and I tilted her head so I could see her face. She smiled lazily and traced her index finger along my clenched jaw.

"What if I'm not ready to let you go?" I said.

"If I stay with you, they'll find us no matter where we go, and they'll keep coming for me. They'll do it because now they know you'll protect me. The more you kill, the closer you'll come to the dark, and that's what they want. They want the darkness for you. Then, they want you to kill me."

"That is never going to happen."

"Maybe someday, in another life, I will find the answer. Henry, you have to hang on until then. You can't die. We have to stop this cycle." Her chin wobbled with emotion. "I wish we could blot out the sun and stop time. They are coming. The future is coming."

I kissed her soundly on the mouth and then pressed my lips to her forehead. "But it's not here yet."

Chapter 28

The sky outside the windows was navy blue, sprinkled with dots of iridescent white light. The world had been washed clean, and the future rushed toward the present. Ari would be gone soon.

The warmth of her body soaked through my flesh where she lay in my arms, both of us tangled in sheets. Her head rested on my shoulder, her fingers splayed over my steady thumping heart, and the rest of her pressed against my side as much as possible. One of her legs settled against mine, and the other curled over the same thigh, as though our bodies had unconsciously attempted to meld into one during sleep.

After the events in the kitchen, I'd walked Ari to her room — my room — so she could rest. She'd asked me to stay. I couldn't believe I had slept in the midst of all this, only waking when Doug returned, followed soon after by William. Since then, I'd been watching her, reveling in the exquisite torment of her scent and the taste of her on my lips, the feel of her silken hair on my skin, her breath stroking over my collarbone, and the sound of her sweet living heart.

My sexual desire for her had not yet abated. I craved her body in ways I was too terrified to explore. I felt entirely inept and feeble in the face of all this new stimulation and information and the emotions scorching my blood. Perhaps Doug had been right that I'd been too long without the companionship of a woman.

I longed to know the quantifiable parameters for romantic love. How could I know if these whirlwind emotions I felt for and around Ari were love? The scientist in me said it was nothing more than a biochemical reaction. I'd been convinced for so long that vampires formed associations as a means of survival, but that those associations weren't the same as love.

The contradiction to this theory was Lottie. My love for her was transcendent, even if it couldn't save her. Then there was Doug and Sarah. I couldn't doubt he had loved her and continued to love her, even after death had separated them.

Ari stirred and murmured in protest as the real world came crashing down. She blinked to clear her vision and made to turn toward the window. The day had been dark enough to open the shutters, but I regretted it now that night soaked the room in silver light that carved shadows over the hollows and curves of Ari's body.

"You let me sleep." She tilted her head to meet my eyes. Weariness made her voice thick.

My fingers slipped from her arm to cup her neck lightly. "You needed it."

She began to twist toward the window, but I caught her chin in between my thumb and forefinger.

"It's night," she whispered.

"You can't leave yet. It's still daylight."

Ari's eyes narrowed, perplexed at my bogus observation. "Henry, I can see the moonlight—"

I rolled us both, pressing Ari into the mattress beneath me. Her hair fanned over the pillow as I dipped my mouth and kissed from the curve of her throat to her ear. "Night is passed, and the day is here again. It's the sun blazing in the sky. Stay awhile."

Her neck arched, pushing her chest and her racing heart into mine. A ghost of a moan passed her lips as she recognized my poor corruption of Romeo and Juliet's parting. Ari's fingers bent at my waist, drawing the tips over my skin and sending rushing heat through my blood. Her legs parted, allowing me to settle between them briefly before she tumbled us back and sat up on my hips, skimming her nails down my chest. She shifted her hips, making her intentions clear.

"Let me be captured then." Ari threaded her fingers through mine and gripped tight. She pushed up onto her knees and sank down, throwing her head back when a shiver rushed over her. "I am content if you would have me so. I have more care to stay than will to go." She smiled and rocked slowly.

Hot desire welled and, with it, a crushing thirst for blood. The muscles of my thighs began to tighten almost immediately. I released Ari's hands and pulled myself up to a sitting position, wrapping both arms around her back. Our mouths crashed in a deep, needy kiss, her tongue sweeping out and tangling with mine. I bent my knees behind her, pushing deeper into the madness of restraint and acute temptation.

Ari clasped my shoulders, anchoring herself as heat pulsed inward and concentrated where our bodies were one, building to a dizzying peak. She closed her eyes and touched my forehead with hers, her hot breath washing over my face. Our mingled scents rose from her slick skin, and I sucked in a deep breath against my better judgment. Her blood roared in my head, muffling the sweet gasps from her ruby lips. The climbing sensations of euphoria were too much when combined. This slow, torturous, intimate dance would be the death of her.

Ari's hair swept over my fingers with each movement, and they trembled with an urgency to twist the silken strands around my fist and pull her head back, exposing the pulsing artery in her throat. Aching hunger threatened to consume me from within.

I stopped breathing and bit down on my bottom lip, tasting the velvet tang of blood on my tongue. Ari's movements slowed, and her body stiffened faintly. My hands slid to her side, my thumbs skimming the underside of her breasts, before traveling to her hips. I flipped her onto her back, conscious of the still-covered wound on her arm, and plunged back into her heat.

"Look at me, Ari."

Her eyes remained closed, and her legs crossed at the back of my thighs, pulling me deeper.

"Ari."

Her eyes snapped open, a look of concentration in her expression, her gaze liquid with sadness and desire. I saw all the loss and the guilt, her ancient soul exposed and raw in the blackness that

captured my reflection...captured me. Her body shook with the effort of meeting my eyes, and I fought the realization this was more
than sex. The exposure to danger brought a level of intimacy and
trust hard to ignore, as was the growing awareness I'd never want
this with another being. A rumble of a growl built in my chest at the
thought of her ripped from me. Our fingers entwined over crumpled,
damp sheets as she cried out and the euphoria shattered within her.
I exploded with mind-blowing intensity and aftershocks vibrated for
several prolonged moments.

I kissed Ari again, tasting salt on her upper lip and dragging our
clasped hands to rest by her head. My weight pressed down on her,
my limbs loose and heavy, both of us, for the moment, utterly spent.
Loath to release her just yet, I sank lower down her body and laid my
head on her chest. Her heart thrummed, and air whooshed softly in
and out of her lungs, blurring the bloodlust I couldn't escape. Ari
untangled her hands and stroked my hair, curling her fingers in the
damp strands.

"I have to go now," she said shakily.

I rolled off and flopped onto my back, clasping her hand again.

She slipped from my fingers, and I turned my head to face her,
but she was already in the process of sitting. When I reached for her
again, she jerked out of my range.

"Ari—"

"Henry, don't," she broke in, breathless and pained. Her legs
hung off the side of the bed, and her shoulders sagged. Under messy,
tangled hair, her spine seemed like a smooth string of pearls covered
in the palest caramel-colored silk.

"I have to. I can't just let you walk away with William and not
fight to keep you here. I want you with me. I want to protect you."

"You can't, and I need to go now. Because if I don't go now, I might
not have the strength to leave you ever. Henry, you don't know what
it's been like. Now that I remember it all, I know I always thought
having to kill the man who looked like the one I loved all those times
was the worst punishment I could imagine for what I'd done, but
this...finding you. You are him, but you're also you, Henry Clayton,
and I was utterly unprepared for *you*."

"This isn't the end," I assured her. I reached forward and lay my
hand over the one she'd pulled away.

A little over an hour later, we were on the pathway outside my garden, and I watched Ari stand on her toes to embrace Doug warmly. William waited in the back seat of the taxi that would take them to the airport and on to an unknown location. We'd already said a tense, awkward good-bye with him promising to take care of Ari. I resented that they'd agreed I shouldn't know where they were headed, and Ari'd made me swear I wouldn't try to track her down. I wasn't sure how long I would keep that promise. I would have begged if I'd thought it'd make any difference.

Ari kissed Doug on the cheek and pulled back.

"I know you didn't always trust me and that it went against your instincts to like me, so thank you for ignoring them and being so good to me. I'm sorry I lied to you."

Doug chuckled. "Don't, Petal. You'll make me all weepy."

The corner of her lips twitched, and she inhaled a breath as though to settle her emotions. She gripped the collar of his leather jacket and dragged him forward for another kiss on the cheek.

"I'm going to miss you calling me that."

His eyes flickered from me to Ari and back again. His lips pulled up in a forced, lopsided grin, and he gestured back to the house with his thumb. "I'm going to give you guys a minute."

I pressed my lips together and nodded in gratitude.

"Good-bye, Arianna Caulfield," he said, and my stomach gave a peculiar twinge. It sounded so final, as if he planned never to see her again. Perhaps he didn't.

"Good-bye." Ari waved halfheartedly as he walked away.

I took a step, intent on reassuring her once more that I would find an answer and bring her back to me. Possibly predicting as much, she launched herself into my arms and trapped my lips, making words difficult. When she pulled away, I pressed my forehead to hers and cupped her jaw. Drawing in a lungful of cocoa and coffee, I forced down the enviable bite of the craving for her blood. Her pulse fluttered under my little finger where it grazed the spot under her ear.

"Don't say anything, okay?" she implored, holding my wrists. "Just kiss me again and let me go."

"Ari—"

"Henry." She cut me off and kissed me with all the passion and despondency of a farewell, slipping her hands around my neck and through the bristly hair at the nape.

She broke away winded and touched her fingertips to her lips, but shed no tears. I was surprised to realize I had expected a teary good-bye. I should have known better. Ari walked away backward and smiled.

"Be a good man, Henry. Don't let me down."

"Ari…"

She covered her ears to block out anything I might say and continued her backward walk to the car. Did she believe I could convince her to stay? Maybe I would have tried again, or maybe I would have told her that I loved her. Neither of us would ever know because I hadn't thought past her name and I still wasn't sure if "love" was the correct word to summarize my emotions.

My jaw creaked with the strain of gritting my teeth.

She stopped briefly at the car, with her arm draped over the frame of the open door, and I could have sworn I glimpsed the yearning to stay she was trying so hard to conceal.

"Until next time," she called out. She was unable to hide the tiny crack in her voice before she climbed in beside William.

It took every ounce of restraint and then some to keep from chasing after her. As it was, my legs locked, and my toes curled in my shoes. My finger joints screamed with tension, and my jaw creaked again. Ice slithered down my spine and spread through every extremity as though an echo of foreboding whistled in the night air.

I half-expected the taxi to stop and for Ari to climb out and dash back up the street. Instead, the taxi followed the curve of the road and disappeared out of sight.

"So, what's the plan, brother?" Doug asked, stopping at my side.

"The plan?"

"Aye, you do have a plan, don't you?" he said, his tone heavy with a mocking disbelief. "You can't just give in."

The ice in my veins bubbled. "No. I can't, but tell me, Dougal, how do I begin to fight what I cannot even conceive of?"

Doug hummed thoughtfully. I shot him a sideways glance to see him watching the empty place where the road vanished around the corner. "How about I buy you a drink inside, and you can fill in the missing pieces." He clapped a hand on my shoulder and turned me toward the house. "I don't hear any fat ladies singing yet."

Chapter 29

1908

Bitter salt wind blew in from the Atlantic Ocean. Turbulent water battered the cliffs further down the beach, throwing up white foam. A full silver moon shone down from behind drifting clouds, nothing more than wisps of smoke. The ocean seemed alive and furious under the night sky. I imagined the foam as souls of those lost to ship wrecks along the treacherous west coast of Ireland, screaming for release from their watery grave.

I inched back a step, just enough that the rolling waves withdrew before reaching my scuffed boots. Gray stones clanked and slipped. Soon the tide would rise up and drown the small cove. I was partial to these moments. No human would dare venture down here on a night like this, and no humans meant no temptation.

Except, earlier I'd passed the window in my drawing room, and I'd been sure I spied a willowy figure in a flowing skirt standing precisely where I stood now, gazing out to the horizon. I'd experienced the strangest pull at my ribs. Nothing like the usual hunger, this went much deeper. As though an invisible cord of communion had pulled me right out of my seat where I'd been reading and toward the window. When I made my way to the water's edge, I found the shoreline empty, devoid of any indication someone had been here.

The sensation dragging me forward was gone, and I presumed I'd imagined it.

My home sat three hundred feet above the cove on a small piece of land jutting out into the water. The dilapidated stone manor had been a castle several rebuilds before, and remnants of the towers where previous residents guarded against intruders remained. The roof over the north reception room had fallen in long ago, and the foundations had been exposed at the very edge of the cliff, leaving the structure to appear as if hanging onto the land for dear life. What survived suited my basic needs well enough.

A warm flickering glow came from one of the lower windows—Dougal had returned.

It'd been twenty years since the terrible night we fled London together, and Dougal had come and gone many times. Often I wouldn't hear from him for several months. He remained a social creature, and my self-imposed isolation didn't suit him well. He'd get restless and more agitated as days progressed, until one evening I'd arise to find the manor empty and Dougal gone to immerse himself in our ever-shifting world.

So much had changed over the last two decades. Humans rushed headlong into experience and invention without ever taking the time to understand the consequences. From what Dougal had told me, the mood over Europe had become increasingly strained. Here in Ireland, mass emigration and an epidemic of tuberculosis had depleted the population. Industry in Belfast thrived, especially in the linen district and the shipyards, but government continued to keep a firm foothold in Dublin Castle. Talk of home rule and whispers of independence from the monarchy prompted an upsurge in unionist activities.

I felt far removed from it all out here, but I knew I couldn't stay forever. While this remote location on the border between the counties of Galway and Connemara provided the solitude I craved, my other cravings persisted. I had long accepted my need to consume human blood and my responsibility for the starvation that led to my insanity. The dwindling population of Galway city and the handful of towns in the county meant traveling further afield so as not to risk exposure.

"What is it you spend hours staring at out here, Henry?" Dougal squinted, looking out into the vista. His nose wrinkled and his lips puckered in concentration. The breeze loosened locks of his blond

hair from a tie at the back of his head. His hair remained unfashion-
ably long. In contrast, he wore a stylish dark suit with a long sack
coat, freshly pressed, over a white shirt and waistcoat. His slim collar
turned down over a wine-colored tie. He would have cut a dashing
sight in whatever city he visited this time.

"I sometimes suppose if I fix my gaze long enough, I might spy
a glimpse of America."

Dougal groaned. "Enough of this self-flagellation, man. You've
done your penance, and it's time to return to the land of the living.
You're breathing fresh air, but you're still trapped in that dungeon."

He was referring to the subterranean room where I had spent
the first months of our time here, chained in irons and fighting the
hideous side effects of starvation. Initially, I couldn't think as the thirst
and insanity escalated. I gorged on human blood until it sloshed
about my stomach and nausea crippled me. Hours later the cycle
would begin again. I never asked where Dougal acquired the bottles of
blood. I lay there, day after day, rambling and straining at my chains.
In brief moments of clarity, I had begged Dougal to end my pitiful
existence. He refused and weaned me back to sustainable levels until
I was strong enough to function. Notions of savage feedings remained
at the forefront of my mind, blurring other thoughts at times. I had
come to accept it was the best I could hope for.

I shook my head. "No penance would ever atone for what I've done."

He scratched his fingers through his hair, dragging it free. "Then,
what is the point of all this?" he asked, his tone exasperated. We'd
had this conversation before. "If you want to go to America, let's go.
There's a whole world out there to explore. It's changing so fast, and
you're missing it all. Do you know there's a regular transatlantic wireless
service between right here in Galway and Nova Scotia? Voices crossing the ocean while you play Ms. Havisham up at Clayton Manor."

"It's not called Clayton Manor," I corrected him with a smirk.
"And I have no idea who this Ms. Havisham is."

The tide continued to roll in, forcing us to retreat all the way to
the mouth of the cave where stone steps cut from the cliff climbed
a steep incline to my home.

Dougal rolled his eyes. "Her yearning for lost love drove her to
insanity, just like your craving for humanity."

"The world isn't going anywhere. Who knows how long we will
endure. We'll see many things."

Dougal's expression took on a condescending scowl. "Ah, at last you've hit on a revelation. You endure. I live." He sighed.

"Don't you ever grow tired of it all?"

"No."

His answer was simple and without hesitation. I knew he meant it utterly, and a solid brick of jealously lodged in my gut.

"Their lives are over in the blink of an eye. The moment they take their first breath they are already dying," he said. "I've seen glorious wonders of the world. I've traveled all over and witnessed mankind at its best and worst. When the humans born today are dust, I will remain. There is a cost for everything, and it's a price I pay willingly for this amazing life. I refuse to regret a moment of the adventure it's afforded me. *If* this ever ends, I don't want to have wasted it."

"I envy your clarity, Dougal."

"Och, this is damned insane. If I'm not fit to convince you, I think I know someone who can."

I cast a sidelong glance in his direction. "Pardon me?"

"This is a last resort, Henry. You have a visitor. William Alexander is waiting to speak with you. Maybe he can talk you round."

William faced a burning log fire in the dimly lit reception room. He had to have built it up. I was sure nothing more than scattered embers could have remained after how long I'd been gone. The room itself was sparse, the only furniture a threadbare rug and two high-backed chairs. The walls were bare of artwork, and where the wall covering hadn't peeled away at the seams, it revealed a patchwork of fresher areas where past owners had hung paintings. Smoke had stained the corners of the ceiling a dark gray, and I read the tall stacks of books scattered around the room by candlelight.

Like Dougal, William wore a tailored dark suit with a high shirt collar. A hat and gloves lay abandoned on one of the chairs, and a gleaming cane with a round brass head had been propped against the arm.

I hovered in the doorway. He didn't turn to greet me, and his figure cast an enormous shadow across the room. I felt like a child called into the study of an angry parent.

"I had thought you dead, Henry, until your friend sent word."

"Then the world would be less one demon."

"Henry," he scolded me with his tone.

"Forgive me, William. I didn't wish for you to see me like this."

His shoulders rose and fell heavily before he spun toward me, his expression forlorn, his brow creased. "Like what? Living like a rat in squalor, cut off from the world…hiding? When my letters were returned, I thought the worst. This is not who you are." His eyes flamed with emotion, and his expression grew progressively outraged with each word. "Did I not treat you as a son, Henry? Did I ever ask for anything from you?"

My jaw clenched, and my fists curled into tight balls by my side. Yes, he had treated me as a son, and I feared disappointing him as I had disappointed my own father. I stood there withering under his scrutiny in my collarless shirt, pants, and scuffed boots, humiliated at all my failures. "You asked me to live."

"This…" He swiped his arm out in a wide arc and toppled one of my book towers. "This is not living."

I lowered my gaze. "My research is a failure. I am a failure. I know I must return to the world, but I don't know how."

"You surrender too easily, and yet you are the strongest immortal I have ever encountered. To survive your experiments and still escape as some semblance of the man you were…It's a miracle."

I snorted a laugh and rubbed the back of my neck to ease the knot forming there. "Miracles are God's work. I don't believe He cares much for saving me."

"Only one road is closed to you. Your journey is far from over, Henry."

I approached him slowly, my eyes fixed on the bottle of scotch on the mantle behind his head. I pulled it down with one hand and a couple of the glasses beside it with the other.

I grabbed the cork in my teeth. The popping sounded obscenely loud against the backdrop of the sudden howling wind rattling the windows. Knowing the bottle would be empty soon, I spat the cork into the flames and poured two full glasses.

William sighed. "I would compel you to see your future through my eyes if I could. So much awaits you."

I swallowed the contents of my glass and reveled in the artificial warmth it elicited through my body. "You shouldn't have come." One hand rested on the high mantle, my head drooped. "You should leave now."

I flashed a sidelong glance in his direction and saw his eyes narrowed and his head tilted, considering my words.

"Speak freely and directly," he said.

Pushing off the mantle, I flung my empty glass into the fire. It smashed against the logs, the flames dancing around the shards. "I am grateful for what you've done for me, William, but you are not my father." White hot anger seized my chest in a vice. As much as I'd learned from him, I needed to find my own way, and his presence made me feel as though I were a chastised child. I had taken his training and perverted it for my experiments. I couldn't bear to look at him. More importantly, I couldn't bear for him to look at me. "I can find my own way."

"Henry——" he began, but I cut him off with a glare.

"Please, William, I need to find my own way."

I closed my eyes and listened to him pick up his cane and hat.

Chapter 30

2010

"You believe her?" Doug asked after I'd filled him in on Ari's story. We sat in the drawing room, sharing a bottle of Glenmorangie. An aching knot had lodged in my gut, and my fingers trembled with nervous energy. I should have been doing something else already, but I had no idea where to start. Did I really let her simply walk away?

"I can't explain, but it feels true, if that makes sense?"

"Can't say it does, brother." He shrugged. "Not with a tall story like this."

I raked my fingers through my hair, tugging until pain tingled at my scalp. "Then what do I do? Presume she's delusional?"

Doug opened his mouth to speak. I held my hand up, hushing him before he answered my rhetorical question. He frowned and crossed his ankle over his knee, drumming his nails on the thick sole of his boot.

"She's not delusional," I went on. "She can't be turned, she took down two vampires, and there's the magic that protected her. It's real."

Doug pursed his lips.

"You know you felt it," I challenged him with raised eyebrows. I placed my elbows on my knees, rolling the half-emptied glass between my palms. My head drooped, and I watched the amber liquid glimmer when it caught the illumination from the lamps.

He huffed out a breath. "I hate to admit it makes a sort of warped sense, at least where you're concerned. I've never met another vampire with such duality. You exist so near darkness, and rage so violently against it." He scrubbed his hand over his face. "Since I was turned, I can count on one hand the people I've loved and still have fingers to spare. Whatever you need, brother."

I mused over the implication of his words and the real possibility those people included Ari. The idea no longer inspired jealousy. If anything, knowing Doug cared for Ari was a comfort. Doug had no concept of half-measures, and he'd give his all to protect her.

"I have to fix this."

"What makes you so sure you can?"

I looked up. "I'm not, but I have to try."

He raised his glass to me and drank deeply. "Ah, what the hell, living forever is overrated. Let's show these buggers they've messed with the wrong vampires." He drank again, draining the glass.

I tossed him the lidded bottle for a refill. "I'll drink to that."

We did. We drank in silence, and Doug's face contorted in a series of grimaces scrunching up his handsome face. His green eyes pinched, and his nose twitched. I could almost see the cogs of his mind whirling.

"What exactly is your great diabolical scheme?" he asked after several pensive minutes.

I closed my eyes and sank into the chair. "If they want Abhartach, perhaps I should give them the death and destruction they crave." *The very thing Ari said would make the darkness stronger,* my mind whispered.

"So, you somehow manage to destroy every member of The Circle, presuming you can find them all. Where does it leave you? You'll still have that thing inside you, and Ari is still human, more or less."

"There is no more or less," I said without opening my eyes. "She's human."

"The point is you'll still want to drink her blood all the time." He snorted a laugh. "Well, not all the time."

I peeked at him scrutinizing me with amused curiosity. I was well aware he and William had heard the activities in my bedroom.

"All the time," I corrected him.

His jaw slackened, and one eyebrow arched into his messy hair as he allowed my meaning to sink in.

I closed my eyes again, and he went silent. I was glad of the moment of peace to form a strategy. Constance would be my way in, although I feared members of The Circle would be like the Hydra, the serpent creature of Greek mythology—remove one head and two would grow in its place. If I began cutting them down, wouldn't it strengthen their resolve and their belief Abhartach had returned to the world? How close would I come to losing myself in the process?

"Maybe there's another way." He clucked his tongue, and I heard him set his glass down, so I opened my eyes again.

Doug scowled and swiped tangled hair from his emerald eyes, bright with excitement from whatever idea was tossing around inside his skull. He hopped to his feet and walked past me to the alcove bookshelves.

"Didn't they call in some Druid magic man before Ari—Cailleach—Ari?" He shook his head as if to clear his thoughts. "Before she killed Eógan. That's how the original story goes too, but it ends with the burial."

I twisted in my seat as Doug scanned the shelves. He plucked a thin volume and slapped it down on my knees, standing over me. It was about death rituals, and I wasn't sure I followed his line of thought. I picked it up and flipped through the pages.

"Have you ever heard of a Sin Eater?" His nostrils flared in obvious excitement.

"Yes. They were charlatans who prayed on grief-stricken families for money."

He waggled his index finger. "Not necessarily. Communities generally ostracized Sin Eaters. They lived solitary, miserable lives, only called on when someone either died or was near death to perform a ritual enabling them to swallow down their loved one's sins for a pittance. Hardly a good gig for con men with get-rich-quick schemes."

"So, what are you saying? Sin Eaters are real?"

"It's a process of sanctification, a purifying of the soul. Almost every culture has stories of some form of shaman, witch doctor, or holy man, some poor sod charged with carrying the weight others couldn't or wouldn't. Elements of the rituals still endure today in some places, with mourners eating death cakes passed over the corpse. Essentially, the mourners are taking on the sins of the departed so their lost loved one can enter the after-life free and clear."

I balanced the book on the armrest of my chair, presuming he'd produced it more for flair than information. "Even if this man who had Eógan buried were some form of magic sin sponge, you're forgetting it didn't work."

Doug collapsed into his chair. "Maybe *he* was a fraud." He picked up the bottle, not bothering with a glass, and drank straight from the neck.

"But you said they weren't charlatans."

"I said not necessarily. You really must widen your horizons, Clay."

"My horizons are as wide as I wish them to be at this moment in time. Can you get to the point?"

He shifted to the edge of his seat as though preparing to impart a secret. "What if we could find such a man? If he were to perform the ritual on you, perhaps he could separate Abhartach, or cleanse you somehow."

"You make me sound like a whiteboard. The things I've done can't be wiped clean."

"But what if they can?" he argued. "No more Abhartach."

"And no more Cailleach," I reminded him with a clenched jaw. "When my curse is broken, so is hers, and Ari would be her last incarnation. I would still be a vampire."

"But you wouldn't have to play whack-a-mole with a demon vampire god piggy-backing inside your body while you're trying to take out the bad guys."

"When did we become the good guys?" I scratched the back of my neck, bemused at the idea.

Doug chuckled. "I think we're down to degrees of bad at this point." His expression turned suddenly serious. "This is the best option we have."

I tipped my glass to my lips and downed the remnants of my whisky, feeling its warmth spread through my body and remembering how Ari's heat seeped into my flesh only hours before. A phantom caress played over my forearm, raising gooseflesh. Such a simple human reaction for an inhuman being. Her scent still permeated the air, already fainter than it had been.

What would she think of this plan to chase down another myth, one even rarer and more fantastic than vampires? I wrestled with the decision, turning it over in my mind. Would she approve? I hoped so, because as Doug had so astutely observed, this was our best option.

"How do we go about finding a Sin Eater?" I asked Doug resolutely. I was fully confident he wouldn't have brought the subject up and dangled it if he weren't already five steps ahead.

"It's been quite a long time, but I think I know where to start looking," he said, his fixed gaze veiled with doubt he struggled to hide.

We left immediately, our journey shrouded by night. Travel to the west of Ireland was far different from what I recalled. This time, artificial light spanned a motorway, and even the small twisting minor roads were a vast improvement on the dirt roads traveled so long ago by my rickety horse-drawn coach.

I had been tempted to hire a small plane and fly us to Connemara, except that Doug reminded me in a country as small as Ireland, the distance could be covered via land by the time I'd procured a plane and cleared a flight plan.

With more than an hour to sunrise, I stood on the stone shore of the cove where I'd once spent many nights contemplating the world. My old home was long gone, mostly collapsed in the water; what remained was barely more than a pile of rubble. The stairs to the crest of the cliff had held out, although a now broken metal grate covered the entrance at the top, embellished by a danger sign and secured with plastic cable ties. Judging by the swirling colors and bubbled letters spray-painted over some of the cliff wall, someone other than me had managed to get down here. I wondered how often the local council had to fix the gate.

Cold water washed over the toes of my boots, turning the tan leather dark brown. I inhaled a lungful of the fresh briny air tugging on my hair and clothes. It felt like a million pinpricks inside my chest. I concentrated on the whoosh of the tide and the slow white roll toward shore to still my racing thoughts. Nevertheless, emotional overload came crashing down on me as I recalled the woman I'd once seen standing in this very spot. Had she been Ari's previous incarnation, or maybe the one before that? Would I have experienced the same emotions for her as I did for Ari, had I been given the opportunity?

A sharp whistle called my attention to the top of the cliff where Doug waved, gesturing for me to join him.

I found him leaning against the side of my gray SUV, his arms folded over his thick chest.

"It will be light soon, and by the looks of that clear sky, there'll be sun," he said as I emerged through the gate. "There's a small hotel about twenty minutes away, and we should probably make use of it."

"What did you find out?" I asked, ignoring his suggestion.

Doug sucked in a breath that caused his chest to expand further and huffed out through his nose. "I often find the local pub is a font of all knowledge for the area."

"Is that why you visited that place so often back then?"

"I was keeping my ear to the ground, making sure none of the locals planned to bother the crazy guy living in the broken down house by the ocean."

Guilt made my stomach flip-flop, because of course I knew he'd been looking out for me. "I know, and I'm sorry."

He shrugged. "I've got some bad news and a lead."

"Don't keep me in suspense."

"The man I heard about when you lived here before is long dead."

"Excuse me if I find your surprise bewildering." I raised an eyebrow and smiled.

He rolled his eyes. "Just get in."

Doug pushed off from the SUV to climb in the driver's side while I took the passenger seat. The engine turned over, and he reversed to take us away from the cliff and toward the road. We weren't about to sit and watch the sunrise, at least that we were agreed on.

"What's the lead?" I pushed.

"There's still family in the area."

"What are we going to do, walk up to someone's door before daybreak and ask them if they know where we can find a Sin Eater?"

Doug's eyes slipped to me before returning to the road. "I'm all ears for bright ideas if you have any." His sense of unease was palpable, and he showed none of the swagger I was used to. I wasn't entirely sure what to make of it. It was a little disconcerting, and I experienced a fleeting sensation of inevitability. Even if I wanted to turn back, Doug wouldn't allow it.

"They'll call the police."

"I'll make sure they don't."

My jaw clenched. We'd driven across the country overnight, and I didn't have anything more to lose by at least checking it out. Doug could make them forget our visit if they needed to. I could buy them off or spin a story if he couldn't. The glass in the SUV would filter enough UV light from the early morning sun to get us to a hotel after.

Chapter 31

Forty minutes later, we pulled up on a grass verge outside a large dormer bungalow with a black slate roof, painted cream dash, and an interesting garden.

"Mountain ash," I observed, "and a crossroad. Aren't crossroads said to enhance a connection to the spirit world?"

Doug pressed his lips together and hummed.

The isolated house sat in the shadow of rugged mountains, on roughly an acre of mature garden at the junction of a road, and was closed in by a wooden railing. It contained a range of trees and hedgerow around the perimeter, some of which I recognized: rowan, fir, the willow tree in the center of the lawn, and a hawthorn hedge. Shades of gold and russet red leaves mixed with evergreens.

I could also smell various herbs in the moist air. Two brick pillars contained a wide slatted wooded gate, and beyond it, a curved gravel driveway led to a blue door.

"I suspect the apple doesn't fall too far from the tree in this case," Doug mused aloud, getting out of the car. "The isolation and the crossroad, the trees…I'd say we have the right spot."

Dozens of small birds scattered to the air from the roof of the house, forming a small black cloud. Chattering and harsh trills filled the quiet, along with a bizarre metallic droning. They ducked in unison and changed direction to fly away.

"Do you see that?" Doug's eyes widened.

"Starlings, right?"

He smirked. "Otherwise known in this part of the world as druids."

I kept my expression guarded, unwilling to reveal hope sparking in my chest. It appeared possibilities existed beyond what I'd previously considered. If reincarnation and individuals capable of cleansing a body of sin were real, why not a cure for vampirism?

The gate wasn't locked, and gravel crunched ominously beneath our feet as we made our way up the pathway to the darkened house. The sky had begun to lighten, dimming the stars. We didn't have time to waste. Doug flashed a nervous smile and rang the doorbell, drawing his finger back as if burned. He glowered at the push button and tilted his head to me, baffled. I snatched his hand and inspected the skin. There was nothing there.

"What was that?" I asked.

"It felt like the charge when I touched Ari that first time, but a thousand times stronger. I think it's safe to say we have the right place."

A light came on inside the hallway, and footsteps padded down the stair. A slim dark shape formed beyond the mottled glass panels at the side of the door, and a woman attempted to muffle a yawn.

"Who's there?" The voice belonged to a young woman with a Dublin accent, the rounder, smooth vowels of the south side of the county.

"My name is Dougal Gunn, and this is my friend, Henry Clayton. We need to speak to you about Daniel Manion."

Metal clinked and rattled behind the door before a lock turned, followed by another, and the door opened a crack. Dark brown eyes peered out though a gap held secure by a metal chain. She blinked a couple of times, her gaze traveling from our feet to the top of our heads. I couldn't get a good look at her. She was tall, and I estimated mid-twenties by her smooth, pale complexion and pretty face, with a delicate splattering of freckles across her cheeks. Her thick eyelashes fluttered, and her heart thumped harder.

"You have the wrong person."

She attempted to close the door, but Doug pressed his palm to the paintwork, wincing in pain. "You want to invite us in."

She laughed, unaffected by his influence. "Funny, I don't think I do."

Taken aback, Doug released the door and shook his hand in the air. His expression of unease amplified tenfold.

"Get the hell off my property," she yelled through the wood.

"So, what now?" I asked him.

His lips flattened into a straight line, and he scratched his temple. I turned my attention to the door, knowing she stood the other side by her rushed heartbeat and stilted breathing. The scent of her blood perfumed the air, but it stirred no hunger, giving off a strange sickly sweet aroma.

"Please, I swear we are not here to hurt you. We just want to talk." I sounded desperate, even to my own ears. When I inhaled, the air rattled through my lungs, my body defeated at the thought of losing this one glimmer of hope. "I need your help...please."

She made no response. After a while, Doug hung his head, and his shoulders slumped.

"I'm sorry, brother."

"I can't give up on Ari. Even if we can never be together, I have to do something. The Circle will hunt her like an animal as long as they have reason to. I will do whatever it takes, Doug." My words were laced with urgency, and a desire to slam my fists against the door took root in my chest. It was stupid idea, but still, my fingers shook.

Doug placed his hand on my shoulder and urged me to turn away, perhaps sensing my mounting frustration in the telltale vibration of my body. I complied unwillingly, looking skyward to gauge how much time we had to get to the hotel. The clink of metal when the door unlocked was unexpected. The hair on my arms stood on end, and a shiver ran through my body.

"Wait."

We spun back at the woman's voice. She stood in the open doorway, backlit by the golden light of the hallway. My rushed assessment had been correct; she was pretty and ruffled from sleep. Tangled chin-length red hair was scooped behind her ears, and black silk sheathed a willowy frame. She crossed her arms, and long delicate fingers tipped with midnight blue nail varnish bunched the fabric protectively.

"You can't come in here unless I invite you," she warned, lifting her chin.

Doug flashed the megawatt smile he reserved for female conquests. "That's not how it works."

Her lips twitched at the corner as though she might smile, and her cheeks took on a rosy hue. "If you say so."

Doug's foot shifted. He was unable to resist the challenge and evidently suffered a memory lapse since it had been just minutes since the house had shocked him. I clapped my hand on his shoulder to stop his advance. The woman rewarded me with a brilliant smile.

"You're a witch," I said plainly, since there was no point in any of us beating around the bush at this point.

She heaved in a breath, and her head shook almost imperceptivity. "There is no name for what I am, although it hasn't prevented many from trying. You can call me Danni Manion." Catching Doug's smirk, she continued with a brief nod. "Daniel Manion was my great-grandfather."

A breeze swept up, disturbing the fabric of her robe so it moved like rippling water across her body. Danni took a small move backward and peered into her garden with wary eyes.

"Well, now we know what you are, and I think you know what we are, can we please come in and chat?" Doug said. "You may have noticed it's getting light."

"Please." She smiled sweetly and moved aside, sweeping her hand inward.

He stepped up first, tentatively jabbing at thin air to ensure his path was clear. Danni closed the door, and we followed her into the kitchen. She flipped the lights as she moved though the large room and drew down a blind above the large ceramic sink and another further down. The room wasn't what I expected, bright with cream cabinets and a sleek dark worktop. It appeared to have been recently fitted. I was surprised at my preconceived notions of what a witch should be. I'd walked in expecting brooms, a cauldron over an open fire, and perhaps a familiar in the form of a black cat curled by the fire.

"Not what you expected?" she asked breezily, taking coffee beans from a double fronted black fridge and pouring them into a grinder. Very soon the bitter aroma of filtered coffee spread through the room and caused a flutter of pain in my chest.

Doug sat at a long oak table at the far end of the long room, scanning his eyes over a selection of family photographs neatly arranged on the wall. Behind him double doors opened into a greenhouse. He'd have to move before long; pink light already streaked over the horizon.

"Why does your blood smell different?" I asked curiously.

"It doesn't," she replied. "You just think it does. It's a protection thing."

"Crafty witch," Doug murmured. I presumed he meant for her not to hear, but the slow smirk that formed on her lips told me she had.

She used her fingers to comb her hair. "Why don't you tell me what you want?" Danni directed the question to me, while securing her hair in clip at the nape of her neck.

"There's a girl," I began, and she laughed, pressing her fingers to her lips.

"Most trouble begins with love."

"I didn't say I love her." My tone verged on defensive despite it being a logical assumption. Very few things concerning a girl could drive a vampire to the door of a witch.

"You didn't have to." Her finger swirled in a circle, pointing at me. "It's all over you."

"There are some bad people after her. They want me to kill her because it will release something inside of me. I want you to remove it."

"Ah," she uttered, pouring three cups of coffee. "You want the Sin Eater." She offered me a cup, and I waved it away. She placed it on the counter beside me regardless and took a second cup to Doug. "I'm sorry, but you've wasted your time coming here. I can't do that."

Her words registered like a fist slammed into the side of my head, and desperation took over.

"If it's a matter of money—"

"It isn't," she said.

"It was a long shot such a thing is possible." I hoped I could convince her to try. "I can't imagine the power—"

"It's not a matter of power either."

Doug attempted to wave away the coffee as I did. She raised both eyebrows in another silent challenge. He pursed his lips, securitizing her as though she was some exotic creature, and took the cup. She waved her hand in a graceful curve over Doug's coffee.

He ducked his head and swiveled the cup, snapping his head back up to her, slack-jawed. "It's blood." His startled eyes met mine and returned to Danni, openly marveling.

"It's coffee," she corrected him, adding in mock surprise. "You thought you were the only one with a bag of tricks? My kind have been around a lot longer than yours."

I picked up my cup and watched the warm red liquid ripple with the movement. The smell of fresh blood wafted into the air.

Danni sat at the end of the table with her own cup, flashing a slender thigh before she adjusted her robe. Doug's eyes lingered a moment longer than appropriate on the silken fabric.

"So, you can help us, but you won't?" He threaded his fingers through his hair, pushing unruly locks from his eyes, and leaned forward in his seat. "Is this a game to you? Do you think we'd be here if we weren't short on choices?"

Danni sipped her coffee, either unaffected or pretending to be unaffected, by his scrutiny. "I admit to being curious. I know of The Circle. I've heard stories, but taking the sins of another…It's a slow torture. I'm not about to put myself through that to ease the conscience of a vampire that I don't know from Adam."

"But isn't that what a Sin Eater does?" Doug propped his elbows on the table and inclined toward her. Small muscles jumped under his skin when his jaw tensed.

"Doug—" I started, concerned his sarcasm wouldn't be welcomed.

"It's okay." Danni cut me off with a raised hand. "I do many things. My family has lived in this area a long, long time, and it's no secret I'm different. I was the result of a brief encounter between my parents, and my mother took off when I was two. She couldn't cope with the family legacy. My father raised me alone on the east coast to get me away from the local 'talk,'" she said, making quotes with her fingers, "but I saw what consuming the sins of others did to him. He was fifty-six when he died. He could've passed for eighty."

"So, why did you come back here?" Doug said with genuine interest in his tone and his eyes fixed on hers with surprising intensity.

Her brow creased. "It's my home, and my family's reputation provides a comfortable living. I do a few placebo spells here and there, some readings and other things. I have a nice house, money in the bank, and I can afford to travel when I feel like it."

"Placebos?" I asked. "You mean you're a charlatan?"

Danni shook her head with a smile. "I've been called worse. But not every broken heart needs a real love spell. Sometimes a shoulder to cry on, an ear to listen, and a little clarity is enough. I provide my other skills only where it's necessary and deserved."

"If you can help but you won't help, why invite us in?" I asked, growing frustrated at this apparent waste of time.

She frowned. "I don't know why. Maybe because I'm a sucker for love, and you're willing to sacrifice yourself. There is something noble in that and unexpected from one of your kind."

Doug shook his head and stood, taking his cup. He walked to the sink and poured the contents out, as if it was the most casual thing in the world. It remained unspoken that he was moving out of the path of the pale sunlight moving through the end of the room. He leaned against the counter near me and scrubbed his hand over his face. He hadn't slept in a couple of days and had to feel it by now.

"Ain't love grand," he groaned bitterly.

"Don't pretend to be so cynical." She chuckled, seeing right through the bravado he liked to put on and curling a loose tendril of red hair around her index finger. "You care for this woman too. You came here stumbling blindly for answers to save her from her fate."

Danni gave off no scent for her emotions, but I got a distinct sense of her eyes staying a beat too long on Doug each time she looked at him. Their mutual physical attraction was obvious and badly timed.

"You say you won't help a vampire ease his conscience." I touched my chest out of habit, although we all knew I referred to myself. "What if I told you this isn't about easing my conscience?"

"Oh?" She crossed her legs the other way, holding her robe this time.

I pulled one of the stools out from the breakfast bar and sat down, a rush of determination urging me on. "She was like you, wasn't she?"

"Who?"

"Cailleach."

"You could say that."

"What else could I say?" I asked, detecting more between the lines.

"I'm not sure I trust you enough to tell you all I know about Cailleach and The Circle yet." She raised her hand and watched her fingers sway in the light. "You have until sundown to convince me."

Danni listened to my entire story, hardly saying a word except to excuse herself from the room on two occasions. Once to shower, when she changed into tight fitting black jeans and a slouching cotton top, and again to take a phone call from a friend. She offered us food when she cooked a small meal of roasted vegetables and spiced rice. We both declined but gratefully accepted a glass of the Irish whiskey Doug spied in one of the open cupboards.

I told her everything, down to my confused feelings for Ari and my willingness to walk away when this was over so she could have some semblance of a normal life.

By the time day waned into evening and the first flickers of stars splintered the clear sky, we were all seated around the long oak table.

"Do you trust this woman is who she says?" Danni said, scooping gleaming red hair behind her ear.

"Of course," Doug answered for me despite pushing the same question earlier.

I nodded. Danni maintained a guarded expression, keeping her opinions beyond the reach of my enhanced senses. She hummed thoughtfully, tension making the skin at her brow taut, the only hint to what she could be feeling. Anticipation and apprehension tossed around in my stomach, building like a wall of water behind a dam. I made every effort to temper my expectations for a positive outcome, but over the day, control had gotten away from me several times, and my thoughts had wandered.

"What are you thinking?" Doug probed.

Her long fingers swiped away wisps of hair which had come loose around her face, and she fixed her large brown eyes on him. I imagined lasers piercing right through his flesh, leaving him exposed to her scrutiny. The energy of the unabashed physical attraction popped and sizzled between them. Under other circumstances, I might have been uncomfortable, but there was a fleeting note of question in her eyes, as if she were testing him.

"Tell me more," she said to me.

"There is no more. I've told you everything."

Her head tilted. "There's always more."

Doug flashed me a knowing glance. I knew him well enough to suspect we'd reached the same conclusion. She was withholding something, and she wanted to find out if we were too. Whatever the elusive information, we weren't aware of it.

Danni sighed. "The Druid who attempted to rid Eógan of Abhartach had a child." Her eyes fixed on me, gauging my reaction. "I'm a direct descendant. I thought perhaps you knew."

I wasn't sure what my reaction should be. I was reluctant to presume I'd understood her meaning, but my jaw clenched, and the tendons in my neck strained at the implied connection. Danni's statement meant something significant and nothing at the same time, and the declaration felt like another test. *I'm not Eógan; I'm not Abhartach. I am Henry Clayton.*

"We had no idea," Doug said.

She smiled. "No, I realize that now. Nevertheless, I don't believe in coincidence. Things happen for a reason, and you found your way to my door of all places."

"So, you'll do it?" I hedged, desperate to ignore the voices whispering questions in the back of my mind and push this faster than feasible.

Danni forced her seat back, the wood scraping over the slate floor. Her blood rushed in her veins, and her temperature rose, at last giving some indication of her emotions, even if I couldn't decipher them. Perspiration glistened over her top lip where her skin caught the luminance of the pendant lighting over the table. She had a small, faded crescent scar about two inches below her right eye. It cut through a few freckles and made me think of star constellations outlined in book illustrations. I hadn't noticed before. It didn't distract from her strange beauty—if anything, it made her face more interesting. The scar's origin was a secret she could choose to share or keep, just like what she knew about The Circle. This woman kept many secrets.

She walked toward me, her dark eyes pensive. One hand lowered to my shoulder, urging me to sit back as far as possible while she leaned over me.

Instinct caused my muscles to contract, and I swallowed hard. My hands went to the armrests, curling over the wood. I concentrated on the pressure of my fingers and the smoothness of the varnished grain to distract from the sudden warmth in my chest where Danni had placed her other hand.

I'd never experienced anything like the suction drawing at my internal organs and causing my blood to boil. All sound and vision disappeared until it left me with nothing but the pounding of my heart in utter blackness. I couldn't feel my limbs any longer, or my skin. Words wouldn't come, and the silence when my pulse slowed and vanished was terrifying, until even the fear dissolved, and darkness became light. I was floating in fire…pure, white, languid flames numbing everything.

"Relax." The voice came to me from the nothingness and soaked into my brain.

My next breath filled my lungs, and each nerve came tumbling back to life. The first seconds elongated like a taut rubber band, and time dragged me through a tunnel to the present. My eyes snapped open to see Danni standing over me with flushed cheeks and her pulse hammering through her body. Damp hair stuck to her brow, and perspiration trickled down her cheek. She swayed and staggered back.

Doug and I both reached for her. I caught her first, and she gave me a small grateful smile.

"I'm okay."

When I was sure she could hold her own weight, I released her and held out a chair. Doug rushed over to the refrigerator and placed a glass of water on the table. Danni took the glass in her trembling hand. Doug narrowed his eyes in question over her head. After a moment to gather myself, I shook my head, disappointed to feel no difference.

His nostrils flared, and the muscles in his jaw jumped. "What went wrong?" he asked Danni, slumping back into his chair.

I remained standing, wanting to trust my unsteady legs again before I took a seat.

She yanked the sleeve of her sweater over her hand and used it to blot the dampness from her face. "Nothing."

"I don't understand. Is that it?" I asked.

Danni's forehead pinched, and her lips formed a small O, forcing out a gust of breath. "I wasn't cleansing you." Her eyebrows rose. "Trust me, it's not that easy."

Hairs prickled across my scalp, and the uncomfortable sensation spread over every inch of skin. "Then, what were you doing?"

Danni drained her glass and stood. "I was taking a look inside."

"That can't have been pleasant," Doug quipped. I shot him an angry glare. "Och, don't get touchy. Sarcasm is my thing. Would you rather I weep?"

"It wasn't pleasant," Danni agreed, although her tone was devoid of humor. "You've done despicable things." She shook her head slowly. "I'll be honest—even if I could take that from you, I wouldn't. There's too much. I wouldn't survive it."

A fissure opened in my chest, and disappointment welled up, threatening to drag me under. I shouldn't have allowed myself to hope, but I did. Before that, I'd anticipated another dead end. I expected anger and frustration, not the sick grief catching words in my throat.

"Brother—" Doug started, but I shut him down with a raised fist, disinclined to listen to any pity or optimism he might offer. I'd allow him to thunder on with plans and alternatives later. I'd listen to his next scheme for ridding us of The Circle, but not now.

"I'm sorry that's not the answer you wanted," Danni said, clasping her hands to hold them steady when they trembled. "I saw how much you crave redemption. There is good in you. I've seen it."

A wiser man would have borne the disappointment with dignity. Not me. My foolish, selfish heart burned in my chest like paper set alight. I stormed to the other end of the room, clenching and unclenching my fists. The muscles in my shoulders ached, and a strange emptiness settled over me. I closed my eyes and saw Ari's face against the back of my eyelids.

Notwithstanding the relief from the constant blood craving, I missed her presence and her smell. I missed how I always wanted to touch her skin and how she always saw deeper than I wanted her to see. How could I have allowed this to happen? How could I have allowed my sense of self to slip and tangle in another person so completely that I unraveled without her beside me? I dipped my head, offering up a silent prayer to heaven for her safety. For as much as I deserved my fate after everything I'd done, Ari's only crime had been to love a man too much to let him die.

"There is no good in me," I ground out though a clenched jaw.

A chair skittered across the floor. "Are you calling me a liar?"

I spun at Danni's infuriated tone. She glowered at me, standing beside her abandoned chair. Her reaction caught me off guard, and a little of my misery evaporated.

"Clay loves his pity parties," Doug teased.

She raised a challenging eyebrow and smirked over her shoulder at him. "I can see that, but he seems to have missed the point and—Clay?"

"Clayton Black, the name I've been using," I answered, hesitating a moment before returning to my seat. "Henry is fine. I think it's safe to say you know me well enough now."

Once we were all seated again, Danni glanced at us both before her eyes clouded with resolve. "You missed where I said 'even if I could.'" Her tongue swiped across her bottom lip. "Look, cards on the table. I didn't lie when I said I don't do Sin Eating. I need to know how much you are prepared to sacrifice, because what I'm proposing won't be without risk. You have to remember that all magic comes with a price. If you are willing to pay the piper, I think I can destroy Abhartach."

"You can?" I asked, needing confirmation before I allowed hope to burrow beneath my skin again.

She smiled. "I won't lie. There's something in it for me."

"What's that?" Doug's eyes narrowed.

"An end to all vampires."

Chapter 32

"Come again?" Doug's green eyes flamed with incredulous amusement. Considering his excellent hearing, the comment seemed redundant.

"Do you think my help comes free?" she countered.

Doug shoved his seat back and hopped to his feet, pacing the floor. He scrubbed his hand over his face, the rough stubble making a barely audible grinding noise, like sandpaper on wood. I maintained a careful composure, lacing my fingers over my stomach with my elbows on the armrests. For me it wasn't a question. I'd happily give anything. I'd forfeit my life if it freed Ari, but this wasn't only about me. It didn't matter that I considered vampirism an abomination of nature: I couldn't ask the sacrifice from Doug and William.

"Say something," Doug demanded. "*All* vampires means us too, right?" He looked to Danni for clarification. "I'm not ready to die."

"Even if it means saving the girl?" she said.

Doug froze mid-step. His head fell back, and he released a growl of torment that reminded me of a wounded animal. He pointed a finger at me, fury contorting his handsome features into a demon's mask and black seeping into the whites of his eyes.

"This is your fault. If you hadn't made me promise to protect her, I wouldn't have allowed her to creep inside my head. Now I'm bound by my promise to keep her safe." Doug's voice rose to an accusation.

I went and stood before him, mindful of my own protective compulsions in light of his threatening stance. He met my eyes, seething anger veiling something I couldn't decipher. I lifted one hand to his shoulder tentatively. His fingers curved to fists, and his jaw clenched.

"You don't have to agree to this, Dougal."

"Damn it all, man." He jerked my hand off and turned away, shedding his anger with another rumbling growl. "Of course I do." Doug's fingers raked through his hair from temple to nape and back again, tugging at the roots. The blond strands stood up like a lion's mane around his head. He heaved a breath, and his shoulders shook with resigned laughter, facing down death with the dauntless courage of a man seeing the prospect of another adventure. "It's been a hell of a ride. I suppose there are worse ways to end than going out a hero."

Danni rose from her seat. Pale blue shadows marred the skin below her eyes. "Hang on to your wooden door there, hero boy," she teased Doug. "You may be in the ocean, and the Titanic may be sinking, but you're not done yet."

It'd been a long day for her with a lot of information to process. She moved unsteadily to the coffee maker as though her limbs ached or weighed more than they should. She didn't bother with a fresh pot, instead filling a mug and placing it in the microwave to heat.

"Blood magic made Abhartach and all the vampires that came after him, more specifically Cailleach's blood." The microwave dinged, and Danni took out her mug, blowing on the dark liquid before sipping it. "The blood on your hands comes from that darkness, and that darkness is in Cailleach, not you. It's blacker and vaster than you can possibly imagine. You fought it, and that alone makes you worth cleansing."

"But you said you couldn't."

"She is the key, the link to everything," Danni said. "If I cleanse Cailleach through your friend Ari—"

"Every vampire will be cleansed," Doug finished for her. "You're going to make us all human again."

Danni nodded. "In the beginning, that's why cleansing Abhartach didn't work. They didn't understand it was Ari's sin and Cailleach's blood that needed to be cleansed."

I scratched my nails over my scalp. I wanted to make sense of all this. I'd been searching for a cure for so long. It couldn't be this easy. All we'd have to do is find a way to contact Ari and have her return.

"You're talking about a cure."

"I am," she said.

"So, when you said you wanted to end every vampire…" Doug allowed his words to trail off, implying the question. We'd presumed she meant to kill us.

"Oh, I meant an end as in death."

Doug made a futile attempt to hide his scowl.

"You said it would kill you to take my sins, so how can you take on every vampire?" I asked.

"I don't plan to swallow down the sins of an entire supernatural race. I plan to hold them long enough for you to make the girl safe and release it. A body won't tolerate the shock of the extraction followed by all that darkness pouring back in."

Doug settled his hands on the breakfast bar and skimmed them outward, widening his arms. His head drooped and shook. "How do you know this will work?"

Her mug clinked into the sink. "I don't know, but if I have a chance to rid the world of vampires, I have to try." She shifted her attention from Doug to me. "If you help me, I will do my very best to save you…both of you."

He pushed off the counter, and his gaze slid to me, a peculiar fear in his eyes. "We'd be human?"

She smiled at him, simmering with excitement and her heart quickening. "That's what I'm offering."

"A chance to be human," he said as though needing to hear it again, needing the confirmation.

"How would you feel about that?" Danni stepped closer to him and dipped her head to see his face.

His eyes darted to me again. "I've never thought about it because I never really believed it could happen. I've always considered Clay's research and experiments as a fool's pursuit." He squirmed, embarrassed by his admission, and faced Danni. "You should know, Petal, if the criterion for humanity is being a good man, I come up short."

"A few minutes ago you were willing to give up immortality to save someone's life." She took another step, winding a strand of hair around her index finger.

"That's one life against all those I've taken," he said with an edge of nervousness.

A small part of me wondered what he was playing at. Didn't he know he was trying to talk her out of saving him?

Danni smiled at him. She was tall, even in bare feet, and only had to tilt her head a little to catch his eyes.

"It's not a weighing scale. It's not about numbers. It about intent. Do you want to be a good man?" A slight flush colored her cheeks.

"Honestly, I don't know. I've been this way for so long, I'm just me."

"May I?" Danni's hand hovered over the center of his chest, where his steady heart held its rhythmic beat.

Doug swallowed, his Adam's apple bobbing, and ducked his head like an animal conceding to a master. They both closed their eyes. Her hand inched forward, and a soft breathy sigh left her lips when it met resistance. Doug's body stiffened, and he grabbed onto her arms. A shiver vibrated through his entire body. I recalled the sensation like burning and the floating in nothingness. I knew I didn't cling to Danni, but I wondered if I'd worn a similar expression. Doug's face scrunched up in concentration, and I watched their exchange with interest.

It passed much faster than I expected it to—a matter of moments, although it had seemed longer when I had been in his place. Perhaps it was because my sins were far greater.

Danni withdrew her hand, tugging hard at a resistance melding her hand to his body. Beads of perspiration dribbled down her neck and pooled in the hollow of her collarbone. Wisps of transparent smoke bled out from her palm—or his chest, I wasn't sure. Either way, the ribbons curled, stretched, and then snapped away from Danni, slinking back into Doug's heart. He sucked in a deep breath, just as I had.

The display of power from Danni was disconcerting and yet comforting. I was glad to have her on our side.

Danni smiled broadly, using one hand to steady herself on the counter and the other to grab a wad of kitchen paper from a roll on the windowsill.

"That was intense," Doug murmured, the heel of his hand massaging his breastbone.

"You love with your entire being, and you've been fighting your nature for a long time," Danni told him. "You are a better man than you choose to believe."

"I'm not sure I can believe that." He sighed out a heavy breath.

"I do," I assured him.

Doug grimaced. "This is strange. I have no desire to die, but I'm afraid it's too late to return to the land of the living." A smile tugged at the corner of his mouth, making crescent creases in his skin. As the smile widened, his eyes crinkled, and he released a startled laugh. "To feel the sun warm my skin or my heart quicken...to be human."

"Wait," I said, hating to bust this happy bubble of enthusiasm. "I need to speak to William."

Danni crossed her arms over her chest. "You know this is Ari's choice, right? If she could destroy Abhartach and rid the world of vampires at the same time, do you think she'd hesitate? If I'd known how to find her before now, if I'd known of her existence, you wouldn't be here." She tilted her head toward her shoulder. "You are...and you sought me out to help you, and so I'm willing to help you in return. I'm risking my life here, and your hesitation isn't inspiring confidence."

I raked my hand through my hair. "I understand, and believe me, I'm grateful. I can't condemn William without speaking to him."

She rolled her eyes and huffed. "That would be a mistake." Her cool tone indicated she once again knew something we didn't.

"Why?"

"The Circle are adept at secrets, some more so than others, even within their own followers. For instance," she began to pace heel to toe, "the specifics of resurrecting Abhartach, aside from it involving a sacrifice, weren't general knowledge. Since the recent turmoil in your world, keeping the identity of upper echelon hasn't been so easy."

"What are you getting at?" I demanded.

"I am honestly sorry to tell you this. William Alexander and his mate hold the reigns of The Circle. He's been involved for hundreds of years."

"You're lying," I spat and noted how Doug inched out, ready to block Danni, not that she needed help defending herself.

"The truth is the truth. You can accept it or not, but you can't change it."

"No. It's impossible." I couldn't wrap my head around what she was saying. How could William have kept this secret all this time? Danni controlled her emotions so absolutely that I couldn't gauge her honesty in the way I would with other humans. Regardless, a knot formed in my gut. "William tried to help me."

"From all I've heard from you today, I believe it would be more correct to say he was grooming you," Danni said me. "I realize this is hard for you to hear, but you must accept it if we are to move forward with this plan."

"How could you know?"

She uncrossed her arms and inched past Doug. "Listen to my voice, my pulse, look at my eyes. I won't try to trick you, and I'm not lying. I told you before, I know about The Circle."

I searched her eyes as they settled on me. Her steady voice gave no weight to my disbelief. The potential betrayal was too much to take. My mind refused to acknowledge it even in its smallest measurement. I walked away from them and pressed my back to the wall, sliding down the smooth surface to the floor. I drew my legs up and circled them with my arms, like a small child protecting himself. I probed my emotions, searching for anger, anything to eclipse this sense of loss ripping my insides. I'd trusted him completely.

"Oh, God." I leaped back up.

By Doug's wild eyes and furious expression, he'd reached his conclusion before I had.

"I handed Ari over to him," I said.

Doug ground his teeth until his jaw creaked. "When they couldn't take her by force, he wandered right in." He snorted a dark laugh, dragging his hair from his face with both hands. Blue veins threaded beneath his pale skin.

"No," I seethed, rage suddenly surging. "I invited him in. I'm the one played for a complete fool. You were right about Constance, Doug."

"You were deceived," Danni assured me. "He used your own emotions to manipulate you. It could have happened to anyone."

"It still ends in the same conclusion," I snapped. "He has Ari. Why didn't you tell us as soon as you heard his name? What game are you playing?"

My feet moved without conscious decision, only pure instinct and fury. My nerves oscillated like a million ants crawling through my body, and my muscles spasmed. Sharp points worried the flesh at the back of my lips when my entire body pitched forward.

The force of my acceleration slammed me into nothing, except the nothing felt like a wall made of iron and concrete. I fell back, crashing onto the floor. Pain reverberated along my spine as the back of my head bounced off the tile. Dust particles swirled in front of my eyes.

Doug crouched beside me instantly, his large palm flattened over my chest to hold me down. I pushed up and was met with a brutal shove. A rib cracked, lancing hot pain into my torso. His snarl, revealing brilliant white fangs, rumbled with a restrained growl.

"Stay down," he warned, directing his fierce glower away from me toward Danni. He wasn't protecting her; he was protecting me.

Danni stood over us, her hand held up and sparks flickering over her palm. Her eyes were wide and dark in her blanched face. Her hair was wild too, as though she had been caught in a wind storm.

"Don't make me regret my decision to help you," she fumed, obviously livid at my loss of control. "I am on your side. Believe me when I say that you really don't want me as your enemy."

I held very still, giving my emotions time to settle.

"Why did you lie?" Doug pushed, his body still trembling.

Danni laughed. She shook her hand and perched it on her hip. "Because you're vampires, and I was still considering whether I should trust you. Besides, she's in no danger. She's not much use to him dead, not yet, and from what you told me, she can take care of herself."

I propped up, flinching at the sharp new throbbing at my side. Doug arched a brow, requiring verification I wouldn't take another crack at Danni. I didn't plan to. Danni's bag of tricks went deeper than I initially credited.

Doug jumped up and pulled me to my feet. His brow creased when I favored my right side, but he didn't apologize for the injury since it was my own fault. It would heal soon enough.

"Where is she?" I asked, forcing down the emotions making my fingers twitch. My temper would help no one right now. Ari had to be my priority, and I needed Danni. I realized I'd been reckless to underestimate her, to suppose control of the situation. However, if Danni could pull off what she promised, none of that would matter.

"I can trace her, but it will take a little time."

I moved my shoulder and hissed when my broken rib grazed my lung.

"I'm sorry," she said softly. "I was defending myself. I didn't intend to hurt you."

"*You* didn't hurt me," I answered, sitting down. "It's nothing."

"I'm also sorry for not telling you about William sooner." She met my eyes with sincerity. "I'm navigating this situation as best I can."

A dark groan burst from Doug's lungs, and an echo of guilt broke through, reminding me this had to be overwhelming for her, and for all her bravado, my little exhibition probably scared her.

"No," I said. "I'm sorry. What happened is my fault, not yours. I'm the one who misjudged William."

Doug clapped his hands once. "Okay, now we're all friends again. Let's get this party started."

Danni lowered her eyes and almost restrained an indulgent grin as she smoothed her hair down. She liked Doug, even if she wasn't sure of me yet. She opened one of the cupboard doors and pulled out what resembled a salad bowl painted gold on the inside.

"Can you get a bottle of water from the fridge, please?" she asked Doug, and he nodded.

"How will you find her?" I followed her to the table.

"Hydromancy. It's a form of scrying with water, sort of like looking in a crystal ball."

Doug placed the bottle beside her. "You are a fascinating woman."

"Thank you." She looked up at him when he made no effort to move from her personal space. "I appreciate you have a vested interest in what I'm about to do, but breathing down my neck is not useful."

"Oh." He staggered back. "Yeah, right. I'll be over here." He pointed to me, mumbling like an adolescent with a crush.

Danni settled into her seat and poured the entire content of the small water bottle onto the bowl. She closed her eyes and slowed her breathing, her heart pumping at a relaxed rhythm for almost thirty minutes.

When she opened her eyes again, they were different. I flashed Doug a sideways glance and noted his slack jaw. Her pupils had expanded, swallowing the brown entirely.

Danni passed her hands in circles over the surface of the water several times, never touching the liquid. Over the lip of the bowl, ripples began to form, although a vision of any images that might have been forming evaded me.

"I see her," she whispered in a voice that sounded far away.

I wanted to prod and ask where she saw Ari, but wondered if this trance state was like sleepwalking. Would I cause Danni harm if I interfered?

"She's not alone. There are others, many others. I see an old building. It's a stone ruin in a clearing. I see woods and a sea of glittering lights from a city below. The water in the distance is like a sheet of black glass." She paused a moment, and the corner of her eye twitched. "There's graffiti on the wall, but it's mostly names. It doesn't say where—wait, I see a sign."

Danni blinked once, and her eyes returned to their previous dark brown, except now a web of blood vessels threaded through the white. "I know where they'll be."

"Where?" I asked.

"They're still in Ireland."

Doug rubbed at his chin. "Can you narrow that down?"

"I saw them at Montpelier Hill."

Frustration cut through me, and my fist came down on the table, causing a fault line crack to race to the center. "The Hellfire Club, where William took me after I was turned."

Doug puffed out his cheeks, and Danni glared at me from the other end of the table.

"My floor tiles and now my table," she scolded.

I cringed and flexed my fingers. "I'm sorry. I'll pay to replace them."

"I'd prefer if you didn't break up my house."

I stood, jittery and eager to be off her property before I broke anything else and Danni changed her mind about helping us. "Let's go."

Doug raised his hands. "Hang on. What are we going to do, storm in there? She said William and Ari aren't alone."

"I don't care. I'll think of something on the way."

My friend's tolerant expression indicated he wanted to say something I wouldn't appreciate hearing.

"What?" I said.

"Ari isn't a damsel in distress waiting to be rescued. They need her. Besides, you aren't the knight in shining armor of this story. You're another villain. Step wrong, and this could end with you evil and Ari dead."

I hated that he was right. I wasn't a hero, just another monster, probably more dangerous than the ones who had her. William took Ari for a reason, and his manipulation knew no bounds. We'd have to take him by surprise.

Danni's brow pinched into a frown. "Doug's right. We need to think this through, and we have time. There was a dark moon in the images."

"So?"

She stood and went to the window behind her seat, pulling on the cord of the blind until it rose all the way to the top. A last sliver of light from the waning moon slashed through the sky over the treetops on the sloping ground at the back of her home.

"Tomorrow night," I stated flatly as I sank back into my seat. My finger trailed along the rough edge of the cracked wood, and the splintered grain scratched at my skin.

"The visions don't always show the present," she explained. "However, at least we have something to work with now. I suggest we use the time we have to rest and make a plan."

Chapter 33

Unlike Doug, who could sleep through a bombing—he had once, in London during the Blitz—rest evaded me.

"Do you often sit in the dark?" Danni asked, flicking a light switch on when she walked into the kitchen.

"I can see just fine."

She smiled and nodded. "Of course, vampire vision."

I remained in my seat, running my thumb over the new crack in the wooden table. I'd tried to sleep, lying down on the couch in her front room after we finished discussing our plans. My mind raced viciously, and every sense seemed amplified. Every nerve was a live wire firing bursts of electricity. How could I sleep when I vibrated with anticipation?

"Doug cares for you very much, doesn't he?"

I was confused why she sought my agreement to her observation, but I nodded regardless.

"I've never been sure why," I admitted meeting her brown eyes for a moment. "I owe him so much."

Outside, the world remained settled in a cloak of night. Wind whistled around the house, and the gutter rattled every now and then above the back door.

"Are you having second thoughts?" Danni asked, sliding into a seat at the opposite end of the table. She wore navy sweats, and her hair was ruffled from tossing and turning. It appeared rest evaded her, too.

"I'm having hundreds." I chuckled grimly. "If you're asking do I want to back out? No. If we can break the cycle, I have to try. Ari would want that. If we succeed, I'll be a human again. I keep saying it in my head, but I can't accept it as anything more than abstract. I'm not sure…"

My hands came together on the surface of the table, the pads of my fingers pressed hard until I felt the strain of the pressure to my knuckles. The mild discomfort kept me focused as much as possible.

"Please, go on," she urged, leaning forward on her elbows. "I've seen inside you. You have no secrets from me, but it might help you to talk."

I chuckled again, this time with genuine amusement. "Is this a part of the service?"

Her lips curled up at the edges. "It might be."

Tension coiled around my muscles like snakes and tightened every part of me until I thought I might break apart like a shattered china doll. My mind reeled with the possible situations Ari could be facing in that exact moment, a small part of me counted Danni's every heartbeat, another part ran through every minute detail of my time with Ari, and yet another part considered musical compositions. None of it blocked thoughts of my family and all the others who had died at my hands. I wondered about the loved ones of the nurse in Howth. What were they going through, not knowing what became of her? Why should I have a chance to live when I had stolen that woman's life from her? That's how it went, on and on, thousands of thought processes all at once, and happening so fast, I barely noticed most of them.

I pulled in a breath and tasted the air, separating every element and committing them to my vault of a memory. However, for reasons I couldn't comprehend, the future, after saving Ari, remained beyond my reach. I drew a blank when I tried to think about what might happen after.

"For over a hundred years, I've only been limited by the world around me. My mind works faster than any advancements in technology. My body defies gravity, defies the laws of nature. Defies heaven. I exist in a prison, contained within flesh walls but with unlimited potential. I think somewhere along the way arrogance set in, and I began to like it."

"You'll miss the benefits of being a vampire," she observed without any obvious judgment.

"I don't know."

Her head tilted to her shoulder, and I shifted under her scrutiny. "The humanity you once prized above everything seems like a price to you now."

"That's not it. I'm not sure there will be anything left of the human I was when the vampire is gone. Can you see it? Do you know what will happen? If you saw where The Circle will be, what else do you know?"

Danni tilted her head to the other side, and her eyebrows pulled together. Her mouth turned down in what I could only take as an expression of pity. "That's a mouthful of questions. If I knew, I wouldn't tell you. It doesn't work that way."

"I don't understand."

"And I'm not sure I can explain." She sighed. "Think of it as leaving your home and knowing there's a deep puddle at your garden gate. You know if you step in it, you'll get wet. So, you don't step in it. You go about your day with dry shoes. Maybe if you didn't notice the puddle, your day would turn out different—better."

"You're saying telling me what will happen will affect the outcome?" I asked.

"I see only what the universe wants to show me. Maybe the universe wants us to get our shoes wet."

Danni leaned back and stretched her arms wide before stifling a yawn. "Excuse me. I think I should probably try to get back to sleep." She pushed her seat back and stood.

I hummed dubiously. "If I was a suspicious man, I might think I've asked a question you don't want to answer."

Danni smiled. "If you weren't a suspicious man, you'd accept the answer I've already given you, because there is no more. In this world, there is one simple truth—what we deserve and what we get are not always the same thing. You should try to rest too."

Chapter 34

I concentrated on the mulch scent permeating the air, mingled with chlorophyll and fuel, waste, and other smells rising from the city. If I allowed myself to think of Ari close by, I might rush into the fray with no regard for the outcome. The Hell Fire Wood between the road and the burned-out hunting lodge at the summit of Montpelier seemed eerily sentient. A stream of cold wind winding through the trees rustled branches overhead. Insects and arachnids slithered and crawled under the dead cover of leaves and broken twigs on the ground. All gave the impression of movement and life, making the wood unwelcoming for the dead things wandering through it.

The city droned in the distance, and Danni's heart beat slow and strong in the midst of several other vampire hearts. She'd called it a glamour, an illusion that wouldn't last but would perhaps buy us some time. We were being watched, but I couldn't see by whom because they maintained their distance.

Dublin had sprawled over the last hundred and forty years, encroaching on the dark countryside as a blanket of twinkling colored lights. However, parts of the Dublin mountains remained blissfully isolated. The deer that once roamed this area were gone, and the hill had become a popular walking spot, as well as a destination for ghost busters and supernatural enthusiasts, thanks to its sinister history.

We weren't looking for ghosts. A disquieting sense of unease caused the hairs on my arms to stand, and ice trickled down my spine. A familiar yearning urgency rose up. My nails cut crescent marks into my palm, and blood seeped over my knuckles.

"What are you doing?" Doug hissed in my ear, smelling the metallic liquid dripping a trail onto the earth.

"I feel...strange."

He did a double take, his green eyes flashing like jewels in the dark. "In what way?"

Doug had laced his fingers through Danni's as soon as we had entered the shelter of the trees. Playing the role of a new vampire meant she couldn't use artificial light and relied on him to guide the way. She showed no indication of listening to our conversation and watched the ground.

Ravenous hunger burned into my gut as though I'd been stabbed with a scorching blade. "I need blood."

"You had blood not two hours ago."

"I know," I growled, feeling my fangs extend from my gums.

Doug shrank back. "Whoa, Clay."

I snapped my fingers out straight and swiped my hands over my jeans, refusing to cave to the impulses crowning as I neared William and my rage escalated. Perhaps it was a part of his plan. He wanted me off balance and easily manipulated.

"It's this place. Evil vibrates here," Danni explained in a low voice. "It always has. It's a psychic hotspot, and all sorts of mystical energies converge. Over time, it became tainted. This place holds a memory of each and every one of the depraved acts committed here. What I don't understand is why you're linked to it."

"Why would I be linked to it? I've only been here once before."

"That you remember," Doug tacked on.

He was right. With no memory of my previous existences, how could I know for sure? A fleeting recollection of pain came to mind, and a growl rumbled through my lungs unrestrained.

"He cut me."

Doug grimaced, confused. "Huh?"

"William. I don't remember previous lives, but I know I bled here. William sliced my hand open and called it wicked blood."

"God damn son of a—" Doug ground out.

"It was a ritual bleeding," Danni explained, "linking you to whatever corruption resides here. With everything against you, your strength of will is astonishing. The battle inside you will be over soon."

Arid thirst scorched my insides, and the lingering scent of cocoa drifted on the breeze when we came into the clearing. Ahead of us, the stark lodge with its sloping roof and gray stone seemed menacing against the black sky. Flickering amber light escaped through the window openings, now barred, and caught the sprays of graffiti and green mold growing on the stone. The building itself appeared to be rotting like old food.

I picked out Ari's scent on the second floor, heard her heart thump faster and quieter than all the others. *How can they stand it?* I licked my lips and swallowed so harshly my jaw clicked.

The vampire who'd been following us through the woods emerged, joining at least fifty others circling the building. They all wore black hooded ceremonial robes that shaded their faces, and some carried flame torches. The entire scene was ludicrous and reminiscent of an old horror movie. Only a handful of the gathered were new vampires. I could tell that much by the scent of their blood and the way they held their bodies as though already accustomed to their strength and agility.

One of the new vampires inched closer as we passed, drawn forward not by obvious intent but as though gravity dragged her nearer to the only human, besides Ari, in the vicinity. Danni's blood remained masked to me, but perhaps the vampire's thirst and keen new senses picked up something others couldn't. Perhaps she didn't realize how she was exposing us. It wasn't a risk I wanted to wager on.

Before she could cry out or reveal Danni as human, I acted. I hung back and turned on the vampire. My hand tore through fabric and flesh, broke bone, and gripped her beating heart. My fingers slid over the slick surface, and her pulse vibrated against my palm. Her knees gave way immediately. The vampire's face screwed up horror, her wide hazel eyes glazing with pain in the split second before I ripped out her beating heart. I wasted no time in crushing it to a pulpy mass before it turned to ashes in my fingers. My fangs bared, I glowered at the few vampires daring to crouch.

"Keep your distance," I seethed in a low voice. "Or meet the same end." Not that it mattered. The hostile crowd was nothing more than ashes already. They just hadn't realized it yet.

Danni didn't turn or show any indication her guard had slipped. Two vampires hissed, voicing their defiance before joining the others to avert their eyes in submission.

Doug glanced back and raised an eyebrow, and I shook my head, silently telling him not to question. Most feared me, and those that didn't had the sense to fear what I might soon become. It'd been Doug's plan for me to slip into the role The Circle so desperately wanted me to play. We couldn't hold their numbers back in a fight, and this was the only way to get to Ari. I was the Trojan horse, slipping through their defenses. Except, instead of a hidden army, we only needed Danni to defeat them.

It wasn't proving as difficult as I imagined to show my dark side. Thirst and rage were an intoxicating cocktail, my nerve endings sparked beneath my flesh, and my muscles strained with a constricting energy. We had a matter of several feet before we entered the doorway, which was concealed by a false wall. If the ground had been soft, instead of hard earth under grass, I might have sunk into it with each step.

I closed my eyes and imagined inky vines creeping around my ankles and slinking up my legs. Tendrils of black smoke curled around my head and slithered into my ears and eyes like glossy, translucent worms, crawling inside my nose and ears. My eyes flashed open, and I skidded to a halt, clawing at my throat and face.

Doug attempted to wrench my hands. Fury exploded from my chest in a violent roar to the sky, and I whipped my arms out, flinging him away as though he weighed nothing. My own pulse screamed in my head, too fast and hot, sending a blinding pain coursing through my brain. I crashed to the ground on my hands and knees, panting air I shouldn't have needed but frantically craved.

"What is this?" I ground out. I couldn't hear my own words.

The scent of fresh human blood enveloped me. I could almost taste the velvet wetness sliding down, warming my insides. I grew hard in my jeans, and tightness spread through my stomach and my thighs.

"Henry." Ari's whispered voice came from the second floor.

Other murmured words echoed behind my back, fearful whispering from the vampires watching me writhe on the grass like a madman. The world around me pitched sideways, and acid burned my tongue. My skin tightened further until I was sure it would split wide open with the slightest provocation. My fingers bent and dug into the ground, catching stones under my nails. It was the only way I could think to lock myself to the earth and to calm the raging sensations. I slowed my breathing, sucking in cool air and allowing the chill to spread everywhere until the spinning stopped and my body began to relax.

Doug's large hand touched my back, but it was too soon. I hadn't reeled the animal in enough, and instinct took over. I launched from the ground and smashed him into the stone wall. A couple of bricks gave way and crumpled to dust. Doug clung to my wrist, my fingers wrapped around his throat, my thumb crushing his windpipe.

He snarled at me and ripped strips of skin from the back of my hand, leaving angry scarlet welts. I blinked, clarity creeping back in. And when I sensed his foot coming up and preparing to kick me away, I tossed him aside.

"Keep your distance," I bellowed at him. "You are alive only because I still have use for you."

His furious vampire features contorted with indignation, and a storm of anger swirled in his eyes.

"Your woman, too." I shot a blistering glare at Danni.

She backed up two steps, her eyes lowered like the others. Any trace of fear or submission was entirely for show. The woman was fierce. My outburst would have terrified another human, but her steady heartbeat never wavered.

Doug scrubbed at his reddened neck and fixed his narrowed eyes on the ground. He knew I was back in control, but I couldn't show weakness. If Doug had even the slightest doubt, he would have launched at me, consequences be damned.

Chapter 35

I combed my fingers through my hair, pushing it away from my face and using the moment to test my tentative restraint before entering the building. A manic voice inside my head laughed and goaded me for my weakness in letting Doug live. I refused to listen to the taunts and tamped down the accompanying guilt and doubt scratching at the back of my mind. I'd spent my life practicing control, teetering on the very edge of a carnivorous temptation to concede to my base desires. This was no different.

Another robed vampire holding a torch waited at the bottom of a set of concrete steps with an aged metal handrail. He swept his hand to the side without lifting his head, gesturing up the stairs. I climbed slowly, following Ari's scent while attempting to block out others. Danni and Doug followed.

William waited to greet me at the top, wearing a robe like the others but with his hood slouched at the back of his neck.

"Henry." He held his arms wide, greeting me as though we were friends.

I stared him down coldly, and his arms lowered. He shifted awkwardly on his feet. Clearly, he'd expected a warmer reception.

How naïve must he have been to believe his treachery and attempts to control me, not to mention stealing Ari from under my nose, would come without consequence.

"I knew you'd find us," he said to me, darting his eyes over my shoulder.

I refused to follow his gaze, although I wondered about Doug's expression. "They are not your concern."

"Of course." His hands pressed together, palm slipping over palm. "Now you know."

I nodded. "It's not enough to know. I also want to understand."

William's shoulders softened, and his back straightened. I tilted my head slowly, watching him with narrowed eyes. His desire for this wretched curse to tear me apart so he could puppet his monster shone through his haunted eyes.

My companions lingered in the stairwell, cowering like proper minions.

"You must know," William said. "You must feel the change inside has already begun."

I stepped closer, leaving no space between us. "I want to understand your deceit," I snarled into his face, spittle causing him to blink.

His jaw tensed, some of his bravado slipping. "I told you what you needed to hear to keep you alive. I knew who you were even when you didn't. Did you really think it was all coincidence?"

I leaned in, inhaling brashly. "Her stink is all over you, William."

Footsteps disturbed paper wrappers and other rubbish strewn over the uneven stone ground. I drew back and allowed a languid smile to curl my lips.

"Constance."

It came together in my mind as an early morning mist burned away by morning sun. Everything was still just the same as it always had been, except now I saw without impediment.

Constance came from the next room, the room where Ari's heart pounded. She sashayed around me, trailing her fingernails across my shoulder blades. I didn't like it; it implied an ownership she hadn't earned and ego she'd soon regret. William held his arm out and folded her into the side of his body. She wore one of the robes too, the hood down like William's, but with the addition of white boots with pointed toes kicking out the hem when she moved. I wondered again what sick fantasy of dark rituals they were indulging with these costumes.

"My boys, together at last," she cooed.

"You're the fiancée."

Her response was to kiss William on the cheek. He didn't react to her at all, indicating this level of affection was nothing new to him. I'd been stupid, taken in by both of them. Nothing more than a marionette dancing for their amusement. The urge to wipe the smug grin from her face coiled in my gut. I bit down on my tongue, absorbing the desire and biding my time.

"For two thousand years, I've been watching and waiting." Constance sighed. No puff of condensation escaped her lips, and her cool breath had no effect on the night air. Her head fell to William's shoulder as she addressed me. "Failure after failure, time after time, the cycle turned, and we were left shrouded in night, hiding our true selves. Then you came along." She moved out of the circle of William's arms and placed her hand above my heart. "I knew you were different. I knew you'd be the one. Together we will rule this world."

I sensed her attempts at seduction like pinpricks against my flesh trying to pierce soft tissue. I'd had enough of her madness. I snorted a laugh and shook my head, winding my fingers around hers and prying them from my chest. I bent the slender digits back, and her eyes widened as realization hit her: releasing the monster meant losing control of the game. My fangs elongated, and I felt my veins protruding. Red ringed the outer edge of my vision like a cloud rolling in.

William staggered and hit the wall with his back. I continued to fold Constance's fingers backward until she cried out, an unrestrained howl of pain. She sank to her knees in front of me. A calculating hate throbbed through my chest, and I wasn't honestly sure of the origin. I had every reason to hate these two, but the hate didn't feel rooted in me. The cruelty came from somewhere else, the part of me that enjoyed making others suffer.

"What," I growled in a voice that echoed against stone, "makes you think there is any *we*? Did you suppose I would thank you for your lies, you petulant insect?"

I flung her hand away, throwing my arm in a wide arc. She got up quickly and shrank back into William's chest, cradling the shattered appendage.

The vampire from the base of the steps appeared on hearing the commotion, but Doug stopped him in his tracks, scuffling to keep him from ascending further while Danni stood back. The musky aroma of fear was overwhelming and came from every direction, bombarding my frayed nerves. It clung to me like sheen of sweat.

"Enough," I thundered, stopping their confrontation.

Danni's eyes flickered in my direction and then away. If her glamour faded, this would all be over.

"I will see the girl now." I didn't wait for permission before turning my back on them. Abhartach wouldn't.

I strode under the opening and emerged into the tall room with a sloping ceiling and a massive hearth. The room was set in darkness apart from the glimmer of quivering light coming in the large window in one wall and a second smaller window high up another wall.

Chains clinked in the corner farthest from the light, and I twisted toward it, my sense of smell off kilter because of the cloying scents thick in the air. I had presumed I'd experience relief or at least a sense of comfort in seeing Ari. I felt neither of those things.

The source of the noise huddled near the ground in a crouch, her bare arms wrapped around her knees. Heavy iron shackles circled her wrists and ankles, the chains attached to them so thick even Ari with her inhuman strength wouldn't be able to breach them.

My heart broke at the sight of her, her dark hair falling over arms covered in gooseflesh and her filthy jeans ripped at the knees. The bandage was gone, but the wound to her arm remained closed. My nose twitched at the stale odor rising from her, mingling with vanilla and her usual sweet scent.

"She put up quite the fight," William said. I silenced him with a glare.

"Cailleach," I said. The name felt right in this circumstance.

A shiver ripped through her doubled body as she stood, the chains clanking, and lifted her head at last. A dark, mottled bruise colored the right side of her jaw along with a small swelling of her left eye. Despite this, her blue eyes fixed on me with a familiar pity for an instant. Her chin trembled before a mask came down, blocking me from any further insight. Her bravery almost made me smile. My spine stiffened, and I gritted my teeth to keep from screaming. My instinct to protect and avenge her injuries battled savagely with a more insidious one to claim my prize and kill her.

Without warning, Ari lunged with a piercing cry. Tendons strained in her neck, and her hair whipped around her face. The chains screeched and rattled but held her in place inches from my face. I made no outward reaction, and she laughed, throwing her head back to expose the gentle curve of her throat.

"Go ahead," she sneered. "Try to kill me."

I ran my tongue over my bottom lip where her breath warmed my skin and scowled at her. I couldn't ask what she thought was going on here, but I had to presume she'd heard the disturbance and believed the worst—that I'd given in to the darkness. Though I felt like jumping out of my own skin, I couldn't tell her the truth.

Instead, I clasped my hands behind my back and pushed my face down to hers. "You're chained like a dog. There wouldn't be any sport in it."

She intentionally jerked at the chains secured to the floor with cement and metal plates. The sound echoed against the high ceiling. "Then, make it a fair fight."

I ran off several swear words in my head and stepped back, earning another attempt to breach the metal. I needed to find a way to make her see I still wanted to fight this, to fight for her, without giving us all away.

William and Constance observed the scene from the entrance to the room. Constance's hand hung limp by her side, probably useless for the time being. Doug hovered behind them, peering over William's shoulder, his face set in a careful mask of indifference. When Ari's eyes slid to the side and she spotted him, her composure slipped for a moment, her shoulders stooped, and she blinked as if refusing to believe her own eyes. A dark flush flooded her cheeks, and her chest heaved with each breath.

Her disappointment left a cold, heavy ache in the pit of my stomach. I edged back, hurt that apparently she expected this of me in some way. She'd readied herself for me to turn on her, but Doug was a different story. His betrayal caught her off guard. She thought better of him than falling in line with bloodthirsty vampires. I hated that she had substantial reason to distrust me, yet on previous occasions she'd always seen through my façades. Why couldn't she see the truth now? Why had she lost faith in me?

"Leave us," I instructed William. Danni required time alone with Ari to perform the cleansing.

He exchanged a curious look with Constance, and her damaged hand conspicuously slipped behind her back. William walked to the window, his fluid movements gave him an air of confidence, and an amused smile played at the corners of his lips. He looked out and crooked his index finger, gesturing for me to join him.

After a quick sidelong glance at Ari, I did and peered out into the night. The vampires outside had pulled closer. Their numbers had swelled to substantially more, enough to stand shoulder to shoulder as far as I could see.

"They are here for you," William told me. "Europe is ripe for the taking and, after, everywhere else. They are ready for their god to lead them into a new world. Now is the time of the vampire race, and Abhartach *must* rise to lead us."

I tilted my head and narrowed my eyes, a sudden dread unfurling in my chest. "With you by my side, of course."

Williams flashed a brilliant smile. "Where else would I be?"

I averted my eyes. His words intrigued me. I wanted to lead them. My fatigued body and mind longed to stop the internal struggle and concede to the stronger, ancient nature. My fingertips trembled from the desire to appease the thirst for violence and destruction. The lines between what was real and what was an act for the benefit of saving Ari were blurring.

"All you have to do is show them you accept who you are, who you've always been," William coaxed. "Kill the girl."

Ari pulled in a sharp breath. A human would have missed the sound. Anticipation pulsed through the room. Belatedly, it dawned on me that William didn't care if any of the legends were real, or if the madness that drove me to such heinous darkness when I lost control was the essence of an ancient monster. He only cared that others believed it, and their belief would bring him power. My self-inflicted starvation and notorious rampage in London had only furthered his cause. Regardless of my actions here, he'd used me to place himself in control of all the vampires below us and countless others. If I didn't kill Ari, he'd continue his hold over The Circle by spinning the story of my weakness and probably instructing them to kill all of us. If I did kill her, it seemed he imagined himself controlling the monster.

Fool.

My attention flickered to Constance. She bit down on her glistening bottom lip, uncharacteristically anxious. She vibrated with longing, and it was contagious, seeping out into the air around her. Constance believed. She feared me—justified fear in this case, since I had a score to settle with both of them.

My shoulders rolled back, and I rose to my full height, raising my chin and considering my next move. A low growl of surrender tumbled from my lips as my fangs emerged again. Moving forward was a risk, but walking away wasn't an option.

"Release her."

William chuckled darkly.

Didn't he understand his betrayals had left me damaged? Anyone with sense knew not to corner a wounded animal. I glowered at him dangerously and drew my lips tight across lethal fangs, bored of his tedious maneuverings.

"I am a predator, a hunter. What hunter enjoys the kill of a snared prey? Where is the challenge? It's too easy."

William scrutinized my face, searching for any sign I planned to bolt or impede his plans. Neither was my intention.

He clapped me on the shoulder as though we'd come to an amicable agreement. Disgust flooded every molecule of my being at what I was about to do, but I draped a curtain across my emotions, arranging my features in a cold mask of menace. In my peripheral vision, Doug scowled. This was a divergence from our plan, and my actions must have confused him. I hoped he'd run with it. Danni kept her distance, lingering in the hallway behind them but positioned so she could view most of the room. The slant of her shoulders indicated strain as though a weight pressed on her. She had said the glamour was temporary, and this sign of her beginning to weaken fortified my resolve.

"Henry." Ari's breathy voice stung my ears and my heart as William unlocked the shackles from her legs. "Don't do this."

I stood behind him and stared her down coldly. "Henry Clayton is gone."

"Henry!" The startled cry burst from Doug's lungs, and he pounced forward.

Even with his lightning speed, he was too slow, and several sets of hands held him back as he reared and jerked violently. The others must have come from the stairwell.

I raised my arm out from my body and pointed toward them. "Restrain him…but if you hurt him, I'll do the same to you."

Ari made use of the commotion and her free legs to kick out at William. He was too close for her to get a decent swing or momentum, but she landed a couple of reasonable blows to his shins and smirked when he winced.

"I'll kill you next," she promised him softly.

No, I'm going to kill him.

William wrenched her wrist free from the first shackle. Her eyebrows twitched, and her jaw tightened, her heightened adrenaline making her blood sweeter. She waited until her second hand was free and backhanded him across the cheek. The smack rang out, and a trickle of blood dribbled from his lip. His tongue poked out and licked it away, and his hand lifted to return the blow.

"William," I roared. "She is mine."

Ari blinked as though dazed, and something in my possessive tone must have broken through to Doug, who eased his trashing to a halfhearted struggle. William dropped his hand.

"Of course, son."

The term of endearment he'd used so many times lodged in my head like barbs stabbing at my brain. What I'd once considered affection now felt like a taunt and a reminder of what I'd lost, only fortifying my conviction.

He didn't wait for any response and moved to the doorway with the others.

Ari held a wide, balanced stance, one foot slightly in front of the other, not five feet from me. Her eyes traveled the length of my body, searching for vulnerabilities, and resting a beat too long on my exposed fangs.

"Like what you see?" I asked.

"Not especially," she retorted in a flat voice. A rose flush climbed her neck and colored her cheeks.

I recalled how her skin blushed when she became excited in my bed. *You're killing me,* I thought while hoping she wouldn't.

"I thought it would be different this time," she said in a low voice meant only for me. The others would have heard it perfectly fine. Ari took a step, moving sideways rather than forward, and bringing her nearer to the tall stone hearth. "I didn't want it to end this way."

I couldn't be sure, but I got the distinct impression she meant with my death rather than her own. Although, she had to know if she killed me, the others would have her head in seconds. I didn't plan to let it get that far.

"It's not over yet." I smiled leisurely.

Her chest heaved, unnatural bursts of adrenaline fired into her blood, and her pupils dilated. The hair along her arms rose as if a static charge passed over her skin. Ari's nervous system was going into overdrive, redirecting energy to her twitching muscles. Her fight or flee instincts were kicking in, except Ari had no intention of fleeing.

She launched her attack with fierce brutality. The instant she had enough room, she swung around and smacked my jaw with her foot. My head whipped to the side, but I grabbed her leg and twisted it. The action caused her to spin at a ninety-degree angle to my body. She made use of my assault by landing another kick to my head with her other foot as it passed. *Clever girl.*

She landed in a crouch. Her leg whipped out and caught me at the back of my ankles. When I toppled back, I made a full arc, somersaulting and landing on my feet. My hands acted without thinking and reached for her, my nostrils flaring as the sweet fragrance of her anger finally overpowered the stale odor of sweat lingering on her skin. Ari ducked, sliding under my legs and bouncing up at my back, slamming her entwined fists into my spine at the base of my neck. My head fell back, and an unexpected yelp lodged in my throat.

We matched each other blow for blow. Ari used her smaller height to weave and duck out of my way, and I landed some serious blows when my fists connected with her body. I told myself with each one that it was necessary to convince the others I wanted Ari dead, that I had to make this look real. The more I threw myself into the fight, the more it felt real. Hurting Ari felt right, like my hands and body had a purpose outside my control. How long could I keep this up before the line between Henry Clayton and Abhartach blurred for good?

Ari fought without holding anything back, pouring everything into punches and kicks until I finally managed to knock her to the ground. She hesitated, sucking in a sharp breath and wincing. I'd broken a couple of her bottom ribs slamming her into the wall. My weight on her stomach and my hands encircling her wrists above her head aggravated the injury. She sagged beneath me for a fraction of a second, her wild eyes looking every direction but at my face. I thought this was it, but as always I'd underestimated Ari.

Her legs swung up over my shoulders, and her feet crossed under my chin. Ari grunted and swung her legs back down, taking me with them. Momentum flipped me over. I toppled, and Ari was on my back straightaway, her knees trapping my arms and her hands straining my neck so harshly, the vertebra along my neck creaked. Dust swirled in the air, and sweat glistened on her flushed skin.

"What are you doing, Henry? Why would you come here?" Her voice broke with emotion and the physical pain of the injuries I'd inflicted on her. My gut twisted in knots, and I pushed any pity or guilt away because this was the only way to save her, not just for today but for always.

She wrenched enough to cause pain but no damage to my spine. Her hesitation gave me the opportunity to toss her off my back. I said the first thing that came into my mind.

"I wanted to block out the sun."

They were Ari's words repeated back to her, words she'd said to me before she'd left with William. Her stuttered heartbeat and frozen limbs told me she remembered. Finally, she knew it was still me behind the smokescreen. It made her falter, and her fingers slipped. I used that against her.

My body jerked up, and she rolled off onto the debris-strewn floor, slightly dazed, screwing up her eyes, and shaking her head. I dragged her to her feet, and she immediately began to scuffle in my arms. I restrained her as though in an iron vice, her back to my chest. I tilted my head back and slightly askew in case she attempted to head butt me. I knew I had to act before she recovered from the shock fully and questioned whether my declaration had been a trick.

I didn't think about the wet thumping in her chest, the delicious scent of fresh blood flowing in her veins. The more I didn't think if it, the more flashes erupted in my mind. My mouth salivated for just one taste of her.

"Henry," Doug called from the doorway, struggling again. "Don't."

It all happened so fast. One second, I held her squirming in my arms, and the next, my mouth locked on the soft skin at the delicate curve of her neck. My teeth drove through flesh, and an eruption of the sweetest, most lush ambrosia crossed my tongue.

I squeezed tighter when Ari pulled and kicked at me, trying to get away. Her scream echoed inside my skull and vibrated against my mouth. I wanted more. I sucked harder, not waiting for the natural spray to push the liquid passed my lips. *Drink. Drink it all.* Her trembling fingers slapped uselessly at my thighs, and her dangling legs kicked at my shins.

We tumbled into a black, weightless void where no thought existed outside of the warmth stroking my tongue. It was a steady slip into oblivion where two bodies entwined.

A sense of peace I'd never conceived of settled within me, and I began to unravel. I'd known only chaos and despair for so long, my constant companions whether I chose to acknowledge them or not. Bit by bit, all the pain and anguish, all the torment and restraint slipped away, my existence condensed to only one thing—blood.

Chapter 36

The galloping pulse roared in my ears, sweeping over me like waves in an ocean where I drifted effortlessly. Soon, I found myself separated from my own body and watching from above as someone who vaguely looked like me drained the life from Ari.

Was this how it happened, how Abhartach took over? I couldn't feel the darkness anymore because it wasn't a part of me. I existed outside of it.

Ari ceased struggling and slumped in the arms of my doppelganger. Her fingers clenched at the denim covering his thighs. The sensation didn't register with me, and it was bizarre to be touched with no sensation of it.

I should have panicked, because this hadn't been my intention. William had forced my hand, and I wanted to convince him of my complicity in his schemes. I had to bite Ari in order to save her, to give Danni the time to save her. If Abhartach finished Ari, she wouldn't be reborn.

I had to go back. Dying would have been easy, a gentle release from the torture of living. It would have been so simple to let go of everything and touch the endless void of solitude after death. Going back meant pain…not pain, agony. After the numbness of floating, how could I endure it? The most wretched detail about life was the realization it could end so abruptly, even for an immortal beast like me. I had spent over a century frozen in a rapidly-moving, cruel, uncompromising, and electric place, yet I had no desire to leave. When death stripped my bones clean, hope remained. I supposed some might call it a soul. That tiny flickering ember kept me tethered to the room and to Ari.

I plunged downward, taking back what was mine. This was my life, my body, and my chance to stop the monster once and for all. My head snapped back so fast that blood dribbled over my lips and down my chin. A feral growl ripped from my chest and rattled my body. Every emotion and sensation I'd left behind bombarded my mind and senses. Ari's heart thundered, trying to pump her remaining blood through her body while the stolen liquid sloshed around my stomach. I'd taken less than two liters, enough to put pressure on her circulation and cause her to pass out but not enough to kill her outright. I wanted more, and not only from Ari. Thirst crippled my mind, and my nerves caught fire, so much that Ari slipped from my arms and slumped to the ground at my feet.

I staggered back and fell to my knees, balling my fists by my side. Emptiness still gnawed at my insides, and I imagined myself desiccating, shriveling to a dry bag of bone and ash. My body swayed as the room spun. I slammed my knuckles into the stone floor to keep from reaching for her again. Dust rose into the air, and I pulled it inside my lungs before I noticed I was breathing. I stopped, relishing the immediate ease of the craving. It allowed me to focus on the thumping of Ari's heart as I reeled in my control.

I pushed off the ground and stood tall. It pained me to leave Ari sprawled like a rag doll, tossed aside by a fickle child. What had begun as a pretense, an act to convince The Circle, William, and Constance that their god had returned, had almost became a reality. I'd almost killed her. I was back in control but aware of how close to the surface the darkness inside me remained. My guarded expression showed none of the disgust tearing at my heart.

The hooded figures holding Doug continued to restrain him, although he no longer struggled to get away. His eyebrows pulled together and creased his brow over black eyes fixed on Ari's prone and battered body. Blood leaked from her throat and stained the floor. The sight of the scarlet liquid made my stomach flip with excitement. I looked away.

"She isn't dead," Constance observed, stating the obvious with disappointment.

"Finish it," William sneered, matching Constance's level of disappointment with his own glee. He'd enjoyed the show, probably more so because the hooded figures holding Doug had witnessed it and would relay the story to the others.

"No," I stated flatly and wiped my face with the back of my sleeve. I was conscious of the fact I'd have to breathe to speak. "I may have need of the girl."

William tilted his body as though about to charge for Ari himself. My feet acted before my brain issued instruction and brought me nearer to her. I bared my fangs, daring him to test me. He eased back and smirked, allowing me to take the lead.

"Let him go," I instructed the hooded vampires. "And take these two outside." I inclined my head to William and Constance.

"Excuse me?" William demanded indignantly. He shrugged his arm away from a nervous looking vampire struggling to hold onto his ridiculous hood.

I laughed darkly and scraped hair away from my forehead, running my blood-slick fingers all the way to the nape of my neck, stepping over Ari's unconscious form to illustrate how little importance she held for me.

"I played along with your charade of controlling me because it amused me. It no longer amuses me." I took another step and grinned. "Let me put this another way. You can do what I say. Or I'll kill you."

When the young vampires surrounding William and Constance shrank back, he understood his plan had worked too well. Especially since I took down Ari without blinking. Every vampire in the vicinity now believed Abhartach had taken me over, unaware I had won the struggle for now.

William flashed me a look of annoyance while Constance, at his side, kept her gaze low in submission to me. I returned William's expression of contempt for my game with a glower of my own. I still had a promise to keep.

"Should I ask less politely?" I said to their vampire guards.

They scuttled into action, surrounding William and Constance in an awkward way that told me they weren't familiar to each other as a group. They lacked the dynamics to work in unison smoothly but were eager to please nonetheless. Not that it mattered. My only concern was getting them outside while Danni worked.

A moment later, we were alone. Danni appeared as if from nowhere and calmly walked past me. Her heart hadn't stuttered once this entire time, although her pale face showed lines of exhaustion around her eyes. This had taken much longer than we'd expected, and I wondered if she still had the energy to finish. As though she'd heard me, her eyes lifted, and she smiled before she lowered herself to Ari's side.

I wanted to go to Ari. I yearned for it so hard it felt as though chains wrapped around my insides and dragged me toward her. However, I couldn't even look at her now. I lingered in the futile hope she would understand my actions one day and forgive me. Each kind word exchanged between us and the memory of every action before she'd left with William sliced an excruciating cut through my unnatural heart.

Breathing was agony I couldn't show, barbed wire inched through my body. My nostrils flared as though inhaling fire. This was more than starvation, or blood lust, this was something else entirely. I understood better why Abhartach became such a monster. He had no soul, no conscience to act as a moral compass when the thirst took hold, only an endless pit of emptiness needing to be filled. He acted on pure instinct without remorse, unable to sate this heinous desire. In each incarnation, the soul simply couldn't exist with such evil and faded away leaving only Abhartach, leading to a confrontation with Cailleach's incarnations. Ultimately, beginning the cycle again. Except this time.

I looked to Doug and held his eyes, hoping he understood he was the difference in this life. I couldn't speak the words of gratitude aloud in case they were heard outside and our hosts discovered my ruse, but he had to know. He had been my protector, my deliverer each time I'd lost my way, and my strength—my friend. He was the reason my soul remained long after it should have burned away.

Doug narrowed his green eyes in question and then tilted his head. After a moment, he dragged in a pained breath and placed his hand on my shoulder. I hoped he understood why I couldn't stay. I crossed my arm over his and echoed his stance, clasping his shoulder firmly in a display of unity. I got it now. Some brothers weren't born from the same parents, but rather forged in the fires of shared experience and bonded by a sense of belonging.

"Stay with them, brother," I said.

"Always, brother."

I choked down the swelling lump lodged in my throat. They'd never get Ari out of here with so many vampires around. We'd all be torn to shreds before we left the woods. Keeping the others outside long enough to complete the cleansing meant I couldn't be with them. I didn't understand how it worked, so I entertained the possibility I might be about to die with the other vampires. The prospect scared me senseless.

Before Doug had time to talk me out of it, I spun on my heels and leaped from the window. The distance from human blood brought no relief from the enduring emptiness. The metallic tang on my tongue didn't help. I consoled myself with the idea it would be over soon, one way or another.

All heads turned to the muted thump. I landed in a crouch and rose slowly, dragging out my performance for full effect. My blood heated, and tension thickened the air so each step forward felt like trudging through molasses. Some jostled for a closer position while others balked at the fierce anger rolling off my body like steam from boiling water. The undulating movements made my stomach lurch, and blood swished inside. Nausea and fear slithered through me like snakes, and the lights beyond the hill seemed to oscillate.

Long strides took me to William and Constance, surrounded by the small group from inside. Orange light flickered from torches and cast them in a disconcerting glow.

"Remove your hoods," I instructed. "All of you." I darted my eyes around, taking slow, careful steps and lifting my arms, drawing them in further. "Why do you hide? Aren't you proud?" My voice took on an edge of manic hysteria. "Don't you comprehend what you have done?"

With trepidation, they began to pull their hoods back, darting their eyes around like frightened deer…if the deer were rabid.

I smiled widely, addressing them as children. It didn't take a lot of imagination since a few were little more than teenagers. "Good. After tonight, you will no longer have to hide." *It wasn't a lie.*

Others amongst the crowd were middle aged, much older than I would have expected for vampires who were generally turned in the first flush of youth. Vampires were attracted to youth and beauty like magpies to shiny surfaces. What stood before me was the cream of the crop, no doubt educated and wealthy, but also greedy and easily manipulated, poised to take over the recently vacated key positions in vampire hierarchy.

"But first, a lesson."

I closed the distance to Constance in a blink and plucked her head from her shoulders like a grape from a stalk. Blood sprayed from the decapitated neck, and I tossed the head away. It rolled, dark hair gathering dead leaves blown in from the wood. The eyes stared ahead, and the mouth gapped, giving her the impression of a thrown away fish head. Howls of shock and a few squeals of delight rose up as I plunged a fist into her chest cavity and yanked out her heart before her body grasped the message that death had claimed it.

The dark urges infesting me eased for a split second at killing something, anything. The monster craved death in any form. I didn't. I tamped down the desire, but I couldn't deny the burning ache to finish William was shared by both the monster and me. He deserved it, probably more than Constance had. Her end didn't bring me the peace I had always believed it would. I'd blamed her for the deaths of my family, the victims of the Ripper, and all the others. However, she didn't do those things. I did. Perhaps I deserved to die too.

At times over the years, I'd imagined what revenge would be like. I'd had a fantasy of my family appearing before me, ghostly vestiges smiling their forgiveness before fading from sight.

That didn't happen. Instead, William looked on, frowning, a vision of a disappointed father. Perhaps he didn't care for Constance as I'd presumed. Perhaps he planned to get rid of her himself and I'd done him a favor.

"Are you avenged?" he asked with a calm air of authority. "Am I next?"

"I haven't decided," I replied, swiping my hands together as if the discussion held little interest. In truth, it did hold little interest. Wicked blood had kept him alive, and without it, he would die with the others…with me.

"What is that?" William's handsome face pinched, and he edged by me to peer into the woods.

The rustling came from all round us, and even those guarding the back of the building came out of formation to inch away from the tree line. I rounded the building, keeping it at a distance so the others would follow my lead. There was nothing visible there, so I turned back.

On the horizon, where the sky had begun to fade from black to navy, a dark rippling cloud swelled. Black specks surged into the undulating shape that was rising and falling, appearing to grow beyond anything in nature. It was like looking at a pixelated image set against the fading night over the city.

It is happening. What, exactly, I wasn't sure. I didn't care as long as the others remained oblivious.

Branches bucked and swayed against the wet slapping coming from farther away. Many whirled at the din and reared back on realizing something was going on, and that something was heading our way. The warbles and chattering in the wind preceded the arrival of thousands of birds.

"What are they doing?" a middle-aged female cried. She stumbled into a young male who jerked his shoulder, allowing her to tumble to the ground.

A shard of pity stung in my chest as I watched her fall. Did she deserve to die tonight? Whatever she'd done in her years as a vampire would struggle to hold up against the things I'd done. I had to remind myself what Danni had said about intent. The female vampire had willingly joined a cult set on world destruction and domination.

A few made to break from the crowd and skidded to a halt after only making it several feet. The swirling form inflated from all sides, streaming in like a cyclone. The chattering filled with a metallic clucking as the birds neared, covering the area like a sheet of lustrous shimmering fabric.

Some vampires cowered or attacked those who accidently rammed them in the determination to flee. Those who made it any distance were set upon by birds. Discarded torches lay on the ground, dimming to nothing on the grass. A couple of vampires waved them about, using them defensively.

The starlings were containing us, and those who didn't stray too far from the lodge were left alone.

William trembled on his knees. He covered his head when a huge tattooed vampire, baring his fangs and brandishing a torch, used his back to springboard into a low-flying formation. My former mentor scrambled to his feet, revolving in slow circles and observing the nightmare scene.

His glare finally set on mine, and blue lines snaked up from his jaw, covering his face as his eyes darkened. "You," he snarled. "What have you done?"

I spun out of the way of two vampires tumbling toward me. The crowd was now too riled to care about us.

I laughed and extended my arms. "You flatter me. I don't possess this level of power."

His head snapped one way and then the other. His fists rolled into balls by his sides as he eyed me skeptically.

It happened as though in slow motion as William lifted his chin, and his attention settled on the window to the room on the second floor where torchlight cast an amber glow. His lips curled back and spittle glistened on his razor fangs.

"The girl." The words were hardly more than a breath. "She has to die."

I positioned myself between him and the building. He drew back, his legs parted for balance and knees bent. William ripped the robe away to reveal an ordinary outfit of jeans and a long sleeved T-shirt. A furious growl tore from his chest, and he dropped the robe in a mound at his feet. It was a startling sight, William surrounded by terrified vampires rushing about to escape crazed, diving starlings, swarming like crazed bees. A shower of feathers fluttered to the ground like massive black snowflakes.

"Do you imagine that has ever been your decision?" I roared at him, side-stepping when he did.

"Don't be a fool, Henry."

My chest heaved, and I clutched my hand to my heart when I felt it sprint for the first time in over a century. Searing pain carved through my brain. It was happening. Danni had absorbed the evil of all of them and was now releasing it back into the world.

A young female behind William crumpled to the ground with wide, shocked eyes. She began to crawl, reaching out in her confusion. A starling plummeted through the air and pecked at her knuckles when she reached the invisible boundary.

William staggered and lunged a step nearer as understanding lit his eyes. "What are they doing up there?"

The pain in my chest exploded outward as though needle-sharp splinters of ice pumped through my veins. Frost crept down my spine, and I shivered all over.

Sensing my weak moment, William pounced, landing a blow to my temple that felt as if it had split my skull. An adrenaline-like sensation flooded my body and numbed the pain instantly. I swung my legs around and rolled back up to my feet in time to yank him back down to the ground as he attempted to jump to the second floor. I slammed him onto the grass and stood over him.

"It's over, William," I said through gritted teeth. "You have nothing."

His human face returned, and his sorrowful eyes pierced through me as the world tilted on its axis and I veered sideways.

"Son, please."

The words grated on my last nerve, and I forced out a long breath, mesmerized by the clouded warm air dissipating in front of my face.

One by one, in quick succession, the vampires around us arched their backs, and a stream of red mist pumped from their opened lips, shooting up into the murmuration of starlings overhead. Their shape took formation once more. A cyclone of screeching feathers created a funnel and sucked the mist higher. I felt the pull on my lungs and the suction constricting every molecule that made up my body.

Air inside the funnel roared thunderously and changed direction. Gusts pushed the birds inward. They toppled over each other as every vampire, including me, looked up, terrified and confused.

I'd always thought my life would flicker behind my eyes in a stream of images at the moment of death, but it didn't. There were no images, only the sound of a child's laughter before an ebony cloud pitched downward and plummeted to the earth, swallowing everything in darkness.

Chapter 37

Why am I still here?

Even as I thought the words, I wasn't altogether sure where *here* was. I was blind and deaf, weightless, and surrounded by a soft blackness. I couldn't feel my extremities. I should have experienced panic or loss…something, at the possibility this was death, that all there was to an afterlife was infinite nothing—oblivion.

Except it wasn't. I didn't disappear, because I was still aware. I couldn't rationalize how my existence continued.

An eternity of this void wouldn't be undeserved in my case, only unexpected. I tried to imagine never hearing Ari's voice or Doug's voice again, never touching Ari's skin or ignoring Doug's advice. It was simply inconceivable.

I hoped Danni had succeeded in cleansing Ari and she, at least, was free. I resigned myself to never knowing how things had ended, or if they had. So, when Ari called out to me, I presumed it was a taunt dreamed up from somewhere deep in my subconsciousness and seeping into my awareness.

I heard her again, and I knew the sweet tones of her pleading were something even my perfect recall couldn't reproduce. She was real. Alive.

Gradually, I became aware of my body, the dim fluttering in my heart, an overwhelming need to pull air into my lungs, and cold. Cold everywhere, as though I'd been ducked into a vat of ice water and half-frozen. Perhaps that was the reason my skin was numb and my body felt weighted down.

I forced my eyelids to lift. The process was sluggish. I thought about what I expected of my body and waited. It seemed an age before anything happened. The action felt alien, as though gravity fought against me. The reward for my effort was darkness and a pale fuzzy outline. It took a moment to recognize the dim scent as Ari, but it was all wrong. I couldn't smell her blood, only the lingering sweet bouquet of her skin and the sour tang of sweat.

The shape disappeared and came back surrounded by an orange glow. In the blurred light, Ari stared down at me, her damp hair falling around her concerned face.

"Henry," she whispered and trailed fingers across my forehead. The sensation was muted, as though she touched me through cotton wool. Regardless, it was still enough to make my heart rush.

"Ari," I said. That sounded like a whisper too, or more like hearing underwater.

I raised my hand and tucked messy strands behind her ear, then the useless appendage dropped, exhausted.

"There's something wrong with me," I said, attempting to bring her into focus and failing miserably.

She smiled, and a weird heated feeling squeezed my heart and rushed outward through my chest.

"No. It worked. We're free."

"Free," I echoed.

Ari tugged me into a sitting position. "You're human." She threw her arms around my neck.

I buried my face in her hair, trying to pull in her smell. The sweet and stale odor scratched at my throat.

"That's being human you feel." She leaned back and held my face in her hands.

I blinked repeatedly. I had no idea why it would help me to see better, but it did…marginally. Some of the sensation returned to my body too. Enough to notice Ari's weight on my thighs and realize I'd placed my hands on her hips at some point.

"How are your legs? Can you walk?"

I rubbed my eye with my thumb and forefinger, seeing an array of stars dance behind my lids. The world was still out of focus when I opened my eyes. It was like the difference between watching a movie in high definition and standard, or through a layer of dust. I wriggled my toes, and pins and needles shot up my calves.

"I'm not sure."

"Why?"

"I think you're blocking my circulation." I smiled. "Apparently that's not a wasted bodily function anymore."

Ari returned my smile and leaned in. Her mouth brushed over my lips, and like the other sensations, it felt off—lacking intensity. My hands slid up her sides and threaded into her hair, anchoring her to me as the kiss deepened.

Before tonight, I'd noticed everything about Ari's body, even the smallest change in her temperature or breathing, or the slightest tremor. This new awareness took a different turn. The kiss lacked intimacy. It required an unexpected level of concentration and still seemed sloppy with teeth and tongues clashing awkwardly. I jerked back when the flutter in my chest became a painful hammering against my ribs, and I sucked in a lungful of air. It wasn't altogether pleasant, but it left an impression of heat everywhere in my body, like a handprint left on glass even when the touch is long gone.

"I forgot to breathe." I panted and blood flooded my cheeks at the admission.

Ari laughed. The bouncing movement of her shoulders disturbed her hair and revealed the puncture wounds at her throat, partially hidden by long tangled stands. The wounds had closed but still looked angry. Dried blood crusted over the small holes, and more trailed down to her collar. I touched the tender flesh where purple bruises marred her skin. My fingers skimmed over her jawline and down to the evenly spaced cuts.

Ari winced and dragged her hair over her shoulder. "I'm fine."

I couldn't tell if it hurt or if she didn't want me to look at what I'd done. In so many ways, I could see, but I was now blind.

"I'm so sorry," I told her, tilting my forehead to hers. "I was try-ing to keep you alive."

"I know," she whispered.

Ari kissed the tip of my nose and jumped up, helping me to stand on my shaky legs. Doug and Danni walked toward us from the direction of the old hunting lodge. He stumbled like a toddler new to using his feet and held onto Danni for support.

"You made it," he said.

I was beginning to get the impression it was my hearing that was affected and not the volume of those speaking around me. "You too." I laughed with relief as we looked each other up and down.

My first instinct was to reach out and embrace him, but I hesitated. It would lead to an embarrassing tumble to the ground, considering the lack of coordination we were both experiencing. This human state would take some getting used to for us.

"Ack." Doug's top lip curled up at one side in amusement. "We're too manly to hug anyway."

My eyes watered, the complex emotions bombarding my mind simply too much for this human body to contain. "I'm crying," I chortled and rubbed the moisture between my fingers.

"Well, I'm too manly," he mocked lightheartedly.

Ari swiped his arm.

Apart from a couple of flickering torches left over from the fray, no sign of what had transpired remained.

"What about the vampires who weren't here?" I asked.

"All dead," Danni replied. "They were all created from the same source and are nothing more than a myth now."

Gray smoke curled in the breeze and added a dark taste to the air when it blew in our direction. Everyone was gone. The vampire race had been obliterated in one fell swoop.

I hadn't believed it possible until the moment it happened. A wave of heat churned in my stomach, and bile scorched a path up my throat. I hoped I wouldn't vomit. There must have been others like Doug and me out there somewhere, vampires who had strived to live the best they could in their circumstances. I refused to believe we were a unique situation. Now, they were gone too, if they existed at all. I couldn't wrap my head around deserving this second chance.

"I'm not sure I understand what happened."

"Cailleach's blood created the vampire race," Danni explained. "I hoped Ari's blood, the same blood, would protect you. Sort of like having a vaccine before the disease infected the community."

"You didn't know it would work?"

"No," she replied. Her gaze slipped between Doug and me.

My arm, slung over Ari's shoulder, tightened to pull her closer. Like everything now, it took effort. I pressed my lips to her forehead. "The cure was in your blood after all. So, you drank Ari's blood?" I accused Doug.

He raised a hand and paused in whatever he was about to say, turning the hand in front of his face as though it was some strange alien object.

"The blood already spilled on the floor," Danni explained on his behalf. "It only took a little."

My eyes strayed again, despite my better judgment. "I can't believe they're all gone."

There must have been something in my voice or my expression giving away my conflicted thoughts. Danni touched my forearm. "This is the way it had to be. It's not your fault they're gone."

I frowned at my feet. "I know, but knowing doesn't make it easier. Most of them didn't ask to become vampires. I don't deserve to be standing here."

"No, you don't," Danni said, "so quit whining. I don't know why any of this happened. Sometimes destiny does things we can't possibly hope to understand. Don't waste the chance I've given you. Earn it."

"How?" I asked.

Her eyebrows twitched up, and a slow smile curved her lips. "That's up to you...and you." She faced Doug, while allowing him to hold onto her shoulder for balance.

"Let's get out of here," Ari suggested.

"Wait." Doug's jaw tightened, and he tested his legs before he inched away from Danni. "Look." He faced east where the sky had lightened and a stretch of color skimmed the treetops. "It's the sunrise."

The world around us had brightened to an array of pinks, purples, and burnt orange. A few cotton ball clouds rolled across the horizon, backed by more clouds streaked like brush strokes on an exquisite canvas. Ari folded closer to my side, and her hand found the place where my chest thudded faster.

A curve of white halo surrounded the sun as it crept higher, chasing light and shadow across the landscape. The muscles in my legs tightened, and my pulse escalated. Prickles of excitement and fear trickled over my skin. Every impulse told me to run, that certain death flooded the newly awakened city below us.

"It's okay," Ari whispered, standing on her toes to kiss to my cheek.

I inhaled deeply and released each breath in a slow exhale that pinched my lungs. I looked over at Doug, grinning into the sun, and bit down the twinge of jealously. No doubt this, like everything else, would come easy to him.

We stayed until the bright ball of liquid gold stung my eyes and faint warmth smoothed the edge from the bitter chill of morning. By that time, I was trembling all over from a combination of cold, exhaustion, and adrenaline, and I was glad to go home. I tried not to think further than the next few hours.

I'd spent the morning and all afternoon on the patio at the back of my house, lying on a recliner and bundled up in several goose-down duvets. Some part of me feared this was all a dream and I'd wake up eventually.

Driven to distraction when first left alone, I'd taken a knife and sliced my palm. It wasn't deep enough to need stitches, but Doug reminded me I needed to look after my body now that supernatural healing was a thing of the past.

After, he'd retired to his room, claiming he wanted to sleep for a week. We hadn't discussed our situation further, but the Doug I knew would adapt and survive as he always did.

Danni had already left; she'd taken my car home. She had no wish to hang around, although I suspected it wasn't the last we'd see of her. She promised to make sure we made every effort to deserve our second chance.

"Hey, handsome," Ari said, brushing her fingers through my hair.

I leaned into her touch, covering her hand with mine and craving more because of the lingering numbness. A white bandage wrapped around my hand. Doug put it there after he found me in the kitchen, bleeding.

I smiled up at Ari. Without the thirst for her blood, I struggled to make sense of my desire for her. That too had muted, but in a pleasant way. There was a softness to the longing now, a gentleness that caressed my senses and brought warmth and a familiar comfort instead of constant, blistering fire.

Ari handed me two steaming mugs and shifted the covers to climb under, placing herself between my legs with her back to my chest. Her freshly dried hair tickled my face. I handed her one of the mugs and sniffed the other.

"It's tea," she said with a smile in her voice. "I know how you feel about coffee."

"Do you?"

Ari twisted her torso so she could face me, confusion carving lines into her brow at my wry tone. "What does that mean?"

I searched her eyes for an answer to the question whirling in my mind, a mind as dull as a well-used blade. "How can you know when I don't? This person I am now, I've no idea who he is. I've wanted this for so long, but I don't know if I ever truly considered what it would mean to be human again."

Her jaw slackened. "Are you saying you'll miss being a vampire?"

"Isn't that funny?" My mouth screwed into a grimace. I bent sideways to leave the mug on the ground and flexed my fingers. "Nothing feels as real as it did before." Warmth flooded my cheeks at my next admission. "Not even you."

She raised her free hand and skimmed her thumb over my eyebrow. I missed the sound of her heartbeat.

"I'm real, I promise. The rest we can work out. It's only been a few hours." Ari smiled and glanced away, her thick eyelashes fluttering against creamy skin. I noticed only because we were so close. She gave me the mug and pointed to the ground, gesturing for me to set it beside the other.

Shifting again to twist a little more in my arms and under the cocoon of blankets, she took my hand and guided it beneath the hooded sweater she wore—one of mine. Her stomach sucked in, and my fingers climbed her lower ribs. The corner of her eye twitched, and I realize I must have touched where Danni had healed her broken ribs, the last of her gifts to us. Ari wore no underwear, and an ember of heat smoldered in my abdomen when she slid my palm over her breast to her heart, allowing me to feel the life-giving organ pound.

"This is real." Ari bit down on her bottom lip, darkening the plump flesh, and a shiver vibrated through her body.

I covered her mouth with mine and kissed her long and deep. The subdued feeling gave it a sensual softness. Ari moaned against my tongue and removed her hand from under the sweater, smoothing it up my neck and into my hair. The ember sparked and spread heat everywhere. My nerve endings came to life and hunger pulsed under my skin. Passion welled up, and the kiss became more, spiraling into a fever.

My heart jack-hammered, and our rushed breathing mingled in guttural sounds as Ari rotated her body and swung her leg over my thigh. She sat on my lap, pulling at my clothes and moving her hips. I bent my legs up to encourage her, frustrated by the lack of strength in my limbs. Her back arched, tilting her head. My tongue swirled in a small circle at the dent under her chin, and Ari whimpered. She eased forward, and I ducked into the curve from her shoulder to her neck, kissing upward until I reached the bite mark. Our movements must have stretched the delicate skin and opened the wound. A tiny bead of liquid escaped, and out of a well-worn instinct or habit, I licked it away. The metallic taste of blood crossed my tongue, and I drew back, shaking all over, panting harshly.

My eyes scrunched shut against the memory of sinking my teeth into her flesh. Ari held my face steady and touched our foreheads together.

"What I did to you in —"

She shushed me, her sweet breath on my face. "You did what you had to. You kept me alive."

A couple of tears spilled down my cheeks as I attempted to talk around the lump in my throat. My fingers bunched into Ari's sweater, clinging to her and relishing her embrace. Swift, painful panic simmered in my heart. I wanted to feel like I did before. The idea of this dulled, numb world being my reality was petrifying. Even the fear lacked definition, as though it held no truth. An overwhelming urge to peel my flesh from my bones took root. Nothing made sense.

"I don't know who I am or what I am anymore. I don't know how to separate the man from the monster. How do I live with everything I've done?"

"I'm not an especially strong person. If I can learn to live with what I've done, so can you." Ari sniffled, and I opened my eyes to see her cheeks were damp and she was watching me with sad blue eyes. "You want me to leave, don't you?"

I couldn't comprehend why I wanted her gone. Sending her away when she was the most real and solid thing in this haze of muted life made no sense. I nodded once, and the sound she made floated somewhere on the cusp of misery and anger. Ari kissed me fiercely, enough for me to feel it in my toes and know her lips would bruise. Maybe mine too.

"I think if you stay, you'll become my crutch, and I care about you too much to do that to you. You've been through enough already."

Ari slid down and lay against my chest. I pulled the covers that had fallen away back up and wrapped us in the marshmallow warmth as the sky darkened.

"I know who you are," Ari murmured. "I've always known. This *thing* that you became because of me, it was never who you were inside. *You* were never a monster any more than a virus inside a human being makes them a virus."

Her thumb ran circles over my waist, and I held her tighter, burying my nose in her hair.

"I won't leave you, Henry. I can't."

I opened my mouth to speak, but she pushed herself up and pressed her fingers to my lips in an attempt to stifle any argument.

"I have defied time, defied death, and defied this curse. I've lived a thousand lives and drowned in an ocean of tears. In all of that, the only constant has been you."

"I'm afraid." As I admitted the words, I felt the raw truth of it and the inferiority that accompanied them. The monster had been my shell, my protector. Without it, I was exposed.

"I'm not."

"No?" I asked cupping her fingers with my hand.

Ari smiled, and her nose scrunched up. "Maybe a little. But all important journeys begin with a healthy dose of trepidation, and this is a new beginning. For both of us."

Epilogue

2013

Rain poured down from the overcast night sky. Cars honked and jostled for position on the buzzing New York street.

Despite Ari's claims to the contrary, I felt responsible for the monstrous acts of my past. It had taken a long time to reconcile the different parts of myself and accept I couldn't separate them out and still end up a complete person. It was an all or nothing sort of deal. Once I'd accepted I could only move forward, things got easier.

I'd been working for various charities. Since I'd only one lifetime left to live, I had more money than I needed and donated plenty — including to a hospital in the name of the nurse I'd killed during my rage about Ari. It didn't go anywhere near atonement, but I hoped it would help someone. I even toyed with the idea of returning to finish my medical studies, but ultimately decided against it. Maybe one day. Although I'd grown used to being human, I wasn't sure I'd make a good doctor. For now, the sight of blood made my knees tremble.

Doug didn't sleep for a week as he'd planned to. In fact, in the early months after we became human again, he rarely slept. When he did, he awoke screaming from nightmares about his village. He eventually faced his demons by going home to Scotland and the place where it started for him, something he'd always managed to avoid before. But he didn't go alone. Doug had moved in with the Sin Eater the previous Spring and was running a small bar in the west of Ireland. He said the faces of his victims remained with him, but he'd accepted they always would.

A group of five people crowded in the door of the bar across the street while I watched from the shadow of an alley. Among them, Ari laughed and adjusted the strap of the bag slung across her shoulders. I'd followed them from the hospital not far away, where she was completing her residency. A tall, good-looking man kept his arm around Ari's shoulder with the casual ease of someone who touched her frequently. I turned away, consumed by unreasonable jealously, and my hands balled into fists.

I pulled in a deep breath and allowed my body to calm. Sometimes old habits returned, and I had to remind myself Ari wasn't some prey I'd marked and stalked from the shadows. She had a life and friends outside of our relationship, and she'd never betray me.

The bar was dark and busy inside. Mahogany, brown leather, and worn brass mirrors gave it an aged appearance. Sports and history memorabilia covered the wood-paneled walls. Tall tables scattered through the center of the room with booths along the side. Music played low enough for the many patrons to talk. A chemical scent I couldn't place but that reminded me of disinfectant circulated with the welcoming grain smell of liquor.

I looked around as I navigated the crowd and eventually spotted Ari at the bar. She stood on her toes, leaning forward over the gleaming wood and waving her hand to grab the attention of the barman, occupied by a busty redhead at the other end.

I came up behind the redhead and slipped two neatly-folded hundred-dollar bills across the counter. "Two Scotch, whatever you have that's good."

His eyes flickered between the bills and my face twice, then, redhead forgotten, he snapped up the cash. She smiled and huffed when she realized she didn't hold my attention. I was watching Ari shake her head in disbelief and walk toward me.

My pulse raged at the sight of her.

"Hello," she said with a forced smile.

"Hello." I'd planned something more meaningful, something witty and endearing, but couldn't remember a word of it. My human mind worked like that now. Sometimes thoughts vanished without a trace, or words on the tip of my tongue refused to come.

The barman returned with two glasses, and Ari nudged the redhead out of her way. They must have known each other, because Ari greeted her by name and said they'd catch up later before the redhead wandered off.

"She works at the hospital. One of these for me?" She dipped her head and gestured to the glasses. I nodded, and she picked it up.

I noted how her fingers trembled and the pads of her fingers flattened against the glass in an attempt to hide it. Ari's hair hung in chocolate ripples around her beautiful face, and she wore make up under her eyes, I guessed to hide dark circles from lack of sleep. However, it couldn't distract from the glow of happiness emanating from her.

I picked up my glass. "You seem happy." I wasn't sure if it was a statement or question.

"I'm celebrating," she replied, as though there wasn't some hidden meaning in my words. "It looks like someone I'd thought I'd lost is going to pull through after all."

That would explain the lift in her mood.

"That's good news."

"Yes." She knocked back the glass and raised it to the barman, indicating for another. He paid attention this time. "And my boyfriend caught an early flight home."

Her face ducked down, and she laughed, peeking up at me from under her eyelashes. Her smile was infectious.

I moved in closer, inhaling her cocoa fragrance.

Her eyes tightened to scrutinize my face. "You took your time," she said, and her smile faded to playful scowl.

"I'm sorry."

"Is it done?" Ari's chest heaved, and I guessed if I held my hand over her heart, I would feel it hammering as fast as mine.

I nodded. "I needed to see it one last time, but it's done now. The house is sold, and some family will make new memories there—better memories. It's time to leave the past in the past." I'd been hanging on to the house in Dublin, unwilling or unable to let go. I was a modern day Jacob Marley with the chains of my past, dragging it behind me and allowing it to weigh me down. But no more.

"I'm all yours, if you'll have me. I can't promise it will be easy. I can only promise to love you."

Ari smiled and slipped her hand into mine, weaving our fingers together to give me my answer.

Acknowledgments

I was four when we moved to a new house and my brother told me vampires lived across the street. There were no vampires, but Bram Stoker, the creator of Dracula, was born there. I grew up surrounded by stories of the supernatural. My great aunt read tealeaves and cards. We watched old horror movies on a projector, using a sheet as a screen, and I heard first-hand accounts of banshees, fairies, and ghosts. So, you could say it's down to my family that I believe in the impossible.

When I started writing, publishing seemed impossible too, but here I am.

It takes a long list of folks to make a book go from the impossible to possible to reality. My family, especially my son, put up with me endlessly talking about books and writing in an often untidy home. My friends are always there to prop me up and slap my wrist when my pity party for one rolls into town and I'm sure every single line I've ever written is rubbish. I'd like to thank Debra Anastasia for always remembering to check in when I don't. Thank you to the ladies of O-Fic Sisters and Autism Mamai for the constant support, no matter what it is that's holding back my words. I have to mention Dawnetta Viars and Irina Porotskaya for helping me make this and every story better every step of the way.

Thank you to everyone in the Omnific Publishing family for the support and friendship I've found there since beginning this wild journey in 2010. Team SW consisted of Kasi Alexander, Sean Riley, Katherine Teel, Kimberly Blythe, Coreen Montagna, Jennifer

Haren, Micha Stone, and Amy Brokaw. I couldn't have created this book without them.

Without you, the reader, there would be no book. I write because I have to. The stories in my head run on repeat until I get them down on paper. I publish to share those stories. Thank you for reading them, for sharing your thoughts on them, and for telling other people about them.

About the Author

Carol Oates came into the world on Christmas morning in an elevator. Raised just across the street from the childhood home of Bram Stoker, author of *Dracula*, it was only a matter of time before Carol's love of all things supernatural emerged.

She began experimenting with fiction at school and keeps the notebook containing her first unpublished novel in her desk drawer. Over three decades later, all her stories still begin life scrawled on paper.

When not writing, Carol can be found exploring history with her son. Luckily, he shares her love of old buildings, castles, and tombs.

check out these titles from
OMNIFIC PUBLISHING
←⟶Contemporary Romance←⟶

Keeping the Peace by Linda Cunningham
Stitches and Scars by Elizabeth A. Vincent
Pieces of Us by Hannah Downing
The Way That You Play It by BJ Thornton
The Poughkeepsie Brotherhood series: *Poughkeepsie, Return to Poughkeepsie* &
Saving Poughkeepsie by Debra Anastasia
Recaptured Dreams and *All-American Girl* and *Until Next Time* by Justine Dell
Once Upon a Second Chance by Marian Vere
The Englishman by Nina Lewis
16 Marsden Place by Rachel Brimble
Sleepers, Awake by Eden Barber
The Runaway series: *The Runaway Year* & *The Runaway Ex* by Shani Struthers
The Hydraulic series: *Hydraulic Level Five* & *Skygods* by Sarah Latchaw
Fix You and *The Jeweler* by Beck Anderson
Just Once by Julianna Keyes
The WORDS series: *The Weight of Words, Better Deeds Than Words* & *The Truest of Words*
by Georgina Guthrie
The Brit Out of Water series: *Theatricks* & *Jazz Hands* by Eleanor Gwyn-Jones
The Sacrificial Lamb & *Let's Get Physical* by Elle Fiore
The Plan by Qwen Salsbury
The Kiss Me series: *Kiss Me Goodnight* & *Kiss Me By Moonlight* by Michele Zurlo
Saint Kate of the Cupcake: The Dangers of Lust and Baking by LC Fenton
Exposure by Morgan & Jennifer Locklear
Playing All the Angles by Nicole Lane
Redemption by Kathryn Barrett
The Playboy's Princess by Joy Fulcher
The Forever series: *Forever Autumn* (book 1) by Christopher Scott Wagner

←⟶Young Adult Romance←⟶

The Ember series: *Ember* & *Iridescent* by Carol Oates
Breaking Point by Jess Bowen
Life, Liberty, and Pursuit by Susan Kaye Quinn
The Embrace series: *Embrace* & *Hold Tight* by Cherie Colyer
Destiny's Fire by Trisha Wolfe
The Reaper series: *Reaping Me Softly* & *UnReap My Heart* by Kate Evangelista
The Legendary Saga: *Legendary* & *Claiming Excalibur* by LH Nicole
The Fatal series: *Fatal* & *Brutal* (novella 1.5) by T.A. Brock
The Prometheus Order series: *Byronic* by Sandi Beth Jones
One Smart Cookie by Kym Brunner
Variables of Love by MK Schiller

New Adult Romance

Three Daves by Nicki Elson
Streamline by Jennifer Lane
The Shades series: *Shades of Atlantis* & *Shades of Avalon* by Carol Oates
The Heart series: *Beside Your Heart, Disclosure of the Heart* & *Forever Your Heart*
by Mary Whitney
Romancing the Bookworm by Kate Evangelista
Flirting with Chaos by Kenya Wright
The Vice, Virtue & Video series: *Revealed, Captured, Desired* & *Devoted*
by Bianca Giovanni
Granton University series: *Loving Lies* by Linda Kage

Paranormal Romance

The Light series: *Seers of Light, Whisper of Light* & *Circle of Light* by Jennifer DeLucy
The Hanaford Park series: *Eve of Samhain* & *Pleasures Untold* by Lisa Sanchez
Immortal Awakening by KC Randall
The Seraphim series: *Crushed Seraphim* & *Bittersweet Seraphim* by Debra Anastasia
The Guardian's Wild Child by Feather Stone
Grave Refrain by Sarah M. Glover
The Divinity series: *Divinity* & *Entity* by Patricia Leever
The Blood Vine series: *Blood Vine, Blood Entangled* & *Blood Reunited*
by Amber Belldene
Divine Temptation by Nicki Elson
The Dead Rapture series: *Love in the Time of the Dead* & *Love at the End of Days* by
Tera Shanley
The Hidden Races series: *Incandescent* (book 1) by M.V. Freeman
Something Wicked by Carol Oates

Romantic Suspense

Whirlwind by Robin DeJarnett
The CONduct series: *With Good Behavior, Bad Behavior* & *On Best Behavior*
by Jennifer Lane
Indivisible by Jessica McQuinn
Between the Lies by Alison Oburia
Blind Man's Bargain by Tracy Winegar

Erotic Romance

The Keyhole series: *Becoming sage* (book 1) by Kasi Alexander
The Keyhole series: *Saving sunni* (book 2) by Kasi & Reggie Alexander
The Winemaker's Dinner: *Appetizers* & *Entrée* by Dr. Ivan Rusilko & Everly Drummond
The Winemaker's Dinner: *Dessert* by Dr. Ivan Rusilko
Client N° 5 by Joy Fulcher

Historical Romance

Cat O' Nine Tails by Patricia Leever
Burning Embers by Hannah Fielding
Seven for a Secret by Rumer Haven

Anthologies

A Valentine Anthology including short stories by
Alice Clayton ("With a Double Oven"),
Jennifer DeLucy ("Magnus of Pfelt, Conquering Viking Lord"),
Nicki Elson ("I Don't Do Valentine's Day"),
Jessica McQuinn ("Better Than One Dead Rose and a Monkey Card"),
Victoria Michaels ("Home to Jackson"), and
Alison Oburia ("The Bridge")

Taking Liberties including an introduction by Tiffany Reisz and short stories by
Mina Vaughn ("John Hancock-Blocked"),
Linda Cunningham ("A Boston Marriage"),
Joy Fulcher ("Tea for Two"),
KC Holly ("The British Are Coming!"),
Kimberly Jensen & Scott Stark ("E. Pluribus Threesome"), and
Vivian Rider ("M'Lady's Secret Service")

Sets

The Heart Series Box Set (*Beside Your Heart, Disclosure of the Heart* &
Forever Your Heart) by Mary Whitney
The CONduct Series Box Set (*With Good Behavior, Bad Behavior* &
On Best Behavior) by Jennifer Lane
The Light Series Box Set (*Seers of Light, Whisper of Light, Circle of Light* &
Glimpse of Light) by Jennifer DeLucy
The Blood Vine Series Box Set (*Blood Vine, Blood Entangled, Blood Reunited* &
Blood Eternal) by Amber Belldene

Singles, Novellas & Special Editions

It's Only Kinky the First Time (A Keyhole series single) by Kasi Alexander
Learning the Ropes (A Keyhole series single) by Kasi & Reggie Alexander
The Winemaker's Dinner: RSVP by Dr. Ivan Rusilko
The Winemaker's Dinner: No Reservations by Everly Drummond
Big Guns by Jessica McQuinn
Concessions by Robin DeJarnett
Starstruck by Lisa Sanchez
New Flame by BJ Thornton

Shackled by Debra Anastasia
Swim Recruit by Jennifer Lane
Sway by Nicki Elson
Full Speed Ahead by Susan Kaye Quinn
The Second Sunrise by Hannah Downing
The Summer Prince by Carol Oates
Whatever it Takes by Sarah M. Glover
Clarity (A *Divinity* prequel single) by Patricia Leever
A Christmas Wish (A *Cocktails & Dreams* single) by Autumn Markus
Late Night with Andres by Debra Anastasia
Poughkeepsie (enhanced iPad app collector's edition) by Debra Anastasia
Poughkeepsie (audio book edition) by Debra Anastasia
Blood Eternal (A Blood Vine series single, epilogue to series) by Amber Belldene
Carnaval de Amor (*The Winemaker's Dinner*, Spanish edition)
by Dr. Ivan Rusilko & Everly Drummond

coming soon from
OMNIFIC PUBLISHING

Going the Distance by Julianna Keyes
The Enclave series: *Closer and Closer* (book 1) by Jenna Barton
The Dead Rapture series: *Love Starts with Z* (book 3) by Tera Shanley
The Hidden Races series: *Illumination* (book 2) by M.V. Freeman
Missing Pieces by Meredith Tate

www.ingramcontent.com/pod-product-compliance
Lightning Source LLC
Chambersburg PA
CBHW020344120726
47904CB00002B/454